A MOST
MISLEADING
HABIT

About the author

Catriona McPherson was born in the village of Queensferry in south-east Scotland in 1965 and educated at Edinburgh University. She divides her time between Scotland and California.

www.catrionamcpherson.com
@CatrionaMcP

To Joy Gladstone and Rob Close with love.
And apologies to Rob for liberties taken with the
buildings of Lanarkshire.

I would like to thank:

My agent, Lisa Moylett; Francine Toon, Jenni Leech, Jessica Hische, Jim Caunter, still Suzie Dooré, and all at Hodder; Marcia Markland, Quressa Robinson, Shailyn Tavella, and all at St Martin's; Sarah Brown (again!); Dick Hoenisch for the inspiration; all of my friends and family for their patience and enthusiasm, especially Neil McRoberts who soaks up more of the fall-out than anyone and is still smiling; the many booksellers and librarians in the US and the UK who have championed Dandy and brought readers to her; the bloggers, festival, convention, and conference organisers who add much of the fun, and the Facebook and Twitter crime fiction fans who make writing much less solitary but still just about possible; finally, my Sisters in Crime who were never far from my thoughts as I wrote the sisters here.

The Women of St Ultan's

Mother Superior
Mother Mary

Senior Sisters
Sister Abigail, cook
Sister Catherine, retired
Sister John, teacher
Sister Julian, laundress
Sister Mary, teacher and acting mother superior
Sister Steven, teacher

Sisters
Sister Anne, gardener
Sister Bridget, housekeeper
Sister Clare, assistant laundress
Sister Dorothy, nursemaid
Sister Frances, schoolmistress
Sister Hilda, housekeeper
Sister Jude, schoolmistress
Sister Irene, nursemaid
Sister Margaret, assistant laundress
Sister Martha, assistant cook
Sister Monica, seamstress and companion to Sister Catherine

Novices
Sister Joan, assistant teacher
Sister Winifred, assistant teacher

Nurses
Nurse Matt, senior nurse
Nurse Pirrie, junior nurse

Prologue

There was not a sound to be heard, nor a creature abroad to hear it. The village lay still and cold in the moonlight, the long street a pale ribbon, the cottages on its either side no more than inky smudges, their windows set too deep to gleam. Only on the stained glass of the church did the moon's reflection catch at the little panes and shatter into spangles.

Inside, silently as midnight came, the villagers bent their heads and clasped their hands. Some were praying, some merely waiting; but others, struck by awe, let their thoughts drift up and out into the moonlight, over the quiet country-side to other churches where other heads were bent in silence, to stables where donkeys might kneel if the legends were true, across the seas to distant lands where prayers were said in strange tongues and people quite unlike themselves were awestruck too.

Peace on earth, they told themselves, thinking of those faraway places. Joy to the world, they thought; the words lately sung, still resounding. Silent night, holy night. If only they had known.

For at that moment, not five miles away, klaxons shrieked and guards bellowed, their boots ringing out on the iron-hard ground as they gave chase. Out upon the hills, hunched shapes flitted and darted between the shadows, each one cursing the moonlight.

Later that same night, not five miles away, a bell would

toll and women's screams peal out as flames leapt merrily higher and higher. Black smoke rising in billows from a chapel roof would hide the moon.

And before the morning came, not five miles away, alone in his bed, a man would quietly die.

I

Gilverton, my husband's home, where I have lived for more than half my life now, is not a bower at the best of times, and the dregs of winter in early 1933 were amongst the worst of times I could remember. There had been a perfect Christmas, with just enough sharpness in the air to feel seasonal and just enough frost underfoot to give some sparkle to one's daily walk, but it was followed by gales and torrents throughout January which had gradually chilled until the downpours of freezing rain became, by degrees, deluges of thick, wet snow. Then, as February neared, the temperature plummeted, the head-high snowdrifts solidified into impenetrable barriers, the roadside puddles and rills froze to make treacherous patches of black ice lurking around every corner, and the coke boiler, which had squatted in the lower regions of the house like a troll under a bridge for sixty years, finally gave one last smoky cough and died.

Disaster, and the more chastening for our knowing it was disaster courted, for we had been leaning heavily on the coke boiler trying to save firewood, since the woodpile was under a cap of frozen snow three feet deep and the yard around it had been turned into a curling rink by a burst downpipe.

Hugh was bereft; the coke boiler was a good friend of his childhood. Advancing maturity had been marked by his father allowing him first to rake, then to stoke, then finally, when

3

he was twelve, to lay and light and regulate the thing. Still one sometimes found him down there leaning on the open firebox door and jabbing a poker lazily into the pulsing orange heap of coke, the way that other men lean over gates and use a switch to scratch the back of a sow.

So I could not, in all conscience, give vent to the many thoughts arising in me while I stood in the boiler room with a sable stole over my mink coat and an India-rubber hot-water bottle tucked into my belt. These were thoughts about my suggestion – not three years before – regarding central heating, gas-fired and reliable, sending piping hot water coursing around the house to pulsate in the coils of radiators and come pouring and steaming out of taps and shower baths in all of our old dressing rooms. I had imagined lying in a gleaming new bath, my hair springing into curls, and looking forward to padding across a warm bathroom to my warm bedroom and, if I realised I had left my book downstairs, slipping along a warm corridor to a warm stairway to cross a warm hall to fetch it.

I stamped my feet, encased in wool socks and alpine bootees, on the stone floor of the boiler room and rummaged about until my hands, in gloves shoved into the pockets of my mink, found the bottom edge of the hot-water bottle hanging from my waistband.

Hugh hit the glass face of the boiler gauge with a spanner and sighed. I could see the sigh in a long white jet of steam.

'Alec rang again,' I said. Hugh grunted. 'He's got lots of room and the road's not bad between us and there.' Another grunt. 'And it would let the servants get a terrific head start on the spring cleaning. We could probably start fishing parties in March in that case.' Hugh cocked his head, mildly interested. 'Also,' I went on, hoping I was not too transparent; Hugh loathes to be managed, 'I don't think Alec's new boiler is that wonderful from what he's said. It would be useful to see where he went wrong . . . Before you start deciding what to do here.' There was a silence. Of course, Hugh would love to discover that 'young Osborne' had wasted his money on an inferior system and nothing would give him more pleasure than to point out its deficiencies. Also, and in direct contradiction, he would find it easier to repair to Dunelgar, Alec's house, if it were only a *little* more comfortable, a little warmer, and not an utter collapse into Sybaritism.

'It's a sad state of affairs,' Hugh said at last, 'when you can't get a tradesman to pop along the road in a spot of frost to take on an honest job of work. Makes you ask why we fought the war.'

Sensing imminent capitulation, I said nothing. It was eighty miles from Edinburgh where the plumber had his shop and Hugh's 'spot of frost' had just the previous day turned a milk cart over into a snow bank so deep that one of the churns sank and was assumed lost until springtime. Fighting wars, for any reason, seemed something of a red herring, frankly.

Hugh sighed again, hit the gauge one last mournful little blow and turned to face me.

'Very well then, Dandy,' he said. 'Ring him and tell him we'll be there for tea.' He looked me up and down. 'But you might need to do something,' he added, gesturing vaguely. 'You look rather peculiar.'

I was wearing one of his dressing gowns over my clothes under my mink and I daresay that, added to the hot-water bottle, it *had* bestowed an unusual silhouette upon me. I smiled tightly and again said nothing, knowing that at Alec's I would not need so much as an angora cardigan around my shoulders. I was lying about his heating system to Hugh.

So that – the demise of the coke boiler – is why, on the Monday the post finally restarted, when the roads were open again, when the unstoppable chain of events began, we were at the breakfast table at Dunelgar: Alec, Hugh and me. We each had an enormous budget of letters after the hiatus at the Dunkeld sorting office and set to with our paper knives and an extra cup of coffee to sort the inevitable bills from the unwanted invitations and, in Alec's and my case, to truffle out the hoped-for pleas from clients who might furnish us with work.

Not that life at Dunelgar hung heavy. Far from it. Alec might be finding it a trial to be all things to all men when he was used to living quietly alone but he was managing it splendidly: entering into Hugh's deliberations over boilers like a master plumber every morning and then turning on a sixpence to sit with me after luncheon talking piffle and throwing bone rings for our dogs along the gallery.

Hugh was greatly pleased by having a man at his disposal. Alec was superior to his usual male companions – the tenants, the factor and our sons – because he was an equal and almost a contemporary who had fought in the same wars at the same rank and smoked the same tobacco. In addition, he was unmarried and unencumbered, not always pleading a wife's case for repairs to the farmhouses and not – I quote Hugh directly – turned silly by his mother. Donald and Teddy do tend to catch my eye and snort when their father gets deep into the breeding of Ayrshire cattle or the relative merits of gravel ditches and pipes for field drains. He had high hopes that, when Teddy came down from Oxford and Donald came back from Europe, they would both have shaken the last of me from their coat-tails. But Teddy spent most of his time with chaps and girls who counted it an evening wasted if everyone came home with both shoes and no piglet, and Donald had got Grant, my maid, to sew a pink silk lining into his dinner jacket to ready him for Italian night-clubs. I had made sure to protect Hugh from most of his sons' news, sharing snippets rather than handing letters over for him to read through.

As for me, I could have lived at Dunelgar forever and

not given Gilverton a single thought again. Grant was taken up with the entertainments offered by a new servants' hall and so left me blissfully alone apart from whisking away my linens each night and returning fresh ones. Alec's cook, who was English, did not hold with porridge or barley or Swedish turnips, even in a cold snap. And best of all my puppy, Bunty the second, who was eight months old and as wild as a drunk monkey, was loved by Alec, accepted by Barrow, his valet-cum-butler, who admired her markings and forgave her her occasional puddles, and soothed and calmed by Millie, Alec's spaniel, who was getting staid now at almost ten, waddling up and down the gallery with her bone ring and only growling when Bunty tried to take it from her.

Hugh, predictably, loathed the puppy with all of his loathing. He had taken against all Dalmatians as soon as he clapped eyes on the first Bunty, lying wriggling on her back in a knitting bag by the fire in my sitting room with a cluster of maids exclaiming about her chocolate-drop eyes and the lines of white velvet between the spots of pink satin on her waving paws.

'A dog who lives outside where dogs belong shouldn't have fur growing in its pads,' he announced. 'None of mine do.' This was true: Hugh's ragged pack of terriers, collies and hounds had nothing but dried mud, burrs and rabbit droppings clinging to their feet and they were the reason that the door between the library, billiards room, gun room and business room and the hallway leading to the dining room, morning room, breakfast room and sitting room – the door, as it were, between his quarters and mine – was kept firmly shut. For it was pure nonsense that Hugh's dogs lived outside. They *slept* outside, on straw, but could be found in a reeking heap in front of the office fire whenever Hugh was at his desk and the carpet was, as a result, liberally strewn with wisps of their bed. 'Better off with a pitchfork,'

I had heard Becky muttering once as she came back into my part of the house with a dustpan full.

Still, this time as last, I was trying to prevent a self-fulfilling prophecy from scuppering Hugh and Bunty's friendship beyond all hope.

'If only you wouldn't bark at her, she mightn't bark at you,' I told him. 'Same with growling.'

'I've never cooed at a dog and I'm not about to start,' Hugh growled. Little Bunty lowered her eyebrows and growled back.

So Dunelgar, where Hugh was diluted by many others, who all talked to the puppy in the sweetest of tones – asking her if she was a good girl and a beautiful baby and telling her not to worry about the silly carpet – was heaven for Bunty. She responded with grace and charm. At the very moment Barrow brought in the post that morning she was under the table, lying across my feet with her tail thumping, barely chewing my shoelaces at all.

There were three hopeful-looking letters, addressed to me at Gilver and Osborne, amongst the demands for subscriptions and announcements of spring weddings. I saved them for last. Alec had set aside two of his own, I noticed, but he became absorbed in one of the personal letters, pushing his plate away and letting his coffee get cold.

My first two were something of a let-down. The wife of a town councillor in Dundee wanted someone discreetly to prove that her husband was embezzling council funds and spending them on a shop girl. I could hardly think of a job I should enjoy less. Then a retired train driver from Saltcoats was after a disinterested outsider to attend the vegetable show at his allotments and ensure fair play. He could not pay any cash, he regretted to inform us, but we could have our pick of his onions. The third letter, however, was something else again. It came addressed to me alone from the Senior Sister of the Order of the Little Sisters of St Ultan

8

– she signed herself simply 'Mary' – and already faint bells were ringing.

'If you read the newspapers or listen to the wireless,' Sister Mary began, 'you might remember the trouble we had here at Christmas time. The newspapermen have tired of it now and turned their attentions elsewhere but our troubles are far from over. The great harm done to our house has weakened us and we are not equal to dealing with mischief as well as recovering and carrying out our duties. We are in sore need of a woman such as yourself and can offer you a measure of comfort here if you should choose to help us.' It sounded almost as though she wanted me to profess a vocation. I read on. 'It cannot take much longer. The moor has been aswarm with policemen for a month now and in the end they shall surely prevail.'

Of course I remembered the events at which she was hinting. Either a breakout from an insane asylum *or* a fire at a convent that killed a nun would be memorable each on its own. Both together, a few miles apart and on Christmas Eve besides, had given the headline writers almost more than they could handle. Still, a little more detail in Sister Mary's letter would have been welcome. I read it over again to see what I might have missed and found myself tutting.

I had long suspected that women who go in for nunnery had some melodrama about them. The early rising, the lying prostrate on stone floors, not to mention the glamorous costume – for who would *not* look dashing swathed in snowy white and with her neck hidden? – and this letter did nothing to change my mind. The great harm, the fickle newsmen, the troubles far from over. '*Aswarm* indeed!' I muttered to myself. Then, finally, I caught the meaning. If policemen were swarming over the moor even now, that meant that the breakout was still in business. There were inmates at large. Did I really want to go and stay in a house full of women then?

9

'What's that?' said Alec, looking up at my muttering. Hugh was behind *The Times*.

'Interesting case,' I said. 'Although interesting isn't perhaps the word, exactly.'

'Same here,' said Alec. 'Interesting, but "case" isn't perhaps the word, exactly. I've been asked to help a friend.'

'Do it,' said Hugh suddenly, letting the paper drop. 'If you've the chance to help a friend, Osborne, do it.' He had a peculiar look upon his face, strained about the eye, and not quite steady about the jaw.

'What is it?' I asked him.

'Friend of mine in the obituaries,' he said. 'Sooty Asher.'

'Oh, Hugh!' I said. 'I *am* sor—'

Hugh shook his head as though to get rid of a fly and went on, sounding angry now rather than stricken. 'He killed himself. Shot his own head off. Got past the Boers, got past the Hun, settled himself in a good job, rising through the ranks, and then bang!'

'Oh dear,' I said. 'Well, you must try to get to the funeral, no matter how the roads are. Where is it?'

'God knows,' said Hugh. 'He lived in Hyderabad. So they'll probably have it there and send a tin pot of clinker back on a ship. You know what Indians are like. Poor old Sooty Asher.'

'What was his Christian name?' I asked. 'Where are his family? I shall write to them and you can sign it, if you like. But I can't call him Sooty.'

'No family,' said Hugh. 'At least . . . I think there was a sister, but it was all rather under wraps. He had a patron, you know. We never asked and never cared.' He glared at me as though I had been unfeeling. 'So there's no one to write to,' he concluded, sounding bleak. Then he rose and left the room.

'You didn't deserve a scrap of that,' said Alec.

'I don't mind,' I replied. 'Gosh, if one can't snarl at one's wife when an old pal blows his head off.'

'Well, at any rate, I think I shall take Hugh's advice and help *my* old pal Tony Gourlay,' Alec said, but he looked over the letter with no great enthusiasm as he spoke.

'Help him do what?' I asked.

'Keep his neck out of the noose,' said Alec. 'His mother writes to tell me I'm their last hope.'

'What's he done?' I said. 'Wouldn't a lawyer be better?'

'If I know Tony, he hasn't done anything,' said Alec. 'He couldn't, even if he wanted to. There was this one time in— And Tony didn't even— Just stood there and waited for— If I hadn't—'

I had grown used to the way Alec spoke of the trenches and was able, just about, to fill in the dreadful words for myself.

'But what has he been accused of?' I said.

'Murder,' said Alec.

'And he protests his innocence?'

'He protests nothing,' Alec said. 'He hasn't spoken for fifteen years. He's got the worst case of shell shock I've ever seen, and that's saying something. He's been mute since before the Armistice, living in a mad house out on the Lanark Moor, that goes by the jaw-dropping title of Hopekist Head. Hardly! Anyway, he lives there, carving wood and digging flowerbeds – rotting in other words. And then suddenly this Christmas he's supposed to have broken out, set fire to a chapel and killed a nun! What is it, Dandy? You've gone paler than Hugh.'

2

We were still arguing about it the next afternoon on the slow train from Waverley to Carstairs Stop.

'Nonsense!' I said, as the ticket collector rattled the door closed behind him and left us alone. There were understandably few travellers making for Lanarkshire this February afternoon and we had the compartment to ourselves. 'If this isn't a remarkable coincidence, then I don't know what is! Elyot and Amanda on adjoining balconies is nothing.'

'Nonsense yourself,' said Alec. 'Nothing remarkable about it. For a start, we had more than a week's worth of post. The letters weren't supposed to arrive on the same day at all. And if they weren't nuns, they'd be happy to have a burly policeman come and protect them and wouldn't have turned to you.'

'Hmm,' I said. 'They could have a burly police matron just as easily. And I still don't agree. When they turned to me they got you into the bargain. You, who was a Dorset man when you knew Tony Gourlay. And yet now when he's in trouble in Scotland, here you are in Scotland and my partner to boot. Coincidence.'

Alec's face clouded and he turned to look out of the window. There was nothing to see but a line wavering in the distance, showing where the unbroken brown land met the unbroken grey sky. I could have kicked myself. Alec landed up in Scotland during what became our first case when his fiancée, Scotch herself, was killed and her father left him Dunelgar in gratitude for solving the murder.

'Sorry,' I murmured.

'Not at all,' he replied, turning back with a smile. He is the kindest of men. 'I don't think you ever knew that I met Cara when I was up here visiting Tony. I left him there in that hellhol— Well, I shouldn't be unkind. The nurses do their best and he seemed quite peaceful. But I left him there, took the train to Edinburgh, and there at a party in Queen Street was a pretty little thing with golden curls and a laugh like a silver bell.'

I said nothing. Alec never spoke of the late Cara Duffy and certainly had not touched on what drew them together all those years ago. The pity of it was enough to make one weep. For him to turn from sorrow and madness and memories of war, embrace light and laughter and a merry future in Cara's arms and then, before the wedding, to be standing at her grave and contemplating a story more wretched than shellshock any day . . . I began to see, at last, why he might be quite as hesitant as he seemed about trying again with another.

'That's a remarkably soupy look you're giving me, Dan,' he said. 'I'd rather have an admission that you're quite wrong and I'm right, as usual.'

'Not as usual,' I said, relenting. 'But in this one instance, possibly. Now, if that was the third of the Calders we went through the next stop's ours. And I think I feel it slowing.'

'West Calder,' said Alec nodding. 'Yes, here we go.'

I missed Grant, as we stepped down. Ordinarily she would be on the platform, hectoring the porter. She had taken it very hard to be left in Perthshire to help with the spring cleaning. It had been confirmation of my view of a nunnery that her eyes lit up at the word and she immediately started applying a constant gentle pressure to be included in the expedition. I explained I would not be changing to an evening gown for supper in the refectory and bed after Vespers and so did not need her. I had not foreseen that without her, and without Bunty, I would feel quite so bereft. I did not even have the familiar comfort of my little Morris Cowley nor even the second-best of the hired motorcar we had arranged to have left at the station for us, there being no taxi at Carstairs Stop, for we had agreed that Alec would take it to the hospital and leave me abandoned at the convent with no escape. To be fair, we had agreed it was less likely I should suddenly need to escape my billet than he his, even though he was to put up at the doctor's house in the grounds and not within the actual walls.

The motorcar was there, just as the Lanark garage had assured us it would be, but it seemed to be attracting some attention. Two housewives, complete with babies on their hips, were standing gawping at it and a policeman was walking around it with his hand on his truncheon as though he expected it to bite. As we trudged towards the tableau, following the porter, we were accosted. There is no other word for the way the policeman spoke to us. 'Is this you leaving this lying here?' he shouted, fixing us with a glare.

'I'll just eh . . .' said the porter, putting down our bags and skipping off back to the ticket office.

'What's that, my man?' said Alec, employing the affability which regularly serves him quite nicely.

'I'm my own man, thank you,' said the policeman. 'Is this your car?'

'We've hired it for our use,' I said. 'Is something the matter?'

'So you knew it was going to be left just sitting for anyone to hop in and drive away?' the man went on. The two house-wives tutted and clucked and one of them gave me a look of pity and disdain that would have done Pallister proud. 'Do you not know there's inmates burst out of the asylum and still not caught yet?'

'We did, in fact,' I said. 'Up on the moor, aren't they?'

The policeman narrowed his eyes at me and shook his head. 'A moor, madam,' he said, 'doesn't have a railing round

14

it like Hyde Park.' He turned back to Alec. 'Don't go leaving this lying out, if you don't mind. I daresay they're both long gone by now but better safe than sorry.'

'Indeed,' Alec said. 'Just the two of them then, eh?'

'It only takes one,' the policeman said darkly and with a final glower he was on his way.

Somewhat chastened then, we chugged along the single street of the village, past a run of little shops, a clutch of low cottages, a forbidding church, and finally an open gate affording us just a glimpse of one of those startlingly modern white cubes with metal windows, before we crossed a bridge and were on our way. I returned to our argument, hoping to end it.

'Well, I daresay if the Gourlays hadn't written to you, I'd soon have had to call you in to help. I could hardly go poking about a home for shell-shocked soldiers to see which one of them put a match to the nunnery, could I?'

Alec spluttered, causing his lit pipe to drop from his mouth. There was a lively moment while he took both hands off the wheel to retrieve it then, when the car had been brought back on course, he turned and glared at me.

'Even if the sisters hadn't written to *you*,' he said, 'you'd have had to help *me* with *my* case. I couldn't go poking about this nunnery Tony's supposed to have been burning down even if I wanted to. And the cold remains of an old fire do seem rather beside the point, frankly.'

Then, into my affronted silence, he went on: 'Sorry, Dan. It's seeing Tony again, I suppose. I haven't been back for ten years and he'd have every right to give me the bum's rush for neglecting him.' I could not help but giggle at his inelegant phrase – truly, the silliness was back and forth between my boys and me like a shuttlecock – and the atmosphere warmed again as we left the very last cottage behind us and began to climb.

Someone with a great deal of money and a great desire

for even more had done his pitted best to conquer this landscape, I thought, peering out at it. A mine had been dug – we passed its locked gates with their faded warning signs. Timber had been grown – we drove along a black tunnel through a pine plantation. Rock had been blasted from the very ground, leaving dramatic cliffs and craters by the roadside.

But the land had won hands down. The pale stone buildings, the mine gates, the black quarry scars, the inkblots of trees, were all such tiny patches and the moor was so very nearly endless, a sea of dun-coloured winter grass, rippled by the wind sweeping down from where the hills lay in quiet folds in the far distance.

As we pressed on into the dying light, it was hard not to imagine that even those distant hills were receding and a fancy grew in me that the moor, from cold malevolence, might be stretching out ever further as we travelled, unrolling before us, drawing us on into emptiness. I shivered.

'The heater's on at full tilt already,' said Alec, noticing. 'But it can't be far.'

'It's not that,' I said. 'It's just . . . you will be careful, Alec, won't you?'

'Tony Gourlay wouldn't hurt a fly,' he said. 'Don't make me tell you how I know, Dan. It would only upset you.'

'But if the others are still around here somewhere,' I said, and shivered again. 'It doesn't bear thinking about. I mean, where are they sleeping? What are they eating?' The third shiver was deliberate; I shook the unwelcome idea off me like a dog emerging from water. 'That policeman must be right. They are surely long gone. Away to Glasgow or beyond.'

'But then who's pestering the nuns?' said Alec. 'If you're right in assuming that's why they need you.'

'Not your friend Tony, at least,' I said. 'I wonder if his family knows about the nunnery's continuing difficulties.

This "mischief" I've been summoned to deal with is surely the work of those same rascals from Christmas Eve, wouldn't you say?'

'That's the spirit,' said Alec. 'A quick recce each, overnight, pool our knowledge tomorrow and we might be on our way home in time for tea.'

I tried and failed to match his sprightly confidence but, even had I managed it, it should not have been for long. Shortly after Alec and I parted, I had the worst case of the willies I can remember. It was partly the moor, partly the month, partly Scotland itself, still after all these years. But also it was secrets and sadness and what, if one were not English, one would call evil. 'Nastiness', Nanny Palmer used to say through pursed lips and over lowered spectacles, but nastiness was a matter of error and outrage. The kind of evil I was about to delve into upon the Lanark Moor came from cold inhumanity and made one too bleak and hopeless even to weep.

We had arranged my arrival by telephone the night before and it had sounded perfectly acceptable: one of the sisters would wait by the gates for me and Alec would drop me off and be on his way. I sat forward when the convent wall rose up, unmistakable, on our right-hand side. It was six feet tall, roughcast stone with spikes along the top, and nothing visible beyond.

'Why on earth,' Alec said, craning up at it, 'would anyone break out of a bin only to break into another one? Especially one working so hard to keep you out.'

'There are probably easier ways than over the front wall,' I said. In fact, I had seen a little gap in the overgrown grass of the verge, a path leading to something that could have been a lych-gate.

'It looks pretty unyielding to me,' Alec said. 'And blimey! Look at that.' Fifty yards further on the spiked top of the wall rose and formed an arch over a pair of extremely solid iron gates, the individual poles so close together that surely barely a hand could reach through.

Behind them, we could see a small dark smudge with an even smaller white smudge contained in it, standing statue still. Alec drew to the side of the road and stopped, then hopped out to retrieve my suitcase and hat box from the boot. The small figure moved forward and the gate swung noiselessly open. Either she was very strong or the hinges were good ones.

'Mrs Gilver?' She had a clear high voice with a trace of a west coast lilt in it and a mild smiling face. 'I'm Sister Monica. Welcome to St Ultan's. Thank you for coming to our aid this way.' She turned to Alec and her smile dimmed a little. 'I'll take the bags,' she said. 'I'm sturdier than I look.'

'If you're sure,' said Alec. 'I could drop them at the door for you.'

'Ocht, no,' said Sister Monica. 'It's hardly a step.' Again she spoke brightly and her smile had widened but I was sure she wanted rid of him.

'Until tomorrow then,' Alec said and climbed back behind the wheel. He drove off and disappeared. I could not quite understand why; perhaps there was a dip in the lane or perhaps a fog had descended, invisible against the moor but effective just the same. Perhaps just the fading light hid him from me. The day was certainly giving up. The afternoon had reached that moment of perfect balance when the land and sky are the same shade of bruised grey, like cold ash. For whatever reason, as Sister Monica clanged the gate shut again, he was gone and I felt myself swallowing hard.

'They'll just be finishing None,' Monica said. 'Sister Mary will give you tea in her study.' Then she seized the bags and beetled off, soon lost beyond a bend in the drive, or into that mist, or under the twilight, or whatever it was. Like Alec, she was gone.

'Thank you,' I called. 'And thank you for coming down to wait for me. It's not much of a . . .' – I felt very foolish shouting into emptiness – 'day,' I finished, quietly. There *was* a fog, rolling down from the high ground, held back by the convent wall but seeping in fingers through the gates. I turned away and looked along the drive. With Sister Monica's footsteps faded and the sound of Alec's engine gone there was silence. I could not account for the soundlessness, could not for a moment tell what was missing. Then it struck me. It was twilight without birdsong.

The last of the pine plantation had been miles back. Outside the wall there was not a single tree or bush. Just miles of nothing. I could see bare branches inside the walls, though, the ordered ranks of an orchard, and did not understand why there were no nests there. I hurried up the drive, trying to enjoy the homely sound of my heels on the gravel and to ignore the creeping notion that I was suddenly and utterly alone.

My mother once got through a punishing Atlantic crossing by loathing and composing critiques of the blameless Constable prints on her cabin walls. And church services in my childhood were passed pleasurably in the study of stone masonry and the search for the green man we knew was somewhere among the carving. So it was a lifelong habit, further honed during a long year of galleries and chateaux at finishing school, to attend to art and architecture, identifying, cataloguing and judging its merits, whenever one came upon a new example. Thus it was less remarkable than it might seem that when St Ultan's hove out of the mist, despite my disquiet of minutes before, I appraised it with a practised eye.

I could not say what I had been expecting and yet it surprised me. A convent, in my imagining, was either Gothic or austere, but here before me was a rather good, solid, Queen Anne house only somewhat spoiled by an addition just visible behind the stable wall that had the air of a barracks about it. It was well kept, the window frames bright with new paint and the roof neat with slates still where the roofers had nailed them. (Scotch houses do have a tendency to let their slates slip, like the unravelling curls of a lady, sans maid, towards the end of a warm evening.)

Sister Monica was waiting on the step by the open door, her breath pluming out into the chill as she recovered from the trot up the drive with my bags.

'They're still at prayer as I said, and I need to get to my work.' She smiled at me. 'Can I show you to Mother Mary's study and have you wait for her there?'

'She's been promoted,' I said, thinking to make a joke, but Sister Monica's face fell and she clapped a hand across her mouth, her eyes filling and horrified. Without another word she ushered me in, across an oak-floored and oak-panelled hall that smelled of strong soap and through a door at the back into a dark room, where she left me.

The study, which must surely have started life as a dining room, was quite twenty-five feet long and perhaps only fifteen wide with fruit and fowl carved on the oak panel above the fireplace. It had the same strong smell of plain soap as the hall and, looking around with the benefit of long experience – for Gilverton has a great deal of carved panelling, I suspected that they washed the floor and walls with it, drying out the oak to a nasty yellowish grey. It needed a vat of beeswax soon or it would start to crack.

The rest of the place suggested that waxing wood to bring out its beauty was not a pressing concern. The brass elephants that marched in a line along the chimneypiece were cloudy from lack of polish and a little green in the corners. The curtains were slub repp and hung to six inches above the skirtings, clearly handed down to this room from elsewhere. The furniture was a mixture of cumbersome stained pine, neither old enough to be quaint nor new enough to be convenient, and some modern cellulosed enamel. I deduced that the nuns had accepted any gifts offered and had spared all expense when shopping.

Hugh would have approved. A good roof and frequent painting of the outside of window frames, combined with not even a whiff of interior comfort, was housekeeping as he understood it. The bed in his dressing room had a horse-hair mattress and an army blanket and both facts made him happy.

There was one exception to the general drabness in Sister Mary's study, though, and it would have made Hugh more unhappy than anything else I could fairly imagine. An enor-mous crucifix was hung high upon the narrow, end wall. I ignored the chair set in front of the paper-strewn desk – a penitent's chair, if ever I saw one, for what was a Mother Superior if not a headmistress really? – and went to look at it more closely.

It was plaster, I rather thought, or at least majolica, with here and there little chips through the paint into its crum-bling whiteness. They did not affect the look of the thing much overall, though, for the majority of the surface was white anyway, the same white used for the flesh of the long and twisted body, the cloth about the hips, and the cross itself. There were only three colours: the hair and crown were painted brown, the eyes drooping half-closed from exhaustion were painted blue and then there was the blood. Three dark blooms of blood at hands and crossed feet, and thin trickles down either side of his weary face, from the bite of the thorns. I looked back at the desk, appalled at the thought of spending one's days paying milk bills and ordering kerosene while that plaster figure, frozen in eternal agony, looked on.

'I know. I agree,' said a voice and I spun round on my heels. She stood in the doorway, dressed from neck to ankle in the same black garment as Sister Monica. Her face was almost as white as her wimple but she did not look ill or wan, simply pale. Her eyes, small and very blue, like speedwell, were twinkling at me, and the shine on the apples of her pale cheeks showed as two dots when she smiled.

'Agree with what?' I said.

'That it's odd to sit at my desk and tend to my daily tasks with such a thing glowering down.' I must have looked startled. 'But He would be here watching over me anyway. And it does stop me from complaining. Our Mother always said He helped her remember that her woes were few, her sorrows light and her debt impossible to repay.' I tried to look equal to such talk but evidently did not succeed, because she went on: 'Now I've discomfited you. I'm sorry. Sit, Mrs Gilver. Someone will be bringing you tea. And welcome to St Ultan's. We've just been saying a special prayer of thanks for your intention and another prayer of good hope for your work here.' She was mistaken if she thought *this* discomfited me any less.

'Thank you,' I said. 'Sister Mary, is it?'

She nodded and, gesturing to the penitent's chair, she walked around the desk and let herself drop with a puffed-out sigh. She moved a stack of paper to one side and clasped her hands on the cleared wood.

'Sister Monica called you Mother Mary and then seemed upset,' I said.

She nodded, heaved another sigh, and passed a hand over her eyes before she answered. I had taken her to be a young woman but as she lowered the hand again I rather thought she was my age, over forty and perhaps close to fifty. Tired with it too.

'Our Mother's name was Mary,' she said. 'Strictly, I should have taken a different name when we were here together. Mary Agnes or Mary Theresa. Somehow I came not to. And now I regret it.'

'Are there rules about such things?' I said, intrigued. But

she did not answer, her mind setting off along a different path.

'Poor Sister Monica,' she said. 'I do it myself ten times a day. Six weeks she's been gone and I'm still saving up funny little things to tell her and wondering if the mutton is cut too thick for her teeth. She had terrible teeth, Mrs Gilver, and wouldn't see a dentist. She said it was a waste of money but I think she was scared of the pain. Doctors, too.'

'Six weeks,' I said. 'So it was your Mother Superior who died in the fire? The newspapers didn't say. At least the ones we take didn't.'

'So I hear,' said Sister Mary. 'We get our news second hand from Sister Jude and Sister Francis at the village school. Of course, it'll all come out when the diocese delivers its guiding words on the succession – if any of them are still paying attention. But they were remarkably restrained at the time. The bishop said "a sister of the order" and the gentlemen of the press left it at that.'

'I'm glad they didn't pry,' I said. 'And a little surprised, I have to say.'

'It's sad how surprised you can be to find kindness, isn't it?' said Mary. Then she laughed. 'See now, if Our Mother was still here she'd call me gloomy for that.' For a moment she let her memories carry her away and when she came back she looked older still. Definitely fifty. 'And here comes your tea,' she said, taking her hands off the desk, although I had heard nothing.

The woman who carried the tray was taking a risk being so close to a milk jug; she had the sourest face I had ever seen. Her wimple cinched her tight under the jaw and behind her cheeks, making the most of her pouched wrinkles. Her mouth was a grim and lipless line, like the line which cut down between her brows, and her eyes were sharp, narrowed as she darted a glance at me.

'Ah, Sister Steven,' said Sister Mary and I forgave the

woman some of it, for that was a burden. 'Thank you. This is Mrs Gilver, come to help us.'

'We have the Father, the Son and the Holy Spirit helping us,' said Sister Steven, banging down the tray. 'And now Mrs Gilver too, eh?' Then she turned without another word and stumped out.

I was well brought up in the best Victorian style, by my mother and Nanny Palmer and Mlle Toulemonde and a bevy of finishing-school-mistresses, and while I curse them at times I thank them much more often, for few are the moments when I am startled beyond the reach of a conventional remark. Sister Steven, though, had bowled me for a boundary.

'Ahh,' I said, and stopped; all possible continuings were either lies or blasphemy.

To my surprise and relief Sister Mary, when I looked at her, was biting her lip and holding back giggles. I lifted my eyebrows and let my breath go and something about my face set the giggles free. She had an infectious laugh, as innocent as a girl, and I joined her.

'Oh, poor Sister Steven,' she said. 'She's grief-stricken and frightened and furious with herself for both, of course, so it's turned her even more stern than usual.'

'Why shouldn't she be?' I said. 'Why the fury?'

'Our Mother has gone to her rest, by God's grace,' Mary said. 'And we submit with obedience to God's will. We should be letting her go and praying for her soul. A fractious nun is disobeying one of her vows.'

'But then why am I here?' I asked.

'Because Our Mother's death was the devil's work. I was telling you what Sister Steven thinks, Mrs Gilver, not me. *I* think we must pray hard, certainly, but also work with all the wit God has given us to see that the devil is done down.'

'The devil,' I said, hoping she spoke figuratively.

'Working through the hand of some poor misguided soul. Just as *He* works through ours.'

I bit into the biscuit as I nodded. It was warm and buttery and studded with bits of candied ginger. The first scrap of comfort I had seen at St Ultan's.

'So,' I said. 'You're ready to row for shore.'

'Just show me the oars,' Sister Mary said grimly.

3

I learned a great deal sitting there in the study on that first day, not only about the dreadful night that had brought me there but about St Ultan's and about Mother Mary too.

'She founded the convent,' Sister Mary said. 'In the 1880s when she was quite a young woman. The house belongs to the Church strictly, but she was accepted into holy orders and sent enough helpers to get things up and running.'

'Was it her family home?' I said, wondering how such an extraordinary thing had come about.

'Nothing like that,' said Mary. 'She was here alone for a while, on a kind of retreat, I suppose you would say, and during it she received her calling.'

'Quite unusual in those days for a young woman to live alone,' I said. 'Was her family Bohemian that way?'

Sister Mary laughed. 'Not at all. Grocers. She was a house-keeper before she was a nun.'

'She sounds remarkable,' I said.

'She was a saint,' said Mary. 'I loved her. We all did. We are lost without her, Mrs Gilver.'

I nodded, although I found it strange. I had always thought of the religious life as bent on breaking earthly bonds like love but I supposed if one lived in close quarters for long enough one's human nature would prevail.

'How long have you been here, Sister Mary?' I said.

'I've always been here,' she replied. 'I'm fifty and I've never been anywhere else.'

That would do it, I thought to myself. If she had entered the novitiate at fifteen and graduated to her black veil in the normal length of time, then for thirty years she must truly have thought of the late Mary as her mother. Thinking it over, I was glad the conversation had taken that turn; it helped me, where I was going, to go gently.

'Can I turn to the events of Christmas Eve?' I said. 'Do you have time just now? And would you like someone with you? One of your sisters, to hold your hand?'

'Oh surely not,' Sister Mary said. 'You need to interview us all quite separately, don't you? To make sure our stories tally?' She noticed my look, which was not a feat of observation, for I am sure my mouth had dropped open.

She gave a sheepish smile. 'I played up the notion of the stranger without when I wrote to you, of course, because I wanted to read the letter aloud at supper before I sent it. But now that you're here I can tell you about the—'

'Stranger within?'

'Something like that,' she agreed. 'Someone was not where she ought to have been that night. Someone is not telling the truth about where she was and so who knows what else she might be hiding? I can't get to the bottom of it at all.'

'Tell me the whole story from the beginning,' I said.

She nodded, drew a deep breath and began. 'We were in the chapel, of course, although it wasn't a Mass. We had no priest, so it was only prayers. But it was perfect, just us waiting quietly. It was a perfect night, too. A full moon, as bright as the eastern star must have been, and the moor as cold as the hillsides of Judea. A more perfect Christmas Eve could never have been. We were at silent prayer, it was the very moment of midnight striking, and the first thing I knew was Sister Anne sniffing. I thought she was weeping – she's a romantic sort of woman – but she smelled smoke, you see. Next Mother Mary herself was sniffing and she got to her feet. "Something's burning," she said. Then we were all at sixes and sevens, rushing about, getting in each other's way, trying to get out of the chapel.'

'You *left* the chapel?'

'We had left the candles burning on the Christmas tree.'

'Christmas tree?' I knew I sounded startled, but Christmas trees were still rather exotic in northern parts, and one might have expected them to be renounced upon entering the cloister.

'In the hall out there. We were holding a children's party the next day.'

They did not seem to have renounced much at all.

She dipped her head. 'But I daresay we would have had one even without the children's party. So beautiful with its star and the little candles. We had a sand bucket and of course we should have snuffed them when we all went over to prayers, but Sister Anne pleaded with Our Mother to leave them lit. "Think of coming back and finding them twinkling," she said. "We can have our cocoa and open our gifts by the light of the Christmas tree. Think how beautiful it'll be." And so, since the candles had never caused us any trouble before, and since our prayers without a full Mass are short . . .'

'But I don't understand,' I said. 'If a Christmas-tree candle fell over, why is a man accused?'

'I'm explaining why we thought what we did,' said Sister Mary. 'It's the only way I can tell it, in order. We all smelled smoke, over in the chapel, and we all thought the same thing and rushed across here to check on the tree.' I groaned, beginning to understand. 'But when we got here all was well. We snuffed the candles then – Sister Anne did it herself; too rattled by the scare to let them carry on burning – and the rest of us went to look for the fire. The kitchen was fine. The quiet room and refectory, recreation room and library – all the rooms with fires were fine. None of our cells have fires but still we checked them and there was nothing to be found. By then we couldn't smell the smoke anymore and we began to wonder if perhaps the gamekeepers had started burning off the heather out there for the Boxing Day shoot.'

I nodded. Many a Christmas at Gilverton has been spent coughing and spluttering if a sudden change in the wind brought the smoke from a heather fire down off the grouse moor and in at our windows. For the maids would not countenance leaving windows shut even in the depths of midwinter; rooms must be aired after breakfast or we would all be dead by luncheon.

'And then Our Mother unlocked the door to go to the other side and check with them – although we knew better than to worry, because the nurses sleep over there and they would have raised the alarm.'

'The other side?'

'The orphanage,' said Sister Mary. I must have looked surprised for she smiled at me. 'Didn't you realise when you heard our name?' I shook my head. 'St Ultan is the patron saint of orphans.'

'So you went to check on the orphans,' I said, trying to coax her back to her story. 'And I take it they were fine?'

At last there was a faint flush of colour upon those pure white cheeks. 'They were, as it turned out,' Sister Mary said, 'although we didn't know that until later. We never got as far as the other side that night. The quickest way through is from this study and— Look, let me show you.'

She stood and lit an oil lamp that sat on her desk, her touch quick and sure, clearly someone who carried out the task every day. I had been just as dexterous before electric lights took over at Gilverton, but I would fumble if I attempted it now.

Taking the lamp with her, she glided over to a door in the corner, unbolted it, unlocked it and stepped through, beckoning me.

I followed and found that we were in a tiny room with a

door in each wall. Sister Mary gestured around, causing the lamp shadows to sail and wheel about.

'That's the covered way to the chapel,' she said. 'And that way goes through to the children's side. This leads to . . . Well, it used to be a little storage room but now it's . . . Well, now it's this.' She unlocked the door and stood on the threshold, holding the lamp up high.

'Oh my God!' I said. Then: 'Forgive me, Sister. I couldn't help it.'

'Our Mother said the same,' she told me. The light was shimmering as her hand shook. I was not surprised, even though she must have seen this numerous times since the night it was first discovered, for the words that had been daubed all over the walls in red paint were beyond brutish. 'Witches' was the mildest of them. Its rhyming partner was there too in letters a foot high, but others were words I had never seen written and rarely heard spoken, the worst only once by a young captain I accompanied on a hospital visit from the convalescent home, when he was having his leg re-broken to set it straight. He had never looked at me again without blushing.

'When did this happen?' I said, wondering if this was the "mischief" she had written of in her letter to me.

'That night,' said Sister Mary. 'Christmas Eve. While we were all at supper. Our Mother was in here tidying away a few papers at sundown and all was well. Then, by the small hours . . .' She waved the lamp and I caught another few gems from the words daubed around the walls.

'Can't you paint it over?' I asked.

'Sergeant Gibb is very forceful and very convincing,' she said.

'I think I've met him and I agree. What has he convinced you of?'

'He says it's evidence,' she replied in a strange, hard voice. 'He told us to leave it and so we're leaving it.'

It was evidence of great wickedness in my view. Sister Mary in her letter had talked of mischief, but this was a far cry from it. It was not even the formless and faceless evil I felt threaten out on the moor; it was particular and personal and gleeful somehow.

'We've moved our papers out, what's left of them,' said Sister Mary, and for the first time I paid attention to what the room might have been before it became an outrage. It was not even ten feet square, windowless, and lined with shelves and drawers. The storage room, Sister Mary had called it and I had imagined trunks and cases, old bicycles and the like. Of course, nuns had little need for any of these.

'Were some of your papers taken?' I asked.

She shook her head and I noticed that once that movement was over, the lamplight was steady; she had gathered herself. 'They were strewn all around and crumpled into balls,' she said. 'Paint poured over them.'

Indeed, when I looked closely, I could see breaks in the paint that had spilled in trails across the wooden floor as it was lashed at the walls. We used to do it with cut-paper shapes when we were children, sloshing paint over everything and then enchanted to see the sharp lines appear when Nanny's careful fingers peeled the shapes away to reveal apples and boats and, as our skill advanced, horses and elephants and, one rainy Easter, a fairground with helter-skelters, roundabouts and swings. Here there were only jagged shapes, no sense to them. Then I blinked and bent to look more closely, Sister Mary lowering the lamp to help me.

There were footprints, enormous things, tracking here and there in the blood-red paint. Size twelve boots, I diagnosed, and after my years of detecting I was pretty sure I knew. They were faint at the toe and sometimes at the heel too. Working boots, the leather contracted from seasons of rain

31

so that the toes turned up, and overdue for the cobbler so that the heels were worn.

'We're keeping them in Sister Steven's cell for the time being. It was the housekeeper's room when St Ultan's was a family home and it has a large cupboard off it that used to be for luggage, I imagine.'

'Keeping . . . the boots?' I said.

'Oh, those boots!' said Sister Mary. 'The footprints are a red herring, apparently. Ask Sergeant Gibb and he'll tell you at great length. No, I mean the papers. All our very old documents are boxed up in there anyway so we added what we could salvage from amongst the paint splashes too, and shut the door on the lot.'

'Returning to the night in question then,' I said. 'What did you do next?'

'We didn't know *what* to do. Sister John wanted to ring the police. Our Mother preferred to pray for guidance.'

'What about you, Sister Mary?'

She looked around at the daubed walls before she answered.

'Me? I just wanted to get the youngsters out, especially our novices – Sister Joan and Sister Winifred – and start to clear it up. Blot it out, I suppose. But Our Mother told us all to go to bed and ask for guidance and said we would talk again the next morning. Christmas morning! When we should have been gayer than any other day of the year.'

'So you went to bed?'

'We did and Our Mother's cell is up there,' she pointed, 'at the north-west corner of the house looking out over the chapel. It's the only one that does. After her prayers, she opened her curtains as she always used to – she loved the moonlight shining in. And then, not until then, an hour later almost, she saw the flames.'

'The chapel!' I said.

'That's why I wanted to show you in here,' Sister Mary said. 'It would beggar belief if you hadn't seen it with your own eyes, but after we found this mess, the smell of smoke went quite out of our minds.'

As it had mine, weeks later, so I could hardly judge her.

'Especially since we couldn't actually smell it anymore once we were back in the house,' Mary said. 'Hard as it might seem to believe, we all forgot. Well, Our Mother and the senior sisters forgot. If any of the youngsters remembered and simply didn't want to push forward at least they've had the kindness not to cast it up since.'

'So,' I said. 'You went to bed.'

'And so even though we had smelled those first wisps, we couldn't save it. All our treasures. Come and I'll show you.'

She led me back into the little anteroom, ringed around with doors, and this time opened a different one. It led to a corridor, modern and workaday but nevertheless looking rather ominous by the light of Mary's wavering lamp. There was just one door at the far end and this she unlocked with a sizeable key drawn from the folds of her habit and then stood aside to let me step through.

'Good God!' I said. This was worse, in its way, than the painted travesty in the storage room. One could still tell that it was a chapel, from the shape of the arched rafters and the rows of pews, blackened and blistered as they now were, but the sarking was gone and the slates had slipped and crashed, splintering into shards that crunched under our feet. Above our heads, the fog was seeping in and the smell of damp and cold and long-dead ash was indescribable. The walls stood and of course here and there some patches of painting showed where gaudy murals had once adorned the place. Sister Mary stood amongst the mess with her head bowed. Just in time, before I spoke, I noticed her lips moving and bent my head too.

After a moment, she looked up and smiled at me, rather a watery smile but with courage in it.

'And why haven't you begun on the work of clearing it and getting it repaired?'

'Evidence,' she said. 'Sergeant Gibb again. Or at least, not evidence exactly. But he told us that once the last of the men are caught and they are all put to trial it would be good to be able to show the jury.'

'I see,' I lied, thinking photographs would do nicely. 'The police are confident that the last two men *will* be caught then? In the end?'

'Every constabulary in the land is looking out for them,' she said. 'And the ports, too.'

'But I thought they were still on the moor?' I said. 'I thought they were still making nuisances of themselves.'

Sister Mary shook her head. 'Who can say? They are somewhere. And someone is.'

'It does seem a bit thick to leave you with this mess if they might be stowing away from Southampton harbour!'

'Well . . .' She shifted from foot to foot. I heard the scrape and crunch of it even though her habit hid it from view.

'Well, what?'

'We've never been a rich house,' she said. 'We do unsung work in a very unsung corner of the land. We've never had patrons or bequests. But surely someone might want to help us now. We've sent letters off. I could show you the copies tomorrow.'

I nodded, although to my mind it was just about the most unseemly thing I had ever heard. To turn the tragedy into the sort of story which might catch the notice of a patron? Monstrous! And it did make me think back to what Sister Mary had said about a stranger within. How much could a nun, with her vows of poverty, wish to be in a 'rich house'? What might she do to attract such riches?

'It was all of you, was it?' I asked. 'That night? *Everyone* charged over to the Christmas tree and was then distracted by the paint?'

Sister Mary nodded and returned an innocent gaze. She clearly had no notion of where my thoughts had taken me.

'And was everyone there?' I asked. 'Everyone who lives here was at prayers?'

Again she nodded. 'Except the orphans and the nurses,' she said. 'Some of the oldest children ask every year to stay up but we're too canny for that! They ask the same at Hogmanay after all.'

I shared in her gentle laughter, while tucking away the titbit about nurses and some quite grown-up children. Then I shook myself. If anyone – and it was a stretch to imagine it at all – could harbour the ambition to have a convent patronised by rich donors and stuffed with the sorts of unknowable things rich convents contain, it had to be a nun, not a nurse, and certainly not an orphan who would soon enough grow up and leave St Ultan's behind him.

Of course, there were many more motives than that rather nonsensical one. I thought I could probably discount the nurses whatever the motive though, for if the convent had burned down they would have lost their jobs, and jobs were not easy to come by anywhere, certainly not in this desolate spot. The orphans, however, offered a much richer seam. They were by definition rough and unruly children, it was safe to say. And among their number, whatever it was, there were bound to be a few actually villainous, resentful of the firm hand of the sisters who were bringing them up and only too ready to lash out and repay the Church that I imagined doled out instruction and judgement in place of the love the children had foregone.

'Where did they get in?' I said, returning to the accepted wisdom that inmates from the hospital had done this. 'When we drove along the lane, the wall seemed pretty much unbreachable.'

'The wall goes all the way around the original house,' Sister Mary said. 'But it's a little lower at what were the stables, where the children's wing was built. And there are no spikes.'

I nodded. It was a similar pattern to that at Gilverton and at home when I was a child. There were always plenty of servants around the nether regions and only the front of the house, where large rooms full of silver and paintings lay empty, was protected by railings and unscalable walls.

'And how about the way between one side and the other?' I asked. I hoped she would think I was continuing to imagine the journey of a crazed escapee, but quietly to myself I was wondering about that burly disgruntled orphan.

'There's no carriage gate,' she said. 'In the old days, the carriages were brought along the lane and up the drive.'

'How inconvenient,' I said, although it was far from unusual.

'The little gate is kept strictly locked,' Sister Mary went on. 'For there's no way to stop the children coming through to the orchard and stripping the apple trees bare. And the only other ways between the two wings are inside. Through the kitchen and the way I showed you.' She swung her lamp towards the covered passage. 'Which reminds me, I must give you a set of keys. You can't come running to me whenever you need to look at something.'

'So both sides are kept apart?' I said, hoping that I had not asked one question too many.

I had.

'No one broke in to the *orphans'* side!' she said. Then she widened her eyes. In the sickly yellow light of the oil lamp their speedwell blue was washed out and looked as unearthly pale as her face. 'The children?' she said. 'Did you think I meant to cast suspicion on the *children*?'

'I've heard of orphans troubled enough—' I began.

'I've heard things too,' she said, speaking more crisply than I had yet heard. 'Of brutal places and broken people. St Ultan's is not one of them. Go and visit them tomorrow and see.'

36

'I shall,' I said, matching her tone. 'I have many things to see and much to learn. What started it, for instance? Did you find the spot?' This return to the simple fact of the fire, to the where and how, away from such questions as the why and who, soothed her.

'In the sacristy,' she said, pointing. 'With petroleum-soaked rags. Sergeant Gibb told us so and he seemed very sure.'

I started to crunch through the broken slates in the direction she had pointed but she laid a hand on my arm.

'Come back and look properly in the daylight,' she said. 'I didn't mean you to tackle it right away. I only wanted to show you where it happened, in the dark. To give you a feeling for how it was that night, I suppose. It wasn't kind, forgive me.'

'It was necessary,' I said. 'I'm quite tough, Sister Mary. I was never faint-hearted and the last few years have worked upon me like the smith's forge.' I gave her a smile. 'I only hope my questions don't upset *you*.' I had taken out my cigarette case as I spoke and struck a match, ready to light one, hoping to show my worldliness.

But Sister Mary cleared her throat. 'We have had to move to other quarters for our prayers in the meantime,' she said, 'but the chapel has not been deconsecrated.'

I blew out the match and looked around me helplessly, wondering where to put it. In the end I licked two fingers, pinched its head between them, and then put it in my pocket.

'But don't be worried about upsetting us,' Mary went on. 'Upset *me* as much as you like. Upset all of us until we take to our beds with the vapours. Except perhaps Sister Catherine. She's over ninety and gets rather bewildered.'

'Well, then my next question is this,' I said. 'If Mother Mary was in her bedroom in the main part of the house and saw the fire from her window, how did she come to die in it?'

Sister Mary – I could just see her in dimness – blinked

at me and worked her mouth a moment or two before she answered.

'She came to try to save it, of course,' she said. 'We all did. She raised the alarm and we all came running. To save our Bible and our altar cloth. Our beautiful statue of St Ultan with the children about his feet. We don't even have so much as a photograph of it. Our candlesticks and our votive stand. We had a painting of the Blessed Virgin that had been here since our first days.'

I was glad she could not see my face any more clearly than I could hers. There was not a painting, tapestry nor book in the whole of Gilverton that would have me enticed back in if I had got out and it was burning. If Hugh, Donald, Teddy, Bunty and the servants were safe, I would walk away without a backward glance. I daresay if I had argued with Sister Mary she would have hidden behind her veil; would have claimed that these objects were sacred and worth the sacrifice. For the Bible, one could mount a defence, but as far as candlesticks went I was unmoved. And I had seen the sorts of pictures of the Madonna which were in fashion in the eighties when St Ultan's swung into gear and I would not have flung a cup of cold tea to save a single one of them.

Sister Mary was speaking again. It was fully night now, probably almost five o'clock, and the only thing I could really see was her white linen wimple and her linen-white face. I shivered, but she was either wearing stout undergarments or was impervious to the creeping chill, for her voice sounded perfectly steady.

'It was like something from Hell,' she said. 'Like one of those pictures by Bosch. I thought they were heretical when I saw one in a gallery in Edinburgh, but he has painted no more than the truth. I knew they were my own sisters but in the flames and smoke, they were . . . monstrous. And the noise! Do you know how *noisy* a fire is? And then we were coughing and sick and once, one of the youngsters' gowns caught fire and we had to throw her down and roll her, beating the flames out. Sister Joan. She trembled for days and she still starts at any sort of racket. The coalman came and tipped a good lot into the bunker and she hurried away whimpering.'

'And did you manage to rescue any of your things?' I said. I knew I sounded acerbic, but could not help myself: I thought nuns were supposed to renounce worldly goods, not make themselves sick trying to stop the goods from getting charred.

'The font,' said Sister Mary. 'It was near the back door and Our Mother had carried it out herself before I even got here.'

'A stone font?' I asked, unbelieving.

'Oak,' said Sister Mary. 'Fumed oak and heavy enough at that. It was a gift, commissioned for us by a friend when the chapel was first reconsecrated for the first nuns who came here.'

Mid-Victorian, in other words. Fumed oak! If I owned any fumed oak, and there was a handy fire, I would be throwing it on.

'And we got quite a lot of the hassocks out,' she continued, but even she did not manage to sound pleased by that little triumph.

'And did anyone summon the fire brigade?' I said. 'Is there one nearby?'

'There was no one on the exchange. It was the middle of the night and it was Christmas Eve. Some of my sisters got a chain of fire buckets going and Our Mother rang the bell inside the chapel. For as long as she could anyway. And I rang the orphan bell myself for a good few minutes, but I couldn't bear not knowing what was going on, so in the end I left off and came back round to see if I could help. I saw her going back in the second time.'

'The Reverend Mother?'

'Yes, she said she was going to try to get the books – the Bible and prayer book were on the altar. Sister Steven and Sister John were carrying out tapestries then, but they were smouldering and . . . it sounds all wrong but when they got them out into the night air, they seemed to burst into flames. It was quite diabolical to see. Three times it happened. They just . . . burst into flames as we looked at them.'

'It was probably the extra oxygen,' I said. 'Inside the building, where the flames were worst . . . Well, I don't pretend to understand it but a fire can use up oxygen and burn itself out.' Hugh had explained it to me once and, although I had not been listening particularly, that much had gone in. 'Did she come out again?' I asked. Sister Mary was silent for so long I thought that was my answer but in the end she did speak.

'She never made it back out,' she said. 'The roof fell in while she was still at the altar. Sister John escaped at the last minute and . . . Well, everyone else escaped. I think it must be right, though, what you said about the fire burning out, because it was worst at the door. Inside, sisters were moving about quite easily. Sister John saw Our Mother – spoke to her, even.'

'Do you know what she—' I began and then thought the better of it. 'Never mind, I shall ask Sister John herself. As you said, I would do best to make sure the stories tally.'

'Oh but I know what Our Mother said to Sister John,' said Mary. 'We all know that. We've been trying to decide whatever she might have meant by it. It's been in our minds every waking minute and in our dreams too, I daresay.'

I waited, with my breath held.

'She clasped Sister John's arm and spoke quite urgently. "Find Ultan. Find Ultan." She said it over and over again. "Find Ultan. Find Ultan." And then she said. "Hide Mary."'

40

'Was that all?' It sounded like the ramblings of someone crazed and desperate, watching her treasures burn, the plaster saint and painted virgin she gave her life to save.

'One more thing. She said one last thing before she let go of Sister John and went back to the altar. She said, "All these years, it was real."'

4

Mary showed me to my room, after silently handing me an impressive ring of keys. I do not know which one of us was more wrung out by the telling of the tale, standing there in the blackened ruins of the chapel where Mother Mary had died. Certainly she left me without more than the words that Vespers was at six and supper at half past. As soon as she had gone I let myself fall back onto my bed like a shot stag.

If I had known how paltry the mattress was and that it was laid over a wooden pallet I should not have done so. I heard a crunch in my neck as my head knocked against the boards under the thin pillow and felt every knob of my backbone as though they had each been rapped with rulers. Had there been any mirrors bigger than tea plates in the whole of the convent I am sure I would have seen, over the next few days, my entire spine from nape to tail turn black and blue.

'Find Ultan. Hide Mary,' I said to myself, as I began unpacking my things. 'All these years, it was real.' I laid my underclothes in one of the two drawers, lined with newspaper, and arranged my hairbrush and sponge bag on top of the chest. There was no wardrobe at all, just a row of five wooden pegs sticking out of the wall opposite the window. Comfort, in short, was not to the fore. Worse even than the pegs was the fact that the fireplace had been stopped up with a piece of board and someone had painted upon it a crude picture of logs burning brightly.

There was, however, a daybed, somewhat softer than the bed proper, with a small Benares table drawn up beside it, and upon it a cushion and a lumpy crocheted blanket in garish colours; the sort of blanket Girl Guides produce in exchange for badges on their arms. Or I thought, taking a closer look, perhaps Brownies.

'Find Ultan, hide Mary, all these years it was real,' I said again, tucking up on the daybed with the notebook I had unearthed from the bottom of my hatbox and gazing at the painted flames. It was irresistible, a mysterious bauble dangled before me and doing its job: distracting me from all sorts of sensible questions such as the nature of the mischief at which Sister Mary had hinted, the telephone number of the station where the bossy Sergeant Gibb might be found, and a full list of the names of nuns I had to interview.

'Find Ultan,' I said. 'Hide Mary.'

A plaster St Ultan with children at his feet, beloved of all the nuns. Of course, she wanted him saved. And of course a plaster Mary would be very dear to their hearts and its loss would weigh heavy. I felt a flicker of doubt even as I thought this. She had not urged this Sister John to *save* them, either of them. She wanted one found and one hidden. But was one lost? And hidden from whom? And why?

I pondered it a while, my gaze following the thick red brush strokes on the fireplace board. It bore the marks of a childish hand as much as did the blanket. Presently, I turned my thoughts to the second part of her message, her last words of all. 'All these years it was real.' It must connect to the earlier utterances somehow, if I put my mind to it.

I drew an utter blank. Every notion I considered seemed more ludicrous than the last. If paint had peeled from a statue of St Ultan or the Virgin and it had revealed itself to be Renaissance marble, chipped away at by some Italian master and therefore priceless, it would still be there amongst the slates and charred timbers.

There was another possibility, rather disrespectful of a lifelong nun and I baulked at the thought even in the privacy of my own head. I could hear the sisters singing somewhere downstairs, like angels and yet still it struck me that if the Reverend Mother had never deeply believed all of the tenets of her faith but then someone – Ultan or Mary – had appeared to her in there in the conflagration, she would have realised how wrong she had been to doubt them. Thankfully, that seemed like nonsense when I regarded it for more than a minute and I breathed my relief out very heartily; I would not have relished telling Sister Mary, much less Sister Steven, such a theory.

I shook my head to remove it, pointing out sternly to myself that if an hour in a convent had me positing miracles then Nanny Palmer had failed, and bent my thoughts to more sensible paths again. A crime had been perpetrated upon the Little Sisters of St Ultan and I needed to think like a solver of crimes. There would be a thread of sense in there somewhere even if the guilty man was quite out of his mind, as one who scattered files, painted obscenities and set fires on sacred altars must be.

I sat up, letting the lumpy blanket fall around my hips. He had not set the fire on the sacred altar, though, had he? He had set fire to the sacristy. I was not entirely sure – for my many years in the Presbyterian north, trailing along to Sunday service with Hugh, had begun to interfere with the knowledge of my early days in the warmth of Northamptonshire and the embrace of high Anglicanism – but I was *pretty* sure that a sacristy was much of a muchness with a vestry: a place where robes and vestments were stored. It was rather a dull part of a chapel to set light to if one were in some sort of mad irreligious frenzy. It was almost as perverse to desecrate a convent by daubing oaths and ugliness on a glorified box room. Why not the refectory where the nuns would have to eat their meals under the dreadful words or the Mother Superior's study? Why not that enormous exhausted figure on His cross?

All of a sudden I was sure I knew. The lunatic, whoever he was, could not bring himself – even in the throes of a great angry passion – to do more than he had. He was a Roman Catholic, well taught and still in thrall. I was sure of it and I sprang up to try to find the telephone and ask Alec about Tony Gourlay.

Skipping down the stairs, I discovered that there was no need. Little Sister Monica was just opening the front door as I turned on the half-landing and Alec himself was standing there, fog swirling around him as he stood hatless waiting to be invited in.

I called out a greeting but Sister Monica hesitated, shifting from foot to foot. One could hear the shuffle of her wooden work shoes against the tiles of the entrance way.

'How did you get through the gate, sir?' she said.

'I parked my car on the verge and climbed over the wall,' said Alec, just like that doing away with any need to quiz the nuns about gates and keys. I had looked at a high wall and seen a solid barrier; Alec had looked at the same and seen a return to boyhood. 'I've a great need to talk to Mrs Gilver,' he went on, 'and Doctor Glass is using his telephone.'

Sister Monica was quite outwitted by this turn of events. She craned over one shoulder and then the other, clearly hoping for a more senior sister to advise her.

'They've all gone in to Vespers,' she said. 'And I'll be late in a minute too.'

Indeed, even as she spoke, the sound of voices raised – but not tremendously highly – in song began to creep through the hall.

'Where exactly?' I said, only at that moment wondering how the convent was functioning with no chapel all these weeks.

Sister Monica nodded to a set of double doors off to the

side. 'We've thrown the library and recreation room in together and fitted them up as a makeshift,' she said. 'We're having recreation in the refectory. It's better for skittles even if the table is too long for snap.'

'Skittles?' I said. 'In that case, perhaps Mr Osborne and I could meet there briefly. It doesn't sound like a . . .' I could not think of a way to say 'holy place' that did not sound sarcastic, although I did not mean it to.

'Ocht, you're right,' said Sister Monica. She was edging towards the closed double doors as though the quiet voices were calling to her like sirens. 'We're at sixes and sevens anyway and what difference will it make? Only go to Sister Mary's study rather than the refec, will you? She won't mind. Sister Catherine sometimes wanders off before the end of prayers, you see, and if she were to go into supper and see a strange man she might be upset. She's over ninety.'

She opened one side of the double door a tiny amount and slipped through, as though trying to keep the sacred music on one side and Alec, the brute, on the other.

'Follow me,' I said, getting to the bottom of the stairs.

'Best check round the corners first, Dan,' Alec said. 'I don't want to kill any nonagenarians who might be wandering.'

I gave him a friendly punch on the arm as I passed, for I could see that he really was upset to be cast as a monstrous despoiler, but quietly into myself I thought it was just about his turn, for I had had it up to my eyes with clients frowning and looking at me as though I were some sort of bawd or moll, and with policemen looking at me as though I might faint or cry for mother if they spoke frankly.

'Blimey,' said Alec as we entered Sister Mary's study and he caught sight of the crucifix.

'Indeed,' I said. There were several extra chairs back against the walls but they looked heavy and so instead of dragging one, I went round behind the desk and took Sister Mary's.

It was a good sturdy leather and horsehair affair, its seat hollowed into a bowl-shape from long wear, and it occurred to me that I had never before sat in the habitual seat of a victim in any of our cases, feeling so definitely the evidence of her lived life through my clothes and my skin. I could see before me, too, two polished patches on either side of her blotter where she had rested her elbows. I put mine there and looked over the desk, at her view.

There was a surprisingly normal array of photographs arranged where the Reverend Mother would have been able to glance at them as she worked. A family – paterfamilias, seated matron and three lounging daughters – was arranged on the steps of a great house with its staff flanking it. In other snaps, fat beribboned babies – a great many babies actually – lolled on nurses' knees or stood unsteadily on boxes beside the aspidistras so beloved of photographers' studios. In one picture, a young man stood in jodhpurs and a pith helmet under blinding sunlight.

'First things first, Alec,' I said. 'Is Tony Gourlay a Catholic?'

'Yes, he is,' said Alec. 'But look, Dandy, never mind Tony Gourlay. He didn't do it.'

'Have you seen him?' I said. 'What did he say?'

Alec took his pipe out of his pocket, glanced over at the lolling head under the crown of thorns and put it away again, sighing.

'He didn't say anything, of course,' he said. 'He's mute. Doesn't speak at all. But I know he didn't do it because I've heard the entire case from Dr Glass – who is not at all what I expected, by the way; neither odd and Austrian nor gloomy – and flimsy isn't the word.'

'Tell me all.'

'I won't if, if you don't mind. I want Dr Glass to tell you all when you meet him. Much better for you to get it from the horse's mouth rather than losing half of it in a Chinese whisper. But the upshot is this: he broke out with a dozen others when the doors were opened,' Alec said. 'But before morning he'd come back.'

'He came back?'

'The only one who came back. Most of the others were rounded up over the course of that day and Boxing Day by policemen and volunteers from the village, but Tony came back of his own accord. Personally, I think that speaks to his innocence, but the general view is that doing something so odd is suspicious in itself. And unfortunately, he came back smelling of smoke and rather singed and dirty. And he . . . Well, to tell you the truth he *did* speak that night. If only this ridiculous notion that he burned the chapel could be laid to rest, his mother would actually have more to be cheerful about than they've had for ten years. He spoke! When he was shocked and scared, he spoke to his friend – a Mr Molloy. That shows that whatever it is that's been keeping him quiet all this time, it hasn't got so deep into his brain that there's no way out again.'

'What did he say?'

'Something rather odd,' said Alec and I felt a shudder run across my shoulders. I was sure Alec was going to repeat the words which had been playing on and on in my mind like a newsreel since I had first heard them, about Ultan and Mary and real all these years. 'He said, "Not a human. A monster."'

The shudder ran back across my shoulders the other way, even colder and more pricklingly, but once it had passed I was left with a conviction I knew Alec would not be happy to hear. But if *he* was blinded by loyalty it was even more important that *I* hold firm to cold hard facts.

'Sounds like the sort of thing a child would say if he'd thrown his ball through a pane in the orangery,' I said. 'A monster did it and ran away.'

Alec shook his head. 'He'll hang, Dandy,' he said. 'He's

48

absolutely harmless, broken and harmless, but they'll hang him for this nun.'

'I don't think so,' I said. 'She went plunging into the fire quite of her own accord. He should be punished for arson if he did it, but I happen to agree that a hanging would be wrong.'

'Good,' said Alec, sitting back. 'I don't think they should even countenance a charge of arson. Not for some smoke and ash that might have come from anywhere – there were bonfires all over the place that night. The gamekeepers from the next estate were driving the grouse into close cover for the Boxing Day shoot, you know.'

'I heard as much.'

'So that means nothing. As for two cryptic sentences and a bit of paint on his shoe soles—'

'Paint?' I said. 'What colour?'

Alec had gone very still. 'Red, as it happens. Why?'

'Oh God,' I said, then flicked a glance at the plaster figure. 'You'd better come through here.' I fished for my keys. 'I need to show you something.'

Alec stood at the door of the storage room and gazed in horror then asked exactly the same question as had I.

'Why don't they clear it up? Paint it over?'

'On the advice of a very bossy police sergeant, as far as I can make out,' I said. 'He reckons all this mess being here for interested parties to come and see strengthens the hand.'

'Tightens the noose,' said Alec. 'I've never heard of such a thing. Why can't they just take photographs?'

'Don't get fierce with me, darling,' I said. 'I'm not to blame. But you see how the red paint is a problem for your friend, don't you?' Alec grunted. 'Perhaps a character witness could help.' He raised his eyebrows at me. 'To attest that he would never use such words as these. He wouldn't, would he?'

'He's a man and he was in the army,' said Alec.

'But,' I began. 'But you're a man and you were in the army. Don't tell me you've said these words.'

'Every man alive has said these words,' said Alec. 'Every army man has sung them in the chorus of songs at the top of his voice. Sorry to disappoint you, Dandy. But what's this?' He had bent over and was scrutinising the footprints in the red paint on the floor.

'Sergeant Gibb has apparently worked out that they're to be ignored,' I said. 'Don't ask me why.'

'It's obvious why,' Alec said. 'Look how faint they are at heel and toe. They were made by a person with small feet in borrowed shoes.'

I took another look, seeing my down-at-heel rustic disappear and be replaced by . . . whom? A nun? A child?

'What size of feet does Gourlay have?' I asked.

'Tiny,' said Alec, with a sigh. 'We used to rib him about it. This suddenly looks rather black, doesn't it?'

In answer I took him back to the anteroom and along the corridor to the ruins of the chapel.

'Here's black for you,' I said, striking a match and holding it up. Alec whistled.

'When you look at this, it's a mercy only one of them died,' he said.

'I think he did it,' I said. 'Perhaps not alone, but he was part of it. And I think the reason he sloshed the paint around a mere box room and the reason he burned the sacristy – another box room, if you think about it – rather than the main body of the church itself was . . . well.'

'Early training,' Alec said. 'Yes, he went off to the Jesuits at Ampleforth when he was seven. That would do it.' He lit another match and applied it to his pipe. I did not have the heart to stop him despite what Sister Mary had said about consecrated ground. 'But it's not right, Dandy,' he went on, once he had finished with all the sucking and gasping. 'He's supposed to be a raving madman bent on killing nuns, but he takes time to put on large shoes? He's a devil who goes meekly back to the hospital to his own room, looking for sanctuary from monsters but he's supposed to have been in cahoots with others, who've evaded capture?'

'Who said he was in cahoots?'

'No one said it exactly but, if someone's still hanging around bothering the nuns, don't you think they were probably the ones who were here on Christmas Eve?'

'I can't make head nor tail of any of it,' I said. 'Sister Mary doesn't think the trouble's coming from the outside anyway. She's sure one of the nuns is behind it.'

'And what *is* the trouble precisely?'

'We haven't got that far yet,' I said. 'That's something to look forward to after supper.' I shivered and it was not only from the cheerless cold of the foggy night pressing all around us. 'This is a horrid, horrid case, Alec. Your bit of it and mine.'

Before he could answer, the sound of a very small handbell being rung with gusto split the quiet night and almost immediately a chirping, bubbling sound rose up. Shrieks and shouts, yells and giggles, filled the air doing battle with the damping fog.

'Ha!' said Alec. 'Just what we need to cheer us up, Dandy. Let's forget the case just for a minute. Let's go and visit the orphans. Dr Glass told me there are a jolly lot of them just now.'

5

We took the third door from the anteroom, I at least feeling
a little like Alice in Wonderland, but this door thankfully
led not to daubed horrors or blackened ruins but along a
perfectly ordinary servants' passage, stone underfoot and
distemper on the walls, with the high windows that let in
light to kitchens but stop kitchen maids from seeing out
and turning dreamy. At the far end was a door that must
once have led to a dairy and thence to laundry rooms and
store rooms and stables and carriage houses and coal cellars
and all of the myriad humble places necessary to keep a
house like this running as the great home it once was.
Through that door now was something very different, both
from its own past and from the quiet sad present of the
convent.

The word 'orphanage' summons Dickens and squalor,
wooden bowls of thin gruel, and saucer-eyed children huddled
together for warmth. St Ultan's orphanage made one think
instead of those watercolours of Norwegian life, with curly
golden heads and creamy smocks and the sun always shining
through the blossomy branches of an apple tree. Of course
here, on a winter's evening in Lanarkshire, the light was
from gas lamps but the smocks were creamy and a few of
the heads were golden. The walls lit by those lamps moreover
were not distempered in brown like the walls of the nuns'
side and there was no oak panelling either. They were
duck-egg blue and lemon yellow, with snow-white paint on
windows and doors and cream-coloured linoleum, highly

impractical but cheerful enough to make up for the hours of mopping.

The first room we entered from the convent was clearly a playroom, fitted up with low shelves, these filled with paste-board books. There was a ring of little chairs with dolls upon them, abandoned in the middle of a tea party. The next room was another of the same, but this with a rocking horse and a number of wooden cars with handles and pedals. I stared at them; Donald and Teddy had had nothing half so ingenious when they were tiny.

Through yet another door we came upon the children themselves. About fifty of them, from toddlers with bars across the front of their chairs to girls and boys of fourteen or so, sitting interspersed along the two long tables and helping the little ones. There were two nuns, each with a capacious white apron tied over her black habit, and two nurses also swathed in snowy white, but it was a fifth adult who leapt up to meet us.

'Mr and Mrs Finnie?' she said. 'We didn't expect you until tomorrow.'

'Ah no,' I said, trying but not succeeding to fit this individual into a convent orphanage in some way. She was a flitting little thing of perhaps thirty, with a daringly short cap of blue-black hair and a tomboy's figure dressed in soft sage-green tweeds of the sort which hug like silk jersey, rather than bagging like potato sacks the way my tweeds do.

'Not to worry,' she said. 'Not the least tiny bit to worry. You are very welcome tonight. Now—'

'You misunderstand,' Alec said. 'We're not the Finnies.'

The little person pressed a hand to her heart and spun around to flash a look at one of the older girls who had half-stood and now sank back down with her eyes wide.

'Oh, my dear Laura!' the woman said, 'your heart must be in your mouth. Sip some water, darling.' She turned back to us. 'They're coming tomorrow to' – here she dropped her voice – 'adopt her.' The girl she had called Laura dipped her head, clearly able to guess even if she could not hear what was being said about her.

'Dear me,' I murmured, then fell back on the safer ground of introductions. 'I'm Mrs Gilver and this is Mr Osborne,' I said. 'We're visiting the convent and we came exploring.' The little woman flicked a quick glance at Alec as I said this and a frown tugged at her plucked brows but she smiled regardless.

'Well, here you see the very best of St Ultan's,' she said. 'Isn't it marvellous?' One of the nurses had risen to join us and all of the children were staring over too, the looks upon their faces either shy, cheeky or plainly curious. I smiled in their direction and as one they turned back to their dinner plates, giggling.

'Hush, children,' said the nurse. 'Don't mind them, madam. They're always full of nonsense if it's been too foul to be out running about but there's no harm to them. Mother Mary was a great believer in happy children.'

At the mention of her name the sprightly little woman beside her caught her lip and looked down, then she seemed to catch sight of her wristwatch, for she gasped, wheeled away, kissed a few heads and trotted out of the door at the far end of the dining room.

'I'm late *again*, Nurse Matt,' she sang out. 'See you tomorrow, my cherubs. Chapter seventeen coming up and we shall be making swords and eye-patches. Sleep tight, angels.'

'Bye-bye, Miss Daff,' shouted a chorus after her and she was gone.

'We didn't mean to disturb your dinner,' Alec said. 'We shall take ourselves back through to the other side.'

Nurse Matt did nothing to change our minds. She was perfectly friendly but the way she accompanied us had something of an air of seeing us off the premises, no matter how cheerily she prattled on as we went.

'These are our playrooms, as you see,' she said. 'We don't keep the boys and girls separate. Mother Mary saw no harm in innocent mingling. We only ask that the boys come through here if they're going to play at knights and dragons and the girls stay through there if they don't want their dollies tumbled.' Such genial matters got us started, but when we were safely away from the dining room, two doors shut between us and all those sharp little ears, she said: 'You're the detectives, aren't you?' in quite a different tone. 'Sister Steven came through and told us you were here. I'm glad of it. I know it's the nuns that are getting all the bother but I won't sleep in my bed until the last of those devils is back where he belongs. How are they getting in? That's what I don't understand.'

'Getting *in*?' I squeaked.

'Sister Mary says all the keys are accounted for so it makes no sense but you can't argue with plain facts, can you?'

'Which plain facts are those?' I said, feeling that same shiver which had become my good friend already in this case.

'Someone has been in here at night who had no business to,' Nurse Matt said.

'Inside the garden walls, you mean?' said Alec. 'Or inside the building?'

'And the question is how,' she went on, not answering him. 'How are they getting in with all the windows and doors locked tight? The children are turning peely-wally from sleeping with the windows shut and I've a headache every morning, but still there's someone getting in somewhere.'

'You're telling us that a stranger has come into the house at night, more than once?' I said.

'Upstairs, prowling around the corridors, moving things,' Nurse Matt said. 'What if he gets through to our side? All those children!'

I tried to look shrewd, brave and detective-like, but inside

I was quailing. Sister Mary, I rather thought, had not quite played the straight bat with me. True, she had hinted that inmates were still at large on the moor, but when she spoke of mischief she put it down to what my sons would call 'an inside job'. If some madman had got himself a key to one of the convent's doors or windows and was walking the halls in the quiet night, I thought I could reasonably double my fee.

Then a different possibility occurred to me, somewhere between the spectre of the madman and the unthinkable notion that a nun would prowl around her own convent frightening everyone.

'Who is Miss Daff?' I said. Alec nodded his approval.

Nurse Matt laughed as she answered. 'It's Miss Udney,' she said. 'Daffodil Udney. From Waterside.' I remembered the white cube by the river down in the village. 'She's . . . well, I suppose you could say she's a patron, or her father was anyway. Perhaps better say she's an unofficial Godmother to the children. Runs the Brownies, organises the entertainments.'

'That woman runs a Brownie pack?' said Alec in disbelief. He was terrified of the Brown Owl from the nearest village to Dunelgar, who bullied all sorts of treats and excursions out of his estate for her charges. They were terrified of her too, as were her gang of helpers; she was quite friendless, but splendid at getting things done.

Nurse Matt laughed again. 'The way she looks is sort of what you might call left over from earlier times. She was a flighty piece, for sure, when she was a girl and that's when she learned thon way of sitting and walking and flinging her hands about, but she's quieted right down, so she has, seen the sober side of life and started doing some good with hers. She's a boon to us now, I can tell you.'

'Will she end up taking orders?' I said, and now Nurse Matt gave a shout of laughter.

'I wouldn't go that far,' she said. 'Not even for the memory of her beloved father.'

The nuns were filing out of the double doors when we got back to the hall. There looked to be getting on for two dozen of them: all ages, from a handful of juniors even younger than Sister Monica, some with the plump cheeks of children and the scared eyes I had looked for on the orphans' side, to an extremely elderly nun, bent almost double, who walked with two sticks and one of the younger sisters hovering at her back in case she should topple. I took this to be Sister Catherine, who was not to be upset by my presence. This evening at least, she failed even to notice me, staring resolutely at the floor as she pegged by, munching as though at ill-fitting dentures. Most of the rest averted their eyes and fairly flitted past us, but from Sister Mary's calm look I surmised that Monica had told her of Alec's arrival.

'It's supper time, Mrs Gilver,' she said, and indeed there was a strong smell of boiled turnip and fried onion permeating the air. 'We eat earlier than you're used to, I'll wager.'

'But you probably rise at some ungo— some uncommonly early hour too, don't you?' I said. 'So it evens out.'

'We rise at five,' said Sister Steven, glaring at Alec and then at me, 'but we don't eat until after Mass, of course.'

'Six-ish?' I said, hopefully.

'We have the Angelus and Consecration, then Lauds at half-past five, private prayer until seven, Terce until half-past-seven prayers and then breakfast at eight.' She swept past us. 'I shall be happy to sit next to you at supper and continue your education once you've finished with your *business*.' She made it sound as though Alec had been brought home stuck to my shoe and needed scraping off with a stick.

He was surprisingly cheerful.

'So,' he said, to Sister Mary and me, 'eleven hours between

dinner and breakfast for you, eh Dan? Well, I'm off down to the pub to see if I can scare up a pie.'

'Don't mind Sister Steven,' said Sister Mary. 'She's fierce because she's frightened. There will be a biscuit jar and a stone bottle of milk in the guest's retreat for you, Mrs Gilver. We don't expect you to submit to our rigours.'

Even that sounded rather grim: onions and turnip, then nothing but biscuits until the sun came up again. I sniffed, and hoping to detect the scent of a rich stew besides, and could not stop my nose wrinkling as I recognised the final component of the sisters' meal. Perhaps in the refectory, the lid had just been lifted off a steaming vat of it.

'Tripe?' I said.

Alec cleared his throat to cover a spurt of laughter.

'Always on Tuesdays in the winter,' Sister Mary said. 'Most nourishing.'

'The thing is, Sister,' I said, 'for ten years Mr Osborne and I have worked in tandem. We discuss everything and we've found, over all those years, that when we put our heads together, that's when we make best headway. Do you see? Now, I don't ask for Mr Osborne to be admitted to your refectory, but perhaps he and I might have supper together off a tray in your study and get started on our deliberations?'

'It's most irregular,' said Sister Mary.

'I would hate to be the cause of your breaking convent rules,' said Alec, practically falling over himself, he was speaking so quickly.

'It would be most helpful,' I said.

'It's not a rule as such,' said Sister Mary. 'It's just come to be that way by chance. I don't think a man has been in St Ultan's except Father Mallen or the doctor for fifteen years.'

'And the police and some firemen, surely,' I said.

'All rather different from a detective,' said Alec. 'I'm quite happy to go to the pub.'

'How long have you lived in Scotland, Mr Osborne?' said Sister Mary. 'You'd no more find a pie in the Udney Arms than you'd find dancing girls. It's a working man's stand-up drinking shop. Now, through to my study with you and I'll send you both a good plate of dinner.'

Alec was in a silent sulk until Sister Monica arrived a few minutes later with an enormous tray. Then for five minutes he was in a silent . . . trance is hardly too strong a word for it. Dinner, quite simply, was a revelation. Tripe and onions in milk with boiled Swedish turnips and mashed floury potatoes had never tasted better, I was quite sure.

'I'll take that if you're finished, Dandy,' Alec said, gazing over at my plate after his had been scraped clean. 'If you served that tripe in a London restaurant and changed the name, you'd start a craze. And angels could lounge on clouds of those spuds.'

'And the turnip?' I said.

'Well, turnip,' said Alec. 'There are limits. But plenty of salt and butter. And no strings.' He pushed his plate away and craned his neck, looking round at the door. 'I wonder what's for pudding.'

'Before Sister Monica comes back with it,' I said, 'let's try to make some sense of what we've learned so far. Then we can buttonhole her. First: Mother Mary's last words. If you thought Tony was cryptic, wait until you hear this.'

Alec listened to my account of the night of the fire, saying nothing, and only grunted when the story reached its climax.

'So there were others in there who walked out and left her?' he said after a pause. 'Surprising.' I had not considered it; but now he came to mention the fact, it *was* odd. 'Unless it was a "captain going down with his ship" kind of thing. She might have sent the last nun out ahead of herself, promising to follow, and then have been overcome. I don't suppose she did anything so useful as to die with one hand round a statue of Ultan and one of Mary secreted in the folds of her robe?'

'Habit,' I said. 'Not that I've heard. But you think the same as me, do you? She was talking about paintings or figures or something?'

'What else?' said Alec. 'But as to the rest of it. "All these years it was real"? There's only one thing I can think of.' He paused. 'Is there anything in the Bible about tobacco, Dandy? This is just about killing me. I could be in Dr Glass's drawing room right now, you know, and he has a pipe-rack that takes ten right there on the table by his armchair, with a decanter too.'

'What one thing?' I said.

'A threat,' said Alec. 'A curse. Or a prediction. "All these years" Mother Mary had been ignoring the warning and then, blow me down, "it was real".'

'That seems rather . . .' I said carefully. The word on my lips was 'far-fetched' but I did not want to quash him; his theory made about as much sense as my notion of the priceless treasure.

'I disagree,' said Alec, who naturally did not need to hear my word to know what it was. 'An enemy, a warning. She didn't think it was to be taken seriously but that dreadful night showed her she was wrong. "All these years it was real."'

'An enemy?' I said. 'Of a woman who makes the orphans in her care happy with toys and yellow paint and whom all the nuns love like a mother?'

'At least let's ask if she *had* enemies,' said Alec. He heard the study door open and sat up very straight, holding his empty plate out and looking like Oliver. 'Ah, Sister Mon—'

This was someone new. She was about twenty-five, I guessed, with freckled skin and a wide, gap-toothed smile which she turned on me at full beam and then, a little dimmer but still politely, on Alec.

'Mrs Gilver. Sir,' she said, in an Irish brogue so thick she sounded as though her tongue was curling around a mouthful of cream as she spoke. 'I'm Sister Bridget. I hope you've enjoyed your dinners. It's not everyone can fancy tripe, not these days, but Sister Abigail is a born cook, is she not?'

'Give her our compliments,' I said, 'and thank her for this.' 'This' was two bowls of steamed pudding, redolent with treacle and cloaked in the silkiest of hot egg custards. Alec all but purred. 'Have you finished eating, Sister Bridget?'

'I have,' she said. 'Don't let it get cold.'

'And do you have to dash off to prayers again?' I asked.

She shook her head. 'It's recreation now, until Compline.'

'Well then I wonder if we could ask you to sit here for a while and help us?'

'Me? Help you? With your detection?' All the smile fell from her face and she shook her head.

'Help us by telling us your little piece of the puzzle,' I said. 'So we can begin to fit it together. Nothing more than telling us where you were and what you saw. We shall do everything else. Now,' I swept on, Alec being quite taken up with the treacle pudding, 'on Christmas Eve, when you left the chapel and came back here fearing for the candles on the Christmas tree and then checked the rest of the house: where exactly did you go?'

She shook her head again. 'I don't know what you mean.'

'Which rooms did you look into?' I asked, hoping she would not quibble further. Mary had said someone was not where she was supposed to be and quizzing everyone seemed the best way to flush that misplaced someone out. It would not work, however, if they all refused to answer.

I had forgotten the vow of obedience. Sister Bridget, as soon as she understood what was needed, did not hesitate.

'Oh,' she said. 'Mother Mary told us all to check our own cells in case a candle had toppled over, so I went up there.'

'And where in the house is that?'

'On the second floor. The attic floor. What would have been servants' bedrooms, I suppose. The novices start there and then move down to the big rooms when they can, but I like my little cell. It's more like what I'm used to: plain and small. Mother Mary's cell's like a ballroom, no way to make it plain no matter how you might try. And I like the view far over the moor too.' She dipped her head. 'It's God's creation,' she said. 'I don't think I'm being proud or greedy to love the view of it, do you?'

'I do not,' I said. 'I don't suppose you looked out that night by any chance, even though it was dark.'

'Oh, but it wasn't,' said Bridget. 'It was the most beautiful full moon. And there were a couple of sheep just on the little rise opposite the big gate there and for a moment I watched them, thinking of the shepherds. But that was earlier when we had retired to pray until it was time for chapel. At midnight, I just raced up there, looked in the door and sniffed and raced back down again.'

'I see. What about even later, when Mother Mary raised the alarm about the fire?' I said. 'Did you hear her calling or did one of the others knock you up?'

'Sister Steven came in,' she said. 'And right there I knew something was wrong because we never go into one another's cells unless it's to nurse someone who's sick. But that night she just burst right in and said "The chapel's on fire. The Mother says to come quickly."'

'And then you rushed out there?' I said.

'I *was* in a rush,' she agreed. 'That's probably it, isn't it?'

'What?' I said.

'It's just that I closed my door,' she said. 'I know I did; it's second nature. But when I came back it was open.'

'Probably someone else double-checking you were safe.'

'Probably,' she said. 'Only—'

'What?'

She was quiet for a moment, gazing ahead of herself. Then

she came back to us with a deep, gathering breath and spoke up as though she had come to a decision. 'I had started undressing, you see. I had taken off my veil and my rosary. But when Sister Steven rushed in, I went out onto the landing. I looked down over the banister and Sister Catherine was standing at the door of her cell and everyone was just streaming past her. She looked so bewildered that I went right down and tried to help her.'

'You're a good girl,' I said, sure that the drama of a fire must have been far more enticing than a nun in her nineties.

'I got her settled back in her bed and said a little wee prayer with her and then when she was quiet I left her. And that's when I thought to go back upstairs for my rosary – didn't feel dressed without it, to own the truth.'

'So you went back to the second floor?' I said. 'Back to your cell?'

'Halfway,' said Sister Bridget. 'I was dithering, and no two ways about it. Halfway back to get my rosary and then I changed my mind again and turned. But I did glance at my door on the way – I couldn't tell you why – and it was shut then.'

I was stumped as to why she was making such a lot of what seemed a tiny detail, but then maybe a door ajar to a nun's cell was a much more serious business than someone like me could know.

'Have you asked around to see who might have looked into your room?' I said. 'To say thank you?'

She shook her head. 'Everyone was gone already,' she said.

'And who is "everyone"?' asked Alec. 'Those in nearby rooms?' He had finished his pudding and every last drop of custard and was back in the game.

Bridget nodded. 'The novices were just ahead of me – Sister Winifred and Sister Joan. And Sister Francis was coming out of her cell when I came out of mine. I heard

Sister Clare in her cell through the wall too. She burst out and clattered down the stairs.'

'But you didn't actually see her?'

'I did not, but I'd know her footsteps anywhere,' said Bridget. 'She's been next door to me for five years and she's like a baby—' she blushed.

'Elephant,' I finished for her, smiling. 'I shall ask around if you like, to set your mind at rest. And if it's not too upsetting,' I went on, 'could you take us through exactly what happened next.'

'Well, when I got to the foot of the stairs,' Bridget continued, 'Sister Abigail was coming out of the refec with a pail of cloths. She must have come through that way from the kitchen. There's not so many doors as using the passage and you can nudge them open.'

'And why did she have them?' Alec asked.

'Mother Mary had ordered them for the sisters to wrap around their faces and help them with the heat. So I went out with her, out the garden door in the library and round the side of the house, and soon everyone was there. *Everyone* was there. I counted. The house was empty apart from poor Sister Catherine, and she wouldn't go snooping.'

'So no one was inside the chapel just then?' I said.

Bridget shook her head. 'They were waiting for the cloths. They plunged into the pail and took them out dripping, but only minutes later when Mother Mary came out again with the font that self-same cloth was bone dry and warm like it had been out on a line on a summer's day.' She turned and looked into the fireplace at the crackling logs there. 'You forget, don't you? When fires are in the grate or under the range? You forget how *hot* they are.'

'Did *you* go inside the chapel, Sister Bridget?' I asked.

She shook her head.

'So you couldn't have heard anything that Mother Mary said?' Alec chipped in.

'But I heard Sister John telling Sister Mary,' she said.

'And what do you think she meant?' I asked gently.

'I've turned my head outside in like an old trunk,' Bridget said. 'And I can't make head nor tail of it. I can't make sense of *any* of it. I know what my sisters think.'

We waited in expectant silence.

'It's neat enough, to be sure. Two men are still on the moor and someone has been inside our walls as shouldn't be, so there it is.'

'But you don't believe it?'

'I don't at that. How's he getting in and what's he after? It makes no sense and I'm sick of trying to understand it.'

There seemed nothing more to be learned after that and I was aware that the custard in my bowl was growing a skin, so we dismissed her. I ate quickly and then turned to a new page of my notebook and jotted down everything she had told me.

'She's certainly got a bee in her bonnet about her open door,' Alec said, when I had finished. I nodded. 'But what do *you* find most remarkable, Dan?'

'We need Sister John,' I said. 'She heard Mother Mary's last words and they're what's troubling me.'

'I'd *dearly* like to speak to Sister John,' Alec said. I looked up, surprised at his grim tone. 'She left the woman in there.'

'We take vows of obedience, young man,' said a voice from the door. 'Was I supposed to drag her out by her hair?'

6

Sister John was exactly what one fears when one hears the word 'nun'. She was quite six feet tall, with a granite face, and a withering look when her expression was at rest. She had enormously bushy grey eyebrows, quite a luxuriant grey moustache about which she seemed unconcerned, and the few times in our acquaintance that I saw her laugh she revealed a mouthful of large grey-yellow teeth. How odd it will sound then, when I say that over the course of my time at St Ultan's I came to look forward to seeing her, as I did none of the others, and to drink her in like a tonic. For she was goodness personified: undaunted, unbending, unwavering goodness. One so seldom sees it in such a pure form.

That first night, however, all I saw was a wilfully ugly woman, striding towards us with her large, red-knuckled hand held out in greeting.

'Mrs Gilver,' she said, after giving my hand a good crack of a shake. 'And Mr Osborne.' She shook Alec's hand so that he came out of it the loser. I think he must have raised his eyebrows or otherwise looked surprised, for as she leaped up to sit on the edge of Sister Mary's desk she dealt with him briskly.

'I don't shy away from males,' she said. 'I never saw "cloistering" as a running away from danger, but as a dispensing with unwanted nonsense.'

'Ah,' said Alec. 'Right then.'

'I'm sorry not to have seen you before this,' she said. 'God knows what Mary's been telling you, not to mention those

66

girls going on about their doors. Mine was safely latched, by the way. But my day is filled with work and prayer, and I wasn't about to give up my dinner either. This is our recreation time and I'm all yours until Compline. I need to tell you right away that I don't believe in this "intruder" who's supposed to be spiriting himself in and out of our walls.'

'To do what, Sister?' I asked.

'Nothing! What am I telling you?'

'But surely there is some evidence to support—'

'Doors opened, drawers forced, keys moved. Mischief, Mrs Gilver. Not the dastardly work of an escaped lunatic, that's for sure.'

'You think one of the nuns caused the fire?' I said, swallowing.

'Stuff!' said Sister John. 'Do you need your ears washed out, young woman? No, of course that broken soul from the asylum put a match to us and gave us the vocabulary lesson through there.'

'How do you think he got in?' asked Alec.

'Easy enough,' said Sister John. 'This wasn't built as a convent – I mean, look around! – and it's got doors everywhere. And low windows on the ground floor. Ah now, the convent where I spent my novitiate. *That* was a cloister. It had one door to the street, for the delivery of food and the removal of dead nuns. And a door to the church. Windows above head height, no windows at all in the cells, skylights instead. If a girl got as far as her full orders in St John's House she was a nun indeed.'

'Why did you leave?' I asked.

Sister John narrowed her eyes until all I could see were the extraordinary eyebrows.

'Not cut out for all the praying,' she said. 'I'm a born teacher. I start out by scaring the little ones half out of their wits. That gets their attention and then I win them round.

I was in the east end of Glasgow for ten years and the school had no trouble in all that time. Then I came here. I didn't think it would work at first. Mother Mary spoiled them all and Sister Mary has carried on where she left off. But no one interferes with my school room and I've had more of our orphans go to grammar school and even university than you would believe. I've got boxes of letters from them.' Then she shut her mouth so suddenly that her lips made a smacking noise. 'Pride,' she said. 'Ever my downfall. I'm close to seventy and it's still catching me.'

'So an intruder might have got inside on Christmas Eve?' I said, reluctantly. I could have listened to her all night and Alec looked like a small boy at story time.

'Easily,' she said. 'And the paint's no mystery. We had pots of it all ready for painting bunting for the party next day. Poor mites. Even I think it was tough luck for them to miss their Christmas party, although I'm not as soft as Daft Udney and Sister Merry.'

I was almost sure that is what she said, but she sailed on.

'Anyway, the point is that the disturbances since have almost certainly been nothing to do with the outside world. One of my sisters is hiding something and it's got to do with whatever the Mother was doing in the chapel that night. The real thing.' I could not resist a triumphant look at Alec. It sounded as though my guess about the meaning of Mary's words had hit home.

'You don't think she was trying to save the place from burning down?' I said. 'Or at least saving specific things from burning?'

'Not a chance,' said Sister John. 'She went plunging past all kinds of beloved objects as if they were nothing at all. She was crazed. Grabbing at us all, chasing us. She knocked Sister Hilda over, flat on her back. I had to carry her out like a fireman.'

'Let us just make very sure, Sister John,' I said. 'Tell us

exactly what Mother Mary said to you. Her voice, her gestures, her words, everything. Because we can't decipher the meaning of her last words. Can't even begin to.'

'Nor can I for the most part,' said Sister John. 'Find Ultan? Hide Mary? She was rambling. But "all these years it was real"? Whatever "it" was, I think she was in the chapel to seize *it* and save it. But she died before she could get it out.'

'Couldn't "it" be either Ultan or Mary?' Alec said.

Sister John shook her head. 'She would never describe them that way. "The Virgin" is what we called the picture – sentimental piece, never cared for it myself – and "Old Uncle" is what we always called our icon of St Ultan. He has – had! – children gathered round his feet. Sister Mary called him that the first time she saw him, so they tell me. It was before my time.'

'How long have you been here, Sister John?' asked Alec.

'Nigh on forty years,' she said. I did a quick calculation and could not make sense of it. But even as I opened my mouth to question her further, she resumed talking and what she said drove everything else from my mind. 'Anyway, chances are they weren't her last words. Chances are she spoke to the sister who was still inside when I blundered out for the last time.'

'And who was that?' said Alec.

'That's what you need to find out,' said Sister John, and her face, never sunny, was dark with anger as she spoke. 'The smoke was so thick by then I couldn't tell. And no one will admit to it. No one will admit being the last to speak to Mother Mary. They all say they were out in the graveyard when I reeled out at last, coughing and choking. That's how I know someone's lying. I want to know who it was I saw and I want to know why she won't come clean. Even if we've got to let strangers into our house to get to the bottom of it all.'

* * *

There were still twenty minutes of recreation before the nuns all went back for Compline, their final prayers of the day, and then retired and so we asked Sister John to send Sister Hilda to us. If Mother Mary had got close enough to the woman to knock her over she must surely have said something.

Hilda's first words did not give us much hope.

'Everyone looked exactly the same,' she said. 'Well, we always do apart from height and shape, especially from the back. And even from the front at a distance. That's rather the point. We did have an Indian sister here for a while – she looked very different, of course – but once she had finished her teacher training she went back. Such a fervent vocation; we get letters still from her mission and she's doing great work. You should see them all in their little cotton dresses with their pigtails, beaming like rays of God's good sunshine. We gave the photograph to the other side to hang in the classroom and we sent a photograph of our little ones back there. Of course they look terribly drab, in Scottish light and with their mousy hair, but it'll be just as interesting to the little ones in . . . I forget the province. India, some-where.'

'So you can't help us build a picture of where everyone was then?' said Alec. Like most men, he has very limited patience for the sort of woman who would have been called in my parents' day 'a rattle'. Sister Hilda was a rattle extraordinaire.

'We all were at the Mass,' she began. 'Well, it wasn't Mass because we had no priest, but midnight prayers, you know. Yes, we were all there. Mother Mary and Sister Mary and Sister Catherine and Sister Steven were at the front.'

'Yes,' I said, interrupting and, also, lying, 'Sister John took us through the earlier part of the evening. But we'd like to ask you about later on, when Mother Mary raised the alarm. You must have recognised your sisters as they left their rooms and went to the chapel.'

'Oh! Oh, yes, of course,' said Sister Hilda. 'My room is

above the recreation room in the south-west corner. That is, the *usual* recreation room. Just now we're using it as the chapel and we're using the dining room—'

'South-west corner,' said Alec.

'I saw Sister Irene and Sister Jude come flying down from the second storey, as I came out of my door. There were more behind them – probably the novices; their cells are up there – but it was Sister Irene and Sister Jude that I noticed, because they were holding up their habits as they rushed downstairs and Sister Jude had taken off her left stocking already and Sister Irene had taken off her right stocking. Or – wait – perhaps – no! It was Sister Jude who had taken off her left stocking and Sister Irene who had taken off her right one.' Alec blinked, frowning. 'Because it put that rhyme in my head. You know the one, "Diddle diddle dumpling, my son John".' And then unbelievably she carried on and sang the whole thing, right through.

'Anyone else?' said Alec, when she had finished.

'In just one stocking?'

'Did you *see* anyone else?' Alec said.

'Sister Martha went flying past me and got jostled in with the novices. Why, there you are! Yes – it was Sister Winifred and Sister Joan behind the others. She went flying past, and I almost bumped into Sister Margaret, who has the cell on the other side. Oh, I should have said. Sister Martha is my neighbour to the east. And past her is—'

'We shall have to draw up a plan,' I said. Sister Hilda stopped speaking and nodded. She did not seem to mind being interrupted, which was very useful to know given how much she talked.

'And did you all stay together – those you've just mentioned and yourself – after you got to the chapel?' I asked.

'Oh no,' said Sister Hilda. 'We got separated almost right away. I waited for Sister Margaret – she's rather dreamy – and by the time we were on our way Sister

Martha and Sister Bridget and Sister Winifred were gone. And then Sister Margaret slipped while we were crossing the hall – the floor was wet, but I cannot tell you what had caused it for I do not know. It wasn't newly washed, for we are far too busy on Christmas Eve to be tackling rough housework and even at other times of the year we always wash the hall floor on Wednesdays. The big linens on Monday of course, and ironing them on Tuesdays and then the rough starts on Wednesday and we begin with the hall because otherwise dirt from the hall would be tramped over the clean floors of the rooms.'

'So Sister Margaret slipped,' I said firmly.

She nodded. 'And I took her arm and that slowed us down a bit. And then as we were going along—'

'Perhaps we could skip ahead,' I suggested. 'What happened after you got out of the garden door in the library and saw the fire?'

'It's *usually* the library, but we've thrown open the doors and joined the two rooms up to make a chapel in the meantime. The books are still in there of course, but if someone wants to read they're using the—'

'But after you went out?' Alec persisted, with a note of strain.

'We didn't *go* out. Sister Margaret had twisted her ankle when she slipped on the water and she had hurt her shoulder quite badly when someone pushed past us and so we went to the kitchen to get a hot bottle for her to put on it.'

'I see,' I said. Sister Hilda gave me a shrewd look but did not respond.

'And did you see anyone else?' Alec asked.

'Sister Abigail came in. She's the cook. She had set the kettles on for tea, I think. At least there was a kettle almost boiling. We had filled Sister Margaret's hot bottle when Sister Abigail came back and asked us what we were doing. As though she grudged a little hot water! Then she set me to

72

carrying teapots and trays of cups through to the library – the library as usually is, I mean, but at the moment—'

'Yes, yes,' I said. 'It's being used as a chapel. So you took tea to the sisters who were battling the fire. Sister Abigail is right. There's nothing like hot sweet tea. Whom did you serve?'

'All of them!' said Sister Hilda. 'I never stopped from that minute on. When the teapots were empty, Sister Francis came in and *shouted* at me! Shouted at me to go and get more. And when I went to the chapel door to ask Mother Mary if those were *her* orders, she knocked me over.'

I was not surprised. I was tempted to give her a bit of a shove myself.

'I was still running back and forward when Sister Mary came to say that it was all over,' Hilda went on. 'She said that the roof had collapsed and Mother Mary was trapped in there. Did you know she rang the bell?'

Alec and I nodded.

'Even though she knew she was trapped, she spent her last moments sending a message of God's love and her blessing to all of us,' said Sister Hilda. 'It was quite beautiful. And I think her spirit opened the doors, too.'

'Doors?' I said, perking up. I had been slumping rather.

'Haven't you heard?' she said. 'At the very moment of Our Mother's death all of the doors in the convent flew wide open. She was telling us to cleave unto one another and that together we should be strengthened, despite our grief.'

Alec and I were speechless, which seemed to delight her. Beaming, she left.

'I know I shouldn't speak ill of the saintly,' Alec said, when she had gone, 'but that woman is a blister.'

'A blister who's given us a lot of useful information,' I said.

'About the meaning of a fire bell and all the doors flying magically open?'

'Well, yes, *that* was rot,' I said, scribbling madly. 'But she backs up Sister Bridget's story about someone going into the rooms. And that backs up Sister John's story that someone is lying about where they were. So. We've got one account of Sister Abigail, Sister Margaret and Sister Fran—'

'Dandy!' said Alec, almost loud enough to call it shouting. 'I am putting my foot down. Abigail. Margaret. Francis. At least while we're on our own. If I hear the word "sister" one more time I shall scream.' He took a long breath. 'I'm leaving now, and I'm going to the stand-up drinking shop at Carstairs Stop for a pint of eighty shilling, or two pints, or however many it takes until that dratted word is drowned in beer.'

I let him out of the front door and then wandered across to where the sound of quiet voices and the smell of candle wax were drifting out through a crack in the double doors. I edged it slightly further open and sidled in. It was a double drawing room with the connecting doors pulled wide so that the twenty nuns could sit in five rows of four in one half and their little altar could be set up in the other. And what an altar it was: an ornate purple and gold cloth, so heavily embroidered that the candlesticks upon it sat askew; there was a lectern to one side with a Bible open on its tilted shelf; and there was a wooden font, definitely fumed oak, at the other side by the garden door. Along that wall, leaning against the bookcases, were a statue of the Virgin, smeared with soot and tar, a painting of the crucifixion with a gaping hole in one corner where the canvas had burned away, and about a dozen hassocks in a higgledy-piggledy pile.

The sisters, who had been mumbling quiet prayers, suddenly rose up in song, a solemn and plangent tune, vaguely familiar, with words in Latin, not at all so. I could hear sweet young voices, some breathy, some liquid, and here and there one or two truly beautiful soaring sopranos. As well as these though, I could hear Sister Catherine rumbling along below the others like a freight carriage on a railway line and was

74

sure I could pick out Sister Steven's rasping voice, very loud and with a confidence which came from devotion rather than from musicality. The rest of them fitted in here and there, adding wayward notes or simple bulk to the throng of voices and somehow, overall, it was pleasing. I felt a great deal of the tension of the day leave my shoulders and, before they had finished and were reciting Our Father, I had yawned more than once into my hand. I was almost glad that there was no supper, much less a nightcap, to be had and that I was free to retire to my room, lock my door, check it twice, and then lie down gingerly upon my meagre bed and submit to sisters' voices, reciting other sisters' names, filling my dreams.

7

As it happened, I fell into sleep as though from a high cliff down to a deep river and opened my eyes upon the grey light of morning with no more than a vague sense of having missed something. I reached out for my little notebook, for sometimes I have found that early morning perusal can bear fruit. Even while I was groping about on the floor, though, I saw it on the Benares table by the daybed and groaned. I was only just warm enough under the bedclothes and the air of the room felt very cold.

Before I had steeled myself to slip out and fetch it, there was a knock on the door and, without waiting for an answer, a nun sidled in carrying a laden tray.

When she looked up and I was able to see more than the top of her veil, I recognised her as one of the ones who had smiled as she passed me last night, yawning in the doorway of the makeshift chapel. She smiled again now.

'Your breakfast, Mrs Gilver,' she said, to my astonishment.

'In bed?' I said, struggling to sit up a little. 'That's a surprise.'

'Ocht, you deserve it,' she said. 'And if anyone has anything to say she can say it to Sister Abigail, which she won't because no one crosses the cook.' It was true of any household I had lived in; certainly Mrs Tilling, at Gilverton, was kept sweet by servants and family alike, lest her syllabubs sink or her sponges grow heavy, and Alec's Mrs Lowie was a tartar who only got away with it because she could cook the various pheasants, grouse and partridge Alec brought down from the moor until they melted on the tongue, and was assiduous about removing shot pellets too. Still, I was interested to hear that the cook held sway here too.

My waitress brought the tray over and set it down upon my lap.

'Thank you, Sister,' I said, gazing down at the perfect, milky-eyed eggs and the two rashers of crisp and greaseless bacon. There was a rack of toast, a dish of very yellow butter and a pot of tea with a curl of steam coiling up from its spout. The china was Indian Tree, rather thick but cheerful at breakfast, and there were a few snowdrops in an egg cup of water too.

'Martha,' she said. 'I'm Sister Martha. I help Sister Abigail in the kitchen.'

'Well, thank you for taking the time to run up here with a tray for me at your busy time,' I said.

'Oh, we're done and dusted, Mrs Gilver,' said Sister Martha. 'We're waiting to see if the greengrocer brings us any oranges to get making marmalade.'

'What time is it?' I said, looking over at the top of the chest where I thought I had left my wristwatch.

'Half-past eight,' said Sister Martha. 'You've missed refectory breakfast.'

And about five separate bouts of prayers, I thought to myself, caught between relief and horror at how the nuns would take to their employee loafing in bed until this time.

'Since you say you've got a little time on your hands,' I said, pouring my tea, 'might I ask you about Christmas Eve.' There were twenty nuns at St Ultan's and I had only bagged three on my first day.

Sister Martha grinned and from the folds of her habit she produced a plain white mug, even thicker than my Indian Tree, and held it out towards the teapot.

I asked her to pass my notebook and she put her hand on it without hesitation, as though she had seen it and realised what it was already. When she had settled onto the daybed with her cup of tea well cooled with milk and well sweetened with four good-sized chips of sugar, she began what was beginning to be a familiar tale. The smell of smoke, the assumption about the Christmas tree and mass exodus to the hall, the dispersal of nuns about the house to check for fire and the discovery of the painted mess in the little box room.

'You didn't go to the kitchens to check?' I said. I placed my knife and fork neatly on my cleaned plate and took up my tea cup.

'Sister Abigail said she would,' said Martha. 'She's fierce about her kitchen. I checked my cell and the W.C. next door and that's all.'

'And, later, who woke you? Sister Steven?'

'Sister John,' she said. 'And sent me upstairs to rouse the novices and the others on the second floor.'

'Who *did* you rouse?' I asked.

'Well, Sister Steven was just going into Sister Joan's cell and Sister Winifred was already out on the landing, so I started on the other side, the west side, I did Sister Dorothy' – I suppressed a groan at yet another new name – 'and Sister Anne,' Martha went on, after a quizzical look at me, 'Sister Monica, and then the other doors started to open – there was so much noise, you see? – so I didn't actually knock up Sister Irene and Sister Jude but they were downstairs almost as quickly as me.'

'Now, I'm glad you mentioned doors opening,' I said. 'I want to look ahead if I may and ask about when you finally came back.'

In a heartbeat, Sister Martha's ruddy face drained until she briefly she looked the twin of Sister Mary, every bit as pale.

'I know I shouldn't think so, but that's the worst of all,' she said. 'The mess in the wee room was bad with all those nasty words and of course the fire was dreadful but the thought of the doors still makes me feel sick.'

'What do you think happened?' I said.

'I think the devil came. I think a burning church on Christmas Eve brought him and he showed us he'd been here.'

'Sister John was rather sceptical,' I said, aware that not all of the air was leaving me as I exhaled.

'Sister John didn't see upstairs,' said Martha. 'I only saw it because I took Sister Winifred up. She was limping from a blistered foot – she'd stamped out flames on a tapestry Sister John carried out. Upstairs there were thirteen doors standing wide open,' she said. 'They weren't like that when the young sisters left them.'

'One last question, Sister Martha,' I said. 'Did you actually go inside the chapel during the fire? I know some did and some like Hilda and Margaret were kept busy outside.'

At the mention of their names, Martha raised one eyebrow and compressed one side of her mouth making a dimple appear in her cheek.

'I'm sure that's so,' she said and I could not decipher the tone in her voice. It was most un-nun-like, certainly. Then she shook her head. 'I was one of the ones passing water buckets,' she said. 'With Sister Francis and Sister Dorothy. The only ones I saw inside were Our Mother, Sister Steven and Sister John. Oh, and Sister Clare and Sister Monica too, until Our Mother sent them out again.'

'Why?'

'She was always that way,' said Martha. 'She tried to treat us all the same but she couldn't help it. It's only natural, I suppose. And it was worst of all with Mary because she was one of the first.'

I had been scratching my head about how John could have been here forty years and yet have arrived after Mary but, as she spoke, a notion occurred to me.

'One of the first *orphans*,' I said. 'She was born here? No wonder she loved the Reverend Mother so.'

'Not born here,' said Martha. 'None of them are actually born here, because we don't have a lying-in ward. Either they come from the cottage hospital at Lanark or they're left at the gate. There's a slot, you know.'

'I don't,' I said. 'Slot?'

'In the wall. Like a pillar box, but for babies. It sounds bad, Mrs Gilver, but it's very practical. Very private. And they don't lie long for there's a bell.'

'The orphan bell!' I said. 'Sister Mary said she rang it on Christmas Eve, but I wasn't sure what she meant by it exactly.'

I thought of all the children I had seen at their supper the day before, and of all the mothers who had, more or less willingly, posted them through a slot over the years. How many people who lived on this moor and down in the villages loved the sisters for their mercy and how many hated them for taking their babies away? And how many of them, besides Sister Mary, had made their lives here.

I was waiting at the gate an hour later when Alec trundled over the brow of the nearest hill in the hired motorcar and tooted the horn.

'Why the *cri de coeur*?' he said when he had stopped and thrown open the door for me.

'I need to go to town,' I said. 'To buy a sketchpad.' It was to Alec's credit that he did not laugh. 'I need to draw a plan of the convent and a map of their movements. Or perhaps it should be called an itinerary. Like a . . . book of hours.'

'How fitting,' said Alec. 'Why?'

'Because it's either that or I agree that there was a miracle,' I said. 'Or a visit from the devil. Or who knows; perhaps both.' I knew my voice had grown wild but I could not help it. 'The simplest explanation for the open doors is that someone was inside the convent while the fire raged and all of her sisters' attention was on it. And I reckon if I interview them all and . . . what's the word I'm after? . . . the names then I shall be able to work out who it was. Only there are two score of them and it's making me want to lie down with a cold compress on my forehead already after only—' I riffled through my notepad '—four.'

'And then will you do something for me?' Alec said. 'Will you come to talk to Dr Glass about Tony? I note you don't think it was him?'

'No I don't,' I said. 'Because upstairs there was no mess made. No paint or flames. This person was snooping. And yes, I think I'd like to speak to your Dr Glass. How incredibly irritating it is that Tony won't talk. Especially now we know he can.'

Alec gave me a look which I interpreted as an admonition on my callousness but he said nothing.

The little sweetshop-cum-toyshop on the main street of Carstairs Stop furnished me with a children's painting pad, quite a foot high and half a foot wide, although the shopkeeper was ashamed of the roughness of the paper and twittered on about a marvellous place in Lanark where I could find a proper artist's sketchpad with paper worthy of my brush.

I assured her I had no need of it and only wanted large sheets to draw plans and make long lists and after that she quivered with the desire to find out who I was and what I was up to.

'Staying at the new hoose, are you?' she said. 'Friends of the Udneys?' Then without waiting for me to answer she assumed an affirmative and sailed on. 'Well, that's lovely for the poor dears. What a loss and what a time to have it happen! Not that there's a good time, but Christmas morning? I ask you.'

Now, of course, our interest was piqued. I had been wearing my sternest expression, for shopkeepers' gossip is always tiresome, and had been holding out my half-crown desiring only escape, but now I closed my fingers over the coin and set my bag down on the counter.

'A loss on Christmas morning?' I said. Alec busied himself looking at a shelf full of tiny lead motorcars and lorries. We had long since learned that gossip is more readily dripped into just one ear at a time.

'Mr Udney died,' the woman said. 'He was lying on his deathbed all through thon shocking night, bells clanging and police haring about on their motorcycles all up and down the village. I only hope none of it reached his ears for he had every right to go peaceful. He earned his rest and no mistake. He was a good man and a good friend to many. It breaks my heart to see it all go so wrong when he tried so hard.'

'People can be very unkind,' I murmured non-committally.

'Them that's never seen troubles,' she murmured back.

I had just opened my mouth to murmur something a little more to the point but then the shop bell clanged and an enormous and ancient woman, wrapped in a shawl, waddled in.

'The kettle's on the back,' said the shopkeeper to her, stepping away and raising the counter lid to allow the new arrival to pass through. 'That's sixpence, madam,' she said to me. Clearly this was a pal and juicier meat was to be shared in the parlour than could be spoken across the counter. I looked out the right change and we left.

'It was an ill-fated night, wasn't it?' said Alec, as we drove off. 'Poor Miss Udney. A fire at her pet orphanage and her father pegging out at the same time.'

'Indeed,' I said. I am always interested to hear Alec express an opinion about a young unmarried woman; even the mildest sympathy, as now. I have learned to hide it though. 'I wonder what they're saying – "them that's never seen troubles"?'

'Dr Glass will surely know,' Alec said and applied his foot

to the accelerator pedal as the road started to rise. I peered in past the gateposts of Waterside with renewed attention but saw only the same glimpse of white stone before we were on our way.

Hopekist Head, the hospital, was a mile farther on than the convent; situated – as its name suggested – at the source of the little stream which trickled, then chuckled and then crashed down from the high moor and joined the river splitting the valley. The house could not have been more different from St Ultan's. In fact, as I stared through the windscreen on our approach, it occurred to me that it would have made a much better convent, just as St Ultan's would have made a better asylum for the insane, its plain lines and calm facades offering peace to troubled minds. The building we were now facing was the wildest extravagance a Victorian architect could imagine, with turrets and gables and odd little windows here and there as though they had been flung and stayed where they stuck. Its outline offered corners and recesses galore, archways to hidden courtyards, and looming casements that would hide anyone standing below. It was far beyond romantic to my eyes; closer to hectic and I thought if I had shell shock, or even if life had simply worn me down, I would be in sore need of somewhere more restful.

It was not helped either by being surrounded with a high fence, leaning inwards and topped off with bundles of barbed wire. And a second house – a modern villa – which stood outside the fence, far from softening the overall effect, simply looked terribly vulnerable and out of place and made me think of a child unaware of a grizzly bear creeping up behind it.

'And Dr Glass *lives* there?' I said as Alec swung towards the villa's front door. 'Right there? Does he have a family?'

'He has a spaniel and a fishing rod and a collection of whisky and pipes that would be the envy of many a family man,' Alec said. 'He's not at all monk-like but he's as devoted to his charges as are your nuns to their orphans any day.'

'And what does he make of the case against Tony Gourlay?' I said.

'He thinks it's twaddle,' Alec said. 'But since the breakout, the locals aren't listening to him quite the way they used to. Come in and meet him. Let's see if he can convince you.'

8

One could not see the towering monstrosity of Hopekist Head from the main rooms of Dr Glass's house and, looking out from the drawing room, I understood a little more how he could bear to live here. The view was of an endless stretch of undulating moorland and of a breathtaking expanse of sky, rolling with cloud. I might have put up with a red brick porch and a pink-tiled fireplace to get that view.

I turned from it when I heard the doctor approaching, his metalled heels ringing out as he strode across the hall floor. Alec was right, he was the least gloomy individual imaginable. He had chestnut hair which clashed with a ruddy face, very shiny cheeks and luxuriant tufted eyebrows in a paler shade of chestnut that would have put even Sister John's to shame. They interfered with the little round glasses that were perched on the end of his nose and which he peered over when he spoke and under when he read, so that one wondered what he needed them for. He was dressed in a pitch-perfect example of the uniform of a country doctor: brogues, flannels, a checked shirt, knitted tie, yellow waistcoat, tweed coat, and even with a pipe in his breast pocket and a stethoscope around his neck.

'Admiring my beautiful moor, dear lady?' he said. 'Aren't I the lucky one?'

'It's quite lovely,' I said non-committal as to his luck.

'And so sit down where you can see it,' he went on. 'Coffee is on its way. How are you getting on with the Little Sisters? Abigail's vocation is a loss to the fine dining rooms of the land, don't you think so? It's digestives here, I'm afraid.'

As he spoke I had heard the rattle of a tray and turned expecting a maid. To my astonishment, though, it was borne by a middle-aged man, neither butler nor footman from his lack of livery. He was dressed in a short, grey-cotton coat and rough grey trousers. When he set it down and turned his back it was all I could do to suppress a cry. STATE HOSPITAL was written across the back of his jacket in stencilled letters. I threw a look at Alec and then at Dr Glass and was annoyed to find them both smiling at me.

'Tom has been my loyal servant for almost fifteen years,' said Dr Glass. 'He came with me from my last place. He's not ill enough for a ward. Does much better here with the fresh air and something to occupy him.'

'What's wrong with him?' I said.

Dr Glass cocked his head and only answered when he heard a distant door closing.

'He hears the voices of his dead comrades,' said Dr Glass. 'But out here in the quiet he's learning not to listen to them.'

I took a cup of coffee and tried to settle myself with a sip.

'And what about Tony Gourlay?' I said. 'Does he hear voices?'

'Poor Tony,' said Dr Glass. 'There is a word for what's wrong with him. Two words. Ambulatory catatonia. That is to say, he walks around and is capable of carrying out simple tasks, but he doesn't talk and doesn't take in what's being said to him.'

'Who assigns his tasks?' I said.

Dr Glass beamed at me.

'Mr Osborne said you were clever,' he said. 'No one. He would be quite incapable of following instructions. He gets himself up in the morning, looks around, decides what needs doing – usually in the grounds – and gets on with it. If he smells food he searches it out and eats and when he's tired he bathes, undresses and goes to bed again.'

He sounded just like Hugh.

'But on Christmas Eve,' I said. 'He looked around, saw an open gate and decided that what needed doing was . . . flight. And then worse.'

Dr Glass shook his head and looked at his half-eaten digestive biscuit as though he didn't recognise it.

'I simply don't understand it,' he said. 'I don't understand the breakout at all. I don't know how the front gate got opened and I don't know how the cells got opened. All of the staff have been thoroughly questioned and all of the keys are accounted for. But, *that* aside, there were few surprises. I've long known who would run if they could and who would stay at Hopekist if all the doors were open all day every day. And the ones who took off that night were exactly those I'd expect it of. Restless men, haunted men. Men who are looking for escape every morning when they open their eyes. All except Tony. This is his home and he's . . . not happy . . . but he's content here. He's at rest, at last. It simply makes no sense that he would run away. And as for what they say he did! Tchah! These people have no more sense than sheep.'

'But he *was* there,' I said.

'Oh, he was *there*,' said Dr Glass. 'Soot and ash all over his clothes. Red paint on his boots. And even if there hadn't been, we'd know something happened to him. He spoke. Do you understand what an astonishment that was? He spoke to us for the first time in years.'

'Not a human. A monster,' I said. 'What did you make of it?'

'Doesn't matter what I make of it,' Dr Glass said. 'There's a young man in our midst who has been hiding his light under a bushel, Mrs Gilver. Sergeant Gibb.'

'We met him,' I said.

'He made no impression on me at all when I went in for a gun licence a while back,' the doctor went on, 'but he's come into his own in this case, I must say. He made a confession from Tony's words, if you please. Mea culpa: "I am inhuman to have done what I have done. I am a monster to have done what I have done."'

I agreed that the sergeant was clever; I had pondered Tony Gourlay's words at length without seeing that – or any – interpretation. Now that it had been suggested, however, it was hard to resist.

'And the two men who're still on the run?' I said. 'Were they particular friends of Mr Gourlay while they were here? Might they have a common aim of some sort?'

As I spoke, Dr Glass's chin sunk lower and lower until it was resting on his chest. When he roused himself again his face was grave.

'This is because the nuns think they've got a prowler, is it?' he said. 'Well, no. Not a chance. Tony lives a solitary life, although he's surrounded by others. The two men we've not got back yet are . . . quite different sorts.'

'Tell me,' I said. I noticed Alec shifting uncomfortably from the corner of my eye.

'One of them – Chick Tiddy is his name – is an out-and-out simpleton,' said Dr Glass. 'He's more or less harmless and can be rendered completely so by a strict regime of medicine,' said Dr Glass. 'Without it he's liable to get rather . . . rowdy. He's inclined to make a nuisance of himself.'

I managed to see through the bowdlerising words and I raised my eyebrows.

'If he were prowling the upstairs corridors of St Ultan's, we'd all know it?'

'Harrumph,' said the good doctor. 'Quite. The surprising thing is that he's managed to keep out of sight and save himself from being caught this long. I would have expected him to show himself to someone long before now. The police are leaning very hard on his mother to discover what she knows.'

'What about the other one?' I asked.

'Well, now, I rather blame myself for Ernie Arnold,' he said. 'I brought him here and I kept him here. He's a Cumbria man. Also rowdy if left to himself and also greatly calmed by his medicine. But strictly between ourselves I've always suspected that Ernie's simple-mindedness is a performance. I've been watching him for years, comparing his behaviour to that of the bona fide idiots we have. And the fascinating thing is that he's been getting better. Which means worse.'

'You mean he's been improving his performance?' I said. The doctor once again looked pleased with my perspicacity and it was hard not to simper a little under his beaming gaze.

'Precisely,' he said. 'He's been watching Chick and the others and seeing how it's done.'

'But why?' I asked.

Alec snorted. 'Because a life up here with nurses and hobbies is far preferable to a life in Preston Jail.'

'What did he do?' I said.

Alec and Dr Glass shared a look.

'He set upon someone,' Dr Glass said. 'A young woman. And rather nastily.'

'So it's likely that he's clean away then?' I said. 'If he's been faking his condition he'd be able to drop the fakery and blend into a crowd, would he not?'

Dr Glass made a quick gesture with his hand just as we heard a movement in the other room. 'That was, as I say, between ourselves,' he whispered. 'I'd be in all sorts of trouble if it were to get out that I harboured a shirker.' Then he turned as a door leading to an inner room opened and a young woman poked her head in.

'Are you in consultation, Dr Glass? Only I can smell that heavenly coffee.'

'Come away in, Cinty,' said the doctor. 'We're just having a wee confab to ourselves. The more the merrier.'

The woman, as she straightened and entered, was revealed to be wearing a nurse's dress of pale blue cotton and a linen apron on top, but her head was bare and something about her demeanour did not chime with what one knows of nurses. She helped herself to a cup, flung herself into a corner of the sofa and took out a cigarette case.

'Mrs Gilver,' said Dr Glass. 'Allow me to present Miss Udney. Cinty, this is Mr Osborne that I was telling you about. They're the detectives come to help us through the last of our troubles.'

'Miss Udney?' said Alec, and, now that I looked closely at her, I could see a vague similarity to the other Miss Udney we had met yesterday in the orphans' dining room. She had corn-coloured hair instead of the glossy black hair and it was more severely dressed, missing the little curls her sister had nudged in with wetted fingertips. The Miss Udney before us had simply parted her locks in the middle and brushed them back behind her ears. Since, however, she had that delightful combination of a heart-shaped face and ears that stuck out a little at the tips, the overall effect was elfin and charming.

'Daff told me she ran into you yesterday,' she said. 'I'm glad to have come upsides.'

'Do you work here, Miss Udney?' I asked.

'I do,' she said. 'I'm a . . . Well, golly, I'm not formally trained so we don't say "nurse", but I'm a sort of a patron-cum-general dogsbody.'

'You mean to say you work in the hospital itself?' said Alec. 'With the men?'

'With some of the men,' Miss Udney said. 'One must make oneself useful these days. Well, I mean to say, look at you two. How did you become detectives?'

I was not to be swayed. My looking into this and that with Alec helping was one thing, the clearly very gently-born

Miss Udney nursing lunatics in an asylum on a moor was quite another.

'I'm interested in Dr Glass's work here,' she said, when I pressed her, 'and I suppose I still feel very much a part of Hopekist Head. We were brought up here, my two sisters and me. There's a dear young man – he thinks he's the thirteenth disciple, but he's very sweet – who sleeps in our old night nursery.'

I blinked and Miss Udney chuckled a little.

'This place was my father's fancy,' she said. 'He moved out of the barracks – it was called Hopekist House in our day – and gave it in trust to the nuns in . . . ooh, it must have been eighty or eighty-one. Just exactly when excrescences like that one' – she waved her cigarette behind her – 'were all the rage. Of course, when we were children we thought it was terrific fun. Never got bored on a rainy day with all those turrets and stairways to gallop about in.

'My mother, in contrast, hated it from the day she arrived here after her honeymoon. But it wasn't until the war began that she made any headway. She wrapped all her loathing of the place in patriotism – Golly, I sound as hard as nails; I mean, she did care about them. But her main aim, eventually achieved, was to get my father to build something modern down in the valley.'

'We've seen it, I think,' I said.

Miss Udney laughed and then coughed a little, having misjudged her smoke.

'Isn't it awful?' she said. 'Poor Mother hated it as much as the other, too. And then she only lived in it a few years. Spanish flu, which puts such things as ugly houses rather in perspective, doesn't it? The village abhors it, of course, and who can blame them?' She sighed. 'One hundred years and the Udneys have managed to find the worst of every passing fashion. Georgian box, Gothic nightmare and cubist calamity. We laugh so we don't cry, my sisters and me.'

'And shall you stay on?' I said, hoping I wasn't being too indelicate. 'We heard the sad news about your father.'

Miss Udney sighed even more deeply this time. 'Oh, I should think so,' she said. 'We're pretty well heeled-in, between the orphans and the patients here,' she said. 'I don't mean to say that either the Little Sisters or dear Dr Glass here couldn't manage quite well without us, and of course it's the Church that's in charge of the one and the government for the other. It was the War Office but it's some committee somewhere now. Still, we do feel our duty and we love our work!'

'What about your other sister?' I said. 'Does she help you here or Miss Udney at St Ultan's?'

'Oh, Bena's good works knock ours quite into a cocked hat,' she said. 'Daddy had quite a spread in India, you know – tea and rubber, the usual things – and Bena's there now, setting up outposts. An orphanage and school and a hospital too. She'd already left when Daddy died, which was dreadful for her, and for him, but one could tell he was proud.'

I am not usually easily bowled over, but I found myself rather smitten by Miss Udney. She had had a life of considerable upset: dragged from her home to see it turned into a sanatorium, her mother dying in that horrid epidemic, her father dying at Christmas time, fires and mayhem raging as she grieved and she looked upon it all quite cheerfully and worked at helping madmen, in a cotton dress and apron. I was smitten and also chastened; for if there had been a convent and an asylum plonked down in the Gilverton estate and I was living in a nasty house a stone's throw from disapproving villagers, I should be miffed in the extreme.

I glanced at Alec and had to press my lips together to keep a grin at bay. If I was smitten, Alec looked as though he had been hit by a mallet. Miss Udney was just the sort of girl he talked about finding sometimes in that desultory way: sensible, cheerful, over thirty. I immediately began planning to get the two of us invited down to the cubist calamity for tea, and only a little of me wondered how these three girls could still be spinsters.

'And when is your other sister expected back from India, Miss Udney?' I said, thinking that he could have the pick of them if it was soon.

'She's on her way now. We had a telegram from Port Said. I do hope this is all put to rest before she gets here. She's a worrier and I could just see her confining Daff and me to quarters if she heard about Chick and Ernie. I think they're long gone. At least, Ernie Arnold could be in New York or Hong Kong by now. If I'm honest, I think Chick Tiddy must have met with a mishap. I'm astonished that he didn't simply come home too.'

'And what do you make of Mr Gourlay, Miss Udney?' Alec said, since she had almost brought him up.

'Poor Tony,' she said. 'As though he could do any such thing. I think he must have seen the fire and tried to help. That's how he got smoky and Daff told me the room with the paint slung about was adjoining the chapel, so that fits too.'

'You think he climbed in over the wall after the fire started?'

'Daff said they opened the gates. To let helpers in, I suppose.'

'And were you as surprised as Dr Glass that Mr Gourlay left the hospital that night?' I said.

She gave this careful consideration and then nodded but only slightly.

'It's sometimes possible to get Tony to follow one if one takes his hand and leads him quite slowly. I've got him in out of the rain that way, many times. One mustn't talk – just take his hand and lead him. So . . . if one of the men was desperate to get Tony out, there would have been a way to do it. But it's hard to see, isn't it? The way I imagine it

93

happening is that they fled – full pelt, in case they were caught. It would take nerves of absolute steel to walk out the front gate slowly enough that Tony would come along too.'

'And that's how it was done, was it?' I said. 'Straight out the front gate?'

'It was hanging wide open when I got back after closing time at the Udney Arms,' said Dr Glass. 'I couldn't believe my eyes.'

'Did you ever find out how it came to be?' I asked.

Dr Glass shook his head.

'It was quite the Christmas miracle, wasn't it?' said Miss Udney, drily. 'All the keys shipshape and both the night supervisors vouching for one another. You know there's been another letter in the paper?'

Dr Glass looked up sharply.

'In the *Gazette*?'

'Anonymous again,' said Miss Udney. She turned to Alec. 'This is the third anonymous letter, Mr Osborne. I'm going to write one of my own telling the editor exactly what I think of him publishing anonymous letters. If someone hasn't the nerve to put his name to something then he shouldn't be saying it.'

'And what was he saying?' Alec asked.

'Same old rot,' said Miss Udney. 'Calling for the hospital to be closed down and moved to "purpose-built facilities in more suitable surroundings".'

'I can see the sense regarding the buildings,' I said, 'but what would be more suitable surroundings?'

'Well, exactly!' said Miss Udney. 'The middle of a desolate moor is the perfect spot for a hospital like ours. If there's a breakout the men can be gathered up again before they get to a big-enough town to disappear. Or at least that should have been the case.' She frowned. 'It's most perplexing. How did they manage to get away when so many villagers and police were looking for them, Dr Glass? How did Ernie? He doesn't have the cunning.'

'I wish I could disagree, Cinty,' said the doctor. 'But I daresay when the spring comes and the ramblers from Glasgow with it, we shall hear news from some footpath up on the high ground.'

Miss Udney nodded but did not answer him, just stared ahead and smoked dolefully for a minute or two. Then she gathered herself and turned to me.

'What did you mean about the buildings?' she said. 'The newspapers haven't got hold of anything, as far as I know.'

I mulled that over for a minute before speaking.

'Simply that, if one were troubled anyway, living in such a romantic sort of house might be a little hard to bear.'

'I detect a cinema-goer!' said Miss Udney with a chuckle and I laughed along with her for of course she was right. Mr Karloff had thrilled Donald, Teddy and me in La Scala in Perth only months before, much to Hugh's disgust, and the scenes of advancing villagers had changed my mind about such houses as Hopekist Head forever. 'Well, if that's all it is then, phew!' Miss Udney went on and, at our puzzled looks, she turned to the doctor silently to beseech him.

'I trust we can count on your discretion,' he said, giving a stern look at Alec and me.

'Entirely,' said Alec. 'Mrs Gilver and I are great keepers of many secrets after all these years. What is it?'

'Well now,' said Miss Udney. 'It's just that where the doctor's house is now there used to be a sort of little summerhouse. A temple, I suppose you could say.'

'A folly?' said Alec.

'A considerable folly,' said Miss Udney, pretending to misunderstand him. 'My father, when he planned Hopekist Head, gave free rein to all the most outlandish notions. A castle wasn't a castle without dungeons and secret passageways and priests' holes galore.'

95

'When was it built?' I said. 'Priests' holes?'

'Well, quite,' Miss Udney said. 'All completely – what's that wonderful German word?'

'Ersatz,' said Dr Glass.

'Ersatz!' she cried. 'They do have a talent for *le mot juste*, despite their other failings, don't they? Of course he didn't want an actual consecrated chapel up here – we always went to Mass with the nuns – but he was insistent on the passageway, even if it only led to a folly. It was tremendous fun for us girls when we were little even if it drove our nurses to distraction.'

Alec grunted. 'Is it still intact?' he said, catching on quicker than me.

'Thank the Lord,' said Dr Glass. 'The folly went when the trustees built my natty little villa here and I'm very grateful to be able to slip over to the hospital on winter evenings without having to go outside into the wind and rain. Besides, it's much safer really than to be always opening and shutting the gate.'

'Gosh,' I said, faintly.

'The patients don't know about it,' said Miss Udney. 'No one does, except Dr Glass, the rest of the staff, my sisters and me. The War Office doctors were rather sticklers. They would far rather have had the poor soldiers in boring wards with high windows, so we decided not to broadcast some of the castle's more unusual features.'

'And look at how well we did,' said Dr Glass. 'When the breakout came it wasn't through the passageway after all.'

'Gosh,' I said again, and I was aware that I was sitting forward in my chair, poised to rise at speed if I had to, exactly how Nanny Palmer had taught me to sit in chairs when I was a girl, and not at all the way I had taken to lolling since the fashions in corsetry changed. 'So there's a passageway leading from this house into the asylum? Open? Used?'

'I came through it myself just now,' said Miss Udney. 'And now I shall go back through it again.' She drained her coffee cup and stood up. 'It was lovely to meet you, Mrs Gilver. You must come down to the Water for tea while you're staying. You too, Mr Osborne.' She smiled a very affectionate smile – wrinkling her nose along with it – at Dr Glass and went back the way she had come.

'Thank you for saying you'd keep that under your hat,' said Dr Glass. 'The letter-writers would have a field day.'

The sun had broken through as we stepped outside and down the brick path to Dr Glass's garden gate and the fresh smell of the very first spring grasses lifted my spirits towards cheerfulness again.

'I feel a bit sorry for the late Mrs Udney,' I said, standing beside Alec as we gazed out together over the view. In the far distance a few cottage chimneys smoked but rather than marring the prospect they lent it an extra air of comfort, suggesting that if the sun should go in or the wind pick up there were firesides and armchairs near at hand. 'First she's dragged off to this godforsaken spot to live in a joke of a castle, then she's ousted from here and plonked down in another architect's joke and she's carried off by that filthy flu before she gets a single one of her pretty daughters well settled. I mean, she must have been trying already in 1918, mustn't she? How old would you say the Miss Udneys are, darling?' There was no response. 'Alec?' I said, turning.

He had walked away from me while I spoke, over to the high gates that opened in the fence around the asylum grounds. He was standing looking in through the railings and, without tearing his eyes away, he beckoned me. I walked over and joined him.

Inside the fence, several inmates could be seen. Some were sitting on benches under the bare limbs of what looked like cherry trees; one was walking, perhaps better to call it pacing, back and forth along the terrace in front of a French window; and one was working in a flowerbed, with a long hoe, gently loosening the soil between clumps of emerging strap-like leaves – daffodils at a guess.

'That's Tony Gourlay,' Alec said, nodding at the hoeing man.

He looked like a labourer, his cap on the back of his head, his cigarette between his lips and his eyes screwed up against the smoke. He was not wearing a grey coat, but only shirt-sleeves, rolled above the elbow showing very brown and corded forearms. His boots were thick with mud and there was mud on one knee of his trousers, from where he must have knelt to deal with some pernicious weed – I have seen Hugh come in from the grounds many times with that single muddy knee.

'He looks very calm,' I said.

'Hard to imagine him scrawling obscenities or burning nuns?' said Alec.

'I was thinking more that if any of the irate villagers, not to mention magistrates or – if it comes to that – jurymen were to see him, out in the sunshine doing a spot of gardening, their hearts would harden against him.'

Alec said nothing, but turned away towards the motorcar and waited for me to follow. Tony Gourlay had shown no sign that he knew we were there and we were too far from him for our conversation to be heard, but I looked back over my shoulder just once as I walked away and he was no longer hoeing. He was standing quite still with one hand shading his eyes, looking right at me.

9

'The first order of business,' I said, striding into the hall at St Ultan's minutes later and stripping off my gloves, 'is to draw up a list of the sisters and start ticking them off when I've spoken to them. I've bagged Sisters Bridget, Hilda, John and Mary and I think I can let Sister Catherine alone, don't you, so that's fourteen to go.'

'Who's up next?' said Alec. He threw a look at the mouse-like novice who had let us in and she ducked her head and scuttled off before we could stop her. I glanced at my wristwatch.

'They've got half an hour's work left before the next batch of prayers,' I said. 'Sister Martha gave me a rough idea of the daily round. I got rather muddled towards tea time but I'm sure of this bit. Work from breakfast to Sext. So I say let's grab someone who won't mind downing tools a little early.'

I made my way to a door in the north-east corner, confident it would lead me to the kitchens without going through Sister Mary's study, and indeed the door revealed itself to be double and lined with faded baize and had behind it a corridor with linoleum on the floor and housemaids' shelves along the walls.

'Steady on,' said Alec. 'You surely don't mean to interrupt Abigail and Martha while they're making the luncheon. Think of the poor orphans who want to grow up to be big and strong.'

I tutted as I pushed open the kitchen door and entered.

'Sister Abigail. I'm Mrs Gilver. We haven't been formally introduced yet. And this is Mr Osborne.'

'Sister Martha's told me all about you,' said Abigail. 'And Sister Mary had us praying for your intention last night and this morning, so we're not strangers.' She gave me an easy smile and then wiped her forehead with the back of her hand. She wore her wimple very high, hinting at a high hairline underneath it and her brows were sparse too, her lashes invisible, so that she looked a little like painted bisque – just round red spots on her cheeks from the heat of her range and very red lips. Suspiciously red lips, I would have said, for a nun, had I not seen that she was unrolling pastry tops over pie plates of bramble jam. I deduced that she had been checking the sugar or perhaps just keeping her strength up. 'These'll be piping hot and glistening gold just as soon as we've finished our broth,' she said, when she saw me looking.

'Beef and barley broth,' said Sister Martha, holding up a steaming ladleful. 'And suet dumplings.'

'I wonder if you could direct us towards the laundry?' I said. 'I'd like to speak to Sister . . .?'

'Sister Julian is in charge through there,' said Martha, 'with Sister Clare and Sister Margaret working under her. It's along that way.' She pointed with her ladle towards a half-glassed door leading from the kitchen and I stepped towards it.

'But – pardon me,' said Sister Abigail, and the red on her cheeks had spread so that her whole face was flushed, 'you can't go to the laundry, Mr Osborne.'

'Why n—?' Alec began and then his thoughts caught up with his mouth. Although he did not blush along with the rest of us he was forced to clear his throat quite firmly. 'Of course not,' he said. 'Well then, Dandy, if you could rip me a sheet out of that capacious sketching pad and advance me one of your pencils, nicely sharpened, I shall get on with drawing up that plan of the premises you've been mentioning.'

'You can't go upstairs!' said Sister Martha.

'My dear la— Sister,' Alec said. 'I had no intention of it. I meant to sit here if you can spare a corner of your table and have you describe it to me.'

While enjoying some early tastings of the broth, I imagined, even before I noticed that Sister Abigail was making a tray of jam tarts with the scraps of her pastry.

'Along that way' turned out to be off the passage which connected the convent to the orphanage; a sensible place for the laundry since surely more washing would originate from fifty orphans than from twenty nuns. And indeed, when I opened the door and entered, it was to see a sister, her sleeves rolled back and tied into white cuffs, flapping what I thought were wet infants' napkins and making bundles of a few together to pass through the mangle.

'Sister Clare?' I said, guessing that this sturdy young creature was the "baby elephant" rather than the dreamy one, as I had heard Sister Margaret described. She did not look old enough to be Sister Julian, the laundry boss.

'Mrs Gilver,' she said. 'What brings you to the Tropic of Capricorn?'

I laughed, for it was certainly hot, and humid besides; the air silky with steam and the walls dripping. Matters were not helped by the fact that there were no little windows in the roof where any of the steam might be let escape, such as one finds in the most efficient modern laundries; at St Ultan's an older building had been turned to account and the sisters who worked here were stuck with the smell of wet wood and stone from ancient arches overhead and must put up with great drops of water showering down upon them.

There was plenty to cause the shower: two copper washtubs going at full tilt, the fires glowing white and pink in the grates below; and the two china troughs of cold water only increased the overall clamminess. Sister Clare fed the leading edge of her soaking pile into the maw of the mangle and cranked the handle lustily until the cloths fell into a basket waiting below. She picked them out and flapped them again, lightly damp now, and I saw that they were not infants' napkins after all, but crescent shaped curves of thick linen. She saw me frowning.

'Guimpes,' she said, and touched the collar at her own neck to explain. I had never wondered how the sisters came to be encased in smooth linen from forehead to breastbone, taking it for granted without questioning the trick of it. Sister Clare turned to the wet bowl and started to pick out another bundle, then winced.

'Oh that Sister Margaret!' she said, lifting a cloth and peering at it. 'She's as dozy as a day-old calf. She's went and left a pin in her guimpes again and I've went and stabbed myself.' She stuck her finger in her mouth as an outside door opened and a middle-aged nun, with her sleeves rolled up like Sister Clare's, came in swinging two empty wicker baskets.

Sister Clare took her finger out with a pop and addressed her.

'You're needing to get her told, Sister,' she said. 'That was another pin in the load she was meant to sort.'

The middle-aged nun sighed. 'You go onto sorting the dirty darks till you've stopped bleeding,' she said, 'and I'll take over there. Mrs Gilver, you're finding us at less than full efficiency.'

I had not thought she had seen me, standing back in the billows of steam as I was.

'I wonder if I might ask some questions as you work, Sister Julian,' I said. 'Both of you – all three of you, really. Where is Sister Margaret?'

'Out hanging up,' said Sister Clare. 'But she'll find a way to do that wrong too.'

'Now, now, Sister,' said Sister Julian. 'Let patience have her perfect work. Fire away, Mrs Gilver,' she went on with an encouraging smile. It crossed my mind to wonder why such a diplomatic nun of such seniority was stuck in the laundry but I could not work out a way to ask without being rude. I pulled forward a little three-legged stool and settled onto it, drawing out my notebook, while Sister Clare began rummaging through a pile of black woollen stockings to clip them into pairs and Sister Julian guddled in one of the troughs, lifting long strips of linen out into an enamel bowl.

'Bandeaus,' said Sister Clare, seeing me looking at them. 'This bit here.' She touched her forehead, where the starched band of white hid every scrap of her hair. 'Mrs Gilver's very interested in how our habits go together,' she said.

'Well, you've come to the right place,' said Sister Julian. 'There are no secrets here. We scrub everything except the scapulae, since they are blessed garments. Each Sister washes her scapula when it needs it.'

'Which part is the scapula?' I said.

'The tabard,' said Sister Clare. 'But we don't wear ours in here. They're hanging up on hooks in the passageway. We'll put them back on when our work is done.'

Again it struck me that I was most unobservant when it came to the clothes of the sisters. I should have noticed that ordinarily their belts were hidden by an over-tunic and that the tunics were missing from Abigail and Martha in the kitchen and from these two here. It was a testament to the success of their habits, I supposed. One simply saw a mound of black with flashes of white and all one really noticed were their faces.

Sister Julian, for instance, had the freckles and hazel eyes which go along with auburn hair, while Sister Clare was ruddy with golden eyebrows and looked like a farmer's girl. I would lay a bet that there were wheaten curls under her veil. Unless her head were shaved, as I had heard tell.

'I'm beginning to get a fuller picture of the night the Reverend Mother died,' I said.

'God rest her soul,' said Sister Clare.

'The two things I particularly want to ask you,' I continued after a moment of silence, 'are who you saw and where and when, while you were all dealing with the fire, and also what you heard Mother Mary say.' I gave them a moment to think about these questions. 'But there is also the matter of all the open doors.'

'Not all,' Sister Julian said quickly. 'Mine was closed.'

'Are you sure, Sister?' said Clare. 'Are you sure you just didn't notice? Because mine was wide open and so was every other one I saw. And what's more so was my cupboard door too.' She turned to me. 'I'm next to where the wee stair turns to the high attics and I've a good deep cupboard. We keep suitcases and travelling trunks in it, because the mice in the attics like nothing better than a good chew at a leather trunk, but I can keep up with the traps in the cupboard just fine.' She turned back to Julian. 'Are you absolutely sure?'

'I am as sure as I'm standing here,' said Sister Julian. 'As sure as these are—' She broke off and peered at the sodden garment she was holding. 'Sister Dorothy's winter drawers.' I was glad Alec had been prevented from joining me. 'Every night when I open my cell door I say a prayer of thanks for the finished day. And I remember quite clearly that I hesitated, because I had already retired once that evening and I couldn't decide whether to say it again. It felt strange to me to open my cell door and go in without it.'

'But your door *was* open?' I asked Clare.

'They all were,' she said, definitely if not actually defiantly.

'And what did you make of it?'

'Maybe a draught,' said Sister Clare. 'The way we were all flying about that night, with the garden door open and sisters in and out of their cells.'

'A draught,' I echoed.

'You never know,' she went on. 'This laundry's a terrible place for phantom draughts. The door to the drying green and the one to the pump room are forever slamming and we can never work out why. And Sister Martha's known the oven door to slam shut right out of her hand. Of course, that might be wind in the chimney.'

'Well, it's a more sensible suggestion than what some of the others are saying,' said Julian crisply. 'But don't say "phantom" that silly way, Sister.'

'So maybe you did leave yours ajar, Sister,' said Martha, 'and it blew shut.'

Julian gave her a speculative look, judging whether to admonish her or let peace reign. I concluded that she was a peace-maker by inclination for, despite Clare giving her another pert look and turning back to her task with what in anyone but a nun one would call a flounce, Julian said nothing.

'So let's turn to earlier, when the fire was discovered,' I said. 'Who woke you up?'

'Sister Steven,' Clare said.

Julian said, 'Mother Mary herself. My cell is only two down from hers.'

'I'm on the second floor,' Clare said.

I wrote hurriedly on one page, turned and started another, turned back and looked up.

'You'll drive yourself demented if you do us both in tandem,' said Sister Julian. 'I'm away out to see to Sister Margaret till you're done with Sister Clare.'

I smiled my relief and waited until she was gone.

'So,' I resumed, 'Sister Steven told you the chapel was on fire and then what?'

'I was half undone,' Clare said, 'and I didn't know what to do so I poked my head out – just in my cap and bandeau and looked at the others. Sister Jude and Sister Irene were just turning on the landing and they had their veils on so I pinned mine on quickly and put on my shoes and went out.'

'And who did you see?' I asked her.

'The novices were ahead of me,' said Clare. 'And Sister Francis was shouting to someone behind me – I think it was Sister Bridget but I can't be sure – and when I got down to the first floor,' she chewed her lip, 'I saw someone. I'm sure of it. But I was flying down so quickly. It was someone along the other end, standing quite still. Huh!' she gave a laugh. 'Probably Sister Margaret. Nothing stirs her stumps and there was no sign of her down at the chapel for ages.'

'Good, yes, let's move on to the time at the chapel,' I said. 'What did you do?'

'I saw Our Mother going in as soon as ever I burst out of the garden door,' said Clare, 'and so I went in after her. Some of the others were passing buckets already and they looked to have a good rhythm, so I went in after Our Mother.'

'Did you speak to her?'

'She spoke to me,' said Clare. 'She was at the altar and she had the books in her arms – maybe just the Bible; maybe not the prayer book – and she looked over her shoulder and saw me. Then she put it back down on the altar – I remember it most particularly, because Sister John and Sister Steven had whipped the altar cloth off and it looked dreadful to see our Bible there on the bare wood. That's why I couldn't defy her.'

'I'm sorry, Sister,' I said. 'I don't know what you mean.'

'Well, she put it down to come back to me and tell me to get out,' said Clare. 'She came striding down the aisle like an avenging angel. Sister John and Sister Steven were there and they're older than me and Sister Steven had a bad cough even without the smoke, but she never said a word to *them*.'

'But you're different, aren't you?' I said.

I had noticed something as she spoke. I had noticed that some of the nuns called the Reverend Mother by her rank. To others she was Mother Mary, but she was Our Mother to some and I think I knew why. 'After all,' I went on, 'you were like her child.'

Sister Clare gave an enormous sigh and nodded her head.

'I came here when I was a month old,' she said. 'She was the only mother I ever knew. She fed me herself with a cloth soaked in sugared milk, like a sickly lamb, sat up with me through the night until I was strong enough to be left. But I'm not saying anything against her.'

'What on earth do you mean?' I could not understand her sudden guilty look. Everything she said so far had been an out and out paean to the woman.

'Well, when we take our final vows of profession, we're supposed to leave our secular life behind,' said Clare. 'We're supposed to renounce our families and our ties to them.' She dropped her voice. 'I always felt ashamed when I was a girl, because my mother was just a girl herself and I never had a father, but once I took my vows all of that was washed away. And all of the orphanage should have been washed away too.'

'You're being very hard on yourself,' I said. 'And awfully hard on Mother Mary.'

'She should have let me stay in the chapel and do God's work,' said Clare. 'Or she should have sent me out as a junior nun who must obey her seniors, but what she said when she came towards me was, "Elsie Bell, get out of here before I spank you."'

She had long since left off sorting through the piles of stockings, and as she said these words she dropped the one she had been holding and fished in her pocket for a hand-kerchief. Finding it, she bent her head and, like the child Mother Mary loved, she burst into gales of sobbing.

IO

I guessed, from the way Sister Clare was swiping so savagely at her tears, that she would rather be left alone to compose herself and that a gentle voice and pat on her shoulder would be unwelcome, so I let myself out of the door through which Sister Julian had gone and found myself in a small, high-walled garden, crisscrossed with washing ropes hung from cleats driven into the mortar and with a row of lavender bushes along the south side.

'How charming!' I said. 'I haven't seen that since I was a child. Gosh, I haven't slept on lavender sheets since visiting my great grandmamma!'

'You won't be sleeping on them here, either,' said Julian, walking over the grass to join me. 'We take washing in from some of the big houses in the county – Stanmore, Castlebank – there's plenty people still appreciate the old ways but can't run to a laundry maid of their own.' A quick frown crossed her face. 'It's getting so there's no point training up any of our girls like we used to,' she said. 'They don't need skill to work in the big town laundries now and to tell you the truth, Mrs Gilver, I hesitate to send them.'

'Sister!' came a cry from the far side of the green. Julian sighed and hoisted a smile onto her face as she walked away.

Sister Margaret had got herself so tangled in the tablecloth she was attempting to hang over a high line that she looked like an Egyptian mummy. Julian unravelled her, inspected the cloth for mud at its edges and tutted, finding some.

'I'll take it back in to Sister Clare,' Sister Margaret said, reaching out her arms.

'You'll do no such thing,' said Julian. 'It's only the edges and it'll brush off when it's dry.'

'But Sister Steven will find it and scold me!' Margaret said. 'She looks for mistakes. She searches for them like a bloodhound.'

'We're too busy to be rewashing everything you spoil, Sister,' Julian said. 'If you would just ever watch and learn.' Deftly, with no more than a few flicks of her wrists, she had the enormous tablecloth folded in three and then the threes in half, corners tugged square and not a wrinkle anywhere. 'Now, lower the stretcher, Sister. There's no need to be waving above your head that way.' With another few spare movements she had it neatly over the line, pegged at the fold and at the flapping corners and up again like a masthead. Sister Margaret only sighed.

'I'm not cut out for this,' she said. 'I want to be at prayer.'

'Six days shalt thou labour and do all thy work,' said Julian.

'They toil not, neither do they spin,' shot back Margaret.

'I've seen you daydreaming your way through your prayers the same as your work, Sister,' said Julian. 'Now, don't get upset,' she added hurriedly as Margaret's eyes filled. 'Go and tend to the double line of little things and see if you can't be answering Mrs Gilver's questions for her as you do. Come on now, there's less than ten minutes until the Angelus just and I want this green filled.' If Margaret had moved a muscle or managed a smile or even wiped her eyes, the kindly Sister Julian would no doubt have left it at that, but the girl just stood like a statue with tears splashing down on what I now knew was called her guimpe and Julian's eyes flashed with temper. 'We can't all be lilies!' she said and marched away.

Of course, that set Sister Margaret off worse than ever and soon she was sniffing as well as weeping, looking less lily-like all the time. She was, when not red and swollen, another of the very pale women I had seen in these parts, with blue eyes and dark lashes. It is a colouring one looks for more in the islands and in the far west, where raven hair and white skin tell of centuries of movement between Scotland and Ireland, the black Irish outwitting the Vikings. I wondered if here in the remoteness of the Lanark moor there was a little pocket of settled people just as isolated as the island folk, passing on their speedwell eyes and alabaster skin.

'Were you born here, Sister Margaret?' I said.

She shook her head. 'No, I wasn't an orphan. But my mother was and the way she spoke of "Mother Mary" and the beauty of the place and the kindness of the nuns – as soon as I was sure of my vocation I thought this was where I was called to be.'

'There's no shame in changing one's mind,' I said. 'Why, Sister John said the very same thing. That she started out on the wrong path and righted herself.'

Margaret nodded and, with a wuthering sigh, finally began to gather herself. With another she looked down at her feet into a basket of small linens – drawers and camisoles and binding tapes, and with her third and final, bent to lift one out and peg it to the lower of two tiers of rope stretched across the corner of the walls just beside her.

'Good,' I said, then kicked myself inwardly for getting brisk with her. Briskness, clearly, was not the strong suit here. 'Dear Sister,' I said, trying again, 'Sister Hilda has already told me most of your movements from the night of the fire – I hope your ankle is better?'

Margaret frowned, clearly having forgotten the ankle she had used to get out of useful work that night, then nodded faintly.

'Yes,' she said. 'I was badly jostled.'

'I thought you slipped on a puddle,' I said, and saw Margaret lift her chin defiantly.

'That's right. I slipped and twisted my ankle and then while Sister Hilda was helping me, one of the sisters bowled past without stopping and knocked against me very hard.'

'Who?' I asked.

'I don't know. I called out to her to be careful. She shouted "Sorry, Sister" back over her shoulder and then she disappeared through the door into the chapel.'

'And did you go in after her?' I knew she had not but was keen to hear the excuse.

'No, we couldn't get the door open,' said Margaret, shamelessly. 'There was an almighty thump and suddenly it was jammed. I think something fell over and blocked it from the other side.'

'Really? No one else has mentioned that. In fact, we've been led to believe that sisters went in and out quite freely. Carrying furniture.'

'But that was the outside door,' Margaret said.

'Oh!' I was catching on. 'You mean you and Sister Hilda went along the passageway from Mother Mary's study?'

'We tried to. But that's what I'm telling you. Something fell in front of the door and kept us out. So we turned back and went the other way, to the garden door from the library.'

'And . . . After that you were on tea-duty, weren't you? So presumably you saw everyone.'

'Presumably,' said Sister Margaret. 'But not everyone came for tea for themselves. Some of the sisters came to get three and four cups together to take back for others and, looking over, we couldn't tell who we were seeing. For one thing, because the smoke was so thick.'

'And?' I prompted. 'Because of the dark?'

She shook her head. 'Because of the light,' she said. 'The flames were so bright. It was hard to pick out any detail against them. And of course all of us wear black, anyway. Do you know what it reminded me of, Mrs Gilver? A shadow-puppet show. Just black figures moving against the light. And then when they got closer they were revealed, red-faced and coughing and not black at all. Pale with ash.'

'So you and Sister Hilda were making tea,' I said. 'And Sisters Dorothy, Francis and Martha were passing buckets. We already know that Sisters John and Steven were in and out of the chapel and that Sister Abigail was in the kitchen. Can you remember who else you definitely saw?'

'Why?' said Margaret. 'I mean yes, of course. I saw Sister Dorothy and Sister Anne and I saw Sister Jude come back from ringing the playground bell at the orphans' side, but why?'

'No reason,' I said. 'I just like to get a clear picture.'

'Of what?' said Margaret, anything but dreamy now. 'Do you suspect one of us of something?'

'Not at all,' I said, trying to deflect her. 'I'm most concerned to find out who spoke to the Reverend Mother. She didn't leave the chapel and so I needn't trouble anyone who wasn't in there. You didn't go in, did you?'

She shook her head. 'But Mother Mary spoke to me,' she said. She lifted her eyes and gazed at the sky visible above the high wall. 'She spoke to me through the bell.'

'Really?' I said, as blandly as I could manage. 'And what did she say?'

'That's why I shouldn't be working,' said Margaret. 'I need perfect peace and perfect silence for contemplation to let the Reverend Mother's message become clear to me.'

'Right,' I said.

'I'm not daydreaming,' said Margaret. 'No matter what Sister Julian thinks.'

'I see,' I said, thinking that if Sister Margaret's wool-gathering ways had begun only after Christmas Eve someone would have noticed the fact and mentioned it. Something snagged at my memory. There was a nun who was particularly upset and not recovering. I could not bring her name to mind at the moment but I had written it down and would find it again and try to catch her after luncheon. I blinked and brought my attention back to Margaret who, for a dreamer herself, looked mightily displeased to see me at the same caper.

'Is there anything else?' she said coldly.

'Just the question of the doors,' I said.

'That's the second time she spoke to me,' said Sister Margaret. 'I think she must have passed into eternal life by the time we all came back inside. I think her spirit was free by then.'

'MM dead,' I wrote in my notebook, for no real reason except to stop the cloying euphemisms from sticking to me.

'And she said to me, "Sister Margaret, my child, the door is open. You must leave this place and find your true home." That is what my open door meant.'

'St Ultan's is going to be rather depopulated then,' I said. 'If everyone with an open door ups sticks.'

'I don't believe there *were* any other open doors,' Margaret said. 'I think some of the others couldn't bear to be left out from the Reverend Mother's message and so they . . .'

'Lied?' I said, thinking back over all of them.

'Imagined that what they wished for was real,' she said. 'I certainly didn't see anyone's cell flung open. Just mine.'

I tried not to but, failing, goggled at her. Was there ever a more self-regarding woman born? It beggared belief that she was blind to any evidence that did not fit her preferred notion, and that she would rather call her sisters fibbers than change her mind. Then I relented a little. Margaret slept on the first floor and at least one of the doors on the first floor really was not open, if one believed Julian's denials. I wondered how she had resolved the disagreement with what her friend Sister Hilda had to say regarding *hers*.

Before I could think of a way to broach the matter, the Angelus bell rang out from inside the house and at the same time a less doleful handbell was rung somewhere on the other side of the orphanage wall. Sister Margaret lowered her head and walked away murmuring to herself and leaving the washing basket far from empty. I followed her at a discreet distance into the laundry where Julian and Clare also stood, heads bent, praying. I noticed that their tasks, unlike hers, were completed, the tops on the coppers and the rinsing trough empty. All three exited the laundry, took their scapulae and donned them, and then I walked behind them back along the passage to the main house, beginning to see the rhythm in the alternating sets of bell peals and murmured prayers.

In the kitchen, the two nurses from the orphanage were just disappearing through the connecting door to the children's dining room, bearing laden trays, while Abigail and Martha, aprons off and scapulae on, were also praying. Clare held the door open for the others and still softly speaking the unintelligible words, all five of them left the room.

'Well, that was something different,' said Alec, sitting at one end of the kitchen table with an expression of utter bewilderment upon his face. 'It was all go, dusting with sugar and testing the seasoning, cutting bread and buttering it and then ding-ding went the bell and one would have thought they were hypnotised. I didn't know where to put myself. But the nurses came and got the soup as if it were the most ordinary thing in the world.'

'It is,' I said. 'They do it three times a day. I only wonder how I managed to sleep through that bell this morning.'

'And how long does it take?' said Alec, with a glance at the range. 'Can't be long from the way they've left that soup bubbling. But while we're alone, come and see how I've got on.'

I drew up a chair and sat beside him to admire his efforts and in fact they were more than admirable. The plan of the house was outlined in clear thick lines with only a little rubbing out at the back where the various passages – one to the chapel and one to the orphanage and one to the kitchen and laundry – got tangled, and I noticed that Abigail and Martha had been no more clear than Hilda about the usual and temporary uses of the ground-floor rooms. Only Sister Mary's study was unchanged and elsewhere, library, quiet room, recreation room and refectory were all scored out and written over.

Upstairs though, everything was clear: there were ten rooms on the first floor and twelve on the second with a bathroom on each and even Sister Clare's cupboard under the attic stairs drawn in.

'Are you sure that's right?' I said. 'Sister . . . someone said there were thirteen cells on the second floor.'

'Thirteen doors,' said Alec. 'Twelve cells and the "necessary". Less of an angelic message, wouldn't you say? With the lav door thrown in too?'

'Wait though,' I said. 'That's still twenty-one nuns. There are only twenty.'

Alec smirked and tapped his pencil on the north-east first floor room where he had written 'Sister Dandy'.

'You better not let the sisters see that,' I said. 'They'll think you're laughing at them, not at me.'

'It was Martha who said it!' said Alec. 'They're remarkably unstuffy when you get past the . . .' he circled his hand around his face, sketching a wimple.

More evidence of their unstuffiness was laid before us not a minute later, when Abigail and Martha came clattering back into the room, put on their aprons again and started to fling open oven doors and gather piles of soup plates.

'You've to have your dinner with us in the refectory,' said Martha. 'If you've space inside you for another bite. Sister Mary told me to set places for both of you on either side of her so she can get your report, for she's no time this afternoon and she's hardly seen you all day.'

'Right, well, good then,' said Alec. 'Can I carry something in for you?'

'Ocht away,' said Abigail. 'We'd not want that waistcoat getting splashed. Unless you're happy to wear a pinny.'

There were limits to how far even Alec was prepared to go, though, and so we went empty-handed into luncheon in the nuns' refectory, looking forward to a quiet word with Sister Mary.

My first thought was that they had bungled the assignment of rooms when the house had been turned into a convent for, although the refectory had a connecting door from the kitchen passage, it had just as clearly once been the Udneys' breakfast room as Sister Mary's study had been their dining room and it was rather a squash to get a table for twenty in there.

Even if we had been set out like dignitaries at a state banquet, however, with ten knives and forks at our places and room for six glasses and a coffee cup, we still would not have been able to hold a private conversation with Sister Mary, for the nuns did not use their mealtime for chitchat and anecdote like other people. They drank soup and ate bread in total silence, broken only by the sound of Sister Catherine conveying the broth to her lips – a racket she was no doubt unaware of, owing to her deafness – and also today broken by what turned out to be a very public conversation between Mary, Alec and me.

I was uncertain what her purpose had been in setting the conversation up, but it became quite clear soon enough. She asked about our progress, we replied that we had completed interviews with six of the sisters and hoped to double that number by the end of the day, picking up speed as we went and the salient points became ever more clear.

'Excellent,' said Sister Mary. 'And at least you know for once that every word you are told is as good as a gospel. It must be very frustrating for you to question witnesses out there in the secular world where people lie and hide things. Here at St Ultan's, in the sight of our Lord, we offer nothing but His own sweet truth to you both.'

I could not be sure whether she suspected one of the nuns in particular of lying to us or whether she merely wanted to remind anyone tempted to lie to us of the gravity of false witness, but I was sure our presence was no more than a means of broadcasting the warning to her sisters.

'We needn't take it on faith anyway,' Alec said, and I was sure that the nuns grew even quieter at this amazing occurrence – a man talking in their refectory! – their spoons not even grazing the bottoms of their soup plates and their water glasses replaced on the table top without the slightest tap. 'It's all dovetailing perfectly. We're building up a very clear picture of who was where and when and what she saw. And there are no anomalies at all.'

This was far from true and I was not sure I could have delivered it so soon after a stern reminder that lying was a sin, even for the likes of Alec and me.

'And why exactly are we being put on the rack and interrogated?' came a voice ringing out from halfway down the long table. It was Sister Steven. 'Do you mean to suggest that one of us saw the fellow and is keeping quiet about it?'

'Sister,' said Sister Mary. 'We are not at recreation.'

'You've seen fit to disturb our meal and ruin our digestion, Sister,' said Steven, 'I don't see why I can't say my piece.'

'What fellow?' said Sister John. 'Are you talking about the night the Reverend Mother left us or are you talking about every night since?'

'It's the same thing,' said Steven. 'One of them is captured and two are still on the run.'

'They're not running very fast or getting very far,' said John. 'Not if they're still here.'

The novices and junior nuns were looking about themselves with frightened eyes like rabbits after the first shot on the hillside and even Sister Catherine had realised that something was amiss and was craning to catch some of it.

'Sisters,' said Mary. 'Please, master yourselves and return to silence. We have no need to be quarrelling. All Mrs Gilver and Mr Osborne are doing is making sure that no one saw something important but failed to realise its significance. There are too many upsetting things about that night for us to do the work ourselves. That is all. They see more clearly from a distance than we can see from so close, through our tears, with our human hearts broken.'

At that, one of the young nuns who sat near the foot of the table burst into sobs and stood, knocking her chair over backwards, to run from the room. We listened to her footsteps, first pattering then slowing, faltering and finally stopping. There was a soft thump and a release of breath from several of the sisters at the table.

'Sister Monica,' said Mary. 'Help Sister Anne up to her cell to rest.'

Monica stood and flitted out of the room.

'Sister Monica is our companion,' said Mary.

'And Sister Anne is our fainter,' said John. There was a gasp and then a few smothered giggles and even Mary had a twinkle in her eye although she managed to keep her mouth solemn.

Sister Anne! I thought to myself. That was the romantic one who was still troubled and nervy. I flashed a look at Alec and he wiggled his eyebrows. Anne had just been promoted to the head of the queue for the afternoon's interviews.

11

I had thought the guest retreat was plain but when I saw the inside of Sister Anne's cell, I was forced to amend my view. Here there was no daybed or crocheted cushion, no knee blanket, no pegs on the walls to hang colourful garments and no wooden dressing table gleaming with polish. The room, once a servant's bedroom no doubt, had been stripped of its sprigged paper and calico curtains and what remained was a narrow iron bed with a grey blanket and a fawn pillow case, a shelf with folded clothes upon it, a small table with a Bible and prayer book and a folded cloth whose purpose I could not guess. There was a fawn cotton bag hanging on a hook on the back of the door – turned to account from an earlier life as a pillowcase, I supposed – where the Sister must keep her sponge and toothbrush, but it was the barest chamber I had ever seen and it brought home to me as would nothing else just what it meant to obey a vow of poverty.

Sister Anne hardly made the little room seem less bare. She was lying in the bed, her capped head in the middle of the fawn pillow and her body hidden under the grey blanket, which was pulled up close to her chin. Her eyes were closed and her cheeks were waxen.

'Sister?' I said. Her eyes flew open. Whoever she might have been expecting, it was clearly not me. 'I've brought you a cup of sweet tea.'

'Mrs Gilver,' she said in a weak voice.

'Sit up a bit and see if you can sip some of it,' I said,

finding from far in my past the voice I had learned to use when I was a volunteer at the convalescent home for officers during the war. I glanced at the thinness of the pillow and at the wide spaces between the iron bars of her bed head and wondered if she had ever tried to sit up in bed before. Before she could protest, I took off my coat, a sturdy one, and rolled it into a bundle which I wedged down behind her. Then I stood and held out the cup and saucer and she had no choice but to shuffle up until she was sitting and, bringing one arm out from under the blanket, take it from me. I sat down at the foot of the bed, for want of anywhere else to perch, and waited a couple of minutes before I spoke again. The tea did a little to revive her and, although her cheeks remained pale, her face lost its waxy sheen.

During my waiting time I considered several stratagems. I had all afternoon and was happy to spend it here. On the other hand, as she began to feel better she might become more able to resist my efforts. Should I be stern since even if she fainted again she could not harm herself beyond spilling the tea? Or should I be kind since it seemed that she met with little kindness from her sisters? Should I pretend to know already what it was that was troubling her and trick her into telling me? Or should I perhaps pretend to know nothing at all and let her feel the triumph of telling me things, even if they were ones I already knew?

In the end I plumped for what I can only call naked yearning. I leaned forward and fixed my most intense look upon her wide eyes.

'Tell me,' I said.

It almost worked too. She breathed out and her shoulders dropped, the very thought of sharing her worries bringing her relief. She moistened her lips and opened her mouth. She even took a preparatory breath. I held mine.

Then somewhere in the house a door opened and the sound of voices and gentle laughter drifted up the stairs. It was one of the two recreation hours, of course, and the sisters were free to chat and tell jokes to their hearts' content. When the door shut again and the noise was cut off, Sister Anne's face was set and her mouth in a firm line.

'Well tell me what you can, at least,' I said, letting her know that I had seen the approach and retreat. 'Sister Martha wakened you, I think, didn't she?'

'I wasn't asleep,' said Anne. 'I wasn't even undressed.'

'And yet I think you were one of the last to come out onto the landing when Sister Steven and Sister Martha came up and started rousing everyone, isn't that right?'

'I cannot say,' said Anne. 'I was at prayer. All I can say is that the moment came when I was aware of noise outside my door. I cannot say how much noise there was before that.'

It was a good point. Teddy, when he was small, had an irritating habit of ignoring summonses that threatened to interrupt his play. Nanny would bellow herself red in the face, tramping around the gardens, looking into hedges and under willow branches for him. When he was discovered he would tell what no doubt seemed like a plausible story to him. 'I didn't hear you when you called from the terrace, Nan,' he said once, when I was nearby. 'And I didn't hear you when you called from halfway over the lawn either. I only heard you the third time, when you were right here.' This was delivered with such lisping innocence and with such a guileless look in his big blue eyes that I had to turn away to stop him seeing my smile. Of course, he was thrashed for it; six good spanks with Hugh's slipper, for the individual evils of ignoring Nanny and telling an untruth were each serious matters and added together were grave indeed.

'Not to worry, Mummy,' he had said at bedtime. 'Daddy can't spank nearly as hard as Nan. Not even close. And his slippers are nothing compared to her rolled-up magazines.'

'I should not have been praying so fervently,' Sister Anne

said, bringing me back from pleasant memories of my little scamp. 'Because I was praying for forgiveness. And my most fervent prayers should be prayers of thanks. I have a great deal to atone for.'

'Forgiveness for what?' I said. I could not help the passing thought that I preferred Teddy's view of crime and punishment to Sister Anne's; there was such a thing as too much goodness, it seemed to me.

'For asking Mother Mary to leave the candles lit,' she said. 'I was filled with remorse because we had to stop our midnight prayers. They were on our minds – shocking that anything but our prayers were on our minds as we knelt there! And so when we smelled the smoke that is where our minds went. If I hadn't insisted and Mother Mary had snuffed them we would have started looking for the fire where we were and we wouldn't have found the paint and she would still be alive.'

I wanted to disagree, for there was no way of knowing what would have happened that night if any of the miserable little chain of events had changed, but I sensed that a brisk denial would turn Anne mulish.

'That's certainly a possibility,' I said. 'But Sister, the person responsible for the fire is the one who put the match to it and each person who went inside the chapel did it willingly. No one was ordered, either to go in or to stay there.'

It took her a moment to decipher my meaning. I knew when the penny had dropped from the sudden startled look upon her face. I half-expected her to rise up and show me out for daring to traduce the memory of Mother Mary that way, but to my surprise she nodded a little and looked less troubled than I had yet seen her.

'She had her reasons.' The words were spoken very quietly.

'Do you know what they were?' I spoke just as quietly as she. And for a moment there was no sound but the two of us breathing.

'I find I don't understand anything,' she said. 'I find that one I thought I knew is a stranger to me. And I don't know what to do about it. I thought I knew where my duty lay and what were the temptations put before me to resist, but I was wrong. Suddenly, I find my path unclear.'

'I am here to help you,' I said.

She shook her head. 'No, you're here to solve the mystery of who killed Mother Mary,' she said. 'Isn't that right?'

The moment was past. As clearly as a dream fades upon wakening, the tenuous thread of communication between us was broken. I took my little notebook out of my bag and wound a good point of lead out of my propelling pencil.

'Indeed,' I said. 'I am here to find out who set the fire that killed the Reverend Mother. So let's begin. Do you know any of the soldiers at the hospital?'

'What do you mean?' she asked, apparently aghast.

It seemed a simple enough question to me and a considerable stretch to find insult in it, but I showed goodwill by adding a little more.

'Did Tony Gourlay come to Mass here, for instance?'

'Oh!' said Anne. 'I see. No, our chapel is just for us. And the Udneys sometimes. None of the men come. They have their own chaplain who does a service there every Sunday and there's communion once a month and Mass once a month, two weeks apart. We have early Mass on that Sunday to let Father Mallen get up there and then back to Lanark for his breakfast.'

'So you can't tell me anything about Gourlay? Or about the other two – Arnold and Tiddy – who haven't been captured?'

'Nothing,' she said. 'I can't see that any of them could possibly have any knowledge of St Ultan's or hold a grudge against us. None of those three were children here or have relatives here.'

I thought this over for a minute. 'Were *any* of the men

up there ever children here?' I asked. 'Do *any* of them have children in your care?'

'I am not,' she began, but her voice was dry and she had to clear her throat and try again. 'I am not acquainted with the poor souls in the hospital,' she said.

'Only,' I said, thinking aloud, 'that would be a powerful reason to try to break out, wouldn't it? If a beloved child was so close by.'

'Our little ones are rarely beloved of their fathers,' she said, with the first note of iron I had heard in her voice.

'But then I'd have thought any man who lived here as an orphaned boy would be the very last chap to harbour animus against the sisters,' I went on. 'It seems a happy place today and from what I've heard about Mother Mary and seen of the sisters who grew up here, it's always been that way.'

'The children are very firmly brought up in the ways of the Church,' said Anne. She hesitated a moment with a pained look but then went on stoutly: 'Mother Mary was very clear on that score, despite all the games and cuddles.'

Again, I had to think for a minute before I replied.

'And so there might be resentment against the Church?'

'But none of them were boys here,' she said again.

'This might be just the closest thing,' I said. 'Tony Gourlay was brought up "in the Church" as you put it and perhaps – if he wanted to hit out at the institution – St Ultan's was the clearest example of everything he abhorred.' She blinked twice very fast. 'Or at least if not the clearest example at least the closest,' I went on. 'And his mind *is* disordered. If he hates the church he was brought up in, perhaps the nearest representative of it – church, monastery or convent – would be the target of his rage.' But even while I spoke, I thought of the young man with his sleeves rolled up and the cap on the back of his head, quietly hoeing the flower-bed.

'Can I ask about something else entirely?' I said, sensing

124

that she was tiring. I took the cup out of her hand and she leaned back and slipped a little downwards in the bed. I did not hold out any great hopes of getting my coat back if she fell asleep against it.

'It's about the doors,' I said. 'You must have been almost the last person to go downstairs to the first-floor landing, I think.'

'I was the last,' said Anne. 'I followed Sister Dorothy.'

'You didn't happen to check the rooms before you went?' I said. 'And leave the doors open?'

'When there was a fire?' said Anne. 'Certainly not. Closing all the doors in a house is the best way to stop the spread of fire and at that moment I didn't know it was the chapel that was burning.' She saw my look of surprise and explained. 'I was a Girl Guide.' There was pride in her voice. 'One of the first. A founding member of our troop in Kilmarnock.'

It did not go along with what I had heard of her fabled romanticism nor what I had seen of her swooning and wanness.

'A Girl Guide?' I said, hoping she might explain.

'Tying knots, camping, building fires from twigs and heather.'

'It sounds very exciting,' I lied. 'The Dunkeld Girl Guides tend more towards sing-songs and relaying messages with coloured flags.'

At my words, her face fell and her eyes grew clouded again.

'Yes,' she said. 'There was all of that too.' Her voice faltered. 'Singing and – yes – the flags and everything.'

'Not as beautiful as your singing here in the convent, I'll wager,' I said, trying to gee her up even though I had no idea what was wrong.

There was no rallying her, however. She turned her face to the wall and said in a small voice that she would be alone. It would have been brutish to insist on talking to her any more and so I left, going slowly over everything I had said and wondering what words had crushed her.

Alec was waiting at the bottom of the stairs, actually sitting on the next to bottom stair, for it was not only the cells which were short of furniture; the whole convent lacked many of the most basic necessities, such as a hall chair to wait in.

'Well?' he said.

I sat down beside him and filled him in on everything Anne had said and everything I had said hoping that he would give me one of his smug looks and reveal the cause of her clamming up that way. On this occasion, however, he was my partner in bafflement.

'She sounds a bit of a ninny,' he said. 'Quaking when you asked about the men, undone by talk of the orphans and then affronted by memories of her days in the Girl Guides.'

'And the worst of it is that I didn't get to ask what she made of the doors.'

'I'm sick of the doors,' said Alec. 'No doubt she would have thought Mother Mary's spirit was nipping in and out of the rooms to turn down the beds like some angelic house-maid.'

'Sister Anne the romantic nun might,' I said, 'but Annie the Girl Guide would probably put it down to draughts like Martha.'

'Clare,' said Alec, making me groan.

'If you have anything to busy yourself with for the rest of the day, darling,' I said, 'I could very usefully sit with all my papers spread around me and try to organise what we've learned into some semblance of a pattern.'

'Of course,' Alec said. 'I've barely started on the men up at the hospital. They're not all as silent as Tony by any means and someone might have something pertinent to tell me.'

He gave me a peck on the cheek and strolled off towards the front door, his motorcar and Hopekist Head, looking very jaunty. The thought crossed my mind that it was more likely Miss Cinty Udney putting that spring in his step than any of the inmates. Certainly I could not imagine Tony Gourlay making him forget the plan of the house he had laboured on before luncheon, but there it was rolled up and tied with a piece of string at the inner edge of the stair he had been sitting on.

The recreation hour was almost at its end and, after it, came the sisters' time for rest and silent study. As they all scattered to their cells I took up residence in the library, currently the front half of the chapel, and spread my many notes and scraps of notes and Alec's master plan over one of the map tables still in there. It had been pushed to the side to make way for the altar and I was almost sure it served no devotional purpose for upon it was a large old-fashioned dictionary and an even larger atlas.

I could not help a glance at the atlas, for the years with Hugh have worn off on me and there is nothing he likes better than a map. It fell open at India, as so many maps from the middle of the last century were wont to do, from families of girls poring over them to trace a brother's journey east to fight the mutiny. I wondered idly if it was left over from the days of the Udneys and looked inside the flyleaf for a library plate. There was nothing there except a pair of initials written in soft pencil at the corner of the page. 'MA', which might have been anyone. Perhaps the atlas had come from another convent with a 'Mother Agnes' although I rather thought that a nun, having renounced possessions, would hardly stamp ownership on one of the convent's books. More likely 'MA' was the original name of one of the sisters who had brought the atlas with her and shared it when she stopped being 'MA' and started her life as 'S something'.

I was wool-gathering and, closing the atlas, I turned to face my proper task. It was cheering to see that I was almost halfway through the interviews, with seven nuns ticked off, one departed and one too old and deaf to be troubled. Nine down, I decided to call it, and eleven to go.

I had, what is more, a running order for them leaving their cells, starting with Mother Mary rousing John and Julian and ending with Anne traipsing downstairs after Dorothy to apply her Girl Guide training to the matter of a fire. I numbered them as far as I could, writing lightly under the names Alec had inked onto the floor plan.

Now, I said to myself – it might even have been out loud; for I do have a habit of muttering when I am alone and concentrating hard – for the doors. 'Open' I wrote under Hilda, Bridget, Martha and Clare. 'Closed' I wrote against Julian's name, although I was not sure I believed it. I hesitated over Sister Margaret, wondering how to record succinctly that hers was open and everyone else's was closed. Then I had a flash of understanding; or at least a glimmer of something closer to understanding than anything that had come before.

If Julian was correct in her insistence then Margaret, coming upstairs, would see Julian's door – closed, John's likewise, the locked guest retreat, and then only Sister Catherine's and Mother Mary's before she reached her own. Martha's cell and Hilda's too were round another corner, blocked from view. Staring at the plan, I could see what might have happened.

It was what Sister Bridget had said about the novices beginning up in the attics and the senior sisters, all except Steven, moving down to the grander rooms later on. The closed doors were all senior sisters – trusted lieutenants – and the rooms that had been searched were the cells of the youngsters, the novices and girls. Now, who searched them? And why? Was the searcher looking for someone, for something hidden, for somewhere to hide? Looking perhaps for somewhere to hide something just *found*? The words 'Find

Ultan; hide Mary' rang in my head again. And although I had no way of really knowing, I was suddenly convinced that the opener of doors was Mother Mary. Officially she had not left the chapel after taking the font out and re-soaking her face cloth, but she might easily have cleared the obstruction from the passage door and gone that way, flitting through the convent and back again without being missed. More than one nun had told me that, in the smoke and confusion, all their sisters looked the same.

As though the Gods themselves were smiling on me, as the nuns gathered for None, the first into the chapel, catching me rolling up my papers, was Sister Mary herself.

'There's no need to rush off, Mrs Gilver,' she said. 'Why not join us? It's troubling me that you've been here almost a whole day and night through and haven't prayed with us yet.'

'I don't know the form,' I said.

'Silent prayer, offered with your whole heart, is dearer to God than any,' she said, which did rather make one question all the chanting.

'In that case, I should be delighted,' I said, trying not to think about the fact that I was lying to a nun in a church. I dropped my voice. 'Do I have time to ask you a question, Sister?'

'About what happened at dinner?' she said, with a wary look over her shoulder at the others who were beginning to file in.

'No,' I said reluctantly. 'I just wanted to make sure. Your cell door wasn't one of the ones found lying open after the fire, was it?'

She gave me a shrewd look. 'It wasn't,' she said. 'But how did you know?'

'Just an educated guess,' I told her. 'Things are beginning to make a little more sense to me, I'm glad to say.'

'And I'm glad to hear,' she said, by which time the chapel

was almost full and the gaze of the sisters upon us made further exchanges impossible.

It was not a Sunday; with that thought I comforted myself. God had told us to work six days and by working glorify His name. That is my excuse for thinking busily through the None prayer about who or what Mother Mary might have been seeking or stashing and about how I was going to find out. My justifications did not extend as far as being able to avoid a start of guilt and sudden flush when I realised that the prayer was over, the nuns were filing out again, and that only I remained in place, kneeling on my hassock with my head bent, while the passing nuns smiled and twinkled and generally thoroughly approved of me.

12

By bedtime the cloistered life was beginning to lie heavily upon me. I could not imagine myself into the place of one of the women who lived inside these walls all day every day. Some of the sisters passed through to the orphanage to teach or lead the children in play or song and three of them popped in and out to the drying green on all but the foulest days. Besides these, someone must be a gardener in other months of the year, for I had seen a tidy vegetable garden as well as the fruit trees – rather hopeful for the Lanark moor, I thought. But Sister Mary, Sister Catherine and the two cooks as well as no doubt many others, never stirred across the doorstep. And none of them as far as I knew went beyond the gate.

So although I had been frightened by the thought of the desperate escapees only yesterday, before supper on the second day I let myself out and tramped up and down the road a while just for the sheer relief of it. And this on a day when I had been down to the village and up to the doctor's house in the morning.

Alec had fared little better and it had taken a long telephone call between the doctor's library and Sister Mary's study for him to shake off the effects of an afternoon spent with the inmates of Hopekist Head.

'I don't know which are worse,' he had said, 'the ones who're doped into submission or the ones who're not doped at all and half a step from exploding at any minute. But at least the exploding ones can tell a bit more about what's going on around them.'

'And did you get any useful information?'

Alec sighed. 'Useful in the sense that it shuts down fruit-less avenues of enquiry. Tony and the two who're still on the lam slept in separate wards, did different jobs – Chick Tiddy sloshes a mop about with more enthusiasm than skill, it seems, and Ernie Arnold was a kitchen assistant. *Is* a kitchen assistant, I should say, rather than give up on the hopes of him being found and brought back again. They didn't spend recreation time together either. Tony reads – he's one of Miss Udney's best customers. She has got up a little circulating library out of her own pocket.'

'Isn't there a library in Lanark?' I said.

'Ah, but a few of the men have the habit of writing in the books, and sometimes quite frank messages. Miss Udney has taken the practical step of lending the books to them with a soft pencil attached to the spine and then just rubbing the words out again. Anyway, Tony reads. Arnold was one of a pretty dedicated card school and Tiddy liked to draw pictures and play draughts when he wasn't out in the grounds with his bat and ball. I couldn't get anyone to say they'd ever seen the three of them together long enough to hatch a plan.'

'It begins to look quite hopeful for Tony then, wouldn't you say?'

'It's a question of timing,' said Alec. 'If the court sits before the two men are found Tony's advocate might have a fair chance of casting the suspicion onto the others. If I were in charge of his defence, I'd say he bumped into them as they fled and they seized his shoes, leaving him no choice but to take theirs, paint and all, rather than limp home in his stock-inged feet.'

'*Did* he come back in someone else's shoes?' I said. 'Wasn't there a name marked on the lining?' I thought of Julian holding up drawers and announcing that they were Dorothy's.

'They don't have enough pairs of shoes to make it worth-while,' Alec said. 'And of course Tony won't say if they're his or not.'

'But at least if he won't talk he can't tell unconvincing lies,' I said, scrabbling around for scraps of comfort.

'Thank you, Dandy,' said Alec rather dryly, seeing through my efforts as always. 'So, if Tiddy and Arnold stay lost, all of that might just work out. But if they turn up and they can show that they took off right away, Tony's in much deeper mud. Might as well call it quicksand.'

'And what about the soot?' I said. 'Or was it ash? Or was it only smoke? I can't remember what you said, beyond the fact that he might have blundered into the aftermath of a heather fire.'

'The police took his coat – singed, I believe – and they've got some expert examining it to see if he can tell what was burning that Tony walked through.'

'Not walked through,' I said. 'Not if the red paint was still there on his shoes, surely.'

After I said this, we both paused a moment, each wondering if I had stumbled on something. The line was rather crackly and given to sudden ghostly snatches of other conversations at the exchange so there was no silence exactly, but it was Alec who interrupted the crackles with speech again.

'Say some more,' he demanded. Alec often does this kind of thing, treating me like some kind of walking, talking note-book where he can turn to refresh his memory of matters he did not trouble to write down for himself or, as now, like a source of rough ideas from which he can drink before, refreshed, he expounds the theories as though they were his own. It is intensely annoying, but it has borne fruit in more than one investigation before now and so I lump it.

'The footprints in the paint are false,' I said. 'They're prints from large shoes worn on small feet. They are not the prints of the shoes Tony Gourlay went back to the hospital in, presumably. So where did he stand in red paint, getting it on him but leaving no prints behind?'

'He was framed!' Alec said.

'And that's not all,' I said. 'The painting was already done at midnight. The nuns saw it then, when there was no more than a whiff of smoke in the chapel. Long before it was properly alight. If he still had paint on his shoes when he got back to the hospital, then he can't have been tramping about in the chapel as it burned. And actually, of course, he wouldn't be! Whoever set the fire would be off like a hare as soon as he put a match to it. The last person who'd have a singed coat would be the fire-starter himself.'

'He was framed,' said Alec again. 'I think one of those two – Tiddy or Arnold and my money's on Arnold, who's the wily one – took him with them precisely because they needed someone to smear with ash and daub with paint who'd trot back to the hospital and not open his mouth. Except he did.'

'Not a human. A monster,' I said. 'Hardly helpful.'

'About as helpful as Mother Mary's last words,' Alec agreed.

I could not speak for him, but it was the first time in the case so far that I had considered the Reverend Mother's words and Tony's side by side, as it were. The notion was troubling.

'You don't think there's a chance they were both speaking about the same thing, do you?' I said. '"A monster, not human, all these years, it was real."'

'Upon my word,' said Alec. 'That makes a bit too much sense for comfort, doesn't it?'

'Not sense,' I said, reluctant to go a single step down the path which beckoned, 'just similarity.'

'I wonder how widely it's been publicised that Tony spoke,' Alec said, turning away from the path himself and back to more solid facts. 'If I were Arnold I'd be keeping a close eye on police reports in the papers, wouldn't you? And if I read that the suspect had told police something about what happened that night, I'd be very worried.'

'Worried enough to bolt from wherever he's holed up, you mean?'

'Or worried enough to try to get to Tony Gourlay and shut him up again,' said Alec. 'That's what really troubles me.'

'I can't see them— Oh!' I said.

'What? What is it, Dan?'

'I've just thought of something that might explain it all. There is a way he could have the paint as well as the ash, you know.' Alec waited in silence for me to go on. 'If he was in the chapel but left by the corridor and went *back* through the office.'

'Why would he do that?'

'To search the convent for someone.' I could feel Alec deflating, even though he made no sound. 'Leaving the cell doors open.'

'I thought you'd decided that was the Mother Superior,' Alec said. 'Because of the rooms she searched and the rooms she didn't.'

'I think "decided" is far too definite a word,' I said. 'I haven't decided anything. It's all just floating around like motes in winter sunlight.'

'That sounds annoying.'

'I'll try to bag another couple of the sisters before bed,' I said, with an attempt at heartiness. 'There's more recreation after supper. Are you coming for supper?'

'Sadly no,' said Alec. 'I'm going to stay here and try Tony again. Different time of day, you know.'

I did not crow over him in the matter of Sister Abigail's cooking, but from his doleful goodbye, I knew he knew.

Since the novices, Sisters Winifred and Joan, were on the rota to wash up the supper things that evening – missing recreation, which seemed hard on them – and since Mary had told me that Sister Joan was still rather unnerved by her experiences on the night of the fire, I decided to tackle them together. They had been mentioned in the same breath by almost everyone and it seemed unlikely that one would have anything to say that the other had not.

They took me through the beginning of the story calmly enough, soothed perhaps by the familiar task. Sister Joan had her sleeves rolled high and was scouring plates in a deep sink of very soapy water and then dousing them in cold water to rinse them before handing them over to Sister Winifred who dried thoroughly and noisily. The sequence of blistering hot and freezing cold water would have shattered Gilverton's china and Winifred would have taken care of any survivors. St Ultan's Indian Tree was sturdy stuff, though, and there were no casualties from the two young women's energetic attentions. Since, moreover, they worked so efficiently together, I did not feel obliged to make any murmurs about a second drying cloth that I might use to help them.

Sister Steven had woken both of them, they confirmed. Both of their doors were open when they, eventually, went back to bed in the small hours. As to the meaning of the open doors, they had not given it any consideration, for Winifred had been limping on blistered feet after stamping the flames out on a rescued tapestry and Sister Joan was, I knew, in a state of even more distress, having actually caught fire at one point in all of the upset and been beaten on the ground with a blanket.

'Only it wasn't a blanket,' said Sister Joan, and a quick guilty look passed between Winifred and her. 'It was Sister Anne who saved me, with her quick thinking,' she said.

'And her Girl Guide training?' I said. 'What was it then?'

'She took off her scapula,' said Winifred. 'It was the only thing to hand. And if she hadn't you might have been burnt, or worse.'

'It still seems wrong,' said Joan. 'I tried to talk to her about it afterwards, but she shushed me and told me not to mention it again.'

'I agree with Sister Anne,' I said, more and more puzzled as to how she got the reputation for being a romantic dreamer. 'If it was the only way to save your life I think God would be pleased to have a scapula used as a fire blanket, or a rosary used as a rope or even a crucifix used as a life-raft. Absolutely.'

The two young women looked horrified. They were both under twenty, though, and life no doubt would toughen them up in time.

'I don't know whether I should confess it,' said Sister Joan. 'I think I've been sacrilegious to allow a sacred garment to be used that way upon me.'

'It wasn't your choice,' I said. 'You were lying on the ground in flames.'

She shuddered. 'But I was very thankful. Pridefully thankful. And I think I should confess. But if I confess and Sister Anne doesn't then Father Mallen will know that she's harbouring a sin and he might refuse to give her the Eucharist and then she'll think I've told tales on her. But if I don't and she does, he might refuse me. So I want to ask Sister Mary but I can't do that without breaking the promise to Sister Anne about keeping it quiet.'

'Did you *make* that promise?' I asked. I could not enter into her worries; strip away the trappings of the church and she sounded exactly like a schoolgirl in the midst of a school-girl spat.

'No, but I made a promise to obey the sisters during my novitiate,' Joan said. 'And be guided by them.'

'How about this?' I asked. '*I'll* ask Sister Anne if she intends to confess. Sister Mary told you to answer all my questions, didn't she? Well then, it's my responsibility that you've spoken of the secret.'

This seemed to calm her and I moved carefully on in my questioning. 'I take it from what you did during the fire that you were near the chapel entranceway? Jolly brave of you both, by the way. Top marks.'

'We were,' said Winifred. 'We didn't go inside because Sister John forbade us, but we stayed close.'

'In that case you can be of enormous help to me,' I said. I whipped the page of my notebook over to a fresh sheet. 'Who did go inside? Mother Mary, Sister John and Sister Steven, I know about already.'

'Sister Jude tried to,' said Joan, 'but Mother Mary shooed her out again. She told her to go and ring the orphans' bell at the far gate. It's closest to the village. She told Sister Jude someone might hear it if she gave it her best.'

'But Sister Mary was already ringing a handbell? Or didn't the Reverend Mother know that?' I said.

The two women shared an uncomfortable look.

'Sister Steven said Our Mother was reaping what she sowed,' said Winifred. 'She said it right there that night at the chapel door, while Mother Mary and she were re-soaking their face cloths in the water bucket. She meant that if Our Mother hadn't been so soft with us, she could have ordered Sister Jude out and not had to make up an errand for her. But do you know what, Mrs Gilver?'

I shook my head, busily scribbling down a note to myself to find out if Sister Jude was a St Ultan's baby.

'It was just as well Sister Jude went and rang that bell in the end,' she said. 'Because even though Sister Dorothy tried the telephone she couldn't get through at the exchange – so if it hadn't been for Sister Jude ringing the orphans' bell no one would have known about our trouble. There's trees between us and the village and no one would have seen the flames. But the MacAllies at Muir Farm heard it and Mr MacAllie came close enough to see and then took off for the village like the clappers on his horse to get help. Of course, there was no help to be had, for the village was set on its heels by the breakout, but Mr MacAllie and his men were wonderful.'

'So,' I said. 'Sister Jude tried to get in and failed.'

'Sister Clare got frogmarched out too,' said Winifred, confirming what I knew.

'I'm more interested in sisters who went inside and *didn't* get hustled straight back out,' I said. 'I want to find out who spoke to the Reverend Mother last, you see.'

'Well, Sister Anne,' Joan said.

'Really?' Now that was intriguing. I knew Anne was hiding something from me but this was the first I had heard of her being in the chapel, privy to Mary's final words.

'She fainted,' said Joan. 'Not today, I mean. She fainted at Mother Mary's funeral Mass and she was muttering as she came round again.'

'Muttering what?'

'You never told me this, Sister,' said Winifred to Joan. She turned to me. 'I dashed off to get a glass of water and Sister Joan stayed with Sister Anne.'

'She had fallen right down on the floor and I sat down and cradled her head in my lap to get it off the cold stone. I was there alone with her.'

'Alone? Wasn't the service full?'

'We had taken her out,' said Joan. 'The other sisters were still inside. And so I was alone with her when she came round and started muttering. She said: "It cannot be true. It cannot be true". And then she opened her eyes and looked at me and said, "Our Mother was out of her mind."'

I was aware of my pulse knocking a little in the base of my throat, not from fear or alarm, but simply from a surge of exhilaration. I was getting near the heart of the thing; I knew it.

'Anything else?' I said. 'Try to think very clearly. Stop washing up for a moment and try to put yourself back there

– close your eyes even – did she say anything else? Imagine that you are back there . . . actually, *where* were you?' I said. I had not questioned the detail of the stone floor, for stone floors and churches go together, but the temporary chapel in the library and recreation room had parquet and the hall outside had polished boards.

'We were in the church in Lanark,' said Winifred. 'St Mary's. It was before we had our temporary chapel consecrated. Our Mother is buried here, of course, but the funeral was in a strange place with strangers all around: townspeople come to gawp. It was dreadful. A lot of them weren't even members of the church – at least they didn't take the Mass – they just sat there and looked at us and whispered. Father Mallen said it didn't matter what brought a new lamb to the fold but it hurt us to try to say goodbye to Our Mother that way.'

'What a pity you couldn't have had it here,' I said. In truth, I have never been much for the more elaborate trappings of death. The funerals of my grandparents in my childhood – all that black crepe and those plumed horses – were diverting enough, but since I have been old enough to take a sober view I much preferred the plain cold ways of Hugh's church and then a block of granite under a yew tree.

'It was Boxing Day,' said Winifred. 'We had hardly begun to tidy up and were nowhere near being ready for the new chapel.'

'I see,' I said, but I was rather bewildered. Surely there was unseemly haste in having the Reverend Mother tidied away into her grave as quickly as Boxing Day. It seemed strange that the police and the Fiscal could be finished with her poor corpse so soon, for the modern way was for pathologists and experts of every stripe to pore over a body when a crime had been committed, coaxing it to render its secrets. It seemed greatly at odds with the scrupulous preservation of the evidence in the little box room and the chapel to have what was, callously speaking, the most significant evidence of all – Mother Mary's remains – under the earth where no one could touch them.

'I can't remember anything else,' said Joan.

'What?' I asked.

She was standing wringing her dishcloth between her hands.

'I closed my eyes and tried to imagine the vestibule of St Mary's but I can't remember anything. Just that she said "It cannot be true" under her breath to herself and then she said "Our Mother was out of her mind" to me.' She turned away and plunged her arms back into the hot water. Winifred had caught up with the drying while Joan was lost in thought and was temporarily without occupation. She threw her cloth over her shoulder and blew upwards to cool her forehead.

'Sister Irene,' she said. 'And Sister Dorothy.'

'What about them?' I asked her.

'They were in the chapel,' said Winifred. I began to gather my belongings together, with a glance at my wristwatch. There were a few minutes left before Compline; perhaps I could question at least one of them.

As I crossed through the hall on my way to the refectory to find them though I saw Sister Mary emerge from her study.

'Ah, Mrs Gilver,' she said. 'That's Mr Osborne on the telephone looking for you. I said I would track you down and here you are!'

'I'm tracking myself, Sister,' I said. 'I'm on the trail of Dorothy and Irene. I don't suppose you would tell Mr Osborne I'll ring him later?'

'Sister Dorothy and Sister Irene are on duty in the orphanage,' Mary said. 'Wednesday is the nurses' night off. Mother Mary always gave them the same night off for they are great friends and they like to go to the pictures in Lanark together. I thought she was too soft, but here I am doing exactly the same.'

'I don't suppose it would be very kind to talk about the fire in front of the children,' I said. 'I shall tackle the sisters in the morning and go to speak to Mr Osborne now.'

At that moment, a bell began to chime and Sister Mary bent her head and turned away.

'While I've got you, Sister,' I said, reaching out and laying a hand on her arm. 'I was surprised to hear when Mother Mary's funeral was held. I mean there must hardly have been time—' I bit my words off. I didn't want to make this woman dwell on the question of what a police surgeon or a procurator's pathologist might do to the remains of a loved one. 'Is it a tradition for nuns to be buried so very quickly?'

'Jews, Mrs Gilver,' said Mary. 'And Mohammadans. Not nuns.' She was twinkling at me but she grew restless at the second pealing of the Compline bell. 'It was Our Mother's own desire,' she said. 'Part of a more general fear of hers, I think. She hated doctors. It was quite a "phobia" with her. And many's the time she begged me to promise her that when she died – no matter what she died of – I would simply put her in the ground and not let any doctor go interfering with her body. She made me promise and not just me.'

I waited for her to explain.

'On Christmas Day, both Sister Steven and Sister John each came to me and revealed that she had extracted the same promise from them. When the police sergeant came back later in the afternoon, the three of us together set upon him with our plea. I did not think for a minute that he would agree. He asked for a moment to make a telephone call in private and then, to our astonishment, he gave us his blessing.'

'And didn't you have to summon a lot of people from around the diocese?' I asked. 'How did they manage to gather so quickly. The trains at Christmas are dreadful.'

Sister Mary smiled. 'Our Mother was of great importance to all of *us*,' she said. 'But she meant little to the hierarchy of the church. We are an independent house, Mrs Gilver.

We're under the archdiocese of Glasgow for pastoral care and guidance, it is true, but we are not part of any large denomination of convents. We are not Dominicans or Carmelites or anything like that. We are the Little Sisters of St Ultan. And everyone who mattered to Our Mother was right here.'

'I had no idea that a convent could be such a—'

'Cottage industry,' said Sister Mary. 'That's what Our Mother called it. That was her mission and her vocation, Mrs Gilver. There were orphans and so, instead of sending them to a workhouse in a big town, she opened an orphanage. It was always the children with her. The rest of it was just a way to get things done.'

I nodded, but as I made my way to the study and to Alec waiting on the other end of the telephone, her words continued to trouble me. If what she said was true, why would Mother Mary have walked into a fire to save the trappings of 'the rest of it'? Why would she leave her beloved orphans twice-motherless for a few books and some tapestries. It was beyond me.

13

It did not take Alec long to relate that Tony Gourlay, even in the evening, could go on and do a clam without make-up and that it had not been worth missing the convent dinner. So there was plenty of time after he rang off to approach Dorothy and Irene, but I did not have the heart for it. As for the rest, half past eight still seemed a ludicrous time to retire but, since the sisters were to rise at five, I could not bring myself to make any of them stay up late with me answering questions. After Compline the gas was turned out and one by one the sisters took up a candle from the table at the bottom of the stairs and ascended. I watched them from my place in the study doorway, the little flames flickering and their shadows dancing and trembling on the walls. With their bowed heads and the way they naturally fell in one behind the other, it had more the look of a procession than a household of tired women going to their rest at the end of the day.

Sister Mary was last. She lit Sister Monica's candle, then her own and turned to me with the taper in her hand.

'I'll linger down here a bit, Sister,' I said. 'I want to walk around and think while it's quiet. I've got a box of matches for when the time comes.'

Sister Mary nodded then snuffed the taper, returning the unused portion of it to the spill jar.

'Our Mother always lit our candles and followed us up,' she said. 'This is the loneliest moment of my day. Some nights I miss her so much I can feel it like a physical ache in my breast.'

'A cold stone,' I said. Her face was invisible behind the candle flame but I saw the shadow of the hem of her veil lift and fall as she nodded. 'That's how it felt to me when my father died,' I said.

'Is your mother still living?' said Sister Mary.

'Ah, no,' I said, 'but my father went first and it was the bigger shock.' It was not exactly a lie but the whole truth was that my mother was an intensely irritating woman who spent the last few years of her life avoiding being burdensome in that very particular way which makes a great deal of work and worry for everyone.

Mary turned away and climbed the stairs. Her soft footsteps crossed the hall above and I heard her door open and then shut, leaving me in perfect silence and near perfect darkness there in the hallway.

There was just enough light to see by once my eyes had grown accustomed to it and I stepped over the hall and into the makeshift chapel, sinking down into one of the back row of chairs. Why would anyone – even a madman – set fire to a church on Christmas Eve, I asked myself. Then I wondered if that was in fact the right question. Would a madman know what night it was? Was the breakout planned for that night especially or was a chance simply taken when it presented itself. If so, then Christmas Eve was irrelevant to the solving of the problem.

Why then, would someone start a fire and wreak the sort of vicious destruction wrought in the office? There were three quite distinct possibilities as far as I could see.

Either he wanted to destroy for destruction's sake, because of a mania, or he wanted to steal something and cause such havoc that his true purpose was disguised. Had that been the case, however, we would have heard what was stolen. The third possibility was, to me, the most likely. He wanted to send a message to one of the nuns or perhaps to all of them; a threat, or a warning, or a punishment, or simply a shock.

If the message was for just one of the nuns, then it followed that there was a connection of some kind between the sender of it and its recipient. A family connection? That was a question for Alec and Dr Glass; for the patients' records must contain everything there was to know of their backgrounds, while the nuns had all left their families and the rest of their lives behind them. I supposed it was conceivable that there might be a romantic connection; for the men were men whether they were hale and hearty or ill and troubled and the women were women, nuns or no. But would they ever have had a chance to meet? I knew that some nuns were nurses, but *these* nuns were teachers and someone had told me that the Catholics among the inmates did not even come to services here.

Besides, I told myself, getting to my feet and turning to leave, it was more likely that the message was sent to all of the sisters, or indeed all nuns everywhere, or the whole of the Church from the Pope on down.

I should have been too embarrassed to go back to the office and pore over the words written there in the daytime with Alec beside me or Sister Mary hovering. While I was alone, though, I thought I would take a good long cold look and see if I had missed something.

I stopped at the bottom of the stairs and used one of my matches to light a candle. Then I went softly through Sister Mary's study, averting my eyes from the crucifix, for the leaping candle flame rendered it quite an alarming thing. I drew the bolt back, applied my key, slipped through into the little anteroom where the chapel corridor ended, and then opened the door to the office and entered, holding my breath.

It is an old-fashioned notion these days, but the words written all around the walls there made me feel – there is no other word for it – besmirched. Nanny Palmer had taught me when I was a girl of fourteen the importance of preventing oneself from becoming besmirched but she was talking about keeping out of empty carriages on a railway train and walking quickly away from any young man at a dance who spoke roughly. If she could see me now perusing these epithets and even writing them down in my notebook, even with the consonants only and dashes for the vowels, she would have burst out in horror, using the strongest language in her repertoire, which was 'Mercy!'

It was not one of the nuns in particular, I decided, standing there, for many of the words were in their plural form, accusing several individuals of the characteristics they described. That said, it was definitely the nuns who were the target and not the whole of the church hierarchy for all of the words were best understood as pertaining to women alone.

Perhaps, I considered, lifting my candle high and looking around to see if I had missed any, not just to women alone, but to the whole of womankind. Perhaps the sisters had been chosen as emblematic of femininity overall or at least at its worst: independent, uninterested in men, unnatural even. Were that the case then the attack might be nothing to do with religion after all and the choice of Christmas Eve might well have been insignificant.

But then there was the chapel. There was no way to deny that *that* part of the night's adventures was intended to desecrate what was holy. One might break into a church to steal silver and paintings and even coins from the collection plate – not that St Ultan's took up a collection, I guessed, for the children's pocket money and the nuns' if they had such a thing would come from the same coffers the collection went back into. Besides, if one had just broken out of an asylum and needed money to make an escape, one would hardly draw attention to oneself by starting a fire, much less would one burn the very candlesticks and chalices one hoped to pinch and fence and convert into bus tickets and suits of new clothes.

No, I decided, the only reason to put a torch to a church was to send the self-same message of hatred and contempt as these words sent to the sisters who saw them. With no reluctance at all, I turned to leave the office.

Then I stopped, quivering and as suddenly alert as a doe in a clearing. I had heard a sound. It was not a door, nor a footfall, nor a voice. It was a sound impossible to describe, except that it was heavy and it was close.

As soon as I had thought that I dismissed it. Noise is notoriously hard to pin down at night and what seemed close to me might be anywhere in that unfamiliar house. I knew that it was not upstairs for I felt no desire to lift my head as part of my avid listening. I looked around and wondered where, if not upstairs, someone might be moving.

My first thought was that Sister Dorothy or Sister Irene might have come through to the kitchen from the orphans' side. Perhaps one of the children was ill and needed some milk to be warmed. I took off at once, back through the study and into the kitchen passageway to see.

All was darkness in there, not so much as the faintest glow from the range, which was banked for the night. What is more, the door to the orphans' dining room was locked and bolted. I supposed the nurses must have a gas ring somewhere on their own side for warming milk and making their bedtime cocoa and early tea. I wondered what time they would return from their trip to the pictures and how the sisters who were babysitting would get back to their own part of the house. Was that what I had heard? I did not think so but I had the plan of the cells and I could easily go and knock on Dorothy or Irene's door to see if they were back and to ask if they had just been moving.

I stopped as I was re-crossing the kitchen. There it was again. The most *peculiar* sound. It made me think of sailing ships and storms, although I was hard pressed to know why. Something about that sound of heavy movement, I supposed, like the creaks of rigging or a high wind making cattle stalls shake in an open-sided byre. It did not seem to be any sort of noise which belonged inside a solid stone house.

Then it came to me and I let my held breath go with a scornful little laugh at my own foolishness. Most of this place was a solid stone house, but just off to the side of the kitchen and very close to the little box room was the chapel, with twisted rafters and collapsing walls. If the wind had got up then of course some part of that structure might have given way.

Once again, as I made my way along the kitchen passage out into to the hall and finally began to climb the stairs to bed, I thought how very strange it was that the mess was left there. The orphans, it was true, had their own playground and were well looked-after but boys will be rascals and I remembered the newsreel films of gangs of them playing amongst the East End bombsites. If I were Sister Mary I should want those swinging timbers and heaps of rubble gone for the sake of the children's safety as well as to put the memories away.

I had forgotten how a candle will gutter if one walks too quickly and I had to pause at the top of the stairs while mine recovered. While I was standing there, I half-thought I saw movement out of the corner of my eye. I turned and peered along the landing but if the shadows were hiding a black-clad figure they were doing it well. I shrugged the notion off and went to ready myself for the night.

There was no temptation to linger in the comfortless bathroom and so it was less than five minutes later that, hastily washed and with a nightcap just as hastily pulled over my unbrushed hair, I got carefully into my little wooden bed and composed myself for whatever sleep its narrowness and firmness might offer me.

Perhaps it was the keen thin air of the moorland – or the clean and nun-like living – I had had far fewer cigarettes than usual and not a sip of wine but I dozed off almost instantly, roused myself just enough to punch my pillow and curl up after what felt like twenty minutes, and then dropped into a deep and dreamless sleep.

I was roused by what sounded at first like a siren, a peal of sound steadily increasing in both pitch and volume. Only the intermittent pauses for breath revealed it to be a voice, yelling with alarm as its owner approached. I shot out of bed and leapt across the floor to wrench my door open. Out on the landing in the darkness the nuns – unrecognisable as such in their white nightgowns and white sleeping caps; they looked like ghosts – were emerging and clamouring.

'Is it a fire? Is it another fire?'

'Get Sister Catherine out.'

'Hold that candle steady and light it from mine.'

'Go down and turn the gas up.'

'No! Not the gas! Not in a fire.'

And finally above all the voices, louder than anyone, Sister John.

'Would everyone please be quiet?' She paused. 'And you! You lot from upstairs, stop pouring down. You'll only make more muddle.' The novices and young nuns from the second storey stopped in their tracks, and Sister Joan edged back and sat on the bottom step.

'Now, who yelled?' said Sister John. 'Don't do it again and tell us the problem.'

'It was me, Sister,' said Monica.

'Is anything on fire?'

'No, Sister.'

The nuns let out a collective rushing sigh and several of them turned back to their cells to collect candles.

'Then what – pray tell – is wrong to make you screech like a banshee in the middle of the night?'

'It's not the middle of the night, Sister. It's quarter to five. I got up to ring the Angelus bell.'

'*And?*' said Sister John, sounding displeased to be contra-dicted.

'Tell us what happened, Sister Monica,' said Mary, chiming in for the first time and speaking in a gentle voice, one more likely to produce results than Sister John's, which produced, as far as I could see, quivering lips and the threat of tears.

'There's been an intruder,' Monica said.

'There have been signs of this famous "intruder" more mornings than not,' said Sister Steven, sourly even for her. 'Why the extra commotion today?'

'No, but there really has been,' said Monica. 'There's a smashed window downstairs where he got in.'

This set all of the sisters a-twitter again. One could tell that they were trembling by the shaking of their shadows in the candlelight.

'What window?' I said. 'Show me. And I must insist that everyone else remains upstairs out of the way until I've looked for footprints and other evidence.'

I thought I was being wonderfully practical, straight to the heart of the matter, all business and no nonsense. I had, however, missed something that Sister John had seen.

'Any signs of him getting out again, Sister?' she said. 'Or might he still be in here?'

14

We all froze, listening and – I am sure – half-expecting to hear pounding masculine footsteps, to see Chick Tiddy and Ernie Arnold, filthy and crazed from weeks out on the moor, come blazing up the stairs ready to murder us.

All we heard was the sound of Sister Catherine's cell door opening and then her voice, loud as the voices of the very deaf often are, asking: 'is it not morning? Has the Angelus bell been ru— What are you all doing standing around here?'

She was dressed for the day and the sight of her reminded the others of the call of duty. They dispersed, leaving Sister Mary, Sister Monica and me to go downstairs and inspect the damage.

It was the French window into the library. Glass lay shattered halfway across the altar from where the pane had been broken and one of the pair of doors was ajar.

'I know it would have been better not to leave the key in the lock,' said Sister Mary, 'but after the fire we wanted every possible means of quick escape, should the same thing happen again. And with the curtains closed across the inside, it was very hard to see it.'

'Unless by a lamp,' I said, stepping carefully around the shards of glass for a closer look. 'Or a storm lantern,' I added. 'Or even a tungsten torch.'

What she had said about the curtains interested me. They were both pushed back from the window now and it seemed odd that an intruder would take the time to do so. If he had smashed the glass when the curtains were drawn shut, surely he would just have shouldered through them into the room and left them that way.

'Could you turn the gas up as far as it goes, please, Sister?' I said to Monica. When she had and it was shining brightly down from the centre of the ceiling, I took hold of the curtain on the same side as the broken panes and carefully pulled it wide, listening for pieces of glass dropping to the floor. Then I bent close to it and studied it minutely. The library curtains were of the same cheap slub repp as those in Sister Mary's study, harsh and rough-textured, what any housemaid would correctly identify as dust-traps the first time she laid eyes on them. Yet there was not a single chip or speck of glass visible anywhere in their threads. I even took Sister Monica's candle – still lit in her hand although we were now in bright gaslight – and played it back and forth. Nothing.

'I suppose the curtains *were* drawn last night as usual, were they?' I said.

Sister Monica looked blank, but Sister Mary nodded firmly.

'They were,' she said. 'I looked at them during Compline. I can't help looking over to the old chapel – to where she died – when we are saying our prayers for her soul. Terce to None when it's light outside I can catch just a glimpse but the morning and evening Angelus and Compline I'm looking at the curtains. I would have noticed if it was different.'

Monica looked rather startled at her superior's admission of a wandering mind during prayers and perhaps it was Mary's sudden show of frail humanity that emboldened the younger nun to ask a question.

'What is it, Sister?' she said. 'What's in our chapel – this one just like the last one – that someone wants so badly?'

Mary gave Monica a long speculative look and then turned to me.

'Do you agree with Sister Monica, Mrs Gilver,' she said. 'Is he searching for something?'

'Do you have any idea what that something would be?' I asked, and her look, as she strove for an answer and then reluctantly admitted defeat, convinced me that she did not. Only a consummate actress could have hidden her secret knowledge and performed such a display all at the same time.

'Besides,' I said, 'I don't think it's necessarily significant that he broke the chapel window. This is the only French window in the house, is it not? And it's directly under Mother Mary's empty room with Sister Catherine's room next closest. If I wanted to break a window without waking anyone, I would choose this one too.'

'But you know the lay-out of the convent,' said Sister Mary. 'You don't mean to tell me that the intruder knows where we sleep? Where Sister Catherine sleeps?'

I would have liked to tell her I did not believe there was an intruder at all, that I was sure the prowler in the night began and ended inside the convent walls and that it had been her own bold speech the previous day at luncheon that had convinced this prowler a clear sign of entry from without would be a good idea. Had Sister Monica not been standing there, all ears and eyes out on stops as well, I would have done so.

'It's hard to imagine how that could be,' I said. 'Don't mind me, Sister Mary. There's always a lot of thinking aloud on a case, but I should have the consideration not to do my musing to you and the other sisters.' I gave her a brisk smile, which did not a bit of good.

'Sister,' said Monica. 'Can I ring the Angelus now? It's very late.'

'That's a good idea,' I said. 'You go ahead and I'll have a first look round and see that nothing's been disturbed. Then later, you can perhaps make a more thorough search and see if there's anything missing.'

Sister Mary's eyes flared and she swept towards the door to the hallway. I followed her.

All of the sisters, dressed and veiled now, were huddled on the stairs like nothing so much as a litter of black-and-white kittens, watching and listening and mindful of the order not to come down, six steps between them and disobedience.

'Sister, the Angelus!' said Sister Julian.

'Sister Winifred,' said Mary. 'Fetch a dustpan and brush, please and start sweeping up. Sister John, lead the prayers, please. I'm going to telephone to the village for Hendry to come and mend the broken window. Sister Steven? Did you pass a peaceful night?'

I swung to regard Sister Steven, unable to guess at Mary's meaning.

Steven nodded, her narrow eyes pinched up so tightly with suspicion that they almost disappeared amongst her deep wrinkles. Then the Angelus bell began and her face relaxed into an instant and beatific calm.

Sister Mary swept into the study with me at her heels.

'Sister, it's not yet six o'clock,' I said. 'If Hendry is the joiner I doubt he's up yet, never mind at work.' She stopped dead in the middle of the floor, causing me to stagger a little to save from walking into her back. It was an extreme reaction to my gentle suggestion, I thought. When I drew beside her and looked into her face, though, I saw that my words had not caused her sudden halt. She was staring into the corner and pointing with a trembling hand.

'Oh no,' she said. 'Not again. He went into the office, Mrs Gilver. Or through to the chapel. What more can there be to be desecrated there?'

'How do you know?' I asked her, peering for footprints as well as readying myself in case he was still in there and came rushing out again.

'The bolt is open,' said Sister Mary. 'I've been keeping

that door bolted since the night of the fire and it's drawn back now.'

'Ah,' I said. 'Well, the fact of the matter is, that was me. I went through to the office last night and I didn't shoot the bolt when I came back.'

I thought she would be angry, but there was nothing in her sudden relaxation except sheer relief. 'Oh!' she said, sinking down into her chair at the desk. 'I don't know how much more I can withstand. Missing the Angelus!' And then as the bell sounded again, just audible from the library, which shared a wall with this room, she fished at her side for her rosary and after the sound died away, began to pray.

While the sisters converged on the chapel, I headed to the kitchen and had helped myself to a scratch breakfast of bread and butter with a glass of milk, which I was enjoying while leaning against the warm stove, when the door from the orphans' side opened and Nurse Matt appeared, in a tartan dressing gown firmly belted over striped pyjamas, and with her hair in a plait down her back.

'Oh! Mrs Gilver,' she said. 'You startled me. I'm just dropping off the extra orders. Flora has a sore throat and is going to want some of Sister Abigail's cinnamon jelly and I've got three of them with bad tummies so it's just arrowroot for them and a pint less porridge. There's always something at this time of year, isn't there?'

I made a non-committal murmur; I was thankful to say that Nanny had always taken care of the throats and tummies of my sons when they were small, my entire contribution being to visit them in the night nursery rather than having them brought to me in the drawing room if they were particularly unwholesome.

'I did think I was running a wee bit late,' said Nurse Matt, with a glance at the kitchen clock and then a quick frown. 'Are they still at their prayers?'

'We've had a disturbance,' I said. 'Some broken glass to be swept up before the Angelus could begin.'

'More trouble?' she said. 'I don't think St Ultan's will weather this, Mrs Gilver, really I don't.'

'You think the convent will close?'

'I think the orphanage will close and the sisters will be left with nothing to do. They'll scatter to other orders, schools and hospitals and orphanages elsewhere.'

'Do you really believe so?' I said. It made sense, in a way; for the thought of prowlers and broken windows so close to all those children did give one a sinking feeling.

'There's them in the village as nothing would make them happier than to see the back of us all,' said Nurse Matt.

'You too?' I asked. 'I knew there had been rumblings about the men up at Hopekist Head and one can understand a little of that. I shouldn't like to be wondering at night where the runaways are and when the next breakout might be. But what's the worry about St Ultan's?'

'Well,' said Nurse Matt, somewhat carefully, 'it was different in the old days, when orphans were more numerous.' She paused and gave me an expectant look, clearly hoping that she need not say any more. I would have gratified her with a knowing nod, if only I had had the slightest notion what she was talking about. As things stood, however, I returned an expectant look of my own. 'We call them "orphans" out of kindness,' she said. 'But true orphans – poor mites whose parents have died – are usually taken in by aunts and uncles, aren't they?'

'Ah,' I said.

'Our orphans could be called by a much plainer name had we a mind to,' she said.

'I'm sorry I was dim, Nurse Matt,' I said. 'As a matter of fact, I remember thinking exactly the same thing when I read *Oliver Twist* as a child. I asked my nanny why he kept on looking for his mother when he was an *orphan* and why no one ever explained to him what an orphan was. It struck me as very cruel to let him keep hoping. And then at the end I thought Mr Dickens hadn't quite played a straight bat with the readers.'

'What did your nanny say to that?' said Nurse Matt.

'She boxed my ears,' I replied. 'Then my brother explained and she boxed his. But returning to your concern—'

'Not *my* concern,' said Nurse Matt. 'I loved Mother Mary like everyone else who ever met her and I'd never have left my post while she was at the helm, but for myself I'd rather be in Lanark or Glasgow where a night at the pictures didn't end with ten miles on a bus and then a long dark walk in the middle of nowhere. But I know what you mean and, as I was saying, it was different in the old days. Our orphans really were *our* orphans then. From the Stop or the Junction or somewhere in the valley, but these days . . . Well, there's better information, for one thing. Mrs Stopes – I hope I haven't shocked you.' I shook my head. 'And the girls are bolder, better able to tell a young man to do his duty and give the child a name. So we don't have the supply to keep St Ultan's well stocked – if you'll pardon me using such a coarse turn of phrase. And so in they come from Lanark and Glasgow and the Urr valley towns. The priest in Sanquhar has beaten a path to us with all the little mites of *that* place and it's a den of iniquity.'

I said nothing, thinking of what I had seen of Sanquhar: a long grey mining town on the road to Dumfries from Ayr with plenty of public houses, like any Scottish town where the men all work and get a packet of pay on a Friday, but I could not imagine why it would attract such censure from Nurse Matt. 'Cannibals over the next hill' Alec calls it when he hears one of the lower classes draw such a firm line between their saintly selves and their exact counterparts from elsewhere.

'Why aren't the Lanark and Glasgow girls enjoying the

same benefits, though?' I asked. 'Even the ones in Sanquhar?' It was not a searching question; I was more concerned to stop her thinking she had set me on my heels with her frank talk. To my surprise, it appeared that somehow I had set her on hers. She rubbed her nose with her finger, which was an unsanitary habit in a nurse, I thought.

'They've always been more rackety than the village girls,' she said. 'And there are more of them.'

Those were two inarguable points, but she was contradicting her potted history of the immediate neighbourhood. She had just finished saying there were plenty of local maidens with the right temperament to keep a whole orphanage afloat until Mrs Stopes came along and educated them.

'Anyway, I'd better away and get myself dressed,' she concluded, giving me a nod I took as advice to do the same, although it was not yet seven and I could not summon shamefacedness over being in my nightclothes at that hour. Still, perhaps it was a reluctance to meet the sisters thus attired that prompted me to make a detour into Sister Mary's study and the chapel corridor when I heard them advancing.

They, after all, were tightly coiffed and pinned and decently veiled, with their black shoes polished and laced, while I was a ragbag of satin and velvet – Grant's recent purchases in the nightwear line had been celebrations of the current vogue for bohemianism – and I was, besides, regretting the slapdash way I had shoved my hair into my nightcap. I could feel it, coiling up into lumpy curls, and knew I must at that moment look like a mobbed milkmaid and would, once dressed, look like a hoyden for the rest of the day; and the next unless I could work miracles with some water and my hairbrush, which did not seem likely.

I would have cut a striking figure had anyone been there to see me, emerging into the grey dawn light among the ruins of the chapel, with my peignoir rippling in the breeze.

At least my slippers were sturdy. Bunty, the puppy, had made short work of two more elegant pairs before I gave in and bought these, in which I could have scaled mountains without either chilblains or blisters threatening. Now even if she seized them I could get them back before damage was done and I thanked her inwardly as I crunched over the ashy remains of slate and plaster. There was a piece of twisted lead hanging from a collapsed roof beam towards the front of what had been the aisle and I fancied it for the part of 'creaker in the night'. When I reached it and gave it a shove though, I discovered it was firmly attached and immovable despite its rickety appearance. I put my hands on my hips and looked around. The pews on either side of me were standing pretty square still, although I gave a few a shake just to check, and there was nothing else – not the frames of the shattered windows, nor the empty hole where the sacristy door had burned away, nor the stone arches, nor the solid framework of roof beams, like a great skeletal ribcage above me – that looked capable of producing that muffled grating I had heard the evening before.

I was just on the point of deciding it must have been the chimney flue cooling or one of the sisters opening her window and that there was nothing more than my own heightened senses making me find it troubling, when I heard a sound that presented no mystery at all. It was a repressed giggle finally bursting out, being rapidly smothered by the giggler, then shushed by the giggler's more self-controlled friends.

I swung around just in time to see a row of little heads duck down below the top of the high wall that separated the chapel escarpments from the orphans' playground.

'Come out again,' I said, tramping towards them, passing right across the ruined wall of the chapel proper until I was standing on the scorched grass of the graveyard, where the first few shoots were just beginning to show again amongst the black. 'Come on. I shan't bite you.'

One by one they popped up again, two little black heads, two little tow heads and one head as red as a robin's breast and glowing as the first rays of sunshine began to strike the top of the wall.

'Good morning,' I said and there was a ripple of answering greetings; they had learned good manners if not perfect behaviour. 'I hope you weren't planning on jumping over to this side.'

'Naw,' one of them piped up. 'We're no' allowed.'

'What *are* you doing?' I asked them. I had made no sound that might have attracted them, I was sure.

Of course five little boys between the ages of seven and ten, as I judged these to be, did not need a purpose to underpin their decision to scale a wall, beyond that of finding out who could scale it fastest, run along the top of it furthest or, jumping from it again, land on the ground with the loudest thump.

'We're saying a wee prayer,' said the red-headed child. He had freckles to go with his flaming curls and a missing front-tooth to add charm to his grin. All in all, he had the innocent look of an utter monkey. If he was the appointed spokesman of the little band he was the last one to listen to.

'A prayer?' I said, fixing my gaze on the smaller of the two fair-haired boys.

'For Grandmother Mary,' he said nodding at a point some-where to my left. I glanced that way and saw the telltale marks of a recent grave, the mound of unsettled earth and imperfect joins between replaced turfs.

'*Grand*mother Mary?' I said.

'She was my mammy's Mother Mary,' said the larger black-haired boy. 'So she's my granny, eh no?'

'Your mother was an orphan here?' I said, thinking that the moral teachings of the sisters must have been somewhat lacking if one of St Ultan's alumni had provided it with new business.

'Aye,' said the child. 'And then she was a nurse in the war and then she was a nurse up the hill and then she died.'

'I'm very sorry to hear that,' I said. 'And what about your daddy?' If he had known his mother and had fallen to St Ultan's only after her death then the chances were that she was married.

'Up the hill,' said the child.

'Your daddy's in the hospital?' I said. 'At Hopekist Head?' I heard it with a callous surge of delight, for if one of the men who had broken out had a son here then at last – at last! – there was a whiff of a reason for the animosity and the attack. If one followed the twisted logic of a deranged man, that is to say.

'How about the rest of you?' I asked, more from not wanting them to be left out than from any great hopes of discovering further connections.

'Naw, we're all Bells,' said the other black-haired boy. 'Jesus' wee lambs.' I gave him a sharp look suspecting impertinence but he returned a frank gaze neither suspiciously innocent nor visibly smirking. Behind them a handbell began to ring.

'Breakfast,' said the red-head and dropped from view.

'I shall probably see you in the dining room,' I said to the others. 'I need to speak to your nurses.'

Two more disappeared.

'Missus?' said one of those remaining. 'Can I ask you something? I'm not being cheeky.'

I nodded, even though in my experience 'I'm not being cheeky' was a precursor of monstrous cheek, every time.

'Are you a turn?' he said. I frowned. 'A musical turn?' I blinked.

'Why on earth—?' I said.

'Is that your costume?' he said.

I had quite forgotten my outlandish peignoir and satin sleeping cap. I looked down at myself and then back up at the top of the wall but the last two boys were gone. I could hear them giggling and the sound of their boots as they ran away. Then I pulled my wrap around me and made for my bedroom to ready myself for the day.

15

Dorothy and Irene, I learned, had not just been drafted in to babysit after coming to the top of the pile in some kind of rota; it was their regular daily work to assist the nurses in the care of the orphans. When I got to the orphans' side, rather more soberly dressed than I had been, it was to see through the dining-room window Sister Dorothy leading a crocodile of hand-in-hand tots over the playground to the kindergarten, which ran along the other side, while Sister Irene disappeared through a door at the far end with a fat toddler under each arm.

'Does Sister Dorothy teach the children?' I asked Nurse Pirrie, Nurse Matt's deputy. I did not fancy disrupting a lesson, but much less did I fancy going to watch and possibly help Irene remove the remnants of breakfast from those two wriggling little bundles.

'No, she just takes them over and goes to fetch them at playtime,' said Nurse Pirrie, who was scalding feeding bottles. Two large prams with a pair of infants in each were parked outside the open kitchen door. All four babies were soundly asleep; unsurprising, given the size of the bottles Nurse Pirrie was cleaning. I had seen shepherds offer smaller dinners of warm milk to muscular eight-week-old lambs. 'Sister Steven is the infant mistress,' she went on. 'Sister John teaches mathematics, geography and history to the big ones and she's training up Sister Winifred. And Sister Mary teaches them English literature, French and singing, with Sister Joan's help.'

They were all, I considered, from those dozing milk-fat little grubs wrapped tightly in blankets in the watery sunshine, up to the biggest of the boys I had seen on top of the wall, doing rather well for themselves. The two classes could hardly have fifteen apiece and I had not missed the way Sister Dorothy had swung the hands of the two children at the head of the procession, nor how Sister Irene's armfuls had squealed with pleasure as she bounced them. There were many children in this land whose parents paid a pretty price for boarding schools but who did not receive half the attentions of a St Ultan's child. I stopped myself just in time before letting into my head the thought that they were lucky.

'I met some of the older boys when they came to the chapel wall to say a prayer for Mother Mary,' I said, leading into the topic.

Nurse Pirrie giggled. 'Aye, they said,' she told me and I shared a self-deprecating laugh with her.

'Including one whose mother was one of your success stories,' I said. 'But whose father is less fortunate, I believe.'

Nurse Pirrie's smile faded and she heaved a hefty sigh.

'Sandy Molloy,' she said. 'That's a sad tale.' She looked out through the doorway at the sleeping babies. She was in her outdoor shoes and hat and a warm coat was waiting over the back of a nearby chair; clearly her plan was to take one of the prams and give the babies their airing. She turned away from them, however, and folding her arms, launched into what was clearly a most enjoyable tragedy.

'Sandy's mother, Rose, was Nurse Matt's wee shadow when she was a child here,' she said. 'Made herself a nurse's hat from a starched hankie and went around the infant ward taking temperatures with a toffee apple stick. So we got her some training. She went off to the war and was a credit to us. It was in France she met George.'

'And then he was sent to Hopekist Head?' I said. 'That's a remarkable coincidence, isn't it?'

'No, that wasn't the way,' said Nurse Pirrie. 'He followed Rose back here after the Armistice and married her. She worked at the hospital even after that, even after Sandy was born, for George wasn't able to work at all, the poor soul. He had a very bad war, Mrs Gilver. A very bad war indeed. It left him so troubled. But it wasn't until after Rose died that he got so he had to be in there.'

'Oh dear,' I said. 'That *is* a sorry tale. What did she die of?'

Nurse Pirrie hesitated a little before answering. And when she did it was in a whisper.

'He was sorely troubled. He didn't know what he was doing.'

'Dear God!' I said. 'Does Sandy know?'

'He does not,' said Nurse Pirrie. 'And as long as we have him here he need not. That's one thing we can do for him, Mrs Gilver, wouldn't you say?'

'Of course, of course,' I assured her, although in truth I had no idea if it were preferable to grow up knowing such a thing of one's father or if it would be worse to hold one view of one's parents and then have a dreadful truth sprung on one in adult life. 'Has he no other relations, young Sandy?'

Nurse Pirrie drew herself up and the next words were sternly spoken indeed.

'He has a grandmother and a grandfather in Kilmarnock,' she said. 'But they didn't approve of their son marrying a St Ultan's girl. And he has an aunt and uncle right here in Carstairs Stop, but they won't give house room to the son of a feeble-minded murderer. So the boy's left with no one.'

'Oh dear,' I said again, for there really did seem no more to say about any of it.

Thankfully at that moment Dorothy returned, her charges successfully handed over to Sister Steven for the morning. She stopped short and glanced at the clock when she saw Nurse Pirrie.

'All my fault, Sister,' I said. 'I've been keeping Nurse Pirrie from her duties. It was actually you and Sister ~~Dorothy~~ Irene I came to talk to, though. Do you have a moment?'

'I have all the time you need, Mrs Gilver,' said Dorothy. 'Sister Mary told us to cooperate fully and we do as we're told.' Her words were perfectly polite but they were spoken without a trace of good humour and without a wisp of a smile.

'Why don't you take my pram, Mrs Gilver?' said Nurse Pirrie. 'I'm not shirking. But you can talk to Sister Dorothy that way.'

So it was that my interview with Dorothy was conducted while we each pushed a behemoth of a perambulator down the main drive, twice round the bare orchard, and back again. The babies slept throughout the entire operation, missing quite a pleasant winter's morning and a remarkably friendly robin, which had not heard of the decision by birdlife in general not to frequent this moor and alighted on the side of one of the prams to be borne along for a few yards, peering at the bright, knitted blankets with each one of its little eyes before it concluded that the patches of colour were not berries and flew off again.

'Who's that?' I said, squinting at a sister who was standing on a ladder propped against an apple tree, tussling with a pruning saw.

'Sister Anne is the gardener,' Dorothy said.

'Really?' I could not help replying. 'Sister Anne? She is a woman of contradictions.'

'What?' said Dorothy. 'What have you heard? Where have you been hearing gossip?'

'I think you must misunderstand me, Sister,' I said, taken considerably aback. 'I only meant that she is rather delicate and yet was a Girl Guide in her early days and a gardener now. What did *you* mean?'

'Nothing at all,' said Dorothy. The chill in her voice sent

a clear message that if I poked at her obvious lie, I would get precisely nowhere. Anyway, she swept on without giving me a chance. 'Now, what is it you want from me?'

'I heard that you and Sister Irene were in the chapel with Mother Mary,' I said.

'A lot of us were,' said Dorothy.

'Of course, but I wondered if perhaps she spoke to you. Only we're having a great deal of trouble working out what exactly she meant to say with her final words.'

'How could it be any concern of yours?' said Dorothy. I thought for a minute whether this could truly be said to come under the banner of 'full cooperation' and then decided that it was nicely judged. It fell short but so subtly I should feel like a sneak if I complained to Mary.

'Well,' I said, 'we're still searching for a motive for the crimes committed against the convent that dreadful night. And the puzzling words Mother Mary spoke – those we have heard so far – strike me as possible clues. If you could add something, perhaps all will become clear.'

'She told me to put a wet cloth over my face,' Dorothy said. 'At least she took mine and gave me her dried-out one, telling me to go and wet it.'

'She did send you out of the chapel then?' I said. 'Sister Joan rather thought that you and Irene were two who were allowed to stay.'

'*Sister* Irene,' said Dorothy, sharply. 'Mother Mary didn't send me out. I dipped the face cloth in the font like she told me.'

'Didn't the Reverend Mother carry the font out,' I said.

'Yes she did and if she'd left it who knows what might have turned out differently that night,' Dorothy said, darkly.

'But there was a water bucket, wasn't there?' I said. 'Mother Mary did not suffocate for want of a wetted cloth.' I could not – pushing the perambulator – fish in my bag for my notebook and search its pages, but I was sure of this. 'The

Reverend Mother came out to the doorway to soak the cloth she had on her face, didn't she? And she spoke to Sister Steven while she was there.'

'Once she did,' said Dorothy. 'To get Sister Jude to follow her out, but when she went back in that time, that was that.'

'And do you have any idea why she was in there?' I said.

'Sister Jude?' she asked, and I was almost sure that she said it only to eke out a little time for thought before she had to answer.

'Mother Mary,' I told her, hoping not to sound acerbic.

'She was trying to put out the fire,' said Dorothy. 'Of course,' she added, not worrying at all about how *she* might sound.

In one sense her scornfulness was warranted, for it should have been – would have been in nine cases out of ten – a silly question. If a building is on fire what does anyone want, what is anyone's goal, except to stop the burning. On the other hand, one puts out a fire by pouring water on it, not by going inside the burning building and fussing around.

'There wasn't any plumbing inside the chapel, was there?' I said. 'A washbasin in the sacristy, or a . . . or anything?'

Dorothy saw the purpose of the question and cleared her throat.

'Well, that is to say, not exactly to put the fire out, no. But to stop it from destroying everything. To save something at least.'

'What?' I demanded quite baldly, although not as baldly as she had been speaking to me.

'The Bible and prayer book and all the parish records from when St Ultan's had a priest.'

'When was that?' I said. 'Really? There was a parish here once?' I looked around myself at the emptiness that stretched as far as the eye could see in every direction. We were on a slight rise just then with a good view of it. There was the

169

moor, a ribbon of roadway across it and the great sweep of grey sky.

'When the Udneys were at Hopekist Head,' she said. 'Before the Great War. The only church at the Stop is the Church of Scotland, of course, and the same at the Junction, Carstairs village itself, and Quothquan. But when the mine was open and the mill was at full flood and the quarry was working and there were men at the timber, there were plenty Catholic families for a parish here. And since the house had a chapel, where was the use in building a new church somewhere else?'

I nodded. It was common in England that a whole village full of peasants had to tramp for miles to get to some church built in the grounds of the great house. The family strolled in fine weather and took a five-minute carriage ride in foul and no one questioned the wisdom. I supposed there was no reason it should not be the same with an outpost of the Church of Rome.

'Did old Mr Udney – a Catholic himself – make a point of employing them?' I said. If it were so then I felt rather kindly disposed towards the old gentleman, for one hears plenty about the closed shops in the shipyards and factories where Freemasons keep all the plum jobs for their brethren and the dirty work is done by the disfavoured Irish and their descendants.

'It just sort of . . . happened that way,' said Dorothy. 'Inevitably. I mean, the orphans, you know. We brought them up and they were confirmed and then they went looking for jobs. It just happened.'

'When was the parish . . . I don't know the word,' I said.

'Well, it all changed with Mr Udney getting old and having no sons to keep the mill or mine going. And then the quarrying work dried up in the war, when no one was building and a lot of the families moved to where the work was. And by then Father Dixon was . . . retired and he'd never been replaced. I miss daily Mass, I have to say. Our quiet prayers are all well and good but for forty years I celebrated Mass every day and I still miss it.'

'Forty years?' I echoed, with a quick look around the side of Sister Dorothy's wimple. I should have thought she was only forty years old herself.

'I'm sixty-three, Mrs Gilver,' she said. 'I went to Mass with my mother and father every day from the age of eight until Father Dixon . . . retired from St Ultan's.'

I noticed the hesitation the second time and filed it away to think about later.

'What a shame the Udney daughters are such conventional young ladies,' I said. 'There's many a girl running mills and mines these days, after all. Girls who've lost their brothers in the war. It's a pity the Miss Udneys run to nursing and looking after babies.'

'It was more of a pity when they ran to nightclubs and parties,' said Dorothy. 'They were wild when they were young, especially after their mother died. And we're glad of Miss Daff. As I'm sure Dr Glass is glad of Miss Cinty. It helps to have the family behind us in such unsettled times.'

'Speak of the d—' I said, for as we turned out of the orchard after our second tour, it was to see the figure of Miss Daffodil Udney ahead of us on the drive, sailing along with her arms swinging, whistling merrily. The wild young thing who only had time for parties certainly seemed happy enough to be on her way to another day with her orphans.

'Miss Daff!' shouted Sister Dorothy and the young woman turned and trotted back to walk beside us.

'Filthy morning, Sister,' she said. 'Well, actually, I suppose not.' She gave a short laugh. 'My poor father suffered most terribly from bronchitis every winter, Mrs Gilver,' she said, 'even before the final pneumonia. We got in the habit of loathing a cold day, on his chest's behalf. But there's no need to be so ungrateful for them now, I daresay.'

'You're being terribly hard on yourself, Miss Udney,' I said. 'It's difficult to feel thankful for a Scotch winter.'

'Well, let me feel thankful for something else then,' she said. 'Come for luncheon with us. Cinty is going to persuade that nice young man of yours and we've hatched a plan for them to pick up you and me at the convent gate at one. Say you will, Mrs Gilver.'

I gave it a little thought, trying to decide whether I could legitimately claim that the Udneys were witnesses worth interviewing in pursuit of the case. Yes, I decided, they were. For there was that one troubling detail I had gleaned from interviewing Dorothy and about which I shuddered to ask any nun.

'I'd love to,' I said. 'One o'clock at the gate?' Then I went off in pursuit of Sister Irene, whose interview would put me past the far end and onto the home straight at last.

16

I was beginning to lose faith in the power of my choreography-chart, as I had started to think of it. All I learned was that sister after sister was exactly where everyone said she was. And although scientists frequently tell us – at least, as Hugh frequently tells me they are telling him – that negative findings are still findings, I was getting sick of it. I began, even, to join the nuns in suspecting there was an intruder after all. Perhaps someone did break in through the French window. Perhaps he shook the shards of glass from the curtains as he brushed through them.

In the interests of thoroughness, I ploughed on, asking Irene my litany of questions and getting the stock responses. She did not seem to mind, used as she was to such rituals. Dutifully she confirmed that she awoke when Sister Martha went into Sister Anne's cell, which was two along from her own and that she did indeed go off to fight the fire wearing only one stocking although she did not know that she thus made a pair with Sister Jude. She told me further that her door was open, as was every other one on the second-floor landing.

'*Why* were they open?' she echoed, when I asked her. I had noticed a lot of them doing that too. 'Someone opened them.'

'I wondered if it might have been Mother Mary,' I said.

Irene shook her head. 'She stayed in the chapel. She'd have sent someone over and we'd have heard who.' Then, she departed from the liturgy and said something new. 'I reckon someone just decided to come back over and spend time looking in the rooms.'

'That's an odd turn of phrase, Sister,' I said. '"Spend time."'

'Well, it's always the way, isn't it?' she said. She was busy changing the napkin of a tiny baby who wriggled on her lap and whom she distracted with coos and clucks while she unpinned him. 'Not everyone is brave, Mrs Gilver. Some of my sisters might well have wanted to find something to do that took them away from the smoke and upset. My father used to say there's them as digs and there's them as leans on shovels.' She did not sound as though she were judging the shovel-leaners, but she did sound very sure of the matter. I was instantly convinced that there was no more to it than that and almost as instantly shame-faced that I had not seen it right away. The fact that it was the cells of the youngsters that had been pried into only added weight to the theory.

'Did you have someone in mind?' I said. 'I've spoken to twelve of your number now including you and no one has admitted it.'

Sister Irene screwed up her face, but that might have been because she had reached the most earthy point in the napkin-changing. I had never witnessed the procedure before and although she was deft and quick it was no treat to witness it now.

'Who have you spoken to?' she said.

'John, Bridget, Hilda, Martha, Clare, Anne, Margaret, Winifred, Joan, Dorothy, Sister Mary and you,' I said, scrabbling desperately through the pages of my notebook. The baby, attracted by the rustling, turned and chuckled, reaching out his hands towards me.

'Hmph,' said Sister Irene. 'Well, the ones I'd have suggested to you are on that list already,' she said. I guessed she meant Hilda, Margaret and perhaps Anne. 'And it wouldn't have been – couldn't have been Sister John or Sister Steven or Sister Mary herself, or someone would have noticed. Sister Julian wouldn't walk away from trouble. Nor Sister Abigail either. Sister Jude and Sister Francis? Now where were they? It's all such a muddle.' She had finished washing the baby and dropped her cloth into the enamel basin at her feet then, without warning or request, she lifted him up and put him down in my lap half-naked and wriggling on his towel while she went to pour the water away. 'Pin him in if you can reach the clean one,' she said.

'I— I—' I said.

She was back, whisking him away again before I had even worked out how to get him lying down and facing the right way.

'Ocht, you're right enough,' she said. 'It does them good to get a wee bit kicking their legs.' She lay him down with his feet towards her – apparently by applying mind control – and took his little hands in her own to play at clapping while he enjoyed his freedom.

'Sister Jude was sent to ring the playground bell,' I offered, glad to have a use. 'I haven't yet spoken to Sister Francis.'

She shook her head. 'Not likely,' she said. 'So who does that leave then?'

'Sister Catherine,' I said. 'But she—'

'Aha!' said Irene. 'Well, there you are then. That'll be it. It'll have been Sister Monica, going back in to check on Sister Catherine and just having a wee keek at the other rooms while she was at it.'

'What makes you sure it would be her?' I said.

'That's her job,' said Irene. 'She's Sister Catherine's companion as well as first-aider. And the convent seamstress. I saw her during the fire but only once. Have you spoken to her?'

'I haven't,' I said. 'But I certainly shall. Thank you, Sister Irene. You have solved a riddle for me. Heavens, there have been such stories flying around. Why would Sister Monica not simply tell everyone the truth?'

'She's compassionate,' said Irene. 'If the others had all their tales of angels and devils up and running before she got the chance she'd not want to make them feel foolish. She's a nice woman, Sister Monica. Spends her days taking care of old Sister Catherine and never complains.'

Before my arrival at St Ultan's I should have thought any nun would be a compassionate and uncomplaining woman. I should have thought, in fact, that every nun would be more or less the same – poor, chaste and obedient – but the longer I spent here the more strongly it was borne into me that they were a cross-section of humanity like every other group of people – regiment, family, or village street. There were sour ones like Sister Steven, sweet ones like Sister Martha, there were down-to-earth sorts like Clare and dreamers like Margaret. Sister Hilda was a rattle and Sister Anne was a still pond. Sister John was shrewd, Sister Mary was kind. They really were as different one from the other as any of us.

As I had the thought, a familiar feeling stole over me and a familiar following sense of dismay was close on its heels. I had missed something. Somewhere in my notes – pages and pages of them, with names and times and rooms and notions as snarled as a ball of wool wrested back from a kitten – there was a speck that I should have seized upon and had not. For taking notes is only half the job; writing them up in the quiet hours is what matters. On this case, the deluge of evidence had overwhelmed me. Disorderly as that was in a detective, though, there was a worse possibility: perhaps somewhere in the swirl of talk, someone had said something and I had missed it, had not even written it down; in which case it was gone forever.

I took the time to ask Sister Irene what she had done in the chapel and was impressed to hear that she had been pouring water onto the floor, hoping to put a break in the fire's path. Perhaps if all of them had done that, instead of rushing about ringing bells and making tea and dotting back over to the house to waste time looking in empty rooms, the chapel might have been saved.

'And did the Reverend Mother speak to you?' I said. 'Can you add anything to the account of her last words, which I admit is baffling me.'

'No, I was one of the first ones out,' said Sister Irene. 'Mother Mary and all the other sisters – the senior sisters – were still in there when I left.'

'The senior sisters?'

'Not all of them,' she said. 'Sister John and Sister Steven. Sister Mary wasn't in there at all and Sister Julian . . . I don't think she was. No, I don't know what Sister Julian was doing, but I'm sure I didn't see her.' She frowned.

'What is it?' I asked.

'Nothing,' she replied. 'It was a terrible night. Like a nightmare. Have you spoken to everyone who was in the chapel, Mrs Gilver?'

'Not yet,' I said. 'I haven't managed to catch Sister Steven since the first evening. To be perfectly frank, I haven't tried. I've found myself rather . . . and – actually – I missed Sister Julian somehow when I visited the laundry.' It was a poor show, I thought, but Irene was not the sort to rub my nose in it.

'Oh, well I'm sure you'll get round us all in the end,' said Irene. She looked down at the baby in her lap, who had had his fill of kicking his legs and waving his arms and had grown still, regarding Irene with large, solemn eyes. I gazed at his perfect little form, the way his slow breaths rounded his tummy and how I could see the flutter of his heart in the soft place just under his ribcage. He was such a tiny scrap to have been left in a basket in a convent doorway in winter. As I gazed at him, I wondered a little about the girl who had borne him and then set him down, turned her back and walked away.

'I've scratched my head over it many times myself,' said Irene, making me blink and look up at her. 'Your thoughts were written on your face, Mrs Gilver. Of course, it's all very well for us, isn't it? We don't worry where the next meal's going to come from and no one's looking down his nose at us. And when it's not our turn to sleep in the nursery we go to our beds away in the other wing and they can cry all night if they like and we'd never know. So it's easy for Sister Dorothy and the nurses and me to think they're little cherubs and blessings and wonder how anyone could put them in the slot and walk away.'

'Now, someone mentioned the slot,' I said. 'But I can't quite picture it.'

Sister Irene, instead of answering, deftly folded the baby into a fresh napkin, pinning him so tight that his legs stuck out in the shape of a catapult, then she laid him in his crib and, standing, beckoned me to follow her.

At the end of a long corridor leading away from the kitchen and the courtyard there was a wooden panel set into the wall. Sister Irene tugged it and it opened to show a deep drawer, rounded on the bottom.

'There's a bell on the outside,' she told me, absent-mindedly picking a few pine needles and a skeletal beech leaf out of the drawer. 'And another handle. The girl puts the baby in there, slides it through and rings the bell. Then the baby's ours. It's registered as born at St Ultan's. And given the name—'

'Bell!' I said. 'Some of the little ones told me they were Bells and I didn't understand them. Gosh, it seems rather callous somehow.'

'Better than some you get other places,' said Irene. '"Found" or "Parish". At least it's a good Scots name.'

'But all the same,' I said. 'You don't call all the girls Mary and all the boys Ultan. Why not give them different surnames too?'

'Can't you guess, madam?' said Irene. 'I wish you'd guess for yourself, because I don't really care to say.'

She gave me a penetrating look and I returned it with a blank and gormless stare, then in the distance we both heard the tolling of the Angelus bell and Sister Irene turned away.

'What sort of a morning have you had?' I asked Alec as I climbed into the passenger seat at one. Miss Udney, clambering into the back, decided that I was talking to her and answered gaily.

'Oh, not so bad. The poor mites with their tummies. Arrowroot is really more of a punishment than a cure, don't you think?'

'Have you got enough room?' said Alec, craning round. 'I was sorry your sister had to rush off early but, looking at you, packed in there like a sardine, perhaps it's just as well.'

'Quite fine,' she said. I found myself fighting against a churlish urge to find fault in her. It might well make me feel elderly to have her hop into the little back seat and leave the front to me as though I were a dowager but if she had claimed the front I should have felt she was claiming Alec too and would only have resented her. 'I'm the baby of the family,' she went on, 'and I'm quite used to having my back to the engine and being squashed into odd corners. How about you?'

'The middle son, but I became the eldest during the war,' said Alec, as he pulled away.

'How was your morning, I think she meant, darling,' I murmured. It was rather sickening to have a woman in her thirties refer to herself as the baby and no less sickening to wonder if Alec was throwing out that titbit so readily as an advertisement of his eligibility. If so then he could be had

179

up for fraud, for his father had settled the Dorset estate on the third son when it looked as though both elder boys were lost.

'Your poor parents,' said Miss Udney. 'All the poor parents really. It was the first time my father had ever been glad of his three girls, I think.' We were all of us silent for a minute or two, just the swish of the windscreen wipers marking time. The damp had resolved itself into proper rain, driven by a determined wind from the west, and the day that had begun so hopefully was now the more usual sort of February day, an ordeal to be got through until one could bathe, don warm flannel and burrow into bed again.

I cleared my throat and launched into one of the matters I was hoping could have light shed upon it by the Udney sisters over luncheon. This one might be easiest broached when we were in the motorcar and could avoid looking one another in the eye.

'Speaking of parents,' I began, 'Sister Irene just showed me the slot.'

'We're passing it now,' said Miss Udney and I whipped my head round just in time to see a weathered wooden handle set into the high wall at the edge of the lane and a small bell, brass but very tarnished from lack of polish, above it.

'An orphan wheel?' Alec said. 'I remember one at St Dominic's in Harrow town. We put a sacked badger in it once, rang the bell and ran away. The priest came to the school and addressed the assembly. Then the whole form was punished because the culprits didn't own up.'

'You didn't?' I asked. That was surprising. Nothing would have stopped the Alec I knew from sticking his hand in the air and taking his six of the best.

'One of the others wouldn't,' Alec said. 'And since we were all out on the same pass, the two of us who would couldn't, not without dropping him in it. So the form missed its quarter-day treat. We got fifty lines of Pliny to translate while the rest of the school got tennis and ices.'

'Poor darlings!' said Miss Udney.

'How did you manage to get a badger into a sack if there were only three of you?' I asked. In my experience badgers were fearsome things.

'It was quite docile,' Alec said. 'Well, dead.'

There was a short silence and then Miss Udney broke into peals of laughter. Alec caught her eye in the driving mirror and twinkled unashamedly.

'But to return to my question,' I said, once the hilarity had died down to a few giggles. 'When I asked Sister Irene why all the orphans who came through the slot were given the surname Bell she went coy and pleaded with me to work it out without her telling me.'

There was a silence from the back seat; no giggles at all and I noticed Alec glance up at the mirror and then raise his eyebrows at what he had seen. I craned round again and found Miss Udney staring at me quite coldly.

'I agree with Sister Irene,' she said and turned away to look out of the side window for the rest of the journey, not speaking again until we had swept up the drive of Waterside and parked near the front door.

'Ah, good,' she said. 'Cinty's back in time. I'll just settle you in the drawing room and go and help her. We don't keep a cook and our one and only girl is a bit of a daisy.'

Hard times have come to many and there are lots of us struggling on with daisy-like girls and helping to serve luncheon. Matters had not reached that pass at Gilverton just yet but there were good friends from the old days whom recently one met in town for tea at a hotel rather than see the change in how they lived at home. I could not help thinking, though, as I got out of the motorcar and took my first close look at the Udneys' place that it was not suited to struggling along without battalions of staff. There was so much glass, walls of glass everywhere, and it needed to be glittering to be at its best. As it was, about three winter months from its last washing, it looked exactly what it was: an odd choice for a house in Scotland where the light does not lend itself to the sort of thrown-wide life of villas in the south of Spain. The same was true, and even truer, of the smooth white plaster of the building's walls. It needed frequent painting and even more frequent washing to be at its best and Waterside, at least recently, had enjoyed neither. There were splashes of mud near the bottom and greenish stains from gutters near the top, even a few flakes missing here and there.

Since there was such an excellent view of the inside through the ludicrous panes of plate glass – really it was like a Bond Street emporium rather than a house – one could tell that the interior was just as 'not quite' as the exterior and, as we were shown in to the drawing room, it became even more clear. The curtains were shoved open and left as they hung; cushions not banged from the night before; books and papers littering the little tables and ash on the ends of the poker and tongs hanging by the fire. Clearly no one had wiped them since last night's fire had died down. It gave a frowsy air to what could have been a striking room and made me feel as though I were intruding unwanted into the Udneys' privacy. Since they had invited me, however, I did not intend to squirm about it.

I plumped one of the cushions for myself and sat down. Alec to my surprise sat right beside me on the sofa.

'Well,' he said softly. 'That was surprising.'

'Hm?' I said. I was studying the pictures. They had been chosen twenty years ago to complement the modernity of the square sofas and blocky tables, and nothing is more dispiriting than what was once avant garde.

'The children named Bell,' Alec said. 'I didn't have Miss Udney down as a prude, did you?'

'I have no idea where prudishness would come into it,' I said. 'I keep telling you.'

Alec snorted with derision and shook his head.

'They're all called Bell because it's a small place and people tend to stay here if they're born here,' he said. I gave him the twin of the blank stare I had bestowed upon Sister Irene. He snorted again. 'And the chances are that quite a few of them are all the work of the same local Don Juan. So it's better to have the brothers and sisters labelled as such, in case they were to grow up and start courting.'

'Good God!' I said. 'Are you serious? Well, no wonder she thought I was an odious creature for piping up about it. What a horrid thing. You really are coarse sometimes, Alec.'

But I was to drop even bigger bricks, even more innocently, before that dreadful luncheon was done.

17

Daff Udney returned with Cinty in tow a minute later.

'You *are* good!' Cinty exclaimed. 'We know you're fore-going one of Sister Abigail's lunches to be here with us eating indifferent omelettes.'

'Not indifferent,' said Daff, loyally.

'But I'm right about Sister Abigail,' Cinty said. 'Daff regales me every night as we're picking the lumps out of my mashed potato.'

I smiled and hoped I managed not to make it too stiff. One tires of hearing others being jolly and brave about their financial misfortunes.

'But never mind all that,' Cinty said, having seen my failure and correctly interpreting the stiffness, 'how are you getting on with the case? Have you discovered anything?'

'Come through to the dining room and tell us all about it,' said her sister.

The dining room was just as smeared and dusty as the drawing room, east-facing and dreary, but the Udney sisters had been too modest about their cooking and served a perfectly acceptable Spanish omelette with some sort of smoked fish inside and then some good oranges and walnuts with the coffee. I might have enjoyed the meal if I had not been beside myself with embarrassment more than half the time.

'It's not so much that we've discovered something,' I began, as we were sitting and shaking out napkins, 'as that I can't go ten minutes *without* discovering something and I've no way of knowing whether it's useful information to be remembered, noted down and folded into all the other snippets until a picture emerges, or if it's irrelevant gossip and will only obscure matters. I did think nuns might be different, for it's usually love or money that turns people secretive, but they're just the same.'

'For instance?' said Daff, her voice sepulchral with fascination.

'For instance,' I said, 'did Sister Mary really mean to imply that Sister Steven staged this morning's break-in or was she referring to something quite separate?'

'Sister Steven?' said Daff, boggling.

'Is she the one with the— ?' said Cinty, twiddling the ends of an imaginary moustache.

'Oh, don't,' Daff said. 'She's a lamb and I love her but even I can't take my eyes off it when she's speaking to me. When she wipes her mouth after drinking soup, it rustles. It positively rustles!'

'What did Mary say?' said Alec.

'It was when they were gathered on the stairs after the broken window had been discovered,' I told him. 'The talk was all of someone entering the convent and what he might have been up to and all the rest of it and then, apropos of nothing that I could think of, Mary suddenly asked Sister Steven in front of all the others if she had slept well. And the only interpretation possible if you ask me was that Mary suspected Steven had staged it. And was accusing her in public.' I looked around their faces to see what effect I might be having. 'Which doesn't seem at all likely. So it's probably something else. And I should discount it.'

'It certainly can't be true that Sister Mary suspects Sister Steven,' Daff said. 'Sister Steven? Impossible.'

'But it can't be completely unrelated,' Alec said. 'I mean ordinarily, Dandy, I absolutely agree. When we're grilling someone and he gets tongue-tied and shifty, it's usually nothing to do with us at all.'

'What do you mean?' asked Cinty.

'Well, someone might not have an alibi for a crime but that's because she was . . . trysting with her swain.' I was glad he had come up with an example; I had been about to say 'kissing the milkman'. 'But in this case, it would be mad to think that Sister Mary was just changing the subject, wouldn't it?'

'You're right,' I said. 'It would be. Well then, if she wasn't hinting that Steven was guilty—'

'Impossible!' Cinty said again.

'—then what could it be?'

'Perhaps Sister Steven is the lightest sleeper,' Alec suggested, 'and if she was undisturbed that means the burglar didn't go upstairs.'

'Burglar?' I said.

'I spoke generally,' said Alec. 'Intruder then.'

'Or perhaps "burglar" is right,' said Daff. 'Perhaps Sister Mary thought he meant to steal something Sister Steven possessed and if she had slept through the whole thing then he failed in his attempt.'

'But she possesses nothing,' I said. 'None of them do. I was in Sister Anne's cell after she fainted and it's practically empty. All the treasures of the convent – that hideous painted plaster Christ, for instance – are downstairs. Besides, I don't quite believe in this "intruder", truth be told. I think something Sister Mary said yesterday suggested to everyone that she doesn't believe in him either. And this morning's little display of broken glass was by way of a demonstration.'

'But hang on,' said Alec, 'if one of the other sisters wanted to steal the treasure chest or whatever it is that's stored in the cupboard off Sister Steven's room . . . For a start she'd know it was there and for another thing she could just slip in and pinch it anytime, couldn't she?'

'You suspect one of the *sisters*?' said Daff, looking quite horrified. 'Of everything? Of the fire? And the vandalism? You suspect a nun? Why?'

'Again, Miss Udney,' I assured her, 'this is simply how detecting is done and nothing to get upset about. We consider much and conclude little.' She sat back again and took a drink from her water glass.

'Well, that's something,' she said. 'I don't think I could have borne it if that were true.' She set her glass down again and sat back. 'I suppose I've got used to thinking of St Ultan's as a sanctuary. A home from home. If one of the sisters killed Mother Mary I think my life would feel very hollow.'

I could not decide if she was admirably open or just very self-regarding. Either way, I gave her a bright smile to cheer her up.

'I'm sure none of the sisters was less than horrified at Mother Mary's death,' I said. 'Even if they didn't all work like slaves to stop the fire.'

'What do you mean?' said Cinty.

'This is another example of the same thing,' I told them. 'There's been all kind of kerfuffle about doors standing open that should have been closed and no one would tell me anything. But it turns out, in the end, to be no more than one of the less courageous sisters making unnecessary checks on the house as an excuse to get away from the smoke and flames. Sister Monica, I think, although I haven't made quite sure. But that's the sort of secret people will keep even though we couldn't care less and the evasion makes our task all the harder.'

'I see,' said Daff. She rose and gathered our omelette plates into a pile, leaving them on the sideboard and sitting again.

'Mind you,' I went on, 'I'm just as bad in my way. I absolutely funked asking a question of Sister Dorothy this morning for no other reason than that I did not want to embarrass *her*.'

'Sister Dorothy?' said Daff. 'What has she done to be embarrassed about?'

'Oh nothing, I'm sure,' I said. 'Only she hinted that there was a story about the late Father Dixon and I didn't press her on it.'

'Not late,' said Daff. 'Not that I know of.'

'Former,' Cinty suggested.

'That's what I suspected,' I said. 'Sister Dorothy used the word "retired" but a retired priest is still a priest, isn't he?'

Both the Udney girls had gone very still again. Alec cracked a walnut and it sounded like a starting pistol.

'Defrocked, was he?' he said. 'What for?'

'We never heard the details,' said Daff, rather sourly. 'But it's nothing to do with the current trouble. Heavens, it was years ago. I can barely remember him at all, just as a pair of large hands clamped on a pair of black knees, and Cinty was a tiny baby. Our mother went off in the carriage to the archbish in Glasgow. I remember most particularly because it was the time of the King's coronation and Bena and I wanted to go with her to see the parade but she wouldn't take us.'

'Bena?' I said.

'Our eldest sister,' said Cinty. 'Verbena. Can you believe it? Hyacinth, Daffodil and Verbena: I ask you!'

She had my heartfelt and experienced sympathies, as I told her. I think Dandelion Dahlia comforted both sisters a little, in that that they saw it could have been worse.

'What was your mother's name?' I said. 'I have a theory that it's only ever mothers with sensible names who lumber their daughters as we have been lumbered.'

'Your theory holds good here,' said Daff. 'Mummy's name was Charlotte. No, it was all Papa. He was the one who insisted. He said it was a family tradition he was keen to carry on. Mummy said it was easier to give in than fight him.'

'Who would we ask?' said Alec. Even I had trouble unwinding the conversation to before the excursion into our woes, and the Udney sisters looked mystified. 'About the defrocking of Father Dixon,' Alec went on. 'The nearest Bishop, is it? Glasgow?'

'Mr Osborne,' said Cinty, 'I wish you wouldn't. It was certainly something very shocking. Mother turned her back on the Church completely over it.'

'It can't do any harm to check—' I began, but Daff interrupted me.

'You've heard how things stand,' she said, 'with the village up in arms over the hospital and starting to rumble about the convent too. Reminding them of a scandal would only make it worse, for the men up top and for the sisters.'

'Not to mention the orphans,' I said, and she beamed at me. 'It does you great credit, Miss Udney, not to resent both establishments more than all the villagers put together.' Her smile wavered as she tried to decipher my meaning. 'It's not every family who could look on house and land given away and find it pleasing.'

She and her sister both laughed a little then and gave one another startled looks.

'I've never thought about it that way before,' said Daff. 'We moved and of course the poor soldiers were to have somewhere quiet to recover and, as for St Ultan's: well, we've loved the nuns since we were babies. Mother Mary was the sweetest, kindest, most motherly woman you could ever hope to meet. She never held our mother's coldness against us and our childhoods wouldn't have been half so much fun without them all. Then as if that wasn't enough they've given us useful employment now we're grown up. What an odd notion – that we might resent them!'

'Yes but Daffy,' said her sister, 'Mrs Gilver has made me think of something, you know. I bet that's why you-know-who has been so cross with us. I don't want to tell tales, Mrs Gilver, but the minister from the Stop – whom one might have expected to show a bit of sympathy to us after Daddy died; I mean, he's not a priest and the church is not known for its warmth, is it? But still – anyway he's been glowering at us pretty non-stop since Christmas and I wonder if it's because we were always supposed to join in the general clamour for the hospital to be closed – unsafe you know, with the breakout – and we haven't. We've let the side down.'

'Supposed?' I said 'Always *supposed*? Do you mean to suggest that the breakout was expected? Do you mean to suggest that the breakout was . . . manufactured?'

'What?' said Daff, and her face drained of all colour. 'What do you mean?'

'Golly, no, that's not what I meant at all,' Cinty said. '*Always* because the villagers have never been that keen on lunatics up the road and *supposed* . . . afterwards, when some of them saw a silver lining. They thought after the worry of the escaped convicts they might end up with the hospital shut down and a nice family installed at Hopekist Head who'd employ girls as maids and men as beaters. A pipe-dream. Those days are gone.'

'But while it lasted,' said Daff, who had recovered, 'we were *supposed* to go along with it. And when we didn't, well then the village turned on a sixpence and found us wanting too. Blasted Catholics almost as bad as the blasted lunatics, you know? If only they could be rid of the whole boiling.'

'But how can you bear it?' I said. 'If you know that's how they feel about you.'

'Oh, they'll settle down again,' said Cinty. 'When the last two men are recaptured and the new Mother Superior is appointed, the village will forget all about it and we'll jog along the same as ever.'

They really were the most sanguine pair. They made one think of turbaned gurus sitting in trees contemplating the sound of silence. If I found myself despised by the villagers of my home estate and knew that they were rumbling away about my father's good works, I should have been furious.

Thinking of the turbaned gurus reminded me of their sister, even more saintly than these two, and I asked after her.

'Ah!' said Cinty, clapping her hands with delight. 'We expect her to reappear any day. We're waiting for a telephone call to tell us she's at Southampton. It will be wonderful to have her home again. Tragically sad, but so wonderful. I can't imagine how she must be feeling. Daddy six weeks dead and she hasn't visited his grave.'

'Where is it?' I asked. 'St Ultan's?'

'Why on earth—' Daff began, then gathered herself. 'No, not at St Ultan's. Certainly not. At St Mary's in Lanark.'

'Surprising,' said Alec. 'It was your father's home and there's a graveyard there.'

They were similar to look at, the two Udney sisters: dark-haired Daff and fair-haired Cinty, but in moments of high emotion it became clear that they were not cut from quite the same cloth. Daff turned pale when shocked – she was the colour of buttermilk at this moment – and Cinty grew a bloom that spread from the neck of her elegant, jersey frock right up to the top of her cheeks.

'We would never have buried our beloved Daddy there,' she said, her voice shaking with emotion.

'Cinty, darling,' her sister said. 'Go and fetch the coffee, dearest.'

Cinty scuttled out and Daff turned to us with a comical look on her face, eyebrows up and mouth turned down.

'You must be wondering what on earth that was about,' she said.

I certainly was but could hardly say so. I glanced at Alec.

'Not so long ago after all, perhaps?' he said gently. 'And perhaps you do know a few more of the details than you have been willing to share with us, Miss Udney?'

She stared at him, then her eyes flared with understanding and, although she tried to hide it, we could see her relaxing.

'We truly don't, Mr Osborne,' she said. 'But I'm glad you understand why we choose not to have Papa buried at a place our mother hated. We might not know what Father Dixon did, but whatever it was it upset Mama dreadfully. And it seemed somehow so ungrateful. I mean, Papa gave a rather good house and a pretty little chapel in trust to the Church and they repay his generosity by plunking down a rascal of a priest who got up to mischief. It would have been dreadful to leave poor Papa resting there for all eternity.'

There was a rattle at the door and Cinty entered, carrying a tray.

'You must forgive me, Mrs Gilver,' she said. 'Such an exhibition. What can you be thinking?'

'I've expl—' Daff began, but her sister sailed on.

'It's the uncertainty about St Ultan's future,' she said. 'If we could be sure that the sisters would stay and the chapel grounds would always be consecrated, then of course. But I can't imagine anything more upsetting than having to exhume a grave and move someone, can you?'

'That's exactly what I was just explaining,' Daff said, in a very loud voice. 'How the old scandal about Father Dixon has put the tin lid on the villagers' view of St Ultan's and it might be long gone before we're half-done mourning Papa. I've told them, Cinty.'

It was quick thinking and she had, in fairness, managed to mesh the two stories quite sensibly, but since Alec and I had not been recently born under a gooseberry bush, we were past being taken in by it. Each sister had thought up a different excuse for Cinty's extraordinary outburst. One surmised that the truth was some third tale we had yet to hear.

With a blinding flash of inspiration, I was suddenly sure I knew what it was and I plunged right in to ask them before they could gather themselves together again after the upset. A pair of witnesses who were changing colour and lying were a treasure trove and I wanted to make the most of it.

'About the villagers and their disapproval,' I said. 'I don't suppose the monster is part of the problem, is it?' Silence reigned in the dining room. 'I mean, I understand that the legend must be long-known amongst them and probably not believed by any except the smallest children . . .'

'But if they got wind of Tony Gourlay's report,' said Alec, catching up and joining in. 'What *is* the local legend, by the way? The one from my childhood village was about a witch who lived in a cave and ate little boys who paddled after sundown. It was remarkably effective at getting us out of the water and into our shoes and socks in time for tea.'

'We had an old man of the woods,' I said. 'In Northamptonshire. He only came towards human habitation when he heard children crying. And so we didn't. Really when you think of it now it was all the work of the nannies and nurses to make their lives easier.' I turned to the Udneys. 'Is it the same here with your monster?'

'Tony Gourlay is as mad as a hatter, poor lamb,' said Cinty.

'But add Mother Mary's last words,' I said.

'Last words?' said Daff. 'What were they?'

Alec and I exchanged a glance.

'You haven't heard?' I said. 'In all your visits to the convent since Christmas, no one told you?'

'I spend most of my time with the orphans and nurses,' Daff said.

'But Daffy,' said her sister. 'You did know. You told me.'

'I don't think so,' said Daff. 'Perhaps Sister Jude or Sister Francis told you. Or Dr Glass. I'm sure I had no idea. We've been at such sixes and sevens,' she said, turning to Alec and me. 'Christmas was awful, of course. The funerals – Papa and Mother Mary—'

'Don't!' said Cinty.

'Perhaps if we told you the last words they might jog your memory,' I said. This whole exchange was bewildering to me.

'What did she say?' Cinty demanded.

'Well,' said Alec, 'she said, "All these years it was real."'

'All these years it was real?' said Cinty. 'Why would she suddenly say that? Who did she say it to? Was that all?'

'Not quite,' Alec said. 'She also . . .' but the words died in his throat as he looked at Cinty. Her chest was heaving and I was sure I saw a sheen of sweat in the hollow of her throat.

'No one seems to understand what the Reverend Mother can possibly have meant,' I said, taking over, but like Alec I did not have the heart to carry on for Miss Cinty Udney was leaning back in her chair, limp and glistening with moisture.

'Perhaps we should be on our way,' said Alec, to Daff. 'Your sister seems unwell.'

18

'I almost laughed out loud when you added that, darling,' I said, as we closed the front door behind us. 'Seems unwell? She practically fainted dead away and slithered under the table. Miss Daffodil might have nerves of steel but Miss Hyacinth certainly doesn't, does she?'

'And what do you suppose it was all about?' Alec said. He climbed into the motorcar and sat staring straight ahead.

'They definitely know something pretty dreadful about St Ultan's in general or Mother Mary in particular,' I said. 'So much so that they didn't want their beloved father buried there.'

'And I wonder if it's connected to the disgraced ex-Father Dixon,' Alec added, 'or if Fr Dixon knew too and far from being defrocked was taken away to somewhere more wholesome.'

'But what could it possibly be?' I said. 'They're nuns, Alec. They take in orphans. They don't even take them in and rule them with a rod of iron. I mean, one hears things about orphanages dishing out stone-cold comfort – visiting the sins of the fathers, or at least the mothers, upon the children – but St Ultan's clearly isn't one of those places. It's a wonderful place for an orphaned child to grow up. And the sisters are good women. I mean, one or two of them are irritating, it's true. But none of them is truly bad.'

'Well, to be fair, Dan,' Alec said, 'you haven't spoken to every single one of them yet. Have you?'

'I've got eight to go,' I said. 'But I can't imagine what I

might find out from any of those eight that might account for Cinty Udney's collapse just then.'

'How quickly could you get round them all?' Alec asked. 'At half an hour each, is there any reason not to have the full set by bedtime?' He started the engine and took off up the drive.

'It's not that easy,' I told him, as he turned towards the moor road. 'They stop for prayers every time you blink, and they have jobs to do. Some of them are teachers of the children.'

'Nab the rest then and get the teachers once the school day is done.'

'And what are you planning to do?' I demanded. 'Really, Alec, the work of this case is hardly split very fairly down the middle. I've got twenty voluble nuns and two chatty nurses to interview and you've got one old soldier who's mute.'

'I'm going to go up to Glasgow to haunt the cathedral close and find out the true story of Father Dixon.'

'Wouldn't you be better to repair to the Udney Arms and pump the local worthies?' I said. 'Surely a pub is the place to hear gossip.'

'Ah, you innocent child,' said Alec, irritatingly. 'There is nowhere on this *earth* for gossip like a very large, very high church. It'll be a perfect hen-house, trust me.'

'In that case, why not go to the station and catch a train. I'd quite like the motorcar for the afternoon. Life up at St Ultan's with no means of escape is beginning to make me feel quite peculiar.'

Alec slowed down and then stopped in a field gate. 'Actually, that's very sensible,' he said. 'The train will be quicker. Right-o.'

He began to edge back and forward across the lane to turn round and retrace our path to the village and the station.

'If you decide on a jaunt, Dandy, promise me you'll come to the village, not go chasing off into the wilderness.'

'Of course not,' I said. 'If I get round all the nuns I'll only be slipping down here to renew my acquaintance with Sergeant Gibb. See if I can get him to share some of his brilliant deductions with me or get him to listen to what scraps I've managed to assemble. I'm not hopeful but it's worth a try. Why are you slowing?'

'Look at that,' Alec said, nodding at the road ahead. We had turned the last corner before Waterside, just in time to see a young man, going at a fair stride with his coat-tails flapping, disappear into the mouth of the driveway. Instinctively, Alec and I both drew back to try to remain unseen. We need not have troubled ourselves. The way the low winter sunlight was striking the windscreen we were rendered quite invisible and, besides, the man had not so much as flicked a glance our way, so intent was he upon his mission.

Alec turned the key and put his foot on the clutch so that we coasted silently downhill to the open gateway. The young man was almost at the front door. As we watched he trotted up the steps and then, to our surprise, turned the handle and let himself in.

'Who is he?' I asked Alec.

'Gabardine raincoat, not buttoned,' Alec said, 'so he came from somewhere nearby. Black shoes, dark suit, bowler hat. Take a guess, Dandy.'

'A policeman?' I said.

'But not Gibb,' said Alec. 'At least, not if that was Gibb who ticked us off about the car.'

'He might be a tradesman, with that bowler,' I said.

'But why would the Udney sisters have peeled themselves from their chairs after we dropped our bombshell and telephoned to a tradesman.'

'You think they rang him up?'

'The timing is just right,' Alec said. 'I didn't see exactly where the police station was when we arrived but I bet he just had time to put his hat and coat on and get along here for us to see him.'

'But why?' I asked. '*What* bombshell?'

'No idea,' Alec said. 'This is getting to be a very interesting case, wouldn't you say?'

We passed the police houses less than two minutes later, adding weight to Alec's notion that the Udney sisters had sought the protection of the law and the law had clamped on a bowler hat and come at a trot with its coat-tails flying.

At the railway station, Alec ascertained that there was a Glasgow train due in less than twenty minutes, that there was a newspaper kiosk and a fire in the waiting room, then he bought a return ticket and bade me farewell.

'Who shall you ask?' I said.

'The Bishop if I can get a hold of him,' said Alec. 'Or there's always the Mitchell.'

I hid my smiles. The Mitchell Library, and in particular its collection of press clippings, were beloved of Alec, even more so than the Central Library and *its* collection in Edinburgh. I cherished a fond hope that one of our cases one day might take us to London and the British Library; I could only imagine what acres of bound volumes and what Byzantine labyrinths of cross-referencing might be found there.

When he was ensconced in the waiting room with his newspaper turned to the crossword page, I set off back to St Ultan's feeling quite liberated. It was not the departure of Alec that lifted my spirits, more that I had become used to the ownership of my little Morris Cowley in the last ten years and returning to a state of dependence on others for my carriage was unwelcome. The drive up onto the moor as far as St Ultan's, though, hardly gave the feeling scope to be enjoyed and almost without deciding to I found myself passing the gate and going onward to the high ground. I had no desire to visit the hospital and the road led nowhere beyond it and so I turned once I was out of sight of one house but before catching a glimpse of the other and pulled off onto a patch of level turf. I opened the door and set one foot on the ground, leaning on the top of the window and drinking in the quiet and the view.

Had I been anywhere else I should have slammed the door shut and wandered away from the motorcar without a second thought, even might have sat down on the grass if I had had with me a mackintosh square or if the ground happened to be dry. I had not forgotten, though, that there were two men supposedly at large upon this moorland and one foot inside, with every hope of hopping in and locking the door should I catch sight of a desperate figure charging towards me, seemed a fair compromise.

Of course, as soon as I thought of the men – Tiddy and Arnold – I could think of nothing else. I cast my eyes around, wondering. There was no cover anywhere as far as the eye could see and the wind scoured across the empty landscape mercilessly. Surely they could not really be here still. They must have got themselves to shelter and made contact with friends who helped them get away. If it were summer perhaps, one could imagine them bedding down upon heather for a few nights between the inevitable squalls of rain, but from Christmas through to February there was surely no hope of anyone surviving in this landscape. There were still forests of pine trees down near the village, but that very nearness made them an unlikely hiding place. The children from Carstairs Stop would no doubt play in those woods and their parents must have searched them thoroughly and repeatedly after the news of the breakout.

No, I decided, the two escaped inmates were long gone.

I even went as far as to put both feet outside of the motorcar and step away from the door, meaning to stroll a few yards this way and that before I turned to my afternoon's work, the better for a little fresh air.

It was then that I saw it. It was no more than a blur of movement against the drained grey of the moor. It flitted across the corner of my vision and in one leap I was back in the driving seat with the door closed and the button pushed down to lock it. Once inside, I peered out through the windscreen and I did not think it was my imagination that I saw another flash of that same quick movement again. It was far enough away for me to be unsure what creature it might be. Larger than a dog, smaller than a horse, too dark to be a sheep and too quick to be a cow; too darting and furtive and careful to be any wild or farm animal whatsoever. There was only one kind of creature that scurried between shadows that way. It was a man.

If, I chided myself, it actually existed at all and was not the product of my imaginings combined with the unusual light and scope of the moorland. In Scotland, one is not used much to an expanse of sky and to the shadows of cloud that scud across the ground below it.

On the other hand, I thought, starting the engine, if he was real then he was a quarter mile from me and rather close to the convent, moving closer at some speed. I let the gear in and set off down the hill towards it, towards him, if he existed, and towards exactly the sort of danger Alec would never forgive me for courting while he was away.

Of course, I saw nothing and by the time I was driving along in the shadow of the high convent wall I had convinced myself there was nothing to see. Thankfully, that did not mean that I stopped looking and so it was I noticed a curiosity that might have escaped the attention of anyone else and even of me nine days out of ten. As I passed the place where the slot went through to the inside and the bell hung above, I could not help but note that there was a dark line around the edge of the wooden drawer-front which had not been there before luncheon.

I stamped on the brake, got out, leaving the motorcar agape in the middle of the lane, and hurried over. The slot was not properly closed. Someone had opened it and feeling reluctant to seal it, had left it ajar. Suddenly I felt sure I knew who had been flitting across the moor towards the convent, darting between the shadows and hoping to be unseen. I was irritated with myself that I had not realised at once it must be a mother, clutching a bundle, ready to ring the bell and leave her infant for the nuns.

But surely, came the thought hard on the heels of the last one, I should have heard the bell. If I had not – and I had not – then the bundle was still in there. I reached out and grasped the wooden handle, steeling myself against the sight of a baby resting in that round-bottomed little cubbyhole, then I pulled the slot firmly open.

Nothing. The drawer was empty. I drew in a breath, sharp with a disappointment I could not explain, and it was then I noticed the odd smell. It had not been present in the morning when Sister Irene had opened the slot on the other side, but it was unmistakably there now: a pungent and not quite pleasant aroma which made me think of the crumbling yolks of eggs boiled too hard and left too long.

It was only too easy to imagine that a poor orphaned mite, soon to be abandoned, might somehow smell exactly like that and I concluded that I had not heard the bell ringing and had missed the baby.

I drove myself in through the gates, stopped at the front door and made my way through to the orphans' side, where Nurses Matt and Pirrie were just finishing off the washing up from the children's dinner.

'You've had a delivery,' I said. Both women looked up. 'A baby?'

'Not today,' said Nurse Pirrie. 'Whatever made you think so?'

I brushed off my mistake and returned to the convent by way of the kitchens. Sister Abigail was one of the eight still left to interview and I knew that a cook is best approached just after a meal, before the next one begins to press itself upon her.

As I pushed open the kitchen door, my nose was assailed by a wave, ten times in strength, of that same sulphurous odour from the slot and I could not help putting a hand up to my face.

'I know!' said Sister Martha. 'You don't need to tell me.'

'What is it?' I said.

'Eggs,' Martha said. 'We sent the children out to check the hedges this morning – we've got some very flighty layers this last wee while. If it was up to me I would have them in the stock pot and start again with hens who'll sit in their boxes in the coop like good girls and not lead us a dance. But anyway, we had upwards of a dozen so we boiled them and mashed them with dressing and made sandwiches.'

'Are you sure they're edible?' I said. 'They smell a bit strident to me.' I was thinking that if I had the care of the orphans' tummies, not to mention that of Sister Catherine – for the very elderly are as delicate as the very young – I should not have chanced it.

'Ocht, yes, they're fine,' Martha said. 'There's such poverty down in the Stop now that the mill's closed. No one would look sideways at an egg just because it's a wee bit over tasty.'

'Alms to the poor!' I said and she nodded. 'I see. And so you put food in the slot in the wall and people collect it?'

Sister Martha blinked. 'In the orphan slot? No, we certainly do not. Sister Francis and Sister Jude took it down to the village with them when they went back to work.' She noticed my frown. 'They teach in the village school. They used to stay down there all day but the Udneys unearthed a couple of bicycles and got them mended – new tyres for the rough lanes and everything – and now they can teach the morning, get up here for Sext and the Rosary, Angelus and dinner and then get back down for the afternoon. They're sometimes a wee bit late for None but they'd not complain. We're a working convent and if there's no work to be done the sisters move to where it is. They'd far rather cycle a few miles and miss a prayer than have to leave us. Especially Sister Jude.'

'Was she born here?' I guessed. Sister Martha nodded. 'What was her name before she became a nun?' I said.

'Oh you're onto that, are you?' said Martha. 'Well, I don't see the harm in it. Yes she was Judith before her vows of commitment.'

'Oh!' I said. 'I meant her surname really.'

'Bell,' said Martha as I knew she would. 'All our infants are Bell. It's the usual way of things I believe, although I have no idea why.'

I had no intention of explaining it to her and, since Sister Abigail was nowhere to be seen, I left the kitchens. I could not resist another visit to the orphan slot, though. It had definitely been ajar a few moments before and it had definitely not been ajar when we left for Waterside. Arriving at it, I opened it and leaned down to sniff. Most definitely of all, one of Sister Abigail's dubious egg sandwiches had been put in here and recently removed, most likely by that fleeing shadow I had glimpsed. I closed it again and leaned against the wall beside it, thinking furiously. Someone within this house had put a parcel of food here for someone without. As to who either party might be, I had no idea. Would a villager rather come all this way up the rough track to avoid being seen to receive charity from the sisters? And which of the sisters would dispense the quiet alms? Jude and Francis, who taught at the school seemed most likely to have formed relationships but they were most able to hand a waxed-paper packet of food to a villager elsewhere. On the other hand, they probably left for their work before the scattered eggs were gathered, since the gathering was done by children before school and their job was to stand before schoolchildren.

Perhaps one of the older orphans, whose mother still lived in Carstairs Stop, was seized with pity for the family who had abandoned him. But could one of the orphans get in and out of Sister Abigail's kitchen?

Of course, the oldest orphans of all had free passage and just perhaps one of *them* had the run of the kitchens. Perhaps Sister Abigail herself was one of the Bells, Jesus' lambs, with the very closest ties to some village family.

I shook my head as I made my way to the main hall and the stairs to Sister Catherine's cell. For every question answered in this case, another three sprouted to replace it. Then I took a deep breath and squared my shoulders. At least one troublesome avenue of enquiry was about to be laid to rest once and for all, I hoped. If Irene was right about Sister Monica, then there might be no more outlandish tales to be told about those damned doors.

19

Catherine's cell was one of the large ones, probably a principal bedroom when St Ultan's was a house, and it was just as well for besides the narrow bed, there was a comfortable chair, almost a chaise like mine, where Sister Catherine was currently tucked up under a blanket, dozing, and a worktable under the large window where Sister Monica was bent over her needle, her nose almost touching the black cloth she was stitching. She had not heard me sidling in.

'That must be the very devil to work with in a north light,' I said, and she jumped a little and then winced as she pricked her finger.

'It's a habit, Mrs Gilver,' she said, once she had taken her finger out of her mouth and inspected it for bleeding. 'Hardly the devil's business at all.'

I felt a tiny flush of embarrassment. It was surprising to find how liberally one's conversation was sprinkled with devils and damnation, here where they stuck out so prominently. Sister Monica was, however, smiling.

'Do you do all the mending?' I said. 'For everyone?'

'The nurses and the sisters who work on that side do for the orphans,' she said, 'and most of the sisters patch up their own linens and darn their own stockings, but I make the new habits, like this one. It's expensive cloth, for one thing, and it matters that it hangs well.' She nodded to the pile of black material and I rubbed a little of it between my fingers, surprised to feel how smooth the wool was, sumptuous almost.

'I'm surprised that you concern yourself with how the habits hang,' I said. 'Isn't that—?'

'To the glory of God,' said Sister Monica. 'It's not pride. For one thing we never see our own, but we see our sisters' and it makes our hearts glad. To have us uniform and neat, our skirts skimming the floors and our veils hanging like . . . well, it might sound fanciful but I always think of the trumpets of foxgloves. It's greatly to the glory of God to have ourselves well turned out for Him.'

'I see,' I said. 'Our farmer at the mains – my husband's tenant – feels the same way about the furrows of a ploughed field. He always insisted it wasn't pride but I don't think I believed him until now.'

Sister Catherine snuffled in her sleep and we both turned. Her veil was crumpled against her neck and her guimpe was askew, showing a few short white hairs at her temple. The blanket had slipped a little and the sight of her stockinged feet, lumpy with bunions and much patterned with patches of darning, made both of us smile.

'Will it rouse her if I were to ask you some questions?' I said, and Sister Monica shook her head.

'She's very peaceful at this time of day,' she said. 'It's in the night she has trouble sleeping. Thankfully, she's quite happy to kneel quietly alone here and pray. She says her quiet night prayers are easier heard by God when He's not beset with everyone else and their clamouring. She doesn't think much about people praying in Australia, I don't think.' She stitched a few minutes in silence, tiny stitches, invisible against the dark cloth; when the seam was ironed it would disappear completely.

'What was it you wanted to ask me?' she said presently.

'Something you might not want to tell me,' I said. 'But I assure you it will go no further.'

'I have no secrets,' said Sister Monica, and her expression was exactly the open book her words described.

'That night,' I began, 'I've been asking everyone what they did, trying to piece it together.'

'We were kneeling at prayer—' Sister Monica began, and I had to purse my lips to stop a groan escaping.

'Actually,' I broke in, 'the earlier part of the evening is well nailed down already. It's the period during the height of the fire I need to talk about. I can't seem to get a proper sense of where everyone was.'

Sister Monica stitched in silence again, but I rather thought that her needle was moving more slowly than before and after a moment, she tutted, unthreaded it, and pulled at an inch of stitching to undo it. She pinned the needle through the cloth of her habit and sat up.

'It was rude of me to keep on with my sewing while you need my full attention,' she said. 'I apologise, Mrs Gilver.' I bent my head in acknowledgement, but privately to myself, I thought that the problem was not rudeness, but rather that my questions were interfering with her steady hand. *That* I found very interesting.

'Yes,' I said, 'where everyone was and what they did. How about you, Sister Monica?'

She said nothing for a second or two and then she heaved quite a sigh before she spoke. 'Ask that question about any hour of any day of my life for the last five years and I would be able to tell you,' she said. 'It's the most precious thing about my vocation, Mrs Gilver. The way my days are like the tides coming in and going out. As sure and steady as the sun coming up and going down. Some of my livelier sisters assume that I feel the burden of looking after my Sister Catherine' – we both glanced at the slumbering figure again – 'for why would I join this order of all others except to work with the children? To teach the big ones or nurse the little ones. But to be honest, when Sister Catherine is taken to her reward, I shall miss the quiet and the certainty of these days. I don't look forward at all to the rough and tumble of the children.'

Even though I was well aware that she might be trying to distract me it would have been beyond the capacity of any detective, nay any woman born, not to ask a little more.

'So what brought you here?' I said. 'You were not brought up at St Ultan's. I can hear the west coast in your voice.'

She raised her eyebrows. It was an expression I did not see upon many faces at St Ultan's for the tight grip of the guimpe rendered it painful. Still, Sister Monica's brow at that moment was as furrowed as one of those neatly ploughed fields.

'I never think of a lady like you being a . . . scholar of dialects,' she said. 'Yes, I was brought up at Largs, away to the west from here. I was born there and I went back there. But in between times, for a year when I was six, I was with Mother Mary. She taught me to read and write and she taught me that I was precious in the sight of God and that my life was to His glory. That's what brought me back again.'

'What brought you here the first time?' I asked her.

'The Armistice,' she said. 'My father came home from the war.'

I frowned and waited for more.

'I was born in 1916,' she said. 'He had been back on a leave – pardon my boldness. And then he came home after the Armistice. He was a fisherman, Mrs Gilver. He needed sons.'

'I know all about the sons of fishermen,' I said. 'I spent a winter at Gamrie with the herring folk.'

'Well, good, then,' said Monica. 'You'll know. Anyway, so by the time I was five and still an only one, my daddy got the idea into his head that leave or no leave I wasn't his. He put me and my mother out and she came to Carstairs – the Junction, where she had an auntie – and put me into St Ultan's.'

'Heavens,' I said. 'Wouldn't your aunt accept you in her home, even though she took your mother?'

'She would have,' said Monica. 'It wasn't that at all. It was more that my auntie worked all day and my mother was very unwell.'

'In her spirits?' I guessed.

'She was expecting,' Monica said. 'And as sick as sick could be with it. Mother Mary was helping her with some potion – Mother Mary and her potions; she didn't hold with doctors, as I'm sure you've been told before – and then she offered to take me.'

'Your mother – wait, I'm not sure I've got this right – your mother was pregnant when your father put her out?'

'They were like two bairns fighting over sweeties,' Monica said. 'My father made the accusation and my mother flounced off in high dudgeon even though she knew she had a baby started. She came to the Junction and waited there for her confinement. When the baby was born – my brother Sandy – she had a photograph taken of him, sitting on Mother Mary's lap. You'll have seen all the photos of the babies, haven't you? And she sent it to my father saying "here's your son, with the nuns in the orphanage where your daughter is too and you can . . ."'

'Put that in your pipe and smoke it?' I suggested.

'Exactly,' said Sister Monica. 'I had eight more years of it. The shouting and the flouncing and the bickering like bairns, and three more brothers betimes, then as soon as I turned fifteen I came home to Mother Mary and a bit of peace.'

All in all, I could well imagine that a night of chaos and terror would send Sister Monica back within the convent walls and to Sister Catherine, the lynchpin of her peaceful life, and I did not judge her for it, although I did rather judge her for keeping quiet and letting rumours fly.

'And so back to that night,' I said firmly. 'Can you tell

me where you went when the Reverend Mother raised the alarm.'

Sister Monica folded the heap of cloth on her lap into a neat square before she answered. I would have thought she was calm were it not for the needle she had pinned through her habit. It winked, catching the light in the movement as her chest rose and fell. The winking was rapid.

'I went downstairs with my sisters,' she said. 'I went rushing down there. And I stayed there. I went into the chapel.'

'You were inside?'

'I was,' said Sister Monica and the expression on her face was one I could not have described if I had spent the rest of the day with a sheet of paper and dictionary, trying.

'Who did you see in there?'

'All of them,' said Monica. 'Mother Mary, Sister John and Sister Steven, poor Sister Joan. Sister Irene and Sister Dorothy. I saw them all.'

'And yet none of them have mentioned seeing you,' I informed her. 'I rather assumed that you would have stayed with Sister Catherine, or at least returned to her. I rather assumed that was why no one had seen you.'

'No,' said Sister Monica simply. 'They didn't see me because I cowered. I got past the door and then couldn't seem to go on or go back. I was worse than useless. I *should* have stayed with my sister. But I rushed down there and straight in and then . . . Have you ever been in a burning building, Mrs Gilver?' I had but I did not want to distract her and so I shook my head. 'It was worse than you could imagine,' she said. 'It was so hot. Doesn't that sound silly? Of course it was hot, but we sit by a fireside every day, three feet away from flames and we're quite comfortable. I think we forget how much of it must go straight up the chimney. Inside the door of the chapel, the full length of the aisle from the flames, it was so hot! And so bright. It was always dim in there, the small windows and stained glass with it and even when the door was open facing to the churchyard wall not much light ever penetrated. And then suddenly it was blinding bright and the air was like to choke me and that's not even the most startling thing of all.'

'Oh?'

'The most startling thing of all was the noise, Mrs Gilver. It was deafening. When they burn the heather off the grouse moor and we see it across the valley, it's silent. But the fire in the chapel that night went at a roar.'

'And how long did you stay?' I asked her.

'I followed Mother Mary when she ushered Sister Jude out,' Monica said. 'She saw me but I'm not sure anyone else noticed.'

I think I understood then what was troubling her. She counted Mary as her true mother and St Ultan's as her home and yet she was not shooed out like one of the Reverend Mother's treasured orphans. She was left to shift for herself.

'So you didn't come back up during the time everyone was outside then?' I asked, hoping a change of subject would soothe her.

'Did someone say so?' Sister Monica looked genuinely puzzled, not at all shifty. There was no flush of discomfort on her cheeks and no clouding of her clear friendly eyes.

'I was clutching at straws, I think,' I told her with a rueful smile. 'It's the doors, you see. I suddenly thought I had answer to the mystery of all those wretched doors. I thought if you had come in to check on Sister Catherine you might have peeped into the other rooms too.'

'No, it wasn't me,' Monica said. 'Have you asked her?'

'Asked who?'

'Sister Catherine, of course. If someone was sneaking around that night she was best placed to catch a glimpse.'

It was a very good point and I felt chastened to have required reminding of it. I felt rather more than chastened, positively startled, when I looked at the elderly nun and found her staring back at me. I had not noticed her rousing, nor heard the change in her breath from sleep to wakefulness.

'Sister,' I began, 'I wonder if I might—?'

'What? I can't hear a word you're saying,' she replied in a loud voice. 'Sister Monica, what's going on?'

Although Sister Monica was more softly spoken than me by far, it is the way of the deaf that they can usually hear a familiar voice over a strange one and, as Monica relayed my questions, the old nun started nodding.

'It wasn't Sister Monica who opened my door,' she said. She gripped the arms of her chair in her rough, reddened old hands and hauled herself up to sitting. 'If anyone had asked me I could have told her that. I'm ninety-two but I've still got some of my faculties, you know.'

My jaw dropped open and the flush I had been looking for on Sister Monica's freckled cheeks now climbed and bloomed upon mine. Of course! Whoever it was who went snooping round the empty cells, would quickly have found out that one of them was not empty.

'My apologies, Sister Catherine,' I said loudly. 'I *should* have come straight to you yesterday. I'm glad to have the chance to hear your evidence now.'

'You're the detective,' said Sister Catherine. 'I was against it from the first minute young Marigold started trying to persuade us to let you come, you know.'

'Who?' I asked. I had a fleeting thought of Hyacinth and Daffodil Udney and could not quite bring the third floral sister to mind.

'Sister Catherine,' said Monica and the old woman tutted so strenuously that she dislodged her false teeth and had to fumble them back into place again with her hand.

'I mean no harm to the girl,' she said. 'I'm sure her vocation is as deep as the blue sea, even if she chose a pet name instead of a— Well, anyway.'

'Sister Mary!' I said. 'Her name was Marigold when she

was a child?' Even to my mind, far from devout, going from Marigold to Mary seemed rather lacking in sacrifice, especially when stacked up against Sister Steven and Sister John. 'Why, Sister Catherine?' I went on. 'You don't need to mince words. Why were you not in favour of me coming?'

'Sleeping dogs,' she said. 'Mark my words, when the dust settles we'll all be sorry we didn't let them lie.'

I had to turn firmly away from the etiquette foisted on me by my upbringing and haul hard to bring up all my detective's resolve, but in the end I managed to press on.

'Since I'm here now and the dogs are awake,' I said, 'I'd be very grateful if you would tell me who it was who opened your door on Christmas Eve.'

'Not Sister Monica,' said Catherine. I waited. 'And not Sister John. Certainly not Sister Bridget.'

She had named the woman she most often saw in her doorway, and the tallest of the nuns and the broadest of the nuns. Inwardly – and only just inwardly – I groaned. Sister Catherine might have some of her faculties left, but she did not have all of them.

'Was your room in darkness?' I asked gently.

'Cell,' said Sister Catherine. 'It's a cell, for all it's too big and over-fancy.' She paused. 'It was. And the lights were on out there on the landing. I only saw an outline.' I sighed and it was not inward at all. The outline of a nun, as Monica had just been so eloquently describing, is a triumph of uniformity.

'Were you asleep, Sister?' Monica asked. 'Did the door opening wake you?' I did not see what path she was starting down; I mistook her question for soothing small talk.

'I was at prayer, of course!' said Catherine. 'Praying for you all down there.'

'And did she just open the door and stand in the doorway then close it again?'

'She flung it open and scurried in,' Sister Catherine said.

'Stopped dead when she caught sight of me and scurried out again.'

'So,' said Monica, gently, 'you saw her moving?' It was a very astute piece of thinking, for a nun, and I applauded her with a flash of my eyes and a quirk of my lips. 'Mrs Gilver agrees with me,' she said. 'And you know I'm right, Sister. I was with you just a week ago when you called out to Sister Winifred to walk with more decorum to Terce and she was the length of the passageway ahead of you.'

Sister Catherine listened, nodding, but after Monica had finished she began to look troubled. 'I don't know,' she said. 'I just don't know. I could tell you who's passing my window or who's running in the orchard with the children, I've seen it so many times. You're quite right about that, Sister. But I've never seen any of my sisters sneaking into a room. I don't know how they would look doing it. I don't know who it was creeping about that night. Except that she was not tall and not plump and I don't think she was old.'

'But she was . . . real?' I said. 'Not a—'

'Ghost?' said Sister Catherine. 'Are you so lost to goodness you let mischief like the talk of ghosts into your silly head? No, she was not a ghost. Nor was she a fairy or a goblin or an elf.'

'But Sister,' said Monica, 'are you sure she wasn't an angel? Or a spirit – good or bad? Are you sure it wasn't a visitation?'

I kept my lips pressed firmly shut on the snort I would have been justified in delivering. For if there were a difference between ghosts and spirits it was a difference lost on me.

'She was very real,' said Sister Catherine. 'I heard her shoe soles squeak on the boards as she turned on her tail and shot out of here again. Not much more real than that is there?'

Sister Monica instinctively lifted her feet in front of her to look at her shoes and I glanced down too, at the sturdy blocks of black leather and the leather soles, buffed almost as soft as chamois from the constant rub of those dry oak boards.

'Do you think you would recognise her again?' I said. 'If all of your sisters were to take turns scurrying in here and out again with you watching?'

'We trust one another here at St Ultan's,' Sister Catherine said, 'never mind how matters are arranged in your world of police and lawyers and prison guards. We don't set traps to catch our sisters out. As I said, Miss Detective, I was against you even being here.'

'Sister!' said Monica, wincing at the rudeness. I, however, am a great devotee of straight talking.

'Very well,' I said, standing. 'Thank you for your honesty, Sister Catherine, and for your assistance.'

'Honesty is not a choice, deserving of congratulations,' said Catherine. 'Honesty is as inevitable, for a nun, as breathing air.'

'Hm,' I said, thinking of the nun who had crept around and then denied it, but my remark might well have been too cryptic for her, for her look of righteousness did not waver as I took my leave.

I paused out on the landing and cast my eye around, imagining the plan Alec had drawn and the marks I had made upon it. Everything had fallen into place. Whoever it was who came back inside, creeping around, must have opened the doors of the first few cells on this landing – Sister Mary's, Sister John's, and Sister Julian's – and closed them again when she was done. Then she blundered into Sister Catherine's room and took fright. She carried on her search afterwards, with the cells of Margaret, Hilda and Martha on this landing and all of the cells on the floor above, but now she was being careful; now she opened them softly and left them open, hoping that the old nun, kneeling quietly at her prayers, would not hear.

I wondered briefly how long she had fretted until she realised that the old nun's poor eyesight had saved her from recognition. It was a very lucky break indeed. So lucky, in fact, that something about it – or something adjacent to it – was troubling me.

I took out my notebook and quickly jotted down enough to spark a memory later *'nun in rooms: knew unrecognised? Knew SC unable to follow?'*

I was roused from contemplation of this troubling little note by a polite cough nearby and I turned to see Sister Mary herself standing at the top of the flight of stairs.

'A telephone call for you, Mrs Gilver,' she said. 'Mr Osborne rang from Glasgow station to ask if you'll meet him off the 5.17. He says he has news.'

'This is rather a lowly errand for you, Sister,' I said. 'Don't you have a . . .?' I was unsure of the word I sought. There were no maids here at St Ultan's and only Sister Catherine, by virtue of her frailty, had anything like a companion.

'I'm a nun,' said Sister Mary. 'I take my turn sweeping the chapel floor and sluicing down the bathroom. There is no such thing as lowly work here.'

'Really?' I said. 'That makes sense of one thing that's been troubling me.' She cocked her head. 'Why Sister Julian works in the laundry. She's a "senior sister" is she not? And in a teaching order. And yet she toils over washing coppers while junior sisters like Francis and Jude take off for the village school each day.'

We were making our way back downstairs by now, companionably side by side, and I could not see her expression; the edge of her veil hid all but the very tip of her nose from view and even that disappeared as she bent her head, pacing in silence. The answer came from below; the penetrating voice of Sister Steven rising up the stairwell.

'All work, offered up to the Glory of God, is noble and honourable in His sight,' she said. 'Sister Julian in her laundry and Sister Abigail in her kitchen are no less exalted than I in the classroom.'

Then Sister John's sweet tones chimed in, at a murmur. 'No one asked about Sister Abigail, Sister,' she said.

'Certainly not,' I said, with a laugh, turning the last corner and seeing them standing there, two identical shapes – one slightly taller and one slightly wider – in the darkest corner of the hall. 'Sister Abigail has found her calling. If that's not disrespectful to her . . . larger calling. But laundered wool and linen are laundered wool and linen, aren't they?' As I spoke I arrived in front of them and I regretted my words. Their habits and veils were as soft and smooth as silk velvet, falling in perfect bell-shapes and reminding me of what Monica had said: foxglove petals. Their wimples were like lilies, smooth and sculpted, gleaming white. They did not deserve my casual disregard of their perfection. For another thing, I saw that I had truly upset at least Sister John. She had caught her bottom lip in her teeth, a most ill-advised gesture which made her extraordinary moustache stand out from her top lip like a brush. Sister Steven laid a hand on her arm and shook it gently.

'I don't miss the fuss and frills of my youth,' Steven said. 'But I daresay that even out in the world things have got less silly than they once were.'

I nodded but the waist string and shoulder straps of my French silk chemise bit into me rather and I was suddenly aware of the slide of the fabric over my body as I twisted round to signal to Sister Mary that I was ready to take my telephone call.

Alec was whistling softly to pass the time and I had a moment to reflect that the girls at the telephone exchanges along whatever route his call had taken to me were rather more lackadaisical than the termagant who reigned at Dunkeld, who would butt in and threaten to pull the plug if a conversation had so much as a moment's silent pause.

'Ah, good, Dandy,' he said, when I made my presence known. 'I've got a few minutes before my train and I wanted to give you something to think about while I'm en route. Quarter past five or so at Carstairs Stop, by the way darling.'

'Did you breach the walls of the cathedral close then?'

'I got in with the secretary on her tea break anyway. The place is run like the head office of a savings bank, lots of women in navy blue, typing, and not a whiff of incense.'

'And how about a whiff of scandal?'

'Ah,' said Alec. 'Now, that's where it gets interesting. Father Dixon did not "retire". He was bundled away quietly but firmly, and lives with a sister in Oban these days, it seems.'

'And do you know why?' I asked. 'And if not, shouldn't you perhaps go back and meet the secretary at five o'clock and take her dancing?'

'She doesn't know,' Alec said. 'And she's sixty if a day, lives with her widowed mother in Renfrew, and it's cribbage night in the parish hall.'

'I apologise for lowering the tone,' I said. 'What am I going to be thinking about?'

'Just this,' Alec said. 'Miss Palmer of Renfrew doesn't know what Father Dixon did. Hardly anyone does. But apparently he was in a position to do some great and grievous harm to the Church if the whole story came out, so he was allowed to scamper off to Oban with an unofficial pension so long as he kept his mouth shut once he got there.'

I waited. Alec does like to make a dramatic rendition if he can and I could hear the drum roll building.

'But I'm not the only one who's been asking recently.' I waited again. 'The other is right there in Carstairs Stop. And we need to find a way to get that person to reveal all.' I tried waiting a third time but Alec was waiting too.

'I'll give you three guesses,' he said, when he realised I was not going to ask.

'Sister Mary.'

'Two guesses left.'

'Sister Julian.' Her name popped into my head unbidden as I remembered the strange little moment at the foot of the stairs.

'One guess left. I'll give you a clue. It's not a nun.'

I racked my brain. The Udneys would have been his parishioners, the men in the hospital must have been among his flock – at least the Roman Catholic ones, like Tony Gourlay. Dr Glass and he might have been close when one was there at the foot of the hill and one was there at the summit, both working for the souls in their care. Then it occurred to me that Alec had said 'Carstairs Stop' meaning the village itself, not 'Hopekist', 'St Ultan's' or 'the moor'. I cast my mind around the villagers I had come across. Only one of them was notable enough to have lodged in my mind at all – I could not have given the name or described the face of the sweetshop owner, for instance, if my life were dangled before me.

'Sergeant Gibb,' I said. There was a long hollow whistling silence on the telephone line; another one which would have seen the Dunkeld exchange take a hand. 'Sorry,' I said. 'I didn't mean to steal your thunder.'

Alec sighed, causing a great fluffy hissing somewhere in the miles of cable between us. 'You never do, Dandy. You never do.'

20

Carstairs Stop was not a sizeable village at all but it was very well served as far as its police force was concerned. There was a pair of new brick villas, sharing a common wall, halfway along the High Street and built onto the side of one of these was a low square police station, with a blue lamp above the door, a notice board inside a glass case and a barred window, suggesting that summary justice might be meted out to unruly villagers on a Friday night when the public house three doors down shut for the evening.

There were no unruly villagers to be found this afternoon. The stone cottages snaking along in a double row that made up the bulk of the village were snugly turned in on themselves for teatime. Lamps were lit, chimneys smoked lazily into the still air and there was a faint aroma of frying bacon and a not quite faint enough aroma of boiling cabbage somewhere.

Alec and I climbed down from the motorcar and perused the villas, looking for hints as to which one was home to the constable and which to the sergeant. The right-hand house, attached to the little station, was trim and nicely kept, with white lace at the windows and a pocket-handkerchief garden where roses, pruned hard for winter, stood in ranks in the cold dark soil. The left-hand cottage was rather more disordered, the curtains of the front parlour indifferently withdrawn, one pulled so wide that it was invisible from the outside and a good eight inches of the other one showing. The glass between the two was marked, just above the windowsill, with the tell-tale round smudge and long smears I knew so well from Hugh's library. A large dog lived there and its training had been patchy.

'This way,' Alec said, pointing to the neat house. 'A policeman with a good housekeeper of a wife is far more likely to advance through the ranks and I daresay a man like Gibb would choose a wife with an eye on advancement, don't you think? Constable Next-Door has been less canny.'

I agreed and we let ourselves in at the gate – freshly painted, with oiled hinges – and walked up a recently swept path to rap the polished knocker on the matching fresh paint of the front door.

The woman who answered chimed with her house exactly. She was dressed in a flowered apron over a woollen dress, thick stockings and sensible shoes below, but her black hair was perfectly waved and she had put on a little rouge and lipstick to welcome her husband home. From behind her came the scent of something warming and delicious – I suspected beef broth – and the sound of a contented baby gabbling to itself.

'Mrs Gibb?' I said.

The woman's eyebrows shot up into the bottom row of waves on her forehead.

'Hardly,' she said. 'I'm Mrs McLintock. Constable McLintock's missus. Sgt Gibb is next door.'

'Will there be anyone in, do you think?' Alec said.

'It's just the sergeant,' said Mrs McLintock. She cast an eye to where a few tussocks of rough grass poked through the shared fence and hung over her neatly turned rose bed. 'As you see,' she added, then at a rise in the level of babbling and a drop in the air of contentment, she bobbed politely and withdrew.

'So much for the great detectives,' said Alec, stepping over the low fence and extending a hand to help me over after him. 'No wife at all.'

221

'But a great need for one,' I said, lifting a cloudy brass knocker and letting it fall onto dull paint. I found myself tutting.

The large dog began barking almost immediately but although it was full-throated it was playful and when the door opened I saw the chocolate-drop eyes and waving tail of a yellow retriever, already sure that we were its great friends. The man with his leg across the gap in the door to restrain our new friend, however, squinting at us through a haze of tobacco smoke from the pipe in his mouth, was a stranger to us. That is, we had glimpsed him rushing to the Udneys but we had never met him.

'The constable's on duty this evening,' he said. His cardigan sleeves emphasised his words.

'It's you in particular we want to speak to, Sgt Gibb,' I said. 'But of course we'll come back at a better time if you're busy. It's Mrs Gilver and Mr Osborne.' I put out a hand to the dog and clicked my tongue against my teeth. She – I thought it was a bitch, somehow – leapt neatly over her master's leg and came to weave around mine, panting happily, that lovely frond of a tail sweeping back and forth and depositing a quantity of long yellow hairs on the purple plush of my coat.

'What a beauty,' said Alec. 'Just a youngster, isn't she?'

'She makes me miss my little Bunty dreadfully,' I said. 'I've got a Dalmatian puppy at home in Perthshire, Sgt Gibb.'

'And I've got an old lady of a spaniel,' Alec said. 'She'd look pretty moth-eaten if she stood beside this one.'

The dog, as though she had understood that a compliment had been paid, responded by putting her front paws on Alec's chest and smiling into his face. Her tail at this new angle might have swept me off my feet if I had stood in its path.

'Mrs Gilver and Mr Osborne?' said Gibb, at last, breaking in to our cooing.

'The detectives helping out at the convent and the hospital,' Alec said. 'What a tangle that is, isn't it?'

'Of course,' said Sgt Gibb. 'Yes, of course.'

'You've heard of us?' I said. 'Well certainly the Miss Udneys would have mentioned it. I'm sorry we missed you at luncheon. Better timing another day, eh?'

Before he had a chance to blink and recover from the fact that we knew about that particular little visit, Alec sailed on.

'And as you'll appreciate, Sergeant,' he said, 'we have a great many questions and problems to put before you. Lots of loose ends and odd little details. But so many that it feels likely the three of us could put our heads together and straighten them out. Wouldn't you say, Dandy?'

'I would,' I said. 'Some of the matters have their roots far in the past and that's where you'll be such a tremendous help, Sergeant. We're putting it together as well as we can – Father Dixon, for instance. But a word from you and it would all be so much clearer.'

'And everyone will be happier with the men back in their wards, the new Mother Superior installed and the convent back to normal,' Alec supplied.

'Shipshape and Bristol fashion,' I said. It was a phrase I had picked up from Teddy, much to Hugh's chagrin. 'In fact, I'd like to get your permission to get cracking on it,' I said.

'On what?' said Sgt Gibb looking pole-axed, as well he might.

'Could we come in?' Alec said. 'There's rather too much to cover while standing on the doorstep, wouldn't you say?'

Gibb, powerless to resist our assumptions, stood back and let us enter, the pretty dog rushing forward, plunging a short way along the corridor and into a door on the right. I followed her, with Alec behind me and Gibb bringing up the rear.

The retriever had lain down on a hearthrug before a

223

neat little tiled hearth where a fire was just beginning to warm the room and somehow her happiness at being there, warm and surrounded by companions, made the gathering less awkward. Gibb even went so far, slightly grudgingly, as offering to make us some tea. We could tell, when he opened the door through to the kitchen, that we had disturbed him in the preparation of his evening meal, for there was steam in the air and the smell of stewing meat, but we affected ignorance and settled in to the visit.

'I'll take Dixon and the inmates,' Alec whispered while we were alone. 'You take the nuns and the Udneys. What do you say?'

I shushed him, for Sgt Gibb was returning with the cups. He put them down on a low table in front of the sofa, saucerless, then left us.

'Fine,' I said once he was gone, but could not say more because he returned immediately with a jug of milk. Then it was teaspoons, a sugar basin, a barrel of biscuits, then finally the teapot itself. Perhaps he did not possess a tray, certainly his bachelor establishment appeared to be run on Spartan principles, but I rather thought he wanted to make sure we did not snoop in his living room while he was out of the way. Of course, that only made me wonder what we would be snooping for and I cast my eye around even more inquisitively than I might have done had he been less twitchy.

I had seen these little brick villas before, a room to the front comprising sitting room, dining room, library and morning room and a room to the rear comprising kitchen, scullery, breakfast room and laundry. There were probably two bedrooms above and perhaps a bathroom if the Lanark constabulary was generous. The doubling of functions meant that here in the main living room there was evidence of a great many different occupations. The newspapers were here, in a pile on the small table beside Gibb's armchair. There was a desk, its roll top open and its cubbyholes and little drawers bursting with papers, to one side of the fire and a small sideboard with a whisky bottle and a set of sherry glasses, dusty and unused, to the other. On the bookcase behind the door there was a selection of cheap paperbacks, westerns and romances interestingly enough, rather than the detective stories a policeman might be expected to favour, as well as a set of folded maps of the counties and a set of matching dictionary, encyclopedia and history of Britain, which spoke of Sgt Gibb being a clever boy at his school and being awarded prizes. The only book that truly surprised me surprised me so much that I decided I was mistaken: I thought that red-leather binding and gold tooling was unique but what would a man like Gibb be doing in possession of a copy of Debrett's? I decided after staring at it for a moment that it must be a Bible, perhaps another prize; this one from a Sunday school of some unknown denomination. Certainly the red was too red and the gold much too gold for the Church of Scotland, but Gibb might well be another of the same congregation as the Udneys and Tony Gourlay, in this crowded little outpost of Rome.

'So, Sgt Gibb,' said Alec. 'Just a little milk for me, thank you. Do you think St Ultan's is so far out of favour that the bishop would keep them waiting? After the business with Dixon, I mean.'

It was a masterstroke. Alec somehow managed to say absolutely nothing and yet imply a depth of knowledge so deep and wide that they could carry on the suggested discussion they had been chewing over nightly for weeks with pipes and brandies.

It worked too. Gibb stopped pouring and froze with the milk jug suspended over Alec's teacup, his face a mask. I had always thought that the sensation of one's scalp shrinking was internal, rather than a true movement of the skin over one's skull, but at that moment a lock of Sgt Gibb's sleek black hair detached from the rest and swung forward over his brow as though it had been dislodged by a shudder. Even the dog detected a change in the atmosphere. She wrinkled her brow and gave a worried look at her master, then she put her head down between her paws and sighed mournfully.

'Dixon?' said Gibb.

'Father Dixon as was,' said Alec. He reached out to take the cup and Gibb, startled into action again, regained a little of his composure. 'He left under a considerable cloud,' Alec went on. 'But it wasn't the fault of the sisters. I'd hate to think of them being punished by proxy.'

'I'm not about to start discussing it with civilians,' said Gibb. 'In fact, I'd quite like to know how you came to hear anything about it.'

'Civilians?' I said. 'Golly, I didn't know it was a police matter. I mean, I heard the story but I didn't think it had gone *that* far.'

'You heard it where?' Gibb said.

'Oh, well you know,' I said. 'It's a small world if one moves in the right circles. But I never heard until this minute that the police were called in. Wait till I tell Barrow, Alec. He'll be pea-green that I got a hold of some gossip before him, won't he?'

Barrow was Alec's valet-cum-butler and a more correct young man could not be imagined; he would neither gossip nor change colour, both on principle. It was, however, the only name I could think of quickly.

'I'm not saying it was a police matter and I'm not saying it wasn't,' said Gibb, rather late and none too convincingly, 'and I'm certainly not saying that St Ultan's was involved in any way. I don't know where you got that idea from.'

'You don't seem surprised, though,' said Alec. 'Changed days, eh Sergeant?'

But this time he had over-reached. Sgt Gibb's face clouded with genuine misunderstanding and I knew that whatever the story of Father Dixon was it had nothing to do with

226

modernity and the loss of the old ways. Before he could think long enough to realise we were faking every scrap of our knowledge I changed the subject.

'Sgt Gibb,' I said, 'the other thing I so very desperately wanted to talk to you about is one which I think a civilian might well take an interest in.'

'Oh?' said Gibb. He had not poured any tea for himself and in fact I saw him cast a yearning look at the whisky bottle on the sideboard.

'It's about the obscenities and the charred remains,' I told him, and was delighted to see that I had grabbed his attention. Alec, seeing the same, sat back and took a sip of his tea. 'In the convent,' I went on. 'The storage room and the chapel itself. I can't agree with your assessment of the dangers. I think the nuns really should be allowed to put things to rights. Some of those fine big boys in the orphanage could be set to shovelling away the fallen plaster and sweeping up, although of course they must be protected from the painted words. Heavens, yes.'

'What dangers?' said Gibb.

'Well, I daresay dangers is overstating it a bit,' I said. 'I mean I do understand that you want to make sure things go your way, but I think you're being quite a bit too single-minded. It's awful for them all to be there without being able to move freely and use their . . . well, their *home*, isn't it when you think about it? It's their home. And poor Sister Steven is sleeping in a nest of paper which has got to be distressing for her. As well as the convent being her home, Mother Mary was her family. She can't forget it for a second even in bed at night when she should be resting, because when she looks around she sees the files and documents that should be in the storage room and can't be because you've got it preserved in aspic.'

'Mrs Gilver,' said Gibb, 'I have no idea what you are talking about.' But his stillness belied his words as did the dog's wrinkled brow as she took another wary look at her master, struck by his tone. 'What do you mean?'

'You want the evidence preserved for the jury to visit and see the damage with their own eyes,' I said. 'At least that's what Sister Mary told me. I assume that's what you told her. I'm relieved to hear that there's more to it than that, because it did seem rather callous, didn't it Alec?'

'So what's behind it really?' Alec asked, chattily.

'Once again,' he said, 'I'm not at all minded to start discussing it with—'

'The likes of us,' I supplied. 'Yes, but the likes of us are exactly who's going to be on your jury when the time comes, Sgt Gibb. And I can assure you that being dragged out from – will it be Lanark or Glasgow? – In any case, being dragged out to the middle of nowhere and made to stand in the ruins of a church would be bad enough. But being made to stand and read those words – there might be ladies on the jury, mightn't there? – Well, let this lady assure you that I would be crippled by embarrassment from that moment on.'

'We would let the ladies and the gents go in separately,' said Sgt Gibb.

'Yes, but then they'd get back together afterwards. The thought of having to sit with the gentlemen and deliberate after such a thing! If I were on that jury I would feel very ill-disposed to the Fiscal and the police and the entire prosecution for distressing me so.'

Alec nodded. 'I'm a man of the world,' he said, 'but I'd wonder at the judgement of whoever made the decision. I'd pay extra attention to all of their evidence. Sorry to say so, old chap. But there it is, I'm afraid, and there you go.'

'But don't be downhearted,' I said, twisting the knife, 'you've done some things marvellously well. Seeing through the big shoes on the little feet was excellent detective work, wasn't it Alec?'

Sgt Gibb hung his head.

'Have I put my foot in it?' I said.

'I was talking to my constable when Sister Mary overheard me saying that,' he said. 'I had no idea she was there. That whole place is a warren of passageways.'

Then he shot to his feet.

I had heard nothing but he dived into the kitchen as though an alarm had gone off. There then followed a set of confused sounds, made of scuffles and whispers, and very shortly he was back again.

'Window cleaner,' he said. 'I sent him away.'

I looked at the line of dog's nose-prints along the bottom of the window and hoped the cleaner would not take umbrage and refuse to return. I also looked beyond the prints at the dying light and wondered how anyone had expected to clean glass by it.

'Now,' I said, 'where were we? Ah yes, the other thing I wanted to talk to you about was the inmates who're still at large.'

'That's not—' Gibb began.

'We'd like to offer our services,' Alec said. 'We had heard that the search was still in progress but we haven't seen any sign of it, have we Dandy? I wondered if perhaps a fresh eye would help. Where exactly are your men looking and how are they organising things? An ordnance survey grid? Are you using dogs?'

'Or do you think perhaps that Tiddy and Arnold are long gone?' I chipped in. 'How could they possibly be survivi— Oh! Sgt Gibb, I know this might sound odd but is there any connection between either of the men and any of the women?'

'Women?' said Gibb, swallowing.

I frowned in puzzlement. I had expected a very forceful sort of chap from the playbills put up by Sister Mary, but this man was a dolt. It took Alec to cut the knot of misunderstanding.

'The nuns,' he put in. 'The convent. Dandy meant the

nuns and nurses of St Ultan's. Although, I suppose you could say that there's a connection to the ladies too, at least to Cinty.'

'What do you mean?' said Gibb.

'Miss Cinty Udney,' I offered. 'Since she nursed them. But, yes, it was the nuns I meant. Can you tell us anything?'

'About what?' Gibb said. When he swallowed this time it was a painful-looking gulp, as though he were trying to get a crust of bread down without any water.

'As we said,' Alec put in, 'about connections. Why though, Dandy?'

'Because I think I saw one of them,' I said. 'I think someone inside is feeding them. Egg sandwiches today. Through the orphan slot. But why would anyone inside St Ultan's do so?'

'You saw one of the escaped men?' Alec said, turning to me with his eyes wide.

'I saw a figure in the distance,' I assured him. 'It could have been anyone really. But who else would be reduced to snatching food from a hole in the wall?'

'Sgt Gibb would be the expert on local tramps,' said Alec and we both looked at the man with expectant smiles upon our faces.

He returned a look I had not seen except when a dog sees a master advancing with a rolled newspaper or a child sees a nurse advancing with a spoonful of cod liver oil. He swallowed another dry crust, this one drier and crustier than the last, and gazed at us in helpless misery.

'I think they had someone in the village to help them with clothes and money,' he said, 'and are gone to Glasgow or London by now.'

'Tiddy is a Cornish name,' Alec said. 'He might even be beyond London.'

'So who's breaking in to the convent then?' I said. 'Do you know about that, Sgt Gibb? It's why we're here. Well, why I am. Mr Osborne is more concerned with Mr Gourlay.'

Gibb turned his terrified eyes first on me and then, as I gestured, on Alec.

'Breaking in?' he said. 'Since they are still holed up on the moor and bent on mischief, you mean?'

'You just said they were in Glas—' Alec said but I spoke over him.

'Holed up?'

'Camped out,' said Gibb.

'Are there caves?' I asked.

'Of course one could be in Glasgow and one still here,' said Alec. '*Are* there caves?'

Gibb took at least a minute before he answered. When he spoke at last it was in a small voice, numb and blank, as though he had been through a great ordeal.

'My dinner's burning,' he said.

Alec and I stood, bade a fond goodbye to the retriever and let ourselves out while Gibb went to the kitchen and his spoiled stew.

'Well!' said Alec, on the doorstep.

'Indeed,' I agreed. 'He's not at all what I was expecting. *He* solved the mystery of the big boots? *He* found all escapees except two? I can't imagine that man finding—'

'The army expression is "the floor with his rear by falling over",' Alec said. 'He must have good men.'

As though to confirm it, we heard a bicycle bell and along the street came our friend from the first day, who had scolded us about the motorcar. He had just missed finding it sitting empty at the roadside again; I hastened towards it to show him we were fully in charge.

He slowed at the gate to the next-door villa, vaulted off his bicycle and over the fence in one smooth movement and stood undoing his clips, looking at us with all the beady shrewdness that was missing from Sgt Gibb.

'Mrs Gilver and Mr Osborne, isn't it?' he said. 'And how's it going up by?'

'We're uncovering more questions than answers, Constable McLintock,' I said.

'Any questions I can answer?' he said. He was unbuttoning his tunic now to glance at his pocket watch. 'I've got five minutes before my tea.'

'Where do you think Tiddy and Arnold are?' Alec said.

Constable McLintock sucked his teeth and whistled.

'Timbuktu,' he said.

I considered pointing out that they had not got there in our hired motorcar, but did not want to annoy him.

'We had the hounds from the Buccleuch hunt out on Boxing Day, you know. His Grace gave up on the wee fox and let the dogs hunt the scent from the men's pillowcases. All week that went on. And we got all but the two of them. I think if that last two were there they'd be found. If, mind you, they'd survived the weather. The week round New Year had a freezing rain and a wind to flay you to the bone. Naw, they're gone. We just can't say how.'

'So you're not still looking then?' I asked him, remembering Sister Mary's phrase; the moor aswarm.

'Not here,' said McLintock. 'They're on wanted posters all over, but I reckon we've seen the last of them.' He tried to do it discreetly but we could not miss the way he turned his gaze to his front door, yearning for the tea his competent wife would have ready for him. Indeed, as we began to say our goodbyes the door opened upon Mrs McLintock, the smell of rich gravy and roasting potatoes and upon the figure of the child we had heard. It was a girl of eighteen months, stout and sturdy, who threw herself down the path towards her father, chuckling with delight and holding out her dimpled arms to be swept up in his. She had the white skin and black hair I was beginning to see was the particular mark of the Lanark Moor, and taking a closer look at her mother, I thought that behind the rouge and lipstick she was as pale as any of them and that her hair, set into ridges, would be just as dark if she let it fall free.

'Are you from these parts, Mrs McLintock?' I said, as her husband swung the baby high and made her shriek with pleasure.

'Born and bred,' she said. 'Janet Bell as was.'

'From St Ultan's?' I thought I understood a great deal suddenly; about how a thrusting young constable like McLintock could be passed over and a bumbling fool like Gibb promoted. Gibb had no 'orphan' in the family to offend the chief constable and the members of the golf, bowling, and curling clubs where all the decisions were made.

'Let's leave the McLintocks to their evening, Alec,' I said, for it was bound to be a pleasant one in that little house where a marriage had been made for love.

21

'That was an interesting thing Gibb said, was it not?' Alec began, as we were drawing away.

'Which in particular?' I asked. 'He made so many surprising contributions I hardly know where to begin to chew them over.'

'Right at the start,' said Alec. 'You mentioned three things currently awry: the convent in a mess, the nuns without a leader and the men still missing, and you suggested we should rectify matters. You said "let's get cracking on it" and he said "on what".'

'Putting the chapel and the storage room to rights, of course,' I replied.

'Of course,' said Alec. 'Yes, of course. That's my point, Dan. How could he think you meant anything else? How could we demand the men to be back in the hospital, much less demand that the diocese make a swift decision? He *should* have known what you meant and I find it interesting that he *didn't*.' He jerked his chin towards my bag. 'Write it down,' he said.

'Gibb: in with the Bishop? Knowledge of where escaped men gone?' I wrote and hoped that would be detailed enough for me to decipher it later. Since I had my notebook out and Alec was driving very slowly, I decided to jot down a bit more, perhaps to have the entire meeting recorded before journey's end. In a moment though I realised he was slowing to a stop rather than simply driving steadily.

Just ahead of us two familiar black bell shapes were walking briskly along the side of the road. We drew in beside them and they turned, that full turn that a nun must make, since her wimple stops her seeing much from the corner of her eye.

I recognised them from chapel and the refectory but I could not put names to them, which meant that these must be the last of the sisters we had to interview. I rootled about in the very bottom drawer of my memory and somehow managed to find what I was looking for.

'Sister Jude and Sister Francis,' I said. 'All done at the schoolroom?'

Sister Jude was a broad, not to say hefty, sort with the look of a farmer's lass – I could imagine her flinging stooks of corn up to a waiting man on top of a haywain – and the brown complexion of the hayfields too. Sister Francis was yet another of the milk-white locals, her black hair hidden but her alabaster skin and her speedwell eyes there for all to see.

'I thought you had bicycles?' said Alec.

'We leave them at the bridge,' said Sister Francis. 'The Days' wee dog is awful for nipping at us if we cycle past him and we'd hate him to get mixed up in the spokes and tumbled. So we walk the High Street and cycle from the bridge end.'

'You are as kind to the animals as your namesake, Sister,' I said and she blushed.

'I wish *I* had been initiated at St Ultan's,' said Sister Jude, in the yodelling voice of a west Irish countrywoman. 'I got the choice of Jude or Ephesia.'

'That was a test of your vocation indeed,' I said.

'Aye, my Mother Superior in Clare was a Tartar. Made Sister Steven look like a fairy godmother.'

'Will your bicycles be safe there overnight?' said Alec. 'If we run you back up? Only we'd like to talk to you both on the way.'

'Ocht, aye,' Francis said. 'They don't have much here at the Stop, but what they have they share and they'd never take what wasn't theirs.'

'A testament to good teaching, Sister,' I said.

'Tcha!' said Sister Jude. 'We didn't get much good teaching done today. The bairns were wild.'

'Oh?' said Alec. He sounded less than enthusiastic about listening to tales of children's nonsense.

'Full of this talk of monsters,' said Jude. 'I ask you! Who'd go telling the children stories about a monster and giving them nightmares?'

I shared a look with Alec. It was difficult to see how Tony Gourlay's words could have got around the village unless Dr Glass or Cinty Udney had gossiped in the pub or sweet-shop. Dr Glass did not seem the type and Cinty had been devastated by the mention of a monster at lunchtime.

'*Is* there folklore about a beast on this moor?' I asked. 'All the English moors have one, but I haven't heard about one at Lanark. My husband can't have either, or heaven knows he'd have shared it with me.'

'No, this'll be from the pictures,' said Jude. 'But it's going round the classroom like wildfire.'

'Actually, Sister,' said Francis, 'it's a . . .' she faltered '. . . a kissing picture on at the Gaumont in town just now. The nurses went to see it on their night off.'

'Anyway,' said Alec, not liking this much more, 'as we said, we have questions for you both.'

'And it was me who mentioned it,' Francis went on. 'To the big ones, to stop them being frightened. I was trying to quash the nonsense but I only made it worse.'

Jude sighed and might have rolled her eyes, but did not berate her sister. I was beginning to appreciate the kindly way they dealt with one another; it surely made for a very peaceful home. Setting Sister Steven aside, anyway.

As Alec began his questions, it became clear that sharing

the details of their own interviews was one way the kindly sisters had passed some of their recreation time, for we did not even have to ask the questions: Jude and Francis started without prompting to tell us that they woke up when Sister Steven was rousing Sister Clare and went downstairs in the general exodus from the second floor. As to what they did when they got to the fire, Sister Francis oversaw the soaking of rags and the safe stowing of bulky items removed from the chapel. A teacher is a teacher, I have found; in the classroom or out of it. She even tried to stir Sister Hilda to greater speed and efficacy in the making of tea.

'But since I didn't have a firework to put under her,' said Sister Francis drily, 'I was wasting my time.'

'And how about you, Sister?' I asked Jude.

'I tried to get a second line of buckets set up,' she said, 'but it was such slow work and people wouldn't stay in their places. No one thought of it when the orphans' side was walled off from ours, I don't think, that the way from the stable yard pump was gone. No one ever thought about what would happen in a fire.'

'Sister Julian did,' said Francis. 'I mind of asking her once. It was when we had just started at the wee school down here and we had a fire drill every week even though it's only tiny and more doors and windows than there are bairns to climb out of them.'

'And what did Sister Julian say?' I asked her.

'She said: not to worry,' said Francis. 'It was a stone building and no gas and plenty ways to get about and get out. I remember thinking it was all very well for her, working in the laundry – that damp you couldn't start a fire with sticks and paper.'

'So, just to make sure,' Alec said. 'Neither of you were inside the chapel?'

Both sisters demurred.

'And so you didn't speak to Mother Mary?' he added.

'Not me,' said Jude, glancing at Francis.

'Me neither,' Francis said. 'She was definitely trying to tell us something, but I didn't catch it and Sister Anne wouldn't—' There was a scuffle in the back seat; a sound I am very familiar with, being the mother of sons. Jude had either kicked or elbowed Francis to shut her up.

'Sister Anne wouldn't what?' Alec said. He went so far as to stop the motorcar and turn round in his seat to glare at them both. They looked steadfastly back, resisting him.

'Sister Anne desperately needs to unburden herself to someone before she makes herself quite ill,' I said.

'It has to be her choice,' said Jude. 'We can't compel her and we've been told not to try.'

'Told by whom?' I asked. 'Of *course* you should compel Sister Anne to open up. Sister Mary assured me that you would *all* do your best to help get to the bottom of things.'

'No one told Sister A—' said Francis and then shut her mouth very firmly.

We were almost at the convent gates and I contented myself with a loud gusting sigh of exasperation. Alec, to my mild surprise, looked rather pleased and when the two sisters had taken themselves off inside, he turned to me and waggled his eyebrows, looking like a very small boy.

'Abigail,' he said.

'What about her?'

'That's what Sister Francis was about to say. It was Abigail who warned them off pestering Sister Anne.'

'Are you quite sure? I assumed she was going to say "Anne", which makes much more sense really.'

'They had said Anne's name twice already,' Alec pointed out. 'Why would Jude shut her mouth like a mousetrap the third time?' That was a very good point and I nodded an acknowledgement of it. 'So I'll take myself off to the kitchen and see what I can get out of her,' he went on. 'What about you?'

'What a sacrifice for you!' I said. 'Going to sit in the kitchen again. I'm off to beard Sister Julian.'

'And then surely that's nearly the lot of them,' Alec said.

'Almost,' I agreed. 'Just Sister Steven to go. And perhaps another attempt on Sister Mary. I've got lots more questions than I had when I spoke to her the first time.'

'Good God, Dan,' Alec groaned, 'don't start going round again!'

Sister Julian gave absolutely nothing away. She might have been a Trappist monk rather than a nun from a teaching order. She answered my questions about Christmas Eve readily enough: confirming what others had told me about trying and failing to persuade Mother Mary out of the chapel; declaring that she had no idea what Mary's last words might have meant; and affecting utter blank ignorance of what Sister Anne might know and why Sister Abigail might want it kept under wraps.

What is more, she did it all with her scant nunnish hair protected by a wimple. I, on the other hand, came away from twenty minutes in the steam-laden air as though from the jungles of Borneo. It was, if anything, even worse at the fag-end of the day, for the last hot water was dashed out of the coppers all over the floor to be mopped off, and then the coppers themselves were rinsed out with cold, so that the fog was thicker than ever.

I was almost glad to hear the sound of the Angelus bell and to see Sister Julian summoned to prayer as surely as a bull is led by the ring in its nose. Clare and Margaret followed her and I was left standing alone as the laundry grew chilled and the last of the condensation ran in stripes down the walls and dripped into the bottoms of the empty sinks and coppers. I felt a chill steal over me. A laundry at work, especially one with sweet Sister Clare inside it, is a cheerful place for all the discomfort, but a laundry empty and growing cold is a miserable spot. I even heard once again the mournful twisting creak I had diagnosed as the wind in the charred rafters of the chapel, and it put another nail in the coffin lid of gloom.

I shivered thoroughly and started to leave. It was unnerving to think that the chapel was so nearby; or to be more precise, it was unnerving that St Ultan's was so short of windows and so oddly blocked off – with its two sides – that one never knew exactly where one was, except in the front rooms. I seemed to spend most of my time elsewhere. I gave myself one last shake, like a dog, and went to find Alec.

One of the nuns was still barrelling along the kitchen passage when I opened the door at the other end. She must have thought I was a senior sister, for she broke into a trot when she heard me.

'Don't worry, Sister,' I said. 'It's only me.'

But either she did not hear me or she did not want to break off from praying to answer me, because she swept through the far door without so much as turning her head, and was gone.

Alec was in the kitchen, sitting at one end of the long worktable with a crumb-strewn plate before him and a contented look on his face.

'Cheese straws today instead of jam tarts,' he said. 'With the leftover pastry from a rabbit pie.'

I could smell the pie, no doubt bubbling away in the oven behind me, and my mouth watered.

'Worth being late for prayers over, by the smell of it,' I said. 'Did you learn anything?'

'I was right,' said Alec. 'Oh Dandy, you would have been proud of me. I came at it sideways from five miles off and she hadn't a clue I was approaching.' Alec took out his handkerchief and wiped his lips; I deduced that napkins were not provided with cheese straws at the kitchen table. 'Sisters Francis and Jude, as well as teaching in the school also take

240

care of the local Girl Guides. And Sister Abigail is the pack leader. The three of them spend a good bit of time alone together, coming and going from the village to the meetings.'

'And?' I said.

'And so, on their journeys, they discussed the matter of cooperation and she persuaded them not to nag Sister Anne to share what she knows.'

'Any idea why?'

'None,' said Alec cheerfully.

'Nor me,' I said. 'But I can add another tantalising morsel of information. Sister Anne is a Girl Guide too. At least, she used to be. She told me.'

Alec absorbed this news in silence, thinking furiously, as was I, about what it might mean.

'Do you suppose,' he said at last, after quite a full minute of quiet, 'that they have discovered how the fire was started?'

'I don't think it's that,' I said. 'It's definitely something to do with Mother Mary's last words. Francis said Sister Anne heard them but wouldn't share them and Sister Abigail sided with her.'

'But everyone heard her last words,' Alec said. 'Either at first hand or in later reports. And what on earth do they have to do with Guides and Brownies?'

'I've got a flicker of a memory,' I said. 'Sister Anne got very upset when I reminded her of something she used to do round the campfire. Oh, heavens, what was it?'

'Did you write it down?' said Alec.

I clapped my hands.

'Got it!' I said. 'Thank you for that very timely little helping hand, Alec. Now, promise you won't laugh. I think Mother Mary's last words were in a secret code.'

'A secret code,' said Alec. He was not laughing but his voice dripped with scorn.

'Yes,' I insisted, 'because it was when I reminded Anne of that aspect of Scouting and Guiding – flags and codes and whatnot – that her face fell and she refused to say another word. At the time I had no idea what was bothering her, but that's it. I'm quite certain.'

I sat back triumphantly.

'Find Ultan, save Mary, all these years it was real,' said Alec. He blew out his cheeks. 'Well, why not? It certainly doesn't make much sense otherwise, does it? Right then, let's sit on Sister Anne till she cracks, shall we? What do they do after this bout of praying?'

'Another bout,' I said. It's Angelus and then Vespers and then supper. Which Sister Anne might take in her room rather than in the refectory, since she's still so sickly.'

'Do you know where it is?' said Alec standing. 'Let's lie in wait and get it out of her. If she's as sickly as all that it shouldn't take long.'

'Alec, you can't mean you're going to go into her cell and sit on her bed?' I said, aghast. 'She'll drop dead.'

'You're right,' Alec said. 'I'll perch on the window ledge. Now, let's get going.'

22

We never made it to Sister Anne. We were crossing the hall, with the murmur of the sisters' voices soothing us through the double door of the library, when I saw someone flit across the head of the stairs on the first-floor landing. A dark figure, the black outline growing so familiar after days with the nuns, but this one with a flash of something pale at its middle.

'Who's that?' said Alec. He spoke softly but whoever it was stopped dead at the sound of his voice and then sprinted away, banging against a wall and then slamming a door. Alec and I both charged for the stairs and raced up them.

'I saw her in the kitchen passage!' I said. 'I knew there was something fishy when she didn't answer me.'

All the doors on the landing were closed. As we stood panting and listening, we heard someone emerge from the makeshift chapel.

Sister Mary called up to us. 'What's going on? Mrs Gilver?'

'Sister,' I said, leaning over the banister to talk to her. 'Are all the sisters at Vespers?'

'Of course,' said Mary.

'Alec, you wait here,' I said. 'I'm going to go and check on the two nurses. Just wait here. And when I get back we'll start searching the rooms.'

'What's going on?' Sister Mary shouted up again.

'There's someone in the house, Sister,' I said. 'Once I check that it's not one of the nurses or one of the orphans, we'll sniff him out.'

'Him?' said Alec. 'It was rather a light footfall, wouldn't you say?'

'Give me two minutes,' I replied. I raced back downstairs, through the kitchen and into the orphans' side where Nurses Matt and Pirrie were supervising the children's washing before their supper.

'Is anyone missing?' I said. 'Any of the big children?'

'Sandy Molloy is at his piano practice,' said Nurse Pirrie, 'but the rest of them are all here. Why?'

I assured her I would explain later and jogged back to rejoin Alec, only to find that he had failed to impose his will on the nuns and that, Vespers over – or perhaps abandoned in the face of another intrusion – they had swarmed out of the chapel and up the stairs to carry out a search of their own.

They were in and out of the cell doors, buzzing with fear and anger, and Alec stood amongst them, with his hands clasped on the back of his head, helpless to stop the ruination of the best chance we had yet had to get to the bottom of things.

'I see how he got in,' said Sister Martha. 'Look! In my cell!'

All of the nuns surged forward to cram into Sister Martha's room, a small chamber across the front landing from the first-floor bathroom, probably once a dressing room for the big front-facing bedroom next door.

I elbowed my way unashamedly to the front.

'Don't touch anything!' I ordered. 'There might be finger-prints.'

'He climbed in the window,' said Martha. 'Look!'

Her window was indeed wide open at one side and peering out into the darkness I saw that the roof of the front porch was an easy stretch from the sill.

'But was your window unlatched, Sister?' Alec asked. Martha's eyes widened as she shook her head.

'No,' she said. 'Locked tight like Sister Mary told us.'

I subjected the window to close study and could see no scrapes or any other signs of misuse on the outside of it.

'Perhaps he only left this way,' I said. I closed my eyes and tried to bring to mind again that flitting figure. He might indeed have been headed to this room. I turned round and looked past the cluster of nuns. 'Where did he come from?'

Sister Steven, just at that moment, was descending from the attic floor. 'Could he have been coming from the staircase?' she said.

'Looks about right,' Alec said. 'Why, Sister?'

'Come and see,' Steven said. She turned and stumped off back up the stairs again, with Alec and me and then the rest of the sisters following.

'Ah,' said Alec, looking into her cell when he got there, then he stood back to let me see.

Her small room was littered with files and papers, even some carbons, as though an office had been ransacked.

And all at once I knew a great many things. I looked at Alec and I saw that he knew them too. We knew the rascal who painted obscenities in the little box room and set a fire in the sacristy was not avoiding the holier places because of his childhood's training in the church. For a sacristy, like a vestry, is used not just for vestments but also for papers, and the storage room was not full of boxes and trunks, but of files and ledgers; files like the ones strewn across Sister Steven's bare floor. The man who set the fire was not bent on sabotage; he was looking for something, and tonight he had finally looked for it in the right place and found it. I thought again of the pale gleam in the middle of the fleeting dark figure and knew what it was. I bent and picked a file from the floor, and gave it to Alec. He understood at once, grabbed it close to his body and bent over slightly. Then he caught my eye and nodded.

'It wasn't Tony Gourlay,' he said. 'This isn't the work of a madman.'

He was right; the monstrous fire and the painted obscenities had been smokescreens. The true purpose of the intruder, on Christmas Eve and every time since, had been to steal whatever was in that file.

'Is there any way to tell what's missing?' I asked Sister Steven, but she just looked around herself helplessly, shaking her head.

'Not quickly,' she said. 'We'll see if we can work it out for you as we tidy things up again. Sister Mary, with your permission I'll have Sister Martha bring sandwiches up and we shall begin right away. Sister?' she went on, turning to John. 'May I beg for your help? And Sister Julian too.'

'Sister Abigail being unable to abandon her kitchens at supper time,' Alec muttered close to my ear. He was right; it was the familiar crew of senior sisters who were chosen to tidy these papers.

'Why not make quicker work of it by asking some of the youngsters to help?' I said to Sister John.

She regarded me steadily. 'We make no distinctions when it comes to work, Mrs Gilver,' she said. 'I think we've told you that before.'

'And it's not a big room,' said Sister Julian. 'We'd be falling over ourselves if there were many more than three of us in here.'

We shuffled out trying not to stand on any of the scattered papers and then, with the rest of the nuns, we made our slow way downstairs. Halfway, Sister Abigail put her nose in the air and sniffed then broke into a trot, with her mind more on her rabbit pie than any intruder.

'This is rather serious, Sister,' I said, drawing level with Sister Mary. 'It's one thing to have unwanted guests at night time but it seems worse somehow for the fellow to make free with the convent during waking hours with you all at prayer.'

'You *were* all at prayer, weren't you?' put in Alec from behind us. 'Only I could have sworn that the figure we caught a glimpse of was a nun. All in black and the right sort of shape.'

One of the novices giggled and Alec cleared his throat. 'The shape of the habit, I meant. Skirts to the floor.'

'It makes a great deal of good sense from the point of view of the miscreant,' said Sister Mary. 'If he wanted to search the cells how much more sensible to come when we are in the chapel than to sneak in and hope not to wake someone at night-time.'

'And do you have any idea what "he" was searching for?' I said. 'In fact, Sister,' I went on as she shook her head, 'it occurs to me that we really do need to sit with you and conduct a proper interview. We've hardly exchanged a word since the evening I arrived.'

'Supper on a tray in my study?' said Sister Mary. 'Just the three of us so we can talk freely?'

We readily agreed to meet her there once we had properly searched the house and grounds. Then I drew Alec into my room, closing the door carefully behind us.

'This is my fault,' I said. Alec gave me a quizzical look. 'I told Sgt Gibb the papers were in Sister Steven's cell.'

'You think Gibb dressed himself as a nun and broke in?'

'There's *something* fishy about him,' I insisted. 'And he was the one who wouldn't let the sisters tidy up the box room and start work to repair the chapel.'

'Or,' said Alec, 'perhaps he rang the Udneys after we upset him, like they rang him after we upset them.'

'An Udney girl?' I said. 'Why? I imagined they rang up Gibb after luncheon because it makes sense to report anything one learns that might help a policeman in his investigation.'

'Except he's such a dud,' Alec said. 'What would be the use?'

'I don't know,' I admitted. 'It's one of the many things I

don't know about this case. I've never felt so much as if I'm going in the wrong direction. As if I know a little less every day.'

Over rabbit pie and mashed potatoes in Sister Mary's study, Alec and I came to the conclusion that with us she made three. She did not know anything. She looked at us guilelessly and answered without hesitation, but had nothing to say.

When we asked what file might be missing, she shook her head, lost. When we asked about Father Dixon's dismissal, she blinked and told us she thought he had retired and had never heard anything to suggest there was more to the story. When we asked her if there was some close connection between Sisters Francis, Jude, Abigail and Anne, she showed every sign of searching her recollection and looked disappointed not to think of anything.

'There's the Girl Guides,' I said. 'They all have that in common.'

Sister Mary pursed her lips, preparing to answer, but try as she did no answer to such an inane remark occurred to her. She glanced at the enormous silent figure, watching over us from high on the narrow end wall, and then she seemed to make up her mind about something.

'I was chosen by Our Mother to replace her when she died,' she said, 'although none of us thought it would be for many years. That doesn't mean I'm versed in all the day-to-day business of St Ultan's. Far from it. I was to be a spiritual leader – if that doesn't sound too conceited – a mother to the young ones as she was mother to me and to my contemporaries. She spoke to me often of the need for kindness and gentle treatment, but seldom if ever did she talk about . . . the pasts of my sisters. Being an orphanage, St Ultan's of all places chooses not to dwell on the past which cannot be changed, but instead do its best in the present for the future.'

'And a fine best it is,' I said. 'One of your youngsters was at his piano lesson before dinner. I'd bet there aren't many orphanages where the children are offered piano lessons, Sister.'

'I would hate to see anything bring our mission here to an end,' said Sister Mary. 'You don't think this file that's been taken has something in it to harm the convent, do you?'

'It must contain something either to harm or greatly to benefit someone,' I said. 'But I believe you, Sister, when you say you cannot enlighten us.'

'It sounds odd to hear you call St Ultan's a mission,' Alec said. 'One doesn't think of missions as existing right here, does one?'

'It was what Our Mother always said.' Sister Mary spoke gently, as ever when she spoke of her beloved Mother Mary. 'She always liked to hear of the orphanage in Hyderabad, their news and their achievements, but she never wanted to go there. She said once that out of great evil, great goodness could be born but that this was her place and that out of small evils, small blessings just as dear could flow.'

'Did you know what she meant?' I asked. 'What great evil?'

Once again Sister Mary pursed her lips to talk as though she expected to find an answer ready in her mouth and then seemed surprised when there was none.

She laughed. 'I have no idea,' she said. 'It's a very clear memory; me sitting on her lap as she rocked me and her telling me about great and small evils and great and small blessings.'

Alec, eating efficiently and with evident hunger, had finished his pie and was signalling to me that I should hurry up with mine. I pushed my plate aside, for in all honesty even the most delectable rabbit pie was quite easily resisted, and followed him out.

'I believe her,' I said. 'I think she's as innocent as a lamb.

In fact, I think it was her innocence that led her to bring us here. I'll bet none of the rest of them – the big-wigs – would have let us within ten miles of St Ultan's.'

'You might well be right,' said Alec. 'But keep your voice down, won't you? And now, see if you agree with me. We need to report this and make it very clear that this was nothing to do with Tony. But who to tell? That sergeant is not only quite hopeless, but we think he might be crooked too. My thought was to ask Dr Glass. What do you think?'

'Splendid idea,' I said. 'He'll have a bottle of port apart from anything. Let's go up there now.'

'Is it safe to leave them?' Alec said.

'We've gone over every inch of the place,' I replied. 'We've double-checked every lock and latch and each of the sisters is on her guard. I think we could fairly go and take care of Tony's welfare for a while, don't you?'

It was black as ink outside, the headlamps making two feeble yellow spots on the lane in front of us, and so we crept along, edging around corners and slowing wherever the track narrowed, and it is a very good thing that we did so, for although the moor was endless it was undulating and, unbeknownst to us, another little motorcar was coming down from Hopekist Head, rather faster than we were ascending.

I was looking out the side window into the blackness when I felt Alec wrench the steering wheel. We lurched off the road until our front wheels were almost in a ditch. There was a long blaring hoot as the other driver registered his feelings and Alec let slip a word which would have been quite at home daubed on the box room wall.

'Oops,' he said. 'Sorry, Dan. What in the blazes?'

He stepped down and I got out on rather wobbling legs. In the headlamp light we saw the Udney sisters, wide-eyed and white-faced, in the front seat of an ancient Crossley.

Miss Daff Udney jumped out of the driver's seat and

came over to us, throwing her arms round first Alec and then me.

'Thank God you're all right!' she said. 'Oh my Lord, could this night hold any more horrors?'

'We're fine,' said Alec, 'but we might need a dray horse to get the motor back on its four wheels again.'

'We need help,' Daff said. 'I was hoping for Dr Glass too but he's having a time of it tonight. One of the men is dreadfully upset about old troubles.'

'Not Tony?' said Alec.

Miss Cinty Udney had rolled down her window and shouted over to us.

'Not poor Tony,' she said. 'It's George Molloy. He gets a bee in his bonnet about his wife every so often and he takes a lot of soothing. Dr Glass is marvellous but it meant he wouldn't come with us and he wouldn't even let us stay there and be with him.'

'Help with what?' I asked.

'So we decided to come and get you and Mrs Gilver,' Daff went on. 'It's a stroke of luck . . . Well, sorry.' She glanced at the car in the ditch and screwed her face up. 'But I'm glad to have met you. You see – I think we've found where the men were hiding.'

Alec and I were momentarily speechless.

'They're not there now. God knows *where* they are now. I've told Sgt Gibb and he's got McLintock out looking too, but after I set a few of the village men to warn the others we were scared to stay in the house on our own.'

'You've found their hideout?' I said. All of a sudden I was piercingly aware that we were all four of us standing like coconuts at a shy, in the glare of our headlamps. I looked behind me into the soft emptiness and felt the hairs on my neck move. I hunched my shoulders.

'Where were they?' Alec said.

'We can show you if you like,' said Daff. 'It's not far.'

We bundled into their motorcar and she set off at the same frantic pace as before, plunging down the road towards the village. When we were past St Ultan's but not yet into the trees she swung off at a gate I recognised.

'Isn't this usually chained up?' I said.

'Daddy's old mining works,' said Cinty. 'Sgt Gibb cut the padlock chain when we told him what we'd found.'

'We're not going down a mine?' I said, not as forcefully as I felt.

'Just into the foreman's office,' Cinty said. We bumped down a very rough track and into a yard. The sweep of the headlamps showed a horseshoe of brick buildings – stables, storerooms, and a smithy, all with rusted iron roofs and boarded-over windows. There was just one slate-roofed building with a chimney and although its windows had also been boarded up one of the sheets was loose and I could see in the headlamp's reflection that a pane of glass had been knocked out leaving a hole about a foot square in the bottom corner.'

'But wasn't this place searched?' said Alec. 'On Boxing Day or afterwards.'

'From what that booby Sgt Gibb told me tonight,' Daff said, 'all they did was check the padlock on the gate and the locks on all the doors. They never looked closely enough to see that one of the boards had been prised off and then just placed back to cover the hole. Idiot!'

She had clambered down and the three of us joined her standing on tiptoes at the high window while she shone a torch into the room beyond.

The signs of recent inhabitation were unmistakable. Two makeshift mattresses, fashioned from stuffed sacks, had been set out on the floor of the room and an orange crate between them held a stump of candle and a single chipped-tin mug. There was a kettle hanging from the hook in the shallow fireplace on the other side of the room and in the grate were not the white ash and nest twigs expected in a long-disused building, but the still-glowing remains of a coal fire. There was a small heap of coal cobbles lying on the floor beside the hearth.

'But what have they been eating?' Alec said, then he turned to the Udney girls. 'Was there a company store here when the mine was open? Might there still have been sacks of meal and tins of biscuits?'

'Upon my word, that's a very clever thought,' said Cinty. 'But no. Daddy's mine was never such an operation as all that. It's a good question, Daff: what *have* they been eating?'

'I think the nuns have been feeding them,' I said. 'I saw someone creep up to the drawer in the wall and away again and I was sure there had been food in the slot.'

'Oh my Lord,' said Daff. 'Someone inside the convent feeding the rogues who've been tormenting them? That's dreadful. And who? Someone in the kitchens? Martha or Abigail? It doesn't seem possible.'

'Look, never mind that now,' Alec said. 'What makes you so sure they've gone away, Miss Udney? Clearly, they were here while everyone was searching, but how can you be certain they've gone.'

It was on the tip of my tongue to say that they had gone because at last, that very afternoon, they had found what they were looking for, but Daff Udney beat me to it.

'Of course, they're gone,' she said. 'Look, they've left the board off and revealed their hiding place. They'd hardly do that if they were coming back, would they?'

Alec and I were quite shame-faced at that, for it should not have been beyond us as detectives to draw the same conclusion. Alec covered his bashfulness by firing questions at the Udneys like a Latin master.

'Did Sgt Gibb go inside? He didn't? Why not? Do you have a key? Well, would you hold that torch up while I go in and have a bit of a snoop about? They might have left clues. Dandy, give me a leg up, would you?'

'Careful of the glass, darling,' I said, but Alec disregarded me as men always do when some woman suggests they are not invincible.

He leaned hard on my shoulder with one hand and grabbed the windowsill in the other, launching himself upwards. I made free with his person as far as giving him a good shove from behind and then he was up, gingerly picking his way over the frame with its glints of glass still along the putty line until, with a cry like an athlete launching himself over a high jump, he landed in the middle of the floor clear of the danger of glass beneath the window.

'I think you're right, Dandy,' was the first thing he said. 'There's greasy paper crumpled up in a ball here. Someone made them a packet of sandwiches recently.'

'Sniff it,' I said, and Alec obliged.

'Pawf!' he said, throwing the paper back down again. 'Not *that* recently.'

'What was it?' I asked.

'Does it matter?' said Alec, his voice still sounding rather thick with disgust. 'Something fishy. Could you hold the torch up a little higher, Miss Udney please?'

We all three of us took turns, for it is very tiring to hold a heavy torch above one's head for any length of time. Those not hoisting the torch aloft stood on tiptoe and peered in over the windowsill but there was little to see, beyond Alec's back and his hunched shadow on the wall beyond him. Eventually he gave a sigh and stood up from his crouch by the further mattress.

'Nothing,' he said. 'At least nothing much. I was hoping for a confession on a scrap of paper. The Secrets of St Ultan's, sort of thing.'

'Secrets?' said Daff. 'What do you mean?'

'"The wrongs nuns have done me", I'd have called it,' I said hoping to cover his slip, for of course the Udney sisters

254

had no reason to suspect secrets of any kind. We had not told them of the missing file.

'There are some calculations scribbled on the plaster in pencil,' Alec said. 'I might just jot them down if you'd pass your notebook through, Dandy. Or better still, you take dictation.'

I sighed but fished for my notebook obediently.

'Of course, these scribbles might be from when the foreman worked in here, but why would he write on the plaster? In any case, it's financial: LSD. Several figures added together and then divided by two.'

He reeled them off and I did my best to copy them down in the light from the torch, although most of its beam was trained through the window.

'That looks to me as though they stole a few items and planned to sell them and split the takings,' I said.

'Sell what, I wonder,' said Cinty, who had been quiet for a while. 'Did they get anything of value out of the chapel? I rather thought not from what Daff's told me.'

'Mind out!' Alec's voice came from just above our heads and we stood back to let him drop down onto the ground beside us. He took a deep breath of air, redolent of old coal as it was, but smelling better than a room where two men had lived on sacks for a month and more.

'What's next?' I said, once I had handed Alec back his hat and coat. 'You said you'd already warned the villagers to stay inside and keep their ears pinned back, Miss Udney?'

Daff nodded, making the torch bob.

'I'm off to the hospital to tell Dr Glass it's certain,' Alec said. 'Could I prevail upon you to take me there, Miss Udney? Or can I drop you at home and borrow your motorcar?'

'We'll take you!' exclaimed Cinty with more vigour than I could easily account for. She sounded almost frantic and I wondered if perhaps the admiration I had seen upon Alec's face when he met her was reciprocated.

'And drop me off at St Ultan's on the way?' I asked. The recent alarums had changed my mind about port in Dr Glass's sitting room. I wanted nothing but cocoa, my narrow bed and peace.

There was no peace to be had that night, though, and I would not see my bed until the sun had risen again in the morning.

23

We heard the bell before we reached the convent walls. It was pealing out frantically, the ringer – whoever she was – not waiting a moment between yanks on the rope so that there was no resonance to it, just a desperate rat-a-tat. Thank God for it. It put us on our guard for trouble and so when Daff Udney swung the little motorcar around the last bend before the gates she managed not to plough into the form of Sister Julian who was running down the middle of the lane at full pelt.

'Oh God!' said Alec. He opened the door and grabbed Sister Julian before the car had barely slowed, hauling her into the back seat, and shaking her. 'What's happened?'

'He was still in there,' Sister Julian stammered. 'I was going for the doctor. The police, anyone! The sisters' bicycles are down at the village and he cut the phone cable. He cut the phone cable. I think he killed her.'

'Sister Julian,' I said, 'what are you talking about? Killed who?' We were in the gates and halfway up the drive and Daff Udney pressed down on the accelerator, spraying a gout of gravel up behind us.

'Mary,' she said. 'He was still in there. And he cut the phone cable. We couldn't— We couldn't. Oh thank God you're here. He cut the cable and the bicycles are gone and we thought we were all alone.'

'Well, we're here now,' Alec said. 'Where was he hiding? What has he done?'

'What has he *done*?' said Julian, turning trembling to face him. 'I told you. He's killed Mary. I think he's killed her.' She leapt down from the car as it slowed and disappeared into a huddle of sisters who were gathered around the front door.

'*Sister* Mary?' I said. 'Tonight? Oh, Alec!'

'Oh God, Oh God,' said Cinty, going to pieces again as she had once before.

'Stay here,' I said to Daff. 'Take care of your sister.' Then I jumped down and followed Alec, who had already got past the crowd at the door. Some of them were praying – Sister Anne and Sister Clare; some of them were trying to comfort others – Sister Winifred with her arm around Sister Jude; and some of them were simply standing helplessly weeping and not even trying to wipe away the tears.

'Where is she?' I demanded.

'Study!' said a chorus. Alec made off at a run and I pelted after him.

The study door was wrenched open before we got there and Sister John, her sleeves rolled to the elbow and her hands bloody, stood shaking from head to foot.

'She's breathing,' she said, 'but we need help.'

Inside the study was a scene of stark horror. The room was dark, the monstrous crucifix gleaming like old bone. Sister Mary lay on the floor at its foot with her head, stripped of its veil and wimple, cradled in Sister Steven's lap. Mary's face was streaked with blood and Nurse Pirrie was pressing a cloth to a wound at her temple. Nurse Matt, crouched beside them, was trying to staunch a second wound at her waist. I could see Sister Mary's letter opener, dark and dull with drying blood, sitting on the floor beside her.

'We can't telephone,' Nurse Matt said. 'The devil cut the wire. If we could only get this bleeding to slow a bit!'

At those words, the stern Sister Steven caught her breath in a gulp and as she let it go, began sobbing.

'Right,' said Nurse Pirrie. 'Mr Osborne, take over from

me. Just keep up a steady pressure. And Mrs Gilver, you take over from Nurse Matt and press steadily on the—'

'I know,' I said and she nodded.

'Mattie,' said Nurse Pirrie, 'try and get a pulse and check for any more injuries. I'm away to get bandages and tape but I'll be as quick as quick can be.'

'This cloth's soaked through,' I said, trying to keep my voice calm.

'This one's worse,' Alec said.

'They'll both do till I'm back,' said Nurse Pirrie and disappeared towards the storage room and the passage to the orphans' side at a trot.

'Here,' said Sister John. I glanced round to see her stripping her scapula off over her head and rolling it into a bundle. 'Maybe it'll help.'

'Fold it into a tight pad, Sister,' I said. 'If you're sure.'

John glanced at Sister Steven, still cradling Mary's head.

'Go ahead,' said Sister Steven. 'And let's pray.'

Alec took the folded pad of black cloth from Sister John and lifted the soaked white to replace it. It was Mary's guimpe, I now saw, and under it a terrible sight. A sunken depression in the side of her face and her ear a bludgeoned mess of shredded skin and gleaming cartilage. I had put the sights of the war-time convalescent home far away from the front of my mind in recent years and I felt my throat grow soft with nausea at confronting such things again. I glanced at Alec. His face was white but his jaw was firm and he even bent for a swift close look before he covered the mess with the new pad again.

'I don't see any brain matter,' he said.

'And her pulse is there,' said Nurse Matt. 'It's weak but it's there.' She stood and, following Sister John's lead, she unpinned her apron-top, pulled the bow loose at her back and made a fresh pad for me.

As I lifted the soiled one, so soaked that a few drops of

Mary's blood fell onto my skirt, I saw that this wound was far worse than the other. It was six inches long and ragged and I caught sight deep inside it of the shining curve of some interior organ and a slick of something yellow and oily. Then the blood welled and I slapped the new compress down hard as much to hide the view as to help Mary.

John and Steven's whispered words faltered but then came back louder and even more fervently.

'. . . sinners, now and at the hour of our death . . .'

'Flickering,' said Nurse Matt, who was taking Mary's pulse again. 'It's flickering, Pirrie!' she said to her colleague who was just then bowling back into the room with a heap of towels across one shoulder and a capacious bag held high in front of her like a shield.

She threw it down and drew out of it a roll of bandage.

'Let go,' she said to Alec and as soon as he took his hand away she whirled out a length of bandage like a streamer and then with deft movements wrapped Sister Mary's head so tightly that her mouth and eye were pulled out of place and she appeared to be winking. I looked away.

'Ready?' she said to me shuffling along on her knees until she was beside me. I lifted the pad again but Nurse Pirrie slapped at my hand to clamp the compress back down again.

'Good Lord,' she said, then: 'Mr Osborne, can you lift her? Her intestine is ruptured. She needs Dr Glass. That needs stitched and flushed out with more iodine than we've got here or she'll be poisoned.'

'It's very faint,' said Nurse Matt, still with her hand at sister Mary's wrist and looking at her fob watch. Both her hands were rusty with blood. In fact all of us were smeared and daubed with Sister Mary's blood by now. Sister John had put her face in hands at some point and had handprints of red on her cheeks so that she looked like a child painted for cowboys and Indians, except for the tear streaks through the stains and for her trembling lips.

'Sister Steven and Sister John,' said Alec, 'go and clear a way for us and get the Udneys out of the car.'

'And tell the sisters to get into the chapel and onto their knees,' said Nurse Matt. 'She needs all their prayers.'

'Is everyone ready?' Alec asked and without waiting for an answer he stooped, gathered Sister Mary into his arms and straightened again. I scrambled up, trying hard to keep pressing against the middle of the mess in her stomach – for although I had seen it I could not tell, as she moved, where the wound was. I could only guess from the heat and the endless surge of soaking blood. Her head lolled against Alec's chest and left a red cloud there.

'Good,' Alec said. 'Now let's go.' I threw one glance back at the crowned head as we left and thought the single word *please*; hardly one of the beautiful prayers He was used to, but surely as heartfelt as any He had ever heard.

The sisters in the hallway cried out in misery when they saw her, and Daff and Cinty, turfed out of the motorcar already when we got outside, were white with terror, clutching one another.

'Is she alive?' Cinty said.

'Just,' said Alec grimly.

'Is she conscious?' said Daff.

No one bothered to answer such a preposterous question.

'How will we get home?' said Cinty and, although some of the nuns turned to glare with disgust at her, I thought she spoke from shock and forgave her.

Alec bundled Sister Mary into the back seat and I jostled in with her, still pressing hard on the folded apron. Nurse Pirrie got in at the other side and took over from me, bending close to see Sister Mary's colour in the low light spilling from inside the front door.

'Hurry,' she said in a wretched voice and Alec sped away, with just the three of us aboard.

The road to the hospital seemed twice as long. We disturbed an owl, which swooped low in front of the car, unearthly white in the headlamp glow. We passed the hired motorcar half in the ditch. A little further on, Alec slammed on the brake as a fox, almost as white as the owl in the lights, streaked across the road six feet ahead of us. At last, though, we saw two pinpricks of light – the doctor's sitting-room windows – and the dark bulk of the hospital wall rose above us. Alec began to sound an alarm on the car horn, long and short blasts in order, and before we had drawn up at Dr Glass's gate, the door was open and the doctor himself was coming down the path in his carpet slippers.

'SOS? What's amiss?' he had time to say and then he caught sight of Sister Mary. 'I'll get a stretcher,' he said. 'Quicker to take her through my house than get the gates opened.'

'What happened?' he said to me when, a minute later, we were hurrying along in the wake of Alec and Glass's tame prisoner, who between them bore her into his house, with Nurse Pirrie trotting alongside still desperately trying to compress her stomach wound.

'Depressed skull and intestinal rupture,' said Nurse Pirrie.

'But what *happened*?' Dr Glass asked again.

'Tiddy or Arnold or both broke into the convent and tried to kill her,' I said. 'She's been hit on the head and stabbed.'

'And you caught them?' I shook my head. There was no time to explain about their abandoned camp and the intruder we thought was gone. Besides, the orderly and Alec had disappeared through a door in the panelling of the hallway and Glass followed them.

I hesitated for a second and then stepped through the doorway into darkness. I was in a tiny stone-lined chamber with a set of steps leading downwards to a dimly lit passageway. Already the stretcher was out of sight and my heart lurched, although I could not tell whether it was fear of being left alone here or fear of following them under the yard wall and up into the asylum.

'Dandy?' came Alec's voice, booming in the empty corridor, and my mind was made up. I started down the steps towards him, offering up a small prayer of my own for Sister Mary, and adding an inarticulate 'God help me' as the door at my back creaked and swung shut.

It was only a draught, I decided, when I got to the bottom of the short flight. A door at the far end had been opened. Gilverton is beset with these pairs of doors too, draughts pulling one open or pushing another one shut as the servants move about the house. We have lost one or two of the more fanciful type but there was no need to fear it, not even here, in a stone passage underground. It really was only a draught. And besides, the fearful things were waiting at the other end through the second door.

It appeared, at first glance, just like a hospital, with red floor paint and green wall paint and a line of chairs outside the door of a doctor's consulting room. It was only when I banged into one of these chairs and it didn't move, that I realised it was bolted to the floor. Rubbing my scraped shin, I slipped inside the room where the stretcher party had gone and was brought to a halt.

It *was* a doctor's consulting room, or at least the anteroom to one, but here one of the chairs had ankle straps and wrist straps, like unbuckled dog collars, and on a hook hung something like a shepherd's crook but with a little band to close the loop and hold a prisoner steady eight feet away from oneself. I averted my eyes and hurried in to where Mary was being moved from her stretcher onto an examination table.

Dr Glass had opened a medicine cabinet on the wall and

pulled out a large brown bottle with a rubber top. He crashed open a drawer and took a needle from a baize tray of them.

'Doctor?' said Nurse Pirrie.

'Sedative,' said Dr Glass. 'Keep her out while I work on her.'

'She's out,' said Nurse Pirrie. I had never in all my days at the convalescent home heard a nurse argue with a doctor that way.

'She needs to stay out,' said Dr Glass. 'If you can't help me you can wait elsewhere. Tom?'

Tom, the orderly, grabbed one of Sister Mary's arms and pushed her habit sleeve roughly back then he squeezed her hard just below her elbow and Dr Glass bent close to see the vein. He brushed my hand away, lifted the compress and bent even closer.

'It's a tiny nick,' he said. 'Worth trying.'

They worked fast, the pair of them. Dr Glass put two stitches deep inside Mary's body, then poured pints of iodine in after it, filling the wound, letting the foul liquid flow in a dark gush over the table and onto the floor. He followed it with what looked like pounds of some white powder and then began to stitch again with steady careful fingers. The bleeding slowed as he worked and when the last of the stitches was in place on her skin he barely needed to wipe away a single drop.

He took much more time over the head wound, pressing the sunken area carefully and asking us to be quiet while he listened, I supposed, for the sounds of broken skull grating.

'I think she's been lucky up this end,' he said at last. 'The bone is badly bruised but there's no fracture in the depression. Her ear though. I don't think I can save much of her ear.' He took up a pair of large shears and at last I had to turn away. I felt Alec's hand under my arm and smelled his pipe tobacco as my face was crushed against his coat.

'Get away back through to my house and put the kettle on,' Dr Glass said. 'Hot, sweet, strong tea. Tom, go with them and help. If you'll help me here, Nurse Pirrie.'

'I—' she said and Dr Glass took pity. 'Well, you go and take care of Mrs Gilver and leave Tom to help me here,' he said.

Nurse Pirrie nodded and the three of us left the doctor and his silent assistant.

'I can't think why I quailed at that,' said Nurse Pirrie when we were through the passageway and back in Dr Glass's hallway. 'Which way do you suppose the kitchen is?' she said, opening doors. 'I've never been in this house before. Only just at a garden party in the grounds one time.'

'It's because you know her,' I said. 'And are fond of her. I almost swooned.'

'Here we go,' said Alec, who had found the kitchen passage. 'You heard him, Dandy. Hot, sweet, strong tea.'

I filled the enormous iron kettle far too full and Dr Glass was back just as it boiled. He was grey-faced with exhaustion and I remembered Daff Udney saying that there had been trouble earlier on in the evening too, a poor soul in torment and the hospital in a state of alarm until he was quietened again. As I had the thought, I half-remembered something else, unsure whether it was something heard or seen, or a question I had meant to ask but forgotten. Too much had happened for any hope of remembering, I decided, and put the troubled feeling aside.

'How is she?' Nurse Pirrie asked Dr Glass.

'She needs someone to sit with her,' Dr Glass replied. 'I've left Tom there for a minute, but I'd rather you womenfolk went through. Take tea and I'll be back to relieve you just as soon as I've had a wee bit rest and rung St Mary's.'

'What a night for you, Dr Glass,' I said. 'How is Mr Molloy after all the upset?'

Dr Glass stared at me without comprehension and it

occurred to me that of course he had no idea we had met the Udneys and heard of the commotion at the hospital. I poured tea into a large, thick white cup, added two spoonfuls of sugar and followed Nurse Pirrie who was ahead of me.

'Second right past the room from before,' Dr Glass said in a weary voice as we were leaving.

'What's St Mary's?' I asked Nurse Pirrie when we were back behind the door in the panelling and making our way down the flight of stone stairs. This time, with no one opening the door at the far end, it did not creak shut and cut us off. I quaked at the memory of last time, nonetheless.

'The cottage hospital at Lanark,' she replied. 'But they'll not be moving her tonight.'

'I hate to think of all those men, though,' I said. 'And her lying there.'

'There's a bad fever at Lanark,' Nurse Pirrie said. 'She might come to more harm in St Mary's for all that. And the doors will be bolted and guarded between the clinic and where the men are.'

I said nothing.

We found her easily enough, for Dr Glass or his orderly had left the door ajar and a lamp glowing.

'Oh, Mary!' said Nurse Pirrie when we saw her, as stark and white as the pillow she rested on, as white as the bandage around her poor head. The dressing on her ear – I tried not to think of her ear – was not quite white, but rather pinkish from her blood and a little yellow from the iodine.

There were two seats in the room and we dragged one to each side of the bed and sank into them.

'Now, you mind and drink that tea down, Mrs Gilver,' Nurse Pirrie said. I did not need to be told twice and although it was sickeningly sweet I could feel it warming me and soothing me from the first sip. I gazed at Sister Mary, drinking in as well the sight of her calm face and clean bandage and the blessed movement, slowly up and down, of her breathing.

If only she were not so very pale I might have felt quite hopeful and I tried to remind myself of her customary pallor and not to attribute it to any sinister cause, for really there was no difference in the whiteness of her face which saw the sun when she was walking or working outside and the skin on her neck which never saw light, hidden under her wimple. I wondered how she would take the news that she had lain bareheaded but for a bandage, for me and Alec to see. Her hair made me think of the down of a duckling. It was as short as a boy's when the barber has trimmed it with clippers and a pure blue-black, the white of her scalp showing clearly. I finished my tea, set the cup down and reached out to stroke it. I had no idea if it would do any good but I kept the stroking up, gentle and rhythmic, and after five minutes her eyelids fluttered.

I looked up at Nurse Pirrie to see if she had noticed, but the poor woman had fallen asleep, half of her tea undrunk, as very shocked people sometimes do.

I stroked Mary's hair again, making sure not to let my hand stray near her dressings. Again, her eyes fluttered.

'Which one of them did this to you?' I murmured. 'And what did you ever do to either of them? Why would they attack you? Why would they come back after all these weeks?'

Even as I thought it, though, I knew I was making a mistake. They had been going back throughout the weeks. They had been searching for something and today they had found it. As to what it was and why it led to this, I had no idea and it hurt my aching head to wonder.

Perhaps I was adding two and two to get five, I thought to myself. Perhaps the thing they had found in Sister Steven's cupboard, the thing they hoped to sell if the sum scribbled on the wall was what we thought it was, had nothing to do with this attack. 'Attempted murder,' I corrected myself. Perhaps they were simply hiding in Sister Mary's study and then set upon her to get away.

But why would they go there rather than jump out of that open window. The study had doors, but they were all dead ends one way or another. A door to the chapel, one to the box room and one to the orphans' side. I shook my head to try to order my thoughts.

'Attempted murder,' I said again, thinking anger would help me stay alert and drive me towards answers. No one could have known Mary would survive such a blow to the head, never mind the wound in her stomach. In fact, it was still too soon to say.

I looked up at her face again. Her breathing seemed deeper and her eyes moved rapidly under her lids. I took her hand. How did it go . . .? 'Hail Mary full of grace,' I whispered. 'The Lord is with thee. Blessed art thou amongst women.' Hugh would have twenty fits if he could hear me. 'Something something fruit of thy womb. Holy Mary Mother of God, pray for us sinners now and at the hour of our death.'

'Amen,' she murmured. It was scarcely more than a breath, and it stilled *my* breath in my throat.

'Hail Mary,' I said again.

'Grace,' she breathed.

'Mary, can you hear me?' I said, a little louder. Nurse Pirrie snorted in her sleep but did not waken.

'Bless,' she said.

I did not understand everything the doctors were discovering these days about the brain and the mind, and what the difference between those two things might be, but I knew enough not to get too excited yet. She had repeated these words countless times a day for countless years and they were probably automatic to her.

'Mary, can you hear me?'

'Lord.'

'Can you say your name?'

'Mary.' I cursed myself for saying it to her, but before I could think up another question she spoke again. 'Cold.' I chafed her hand. 'Usher.'

'Usher?' I said.

'Arsher. Mary. Cold. Arsher.'

I was silenced. 'If these were her dying words then, just like Mother Mary before her, she was speaking in some kind of code and I could not decipher it. She took her deepest breath yet.

'Marygold Arsher.'

A wave swept up over my body as though a giant brush had taken a swipe at me. She was answering!

'Marigold Archer?' I said. 'Was that your name when you were a girl?'

A tiny frown plucked at her brow.

'Usher,' she said.

'Marigold Usher,' I repeated and the frown was gone. I stroked her hand for a moment to let her rest and then tried again. 'Who hurt you, Sister Mary?'

'Sister,' she said, very faintly. I stared at her. One of the sisters had attacked her. Or was she echoing my words?

'Who did this?' I asked her.

'Mother,' she murmured. There was a long pause. 'Mary.' That was even fainter, just a curl in her breathing.

'Mother Mary?'

Then she spoke so softly and let the word trail away so gently that I could not tell what it was. 'Gone', it might have been or 'God' and I did not know which was more pitiful: that even now grief had assailed her at the thought that her beloved Reverend Mother had gone or that, asked who did this, she replied that it was God's will.

I decided to go back to offering comfort instead of interrogating her.

'Hail Mary, full of grace,' I began again. 'The Lord is with thee.'

I said it ten times before my exhaustion took over and I slipped into a doze. Ten Hail Marys is no doubt the punishment for some negligible sin. It was not punishment enough for my stupidity in not understanding what she was trying to tell me.

24

I woke, frozen and stiff, with my head on the sheet and Sister Mary's hand resting in mine, hardly aware of where I was or what had startled me.

'Mercy!' said Nurse Pirrie suddenly, sitting bolt upright in her chair as a door banged somewhere close by. It was still dark but the lamp over Mary's bed burned on. I peered at her and saw her chest lift and fall.

Dr Glass, still in his cardigan and carpet slippers, had come in the door followed by Alec, grey-faced and dishevelled, with his hair sticking up.

'What time is it?' I croaked.

'Four,' said Alec.

Dr Glass came over and bent close to the bed. 'Well, isn't that something?' he said, beaming. 'Look at that.' Nurse Pirrie already had Sister Mary's wrist pinched in her grip taking a pulse and a smile as wide as the doctor's spread over her face. 'I might have fussed on and upset her if I hadn't fallen asleep over my whisky. It's for the best.'

'I'll go straight down to St Ultan's and tell them she's better and resting,' Alec said.

'She woke up,' I said. 'Tell them she woke and was speaking, Alec.'

'Speaking?' said Dr Glass. 'Are you sure, Mrs Gilver? Are you sure you weren't dreaming?'

'She said her name and a few words of a prayer,' I told him, and he seemed willing to believe that much.

'Could she tell you anything about what happened?' said Alec. 'Did you ask?'

'I did but she was muddled,' I said. 'She spoke of Mother Mary and God and her sisters. Nothing useful.'

'But good reason to rejoice,' said Nurse Pirrie. 'You go and tell them, Mrs Gilver. And I'll wait here with Sister Mary.'

She was as croaky as I was and she had just as much blood on her uniform, odd without the apron, as I had on my coat and skirt, but the temptation was stronger than I could bear, to go to St Ultan's, wash and undress and crawl into my narrow, hard little bed for an hour or two before one of Sister Abigail's breakfasts.

'Come on, Dandy,' Alec said. 'Poor things down there with the phone line cut. They'll not want to ask me everything they could ask you.'

I nodded and got to my feet, easing myself up with some groans to help. I squeezed Sister Mary's hand and brushed her hair softly one last time.

'Black as pitch,' said Nurse Pirrie, pulling at one of her own iron-grey curls. 'Same since she was a child.'

'Should we cover it?' I asked. 'Will she be mortified to wake and find that she's bareheaded.'

'Not in her sickbed,' said Nurse Pirrie. 'Nuns are very practical people underneath it all.'

'And I'm forbidding any use of that blessed contraption over her dressings anyway,' said Dr Glass. 'I don't approve of them at the best of times, half-blinding them like blinkered ponies and giving them stiff necks like billy-o. The weight of the veil has to be felt to be believed.'

We stopped in a little sluice room to let me wash the blood from my hands. Alec had cleaned his own and sponged his coat already. When we came out into the passageway again Tom, the orderly, was lurking, looking more disreputable than ever. Alec gave him a polite nod as we passed but the man cleared his throat and stepped forward.

'The doctor said you found the hideout,' he said. 'His voice was soft and yet strained as though he did not much use it. 'And so you might be close to finding the men. Would you like to tell young Tony that?'

'Good grief, that's right,' said Alec, turning back. 'It went out of my mind completely.'

'Alec, we're supposed to be taking news to the sisters,' I reminded him.

'I could take you through to have a bit of a chat with him now, if you like,' the orderly went on. 'He's always up with the lark and it's quiet this time of day.'

'Ten minutes won't make a difference, Dan,' Alec said.

'Through?' I echoed. I glanced towards the door leading along the passage to the doctor's house and then at the other, much stouter, that closed off the clinic from the part of the hospital where the men were housed. It was as unsettling as St Ultan's, with the convent and orphanage and chapel: everything separated and yet still linked together.

'Will you come with me, Dandy?' Alec said. 'I'd like you to meet him and see for yourself. Dan? Are you listening?'

I blinked and shook my head. 'Sorry,' I said, 'I was thinking of something, or trying to anyway . . . I'm still half asleep. What were you asking me?'

'I don't wonder after the night you've had, madam,' said the orderly. 'Drooped over like that. I looked in a couple of times to see if you needed anything and I thought to myself – that'll be a stiff neck in the morning.'

I smiled repressively; the smile my mother used on chatty hansom cab drivers and pushy flower-sellers. I did not like to think of him looking in on me while I slept.

'I was saying, come with me to meet Tony Gourlay,' Alec said.

'And I'll bring you a pot of tea,' said Tom. 'Or I can bring it through to the doctor's parlour if you'd rather, tuck you up on the sofa there.'

It was the thought of being tucked up by this peculiar little man – although I doubt he had meant it literally – that spurred me on to accept Alec's offer and a minute later we were waiting while Tom picked over a bouquet of large keys and opened the first of the doors into the hospital proper.

It still bore the marks of having once been a family home. There was an air of splendour about the arched doorways and the stone architraves, not to my taste and reeking of Victorian sentiment, but much more lavish than the builders of a hospital would have gone in for. We followed Tom across a hall out of which rose a splendid winding staircase, looking odd now with its linoleum covering and a plain, white-glass gas lamp hanging in place of any kind of chandelier. At the far side was the old dining hall, arched overhead like a room in a castle and with a fireplace large enough to roast an ox. Along at the other end was a pair of French windows, their glass now barred but their stone surrounds as grand as ever and, in the winks of approaching daylight they let into this gloomy chamber, two men dressed in rough work clothes were sitting with early tea and the first cigarettes of the day. The steam and the smoke rose in four slow drifts and the tableau was a peaceful one. For the first time I saw that Hopekist Head might not be the dread Bedlam I had imagined, but instead a sanctuary and a haven.

One of the men turned at our footsteps and then said, in the voice of a local, 'Here's your friend again, Tony boy.'

'Mr Molloy,' said Alec. 'Hello, Tony, old chap.'

'Oh!' I said, and then could find no way forward. I had met this man's son and I knew more about him than he could surely want me to. He was the wife-killer. I took a step backwards.

'Here's Dandy, Tony,' Alec said. 'Remember I was telling you? Mrs Gilver?'

I had never heard him so gentle before, and I had heard him very gentle. I could not bring myself to rush away from a friend he treated with such tenderness and so, setting my mind against the knowledge of Mr Molloy's past – for surely he must be docile now or they would hardly let him sit here unrestrained, I moved forward to greet Tony Gourlay.

'I've heard a great deal about you,' I said. 'How do you do?'

Alec drew out a chair and I sat, then Tom went bustling off, presumably to fetch our tea. I bristled with the thought that we were now sitting unguarded with two lunatics inside an asylum. I could feel a stain rise up on the skin of my throat as my body refused to bend to the will of my conventional, polite, brain.

'We've got news for you, Tony,' Alec said. 'I really don't think you'll be tried for the fire on Christmas Eve. There's been another break-in and an attack on another nun.'

'What nun?' said Molloy, starting forward in his seat. I shrank back in mine a little.

'Sister Mary,' Alec said, putting out a calming hand. 'Don't upset yourself. I'm sorry I said it so baldly.' He turned back to Gourlay again. 'Clear evidence of your innocence, I'd say. You'll be left in peace now.'

I watched Tony Gourlay for signs that he understood or even that he was listening, but he continued to smoke his cigarette, held curled in his hand like a working man hiding it from the foreman, and he did not look at Alec, much less at me.

'Is she dead?' said George Molloy.

'She survived,' I told him.

'And the rest of them? Sister—? Are they all safe?'

'They are,' I assured him.

'Good,' said Molloy. 'That was a bad business. Who'd hurt a nun?'

He spoke as calmly and conventionally as anyone else I could imagine and I struggled to repress the question on my lips: who would hurt his wife?

As though he read my thoughts, Molloy went on: 'The nuns at St Ultan's brought my wife up from a tiny baby, you know. My poor dear wife loved them all.'

'I did know,' I said. And, I thought to myself, now they are bringing up your son.

'Tiddy and Arnold have run away,' Alec said. 'They're gone, Tony. They were hiding out in one of the buildings down at the old mine but they're gone now.'

'What?' said Molloy. 'Hidden for six weeks? Someone's having you on. The same someone that let them out and then swore blind they escaped.'

Again, what struck me about him was how rational he seemed. It was exactly the question that had been troubling me: how *did* Arnold and Tiddy stay hidden so long; how did they get past a padlocked gate and a wire-topped fence; and what did they live on? Then another question bubbled up from deep inside me.

'It's got stuck on them like it got stuck on me, has it?' Molloy was saying, distracting me.

'What?' said Alec.

'They've never done this!' he exclaimed. His voice was a just a touch too loud and that was the first inkling of trouble. 'It's got put on them and there it'll stick. Just like me.' He lunged forward suddenly. 'I never killed my Rose, missus. I never lifted a hand to her. I was proud of her. Clever as a bag of monkeys, she was. She saw everything, my Rose. Saw it all and lost her life for it.'

'What do you mean, Mr Molloy?' I said. I was more than half-sure all of this was just the raving of a long-locked-up madman, but I could not resist the vague hint nevertheless. For there were certainly secrets to be known somewhere.

'She never told me,' he said. 'Said it was safer for me not to know. Knew me too well, how I talk when I had a drink on me. She wouldn't say, but she went out that night. Into the lion's den, to right a wrong, she said. She was brave and true, my Rose. There's women as brave as any soldier, you know. Made of honour and iron. I've met two at least in my life and both of them have torn my heart in two.'

'Two?' I said.

'My Rose and—' he stopped himself. 'More than two. All of the nuns. Every one of them.'

But he couldn't possibly mean that all of the nuns had torn his heart. I wondered whose name he had bitten down upon before it escaped him. Could it possibly have been Mother Mary? Did he know something?

'On Christmas Eve,' I began. 'Where were you when the breakout began?'

'Breakout!' he said. 'That'll be right. As if I'd sit here with men out, making trouble for the sisters. As if I'd just sit in my cell and let them! I knew nothing of it. I knew nothing this time just like when my Rose was taken. Nothing! She went to right a wrong. And I never saw her again.'

'There, there,' Alec said. 'Don't upset yourself.'

I happened to be looking at Tony Gourlay as Alec spoke, and I saw in his face the first spark of life. His look sharpened for a fraction of a second, with amusement or its bitter cousin, before turning blank again. He must have heard so many bland attempts at consolation over the years. He must be sick to his teeth of people dismissing his terrors even while they pretended to sympathise. I had always thought the worst of madness must be the loneliness of no one believing you when you yourself believed – nay, *knew* – that all your demons were real. I decided to ignore his bravado regarding how he might have stopped a breakout if only he had known, and concentrate instead on the old horror that must surely underlie all his ramblings.

'How awful for you, Mr Molloy,' I said. 'Did she really say no more than just that?' He turned to me with a watchful look on his face. Perhaps sympathetic visitors just as often pretended to believe his ravings as they dismissed them. 'Did you understand what she meant by "the lion's den"?'

I had decided to treat his story as I did anything anyone ever told us while we were detecting. I would winkle out as much of the detail as I could and try to work it into what we already knew. That way, I thought, he might feel that for once he was properly being listened to. In point of fact, as I made this swift decision, I felt myself swell with pride, and not being a nun I felt no shame on the heels of my pridefulness.

'St Ultan's,' he said. 'It was the nuns she was going to. She told me that. "I've worked it out, Geordie," she said. "They're all the same." And then she kissed our lad lying in his cradle and went out and that was the last time I saw her living.'

'All the nuns?' I said. 'What a tantalising thing to be left with, Mr Molloy. Did no one ever manage to work out what she meant? When you told them?'

'No one listens to me, madam,' he said. 'No one's listened to me since they found her.' He ground out his cigarette and finished his tea with a smack of his lips. 'Found her in the outhouse the next morning, her throat slit to the back with my razor and her ring finger cut off. Found her wedding ring in my coat, hanging on a hook on the back of the lobby door and the baby outside in the yard in his pram bawling his head off. Woke the neighbour and she went for the constable. Nobody's listened to me since.'

He had started rocking to and fro as he got through this grisly tale and, as Tom approached with the tray of tea, the rocking grew faster and the arc of it wider until it looked as though George Molloy might tip right off his chair.

'Now, now,' said Tom. 'What's all this?'

'It was the nuns,' said Molloy. 'Killed her and stole the baby. Cut off her finger to get to the ring. Left the baby out in the cold. Witches they are. Witches and devils. They're

278

all the same. I've got to save her. I've got to get her away before they kill her too. Honour like iron. Stronger than me.'

Tom put the tray down out of his reach and then with a gentle hand under one elbow he helped Molloy up out of his seat and drew him away. We could hear the babbling long after they left the room, fainter and fainter until at last a door closed and left silence.

'Gosh,' I said. 'Poor chap. He really believes all of that, doesn't he?'

'Every word,' said Alec. Then he looked at Tony Gourlay, who was smoking his cigarette down to the last pinch. 'I hope that didn't upset you too much, old man?'

Tony might have been floating in a rowing boat on an empty lake for all the concern he showed about the scene around him. For some reason I found his sanguinity intensely annoying. Poor George Molloy at least suffered, even if his sojourn at Hopekist Head had begun with an act of wickedness and Gourlay himself had never harmed a fly, if one did not count Germans anyway.

'Good to meet you, Mr Gourlay,' I said, standing. 'Until we meet again then.'

Tony Gourlay took my hand and bowed over it very slightly. I had no way of knowing whether this intercourse was unusual for him but I saw Alec's eyes widen.

'Did you really see a monster?' I asked, keeping hold of his fingers in mine. He raised his eyes and again I saw that small spark of interest in them. 'On Christmas Eve when you were outside the gates,' I went on. '*Did* you see a monster?'

Of course, I did not expect him to answer me. Even when he opened his lips and wetted them with the tip of his tongue I thought perhaps he was just getting rid of the last dryness from his cigarette paper – he really had smoked it down to nothing and that can leave one's lips most uncomfortable.

My mouth dropped open and my eyes grew wide as the words drifted out in a whisper on his breath.

'They're all the same.'

Alec was beside himself.

'I must telephone to his sister immediately,' he said, charging through Dr Glass's house towards the motorcar parked at the door. 'This is tremendous. Not only have we established his innocence – in a matter of days, Dandy! – but he has spoken again. Twice in a few weeks! I wonder who it was he spoke to first time. It wasn't Dr Glass, I know that much. Perhaps it was Cinty Udney. Perhaps all he needs is some female companionship; in which case, his sisters could come and put up at a hotel in Lanark and be here with him every day. Hurry up, Dan! Let's get to St Ultan's to their telephone.'

'It's broken,' I reminded him.

'Oh, rot!' said Alec. 'It's only a cut wire. I can bodge that together in no time.'

'And it can't have been Cinty Udney he spoke to when he got back to the hospital,' I pointed out, 'because she was at her father's deathbed.'

'Well, all right then. It's not the woman angle,' Alec said, leaping into the motorcar and starting up the engine. 'But would you be willing to come back and sit with him to see if it's you in particular?'

'For as long as we're here,' I said. 'And always assuming I shan't run into George Molloy again. But we'll be on our way now, won't we?'

'Will we?' said Alec.

'The case is solved,' I said. 'Tiddy and Arnold have taken off and won't bother the nuns any more. It's up to the police to track them down and bring them to book for the attack on Sister Mary. And your work is certainly done, isn't it? Gourlay's head is out of the noose.'

'That's true,' Alec said. 'Look!' We were cresting the hill at the head of the long low descent across the moor to the convent and we could see, from our vantage point, a pair of horses, their breath pluming and their flanks steaming in the frosty morning. Their owner, just at that minute, was hitching them to the little hired motorcar in the ditch where we had left it the previous evening. The farmer, as I guessed this to be – the ever helpful Mr MacAllie – shouted and waved his switch and the chains straightened and then strained as the horses paddled their hooves. Then with a rush the bumper dropped and the wheels were back on the hard-packed earth of the track. The horses trotted on a few yards with the car rumbling behind them before the farmer pulled them up and went to work to set them loose.

'Perfect timing,' Alec said. 'If you let me off I can follow you down to Waterside and return the ladies' car.'

'Stopping off at St Ultan's with the good news first,' I reminded him.

'No need,' he said, pointing again. Two of the sisters were trudging towards us, heads bent and hands hidden in their sleeves. I remembered Molloy's frantic words – 'they're all the same' – and Tony Gourlay's soft echo of them.

'What did you make of what he chose to say?' I asked Alec.

'Tony? Nothing. I thought he was just repeating what he'd heard Molloy telling him.'

'And so what about his words that other night?' I went on. 'Do you think it could be the same again? That he was repeating what someone told him? Some chance remark he had heard?'

'It's a thought,' said Alec. 'But who?'

Before we could discuss it any further, we drew close to the two nuns, who revealed themselves to be Sister John and Sister Steven.

'Great good news, sisters,' I shouted, hanging out of the

side window to hail them. 'She woke up and spoke to us, but she's sleeping comfortably now. We were just on our way to tell you.'

'Thanks be to God!' called both of them in chorus.

'Thanks be to Nurses Matt and Pirrie and Dr Glass,' muttered Alec.

'Don't, darling,' I muttered back. 'Look at them. They've been on their knees all night, I'll wager.'

I had never seen any of the St Ultan's sisters look so bedraggled. The knees of their habits were dusty and their veils were hanging crooked and crumpled. Neither of them wore a scapula and Sister John had a rough cloak over her habit, while Sister Steven seemed to have borrowed a gentleman's overcoat.

'Would you like us to take you up?' Alec said, hanging out of his own window as we neared them.

'Not a bit of it,' shouted Sister Steven. 'We are praying as we go and we don't want it cut short. But thank you.'

'The police have been,' said Sister John, stopping to rest with a hand in the small of her back as we drew level. 'Finally! The Miss Udneys set off right after you two left us to go and summon them, but it took until half an hour ago for McLintock to show his face and there's been no sign of Gibb yet.'

'No loss,' said Sister Steven, who had evidently settled back into her customary mood of cold sourness after the upsets of the night.

'And is Sister Mary to be taken to St Mary's in Lanark or is she to be looked after at Hopekist Head until she comes home?' said Sister Steven.

'To her sisters,' said Alec. 'Such a lot of Marys and sisters in this case,' he said. Sister Steven glared at him and even Sister John gave him a rather penetrating look. He rubbed his hands over his face and smiled. 'Forgive me, Sisters. I've been up all night and I'm rather foggy.'

'We've all been up all night, young man,' said Sister Steven, 'but not all of us have had Dr Glass's decanter at our elbow.'

'More's the pity,' said Sister John, and when Sister Steven swung round to glare at her, she stuck her tongue out. It was so unexpected that Alec and I both laughed, quite loudly, and Sister Steven, with a murderous set to her jaw, stumped away before we could apologise.

'Poor thing,' said Sister John in parting. 'She feels responsible. Having the papers in her cupboard all these years and never getting round to sorting them out so that now she has no idea what was stolen. She's feeling it dreadfully and she can't even confess it for it's no sin.' She tucked her hands away in her sleeves again and made as though to leave us.

'Wait a moment, Sister,' I said. 'What did you just say? I thought the papers had only been moved into Sister Steven's cupboard after the fire?'

'Oh yes, that's right,' said John. 'The newer papers. But the old ones – ancient old stuff from when we had just begun. Well, we moved some of that in there a few years back to relieve the strain on the little records room, you know? Why, Mrs Gilver? Why does that trouble you?'

I shook my head. 'I can hardly say,' I told her. 'Just sorting through the facts and putting them in order. I won't keep you, Sister. Give my best regards to Sister Mary if she's awake when you get there.'

'Is that true?' said Alec when we were once more on our way. '*Do* you know why that little morsel bothered you?'

'Alec, I'm shocked,' I said. 'Are you suggesting I would lie to a nun?'

He gave a gruff laugh and said nothing for a moment. When he spoke again it was on another subject altogether. 'They're not nuns,' he said. 'Dr Glass mentioned it last night.'

'*What?*'

Alec laughed more heartily. 'Nuns are the ones in enclosed

orders who pray all day and never see anyone,' he said. 'These are religious sisters. Quite different, you see.'

'I do see,' I said. 'But I disagree. I'm with Molloy and Gourlay on this point, Alec: they're all the same.'

Alec nodded absent-mindedly and began to whistle under his breath but he had only got a few bars out when his whistling grew quiet and stopped. 'You talk quite often of a feeling of something just out of sight, just out of earshot,' he said.

'Ah,' I chipped in. 'You've got that too, have you?'

'Very much so, just at the moment,' said Alec. 'It's like . . . have you ever had rats?'

'What do you mean "had rats"?' I asked.

'In the trenches,' he said, and I grew very quiet and still as I always did, even after so many years, on the rare occasions when he spoke of the war. 'In the trenches, the rats were almost worse than the shelling. And I grew to loathe that moment when I entered a bunkroom or one of the offices, telegraph office or what have you, and had to light the lamp to see them all just sitting there.' He shuddered and I joined him. 'So we got in the habit of banging doors open and stamping in. Hearing the scuttle was bad enough but at least they were out of sight when the lamp started glowing. The most we ever saw was the last bit of a tail tip disappearing.

'And that's what I feel like now. As though every time I turn round I just see the last wisp skittering out of sight.'

'I know what you mean,' I said. 'Only we're not stamping and crashing. Or not deliberately anyway. I'd love to see the whole rat sitting on the table where I could get a look at it but no matter how stealthily I creep in, it's too fast for me.'

'Exactly,' Alec said. 'Someone has said something to us.'

'At least *one* someone and at least *one* something,' I agreed. 'I rather think that a whole bevy of someones have each handed us a little glittering piece of metal. And if we fit them together properly we'll find we've made a key.'

'Rather poetic today, aren't you Dan?' Alec said.

'Better than rats,' I said stoutly. 'Now let me down here and I'll drive the other car to the Udneys. If we catch up with MacAllie and his horse we can thank him. Have you got a half-crown handy?'

'I've got a shilling,' said Alec. 'If you want him to have a half-crown for ten minutes' work, be my guest.'

But Mr MacAllie, busy famer that he was, had made good speed and was nowhere to be seen on the road. I swept past the gate to his farmyard and on past the drive to his house, where all was still in darkness, and carried on down to Waterside, into the trees, over the bridge and sharply in at the gateway. It was a testament to my poor night's sleep at Mary's bedside and the fact that I had drunk not a single sip of the pot of tea Tom had brought me, that I only realised what I had seen once I was past it. Alec, despite the whisky, was not so dull-witted; he spotted it in time and sailed past the entrance to the drive to go and investigate. I, hesitant to back out onto the road, left the motorcar and went on foot.

A short distance along the road towards the village proper, just before the first of the straggle of cottages, a small knot of people – among them Sgt Gibb – was gathered looking into the hedgerow. A couple of the women had their hands over their mouths and when a small child toddled up it was shooed away like a hen from the kitchen.

Alec parked and jumped down, striding over with such a confident air that everyone gathered, even Gibb himself, turned slightly towards him as though for guidance. Alec turned and looked at whatever had drawn their attentions and then, glancing over his shoulder at me, he beckoned me with a great sweep of his arm.

'Dandy, you won't believe it,' he called. 'Hurry.'

25

I was already trotting but at his words I broke into a fully fledged run, my mind dancing and scattering over a nightmare mix of dreadful possibilities. Fire, scrawled oaths, abandoned infants, precious documents thrown into the muddy puddles of the roadside ditch, or another injured sister – for some reason Francis and Jude were worrying me, perhaps because the place they left their bicycles must be near here somewhere. When I arrived at Alec's side and turned to look at the sight drawing such a crowd even this early in the day I had my eyes half-closed in a kind of pre-emptive wince.

It took a second or two to understand what I was seeing and then they opened wider than ever in my life before. Or, I rather think, since.

At the side of the lane there was a hedgerow, of the usual muddled, Scottish kind. Not the centuries-deep wall of roots and litter one finds in the south but a shallow ditch choked with brambles and hopeful saplings and behind it a straggle of hawthorn and gorse serving to mark off the start of the field beyond. At the point where the crowd had gathered was a thin patch, perhaps where a hawthorn had been damaged and left to die in the winter wet – I am something of an expert in the management of hedges after all my years with Hugh – and in the gap lay a pair of legs in sodden, striped trousers, feet in rough black boots. I glanced at Alec, who glanced at Sgt Gibb. Gibb nodded, giving us permission, and Alec handed me over the ditch to take a closer look.

There was a ripple of disapproval from a few of the house-wives and I sought to reassure them.

'I am a detective,' I said. 'I have seen worse than this in my time.' They stared stolidly back at me, ruddy cheeks turned a peculiar shade of blue by their disgust and their colourless eyes rendered even more colourless by the frowns drawn down above them. This little gaggle happened to have none of the white skin and speedwell, I noticed, and their hair was shades of mouse and ginger, not the shining blue-black of so many other locals. Perhaps they were all sisters and lived in adjoining cottages nearby. I gave a smile, unre-turned, and then applied my attention to the ground at my feet.

He was quite dead; that was clear without any taking of pulses. He lay on his back with his mouth wide open and I could see that the inside of it had dried and his tongue grown wooden in the hours since he fell. I looked away. Even the sight to be seen on the front of his rough, striped coat was better than that. The blood had spread over his chest in a perfect circle, like a flower. A chrysanthemum was my fanciful thought, from the rusted colour of it and the way it had puckered up the cloth as it froze.

'Suicide?' I asked Alec, for in one of the man's flung-out hands there was a pistol, still gently held in his curled fingers.

'In his chest?' said Alec. 'Here at the side of the road?' His words made me look about myself, for any sign of what brought the man to this spot and when I did I saw something that made me gasp.

'No!' I said. 'Surely.'

Halfway across the field, there was another mound of that same dark and light striped cloth, just visible from where we stood, although hidden from the lower level of the road. Alec and I made our way towards it, stumbling in frozen ruts left by cattle's feet.

This one was face down, the frosted chrysanthemum on

his back and the pistol flung from his grasp as he fell. His fingers were dug into the earth although his feet in their rough boots lay slackly pigeon-toed.

'Did anyone hear the shots?' I shouted back to the crowd of villagers. It had grown by two or three and men among them.

'Aye,' one of the men shouted. 'We thought it was maybe the polis.'

'Hoped it was,' said another.

'They saved us the bother,' said Sgt Gibb. 'I'll still need to get onto Lanark, mind. Maybe Glasgow.'

Alec had crouched down at the side of the corpse and was feeling about underneath him, with a grimace of distaste on his face.

'I wish I could turn him over and get into his pockets,' he said.

'Why?' I could not imagine many things I would like to do less than search the pockets of either man. 'Why not search the other one? At least he's face up. I wonder which is which.'

'I'd lay bets that this is Arnold,' Alec said. 'The wily one. And that's Tiddy by the gap in the hedge. The mild one. I think Arnold was running away with the loot.'

'What loot?' I said.

'Exactly,' said Alec. 'Whatever it was they searched for in the convent on Christmas Eve and kept going back for and finally found. Is Gibb watching?'

'Not closely,' I told him. 'He's trying to shoo away the onlookers but he does keep glancing. Oh, but here's Constable McLintock. That's that then.'

McLintock got rid of all the bystanders: village men, women and children and then Alec and me. He even went so far as to leave Sgt Gibb standing guard while he went to organise an Inspector and the Fiscal and stretcher men from the mortuary, as though double murders were quite a part of his daily round.

There was nothing left for us to do but trail back to Waterside to return the Udneys' car. Cinty and Daff were standing at the front door when we arrived.

'Ah, sorry,' I said. 'You must have been wondering why I abandoned a motorcar halfway down your drive. Let me explain.'

'What? Oh, yes of course,' Cinty said. 'But actually, we've had a telegram to say that Bena is on her way. She's on the milk train and should be here any minute.'

'We shall leave you to your reunion,' said Alec, lifting his hat and stepping back. I began to shuffle aside too, horribly conscious that the unfortunate Bena was coming home to a house without her father, having missed his funeral.

'No!' said Daff. 'Not at all. Come in and tell us the news of Sister Mary. I mean, we've rung up Dr Glass already and we know she's comfortable, but he says you sat with her, Mrs Gilver. Tell us everything. We're so fond of Sister Mary – as we were of her Mother before her.'

'Daff!' said Cinty. 'Her Mother before her?'

Daff giggled. 'I'm beginning to sound like a proper old maid,' she said. 'The three of us together here are months from bath chairs and ear trumpets. But do come in, Mrs Gilver and Mr Osborne.'

I could smell coffee, rich and delicious wafting through the house and was powerless to resist any further.

'I'm afraid we have some more shocking news to relate,' I said, as we went inside and back to the dining room where we had been served luncheon. Either this terrifically modern house did not possess a breakfast room or the Udneys in their retrenchment had stopped using it. 'Although there is relief in it too.'

Daff Udney poured us both a cup of coffee from a tall pot sitting over a burner on the sideboard and then raised her eyebrows with polite interest.

'They've found Arnold and Tiddy,' Alec said. Daff went

to stand behind Cinty's chair and put a reassuring hand on her shoulder.

'See?' she said. 'I told you you were safe. Do you know, I had to sleep on the sofa at the bottom of Cinty's bed last night, Mr Osborne? She was convinced the pair of them were creeping around the house trying to break in.' She shook her sister fondly and dropped a kiss on the parting of her hair.

'Well, actually,' Alec said, 'they were found not far away at all. Between here and the village.'

'Between here and the Stop?' said Cinty, her face draining. 'Right outside?'

'Dead,' I said. It is not usually a comforting remark to contribute but in this instance it did wonders for Cinty Udney. She sat back in her chair and let her hands drop from the table edge until they hung straight down.

'Both of them?' said Daff.

'They seem to have shot one another,' said Alec. 'I know it sounds like something from the Wild West pictures, but they do appear to have shot one another.'

'Where did they get guns?' said Cinty, in an awestruck voice. I felt a blush creep across my cheeks for of course that question should have occurred to me instantly.

'A pair of pistols,' Alec said. 'Army issue. Well kept but older than the last war. I wondered myself.'

'Oh no,' said Daff. 'I think I know exactly where they got them.'

'Was that what they stole from the convent last night?' I said. 'Pistols?'

Daff looked almost pleased at my mistake, which was odd.

'If only,' she said. 'But the only person I can think of anywhere around who owns a pair of old service pistols is . . . Well, it's Dr Glass, I'm afraid.'

'But he surely would have checked—' I said.

'Of course,' said Daff.

'And he surely would have told the police—' I went on.

'He surely *should* have,' said Cinty. 'It's unforgivable of him to keep it quiet. I feel quite . . . he *knew* how frightened I was. And he never said a word.' She looked like a small child who had just had a treat taken away and I wondered how deep her feelings went regarding Dr Glass and how sharp a shock it was to find out that he had been careless towards her.

'Stupid man!' said Daff. 'The hospital will never survive this. All those poor patients!'

At that moment, their maidservant entered the room with a laden breakfast tray.

'Oh my,' said Daff. 'We don't run to silver chafing dishes these days. Maggie just brings us two plates and a rack of toast, I'm afraid. You wouldn't go and get two more, Maggie dear, would you? Some extra bacon and a couple more eggs if the hens have been kind.'

'I wouldn't hear of it,' I began, but Alec had smelled food and there was no shifting him.

So it was that he and I were there to witness Verbena Udney returning home. I heard nothing and Alec was applying himself with his usual fervour to his plate, but Daff and Cinty both suddenly raised their heads and then stood up. I supposed that they knew the noises of this house very well – if houses as new as Waterside had noises – and they recognised the sounds of arrival.

'Darlings?' came a voice from the hall.

'Darling!' called back the two sisters. They threw down their napkins and made for the door, which was flung open before they reached it. I had a brief glimpse of a raven-haired elfin little figure, wrapped in furs and shod in stout travelling boots, and then Daff and Cinty engulfed her in a hug and stood shrieking with tears and laughter; a startling spectacle for three Scottish sisters to mount even in an empty room, unbelievable before witnesses. Alec gaped and I joined him.

At last the three of them broke apart and Bena Udney caught sight of us.

'Hello,' she said, coming forward, her blue eyes very bright and bird-like in her ruddy face. 'You must think us mad. Let me explain. I'm—'

'They know,' said Daff. 'Mr Osborne, Mrs Gilver. Let me present my sister, Verbena. Bean, these are detectives.'

Verbena opened her eyes very wide at that and I could see the telltale signs of foreign travel and neglectful toilet. The white lines around her eyes attested that her face had been as pale as Daff's before it was burned by the Indian sun.

'Detectives?' she said. 'What have you been hiding from me? Don't tell me you can't find a will?'

'Bean!' said Cinty.

'Oh, I know I should be sniffing into a lavender hankie,' said Verbena. 'But it's been nearly two months and he was over eighty. *Is* there trouble with the will?'

'Not a scrap,' said Daff. 'Isn't she awful?' she put in, in an aside to Alec and me. 'He's left us everything in thirds. You, darling, own a third of not much, and the interest off even less.'

'So why the detectives?' said Verbena, plumping down.

All four of us drew deep breaths and wondered where to begin.

It was not our story to tell, I decided, at least not to the third Udney sister, and so we withdrew from their reunion, pleading the attention we owed the nuns and the desperate need for shaving things and toothbrushes.

Daff showed us to the door alone; Cinty being too overcome by her sister's presence to tear herself away even for that long.

'She feels things most dreadfully,' Daff said. 'If Dr Glass really does get shut down over this she'll go into the slump of slumps. We'll have to try to get her away for a while and cheer her up.'

'India?' I said.

Daff laughed rather harshly. 'Heavens, if she saw the poor little children on the streets and those wretched skinny cows everywhere she would lie down on the ground and die crying,' she said. 'No, I was thinking more of Brighton or somewhere. Normandy if we could run to it. Away from moors, and quarries and forests and mines.' She sighed. 'I love my home, but it hasn't been very lovable just lately.'

'Miss Udney,' I said. 'You've just reminded me. Here's something I meant to ask you last night.' She waited, looking just a little nervous. 'What made you go to the mine office?'

'What?' she said. 'Well, we didn't set out to go to the office. It's just that we saw the board off the window.'

'But what made you go into the mine works at all?' I asked.

'Oh!' she said, smiling. 'I see. Didn't I tell you? Well, there it is, as I've just been saying. Cinty thought she saw a dog. She was convinced she saw a terrier slipping under the fence and she wouldn't rest until we went to see if it was a stray. I told her it was bound to be a fox, but that's Cinty all over, you see. She does feel things so terribly.' She looked back over her shoulder fondly. 'Yes, I really do think I shall try to get her away.'

'Permanently?' Alec said. 'Might you sell up and go?'

'I'd miss the orphans,' said Daff. 'And the sisters. But I'm sure they have both along with sunshine and sea air in Normandy.' Then she sniffed and smacked her hands together. 'We shan't rush off. We need to see how Sister Mary goes on. And we need to be here to lend voices of support to poor Dr Glass once the village gets wind of this last bit of scandal.'

'And they will, won't they?' I said. 'The bush telegraph at Carstairs Stop is better than any I've known.'

'What did you mean by that?' Alec said, as we walked back to the motorcar. 'About the jungle drums?'

'Don't you think so?' I said. 'Don't you think gossip spreads faster than measles around here?'

'For example?'

'Tony Gourlay's "monster" for one. And . . . I retract my claim. At least, there's something else but I can't put my finger on it. Oh, look.'

We had lingered so long at the Udneys' that we passed Sisters Francis and Jude on their way down to the village to open the school.

'It's not really a kindness to give them a lift and leave them without their bicycles in the morning, is it?' Alec said, slowing and signalling with gestures his willingness to turn around and take them down the hill. They signalled back that they were happy to walk and we speeded up again.

'Jungle drums,' I said.

'What about them?' Alec said. 'And shall I drop you at the door, Dandy? And carry on up to Dr Glass? Or shall I wait for you and take you back up to see Mary?'

'Um,' I said, stupidly.

'I'd rather like you with me,' he said. 'I'm not looking forward to asking Glass about those pistols at all. I'm assuming we won't need to break the news. Don't you think the police will already have told him? Or that he'll have heard somehow.'

'Bush telegraph,' I said.

'Quite,' said Alec. He swung in at the convent gates, now open again onto the moor. I guessed that the news of Tiddy and Arnold's deaths had reached the sisters somehow, although Alec had not had the chance to twist together the wires of the telephone line.

'Do you know, darling?' I said, 'I'd rather like to pack up my things and go to an inn in Lanark while we tie up the loose ends. Or even just tie them quickly and go home. I'm getting a bit sick of my cell, to be frank. And that blessed Angelus bell too.'

294

'It must be a nuisance if it's just clanking on and not actually speaking to you,' said Alec.

As he spoke, I caught sight of Sister Anne, with a rough apron covering her habit and her veil pinned back between her shoulders. She was still winter-pruning, busy with one of the apple trees closest to the drive, a pair of shears glinting in her mittened hands.

'Hallelujah,' I said.

'Hm?' said Alec.

'This case has been woefully short of them, but I've just had one of those breaks in the clouds, darling. A combination of what you said and seeing Anne. Pull over, Alec, would you please?'

I jumped down and strode over to where Sister Anne stood on top of a short set of steps.

'It's good to see you up and about, Sister,' I said. 'And to see roses in your cheeks. Have you heard the news?'

'Sister Mary is resting comfortably and those two troubled souls have gone to God's judgement,' Anne said. 'We shall pray for his mercy upon them, of course,' she went on, looking down at me. 'But I can't say I'm not relieved. Will you be going now, Mrs Gilver?'

'Here's your hat!' I said, unable not to smile. 'Yes, we'll be going. I just have one last question for you.' She stopped her pruning then; froze with the shears bitten halfway through a dead branch. 'It's about Mother Mary's last words,' I said. 'And the things you learned in the Guides.' The shears fell out of Sister Anne's hands and she made no move to snatch at them. They dropped onto the grass and lay there among the frosty blades.

'Her last words weren't spoken, were they?' I said. 'They were rung out on the bell.'

'I don't know what you me—' she began.

'And you deciphered the code.'

'I didn't.'

'Well, I daresay if that's a lie you can simply confess it, can't you?' I said. 'It always seems rather convenient to anyone not of your faith, you know.'

'I don't know what it was she said,' Sister Anne whispered. 'Her words were hard to understand and the message she rang out was hard to understand too.'

'Tell me,' I said. 'Perhaps I'll be able to work it out.'

'I've forgotten it,' she said.

'I don't believe you,' I replied. 'And I wouldn't have to confess to saying so even if I went in for such things, because I'm speaking the truth. Are you, Sister?'

'Please,' she said. 'I am greatly troubled. I have a burden I can't share and I can't put down and I don't know what to do. Please leave me alone with it.'

'I can help you,' I said.

'No one can help me,' she said.

I stared up at her and she stared down, but there was more resolve in her than in me and after a moment, when the cold was seeping into my boots and up my legs, I bent, picked up her shears, handed them to her and walked away.

26

Of course, it was wonderful to get home to the puppy and my own bed and my sitting room and a visit from Donald, who came for tea on Sunday.

'You don't seem as jubilant as usual at the close of a case, Mother,' he remarked.

'Tsst,' said Hugh, who was attempting to train little Bunty by hissing at her like a snake whenever she did something naughty. Bunty loved the noise and barked with joy to hear it.

'Grant was very fierce about the state of my hair,' I said. 'She has scrubbed the jubilation right out of me.'

'No,' said Donald, 'it's more than that. You did *solve* it, didn't you?'

'Well, it's solved,' I said and sighed. 'And we were there when it got solved. I'm not sure we actually did anything to help.'

'Saved that nu— woman's life,' said Donald. We were bowdlerising for Hugh, referring to Hopekist Head and Waterside and men and women, rather than the convent and the asylum and inmates and nuns. 'And Mr Osborne's friend is off the hook, isn't he?'

'Don't say "off the hook",' Hugh told him.

'Tsst,' I said. Donald giggled.

'Yes, Alec's end of things couldn't have worked out any better,' I went on. 'The Gourlays are delighted. But Alec and I – Gilver and Osborne – are not. We've made a pact that either we puzzle it out today or we give up. He's on his way now, or should be.'

At that moment, Becky opened the door and announced Alec. He came in, like a wet washing day, and threw himself into a chair. Bunty stopped annoying Hugh and bounded over, launched herself into Alec's lap and began to lick his face. Alec screwed his eyes shut, pressed his mouth closed and let her have at it until she was done, then reached for a napkin and started mopping. Even I thought that this was a shocking encouragement of bad manners in a dog, but I said nothing.

'Anything?' he said, once the mopping was completed.

'Nothing,' I said. 'No answers. Just more questions.'

'Right,' said Alec, clapping his hands. 'Here goes then.'

'Well, if you'll excuse me, Osborne,' said Hugh, putting down his cup. He counts Alec as a friend but the sight of a dog being spoiled was unbearable.

'Actually Hugh,' I said, 'it would be very useful if you could stay. You've seen things in the past more than once when Alec and I have missed them, and we must be missing something here.'

'Very well,' said Hugh, gruffly, hiding his thrill at such flattery. Donald's eyes were dancing. 'Give me a quick run down.'

I nodded at Alec; Hugh would rather listen to him than me. As he spoke I thought back over the case: the breakout, the fire and red paint on Christmas Eve; the intruder flitting around, smashing windows; the documents disturbed in Sister Steven's cell; the last words of Mother Mary and the message she rang out in Morse code on her chapel bell; Tony Gourlay's few mystifying words; Rose Molloy's words, even fewer and just as mystifying; the puzzle of Sgt Gibb – reputedly so sharp and actually so dull and besides so wary; the puzzle of Dr Glass, keeping service pistols and bullets where they could be stolen and keeping quiet about the theft of them. The Udneys had been right about how well *that* piece of news would be received and things looked black for the hospital. I was loath to think about Tony Gourlay losing his sanctuary, never again being able to sit in the early light with a cup of tea and a cigarette and look out at his beloved garden. What I thought of most of all, though, was Eddie Arnold and Chick Tiddy getting out of the asylum and hanging around a few miles away trying to find a mysterious item hidden in a convent; then, having found it, attempting to kill the convent's leader and actually killing themselves in what looked like a senseless squabble. That was the biggest puzzle of all, although there were many little ones: the big shoes on small feet; the egg sandwiches in the orphan slot; the sins of Father Dixon. Those had been nibbling at me constantly since I first heard of them.

As Alec wound up, I readied myself to give a clear summary of the new problems; the things which had only begun to trouble me since I returned home to pore over my notes writing them out in tables and trying to make sense of them.

'One thing that has occurred to me,' I said, 'regarding the sister who went around opening the doors and peering into all the rooms on Christmas Eve—'

'We've solved that,' Alec said. 'She was startled when she came upon Sister Catherine and after that she was trying to be quiet. That's why she left the doors open.'

'Yes, but there are two things wrong,' I said. 'First, she shouldn't have been startled. All the sisters knew Sister Catherine was in her room.' I let that settle and waited to see if anyone, by which I meant Hugh, would argue. He did not. 'And also, Sister Catherine should have recognised the Sister who came *into* her room. She had lived with them for years, and she knew them all.'

'But we kept hearing it,' Alec said. 'They're all the same. Rose Molloy said it years ago and Sister Monica said it too – they are deliberately all the same. Uniform. Interchangeable. And we heard over and over again that they couldn't tell who was who in the fire that night. They all said so.'

'We have no way of knowing if that's what Rose Molloy

meant,' I said, 'but they are not all the same to one another. However, we did – you are quite correct – hear the sisters saying that they didn't know who was who. But they were wrong.' I paused. 'They knew exactly who was who. When asked, they all accounted for one another absolutely. But in addition some of them said that there was one sister, in the chapel, with Mother Mary, and no one knew who *she* was. It's not that they didn't recognise *anyone*; it's that they didn't recognise *someone*.'

'But they'd just have seen her going in,' said Donald.

Alec clicked his fingers. 'No!' he said. 'Two of them saw her going in and they only saw her from the back.'

'Exactly,' I said. 'Just as I saw her from the back in the kitchen passage. Sister Hilda and Sister Margaret saw her in the covered passageway to the chapel. She barged past them, went in and bolted the door.'

'A secret passageway?' said Donald. 'Golly.'

'Not secret,' I said. 'Not even the passageway from the doctor's house into the hospital is secret, although it's underground. And the passage to the chapel at the convent is a modern affair. Look, I've drawn plans.' I handed over my sketches of the two houses.

'So who was it?' said Alec, bringing us back to the main question.

'It was no one,' I said. 'Everyone is accounted for. I've drawn table after table after table. The sister who barged past those two in the passage was no one at all.'

'Were they lying?' said Hugh. In spite of himself he was caught up in it now.

'I would think those two were lying about her rushing to get in there, if it weren't for the fact that she was seen by so many once she was inside.'

'Definitely "she"?' said Donald. I turned to him, trying to keep the surprise from my face. He was hopeless at school and dreamed his way through meetings with factor and stewards. That question was the first sign of native wit I had ever seen in him.

'Excellent point, Donald,' I said and he beamed, bending over the house plans again to hide it. 'It could have been Arnold or Tiddy in a habit. He could have put the habit on again when he came back to attack Sister Mary. It might have been him I saw too. And him we both saw with the papers clutched to his chest, Alec.'

'And here's a thought, Dan,' said Alec. 'If Tony saw him running away on Christmas Eve, do you think a man – unshaven and wild – in a habit, would strike him as monstrous?'

It was the closest thing to sense I had heard about the monster so far. And yet . . .

'I just have a great deal of trouble believing that Tiddy and Arnold are actually behind all this,' I said. 'How and why? I can't begin to imagine how and why?'

'And so where does that leave us?' said Hugh, sounding exasperated.

The door of my sitting room opened and Grant entered. Little Bunty galloped over and gave her an effusive welcome; Bunty adored Grant and it was mutual.

'It leaves us waiting to hear what our assistant has made of the files,' I said. Grant had been holed up with all of my notes all morning and had taken herself off for a walk this afternoon to – as she put it – 'get the juices flowing'. 'Well, Grant?'

'Well, madam,' she said. She spread her feet and put her hands behind her back ready to stand and deliver her report. She was very delicate when Hugh was there, dreading to frighten his sense of propriety, but I was not about to have her be treated as though at court martial or in the head's study.

'Take a seat,' I said. Hugh's face grew black and even Donald's eyebrows rose.

Grant sat on the extreme front edge of the hardest chair, like my grandmother on an afternoon call to an enemy.

'Well, madam,' she said again. 'I agree with you that there's more going on than two madmen breaking out, causing mischief and killing one another. Rather convenient, apart from anything. And Father Dixon interests me greatly although I couldn't find a loose end to pull. But there are a couple of questions I think you probably could get answers for.' She cleared her throat. 'Ready?'

'Panting,' I said. Grant loves nothing more than a dramatic pause.

'As to the question of Father Dixon first. And the notion that he might know something scandalous about the sisters. I don't think so. The convent has been there for fifty years. The nuns do wonderful work and bring up happy children who leave and go onto great things. Even the orphans in India who don't know them love them.'

'No—' I said.

'How do you know that?' said Hugh. 'About India?'

'Benares table, Indian tree china, snap of a man in a pith, and brass elephants,' Grant said rattling out the list with tip-top efficiency. 'Lots of presents to the sisters sent from grateful orphans in the subcontinent.'

'No,' I said again. 'I'm sorry, Grant. My notes have misled you. The Indian orphanage was set up by the Udney sisters, not the Little Sisters.'

'Oh,' said Grant. 'Why all the elephants and so on then?'

'I've no idea,' I said. 'Perhaps there was just one grateful orphan who "graduated" from the orphanage and went to India and he sent everything. Photo of himself and all the other trinkets.'

'Hmph,' said Grant, rather crestfallen. 'Perhaps. Well, anyway, turning our attention to my second question: why was Sister Mary not named Marigold Bell? You said she gave her name as "Usher" or "Archer", unclear which because she was so groggy. But definitely not Bell.'

'Perhaps she was one of the earliest orphans and it was before the "Bell" system was set up,' said Alec.

'What's this?' said Hugh.

'Nothing,' I told him, with a significant look at Donald.

'And related to that perhaps . . .' said Grant. 'About these books that Mother Mary went into the chapel to lay her hands on. You assumed that she meant the Bible and prayer book, didn't you?' I nodded. 'Madam. But what if she didn't?'

'Crikey,' said Alec. 'You're right, Grant. We've been very stupid. The box room in the convent was full of files and ledgers – or in other words "books" – and the sacristy in the chapel might have been full of them too. If Mother Mary got "the books" out, and they ended up in Sister Steven's cupboard, that might have been what Tiddy and Arnold were after. Oh, brava Grant!'

Grant, unusually for her, went rather pink.

'That makes a great deal of sense, sir,' she said, 'but it's not what I meant. I was thinking about the atlas and dictionary Mrs Gilver found, with the bookplate in.'

'Ah,' I said. 'But what about them?'

'I took the liberty of telephoning,' said Grant. 'I asked Sister Monica what Mother Mary was called before she took holy orders.'

There was another enormous pause.

'Well?' said Alec.

'Amaryllis,' said Grant.

'What a ridiculous name,' said Hugh. I rather thought he was getting lost and feeling angry about it.

'That's nothing,' said Alec. 'There's a Verbena, a Daffodil and a Hyacinth too.'

'Women!' said Hugh.

'Actually, with those three, it was their father,' I took great pleasure in telling him. I turned back to Grant, 'Amaryllis what, though?'

And the truth hit me like an anvil.

'*Oh!*' I said.

'Yes,' said Grant.

'Good grief!' said Alec.

'But she was a nun!!' said Donald, I was slightly disturbed to realise that he had cottoned on so quickly.

'What are you all talking about,' demanded Hugh.

'Marigold Usher or Archer – except we now know it's "Archer" – was indeed the very first orphan at St Ultan's,' I said.

'You never told me it was called St Ultan's,' said Hugh.

I shrugged and returned to the irresistible unravelling. 'Marigold Archer was the daughter of Amaryllis Archer, who became Mother Mary. Oh my giddy aunt!'

'Father Dixon knew,' said Grant, 'and covered it up.'

'And she was given the house to keep her quiet?' said Alec. 'The house she turned into a convent?'

'Not exactly,' I said. 'The house was given in trust to the church to be used as an orphanage where Marigold might be brought up. I rather think the convent came second.'

'Given by who?' said Donald. '*M*,' he added before Hugh could nag him. I glanced at Hugh. He was frowning and paying no attention as far as I could tell.

'Marigold's father, of course,' said Grant, then blushed. 'The man of the house where Amaryllis worked as housekeeper.'

'Of course!' said Alec. 'Heavens above!'

'What?' Donald asked.

'He didn't just seduce his housekeeper,' Alec said. 'Good grief, he seduced every girl in the valley.'

'Darling, please!' I said, wishing I could send Donald out of the room, astonished that Hugh had not exploded.

'All those black-haired, blue-eyed, white-skinned children!' said Alec. 'All those so-called orphans. Good Lord, Dandy. Do you think the Udney girls *know*?'

'I think the Udneys know very well,' I said grimly. The thud of things falling into place was practically deafening me. 'I think the Udneys know a lot more than they ever let on and I think they know a lot more than poor Arnold and

Tiddy. I think they hated the hospital and the convent, resented the nuns and the men and wanted the whole estate back in their hands. I think they've been laying the ground-work for years and they've hidden it beautifully.'

Everyone was silent for a long moment while this idea settled into our minds. I waited to see if any bits of it did not fit but all I could see was the new idea fitting perfectly, solving problems and making sense of everything.

'Cinty helped arrange the breakout, from her foothold in the asylum,' Alec said. 'Daff was in charge of the mischief at the convent. They hid the men as long as they needed to and then they killed them. But are we really saying they did this while their father lay dying?'

'Do you think Bena is in on it?' I said.

'She was in India the whole time,' said Alec.

'Who was in India?' said Hugh, suddenly with us again. 'When was this?'

'Over Christmas until a few days ago,' I told him. 'The third Udney sister was in India visiting the orphanage there. Why?'

'You never told me it was called St Ultan's,' said Hugh again. He drew a huge breath and let it go slowly. 'And it's not Usher *nor* Archer. It's Asher.'

'How do you know?'

'My pal, Sooty Asher, who died. Do you remember?'

'Of course,' I said.

'He was born fatherless, brought up in an orphanage, and then went to India where he apparently killed himself for no reason.'

'Yes?' I said. I had a very peculiar prickling feeling creeping over me.

'His name was Ultan,' said Hugh. 'Ultan Asher. Odd sort of name. Not one you'd forget really.'

I turned to Alec. 'I'd call *this* a bit of a coincidence, wouldn't you?'

Alec nodded and gave a long, low, mirthless laugh. '"Find Ultan. Hide Mary." She knew the Udneys were after her children.'

'But what about the last bit?' said Grant. 'All these years it was real.'

'I still don't know,' I said. 'But we know enough to go down there and tell Constable McLintock. I wish we knew how they got in.'

'I think I know,' said Donald. 'Secret passageways. I'm looking at your plans, Mother. And I don't see why the new passage to the chapel was necessary except to replace an old one. One that didn't work any more after they built the orphanage wing.'

'Secret passageways?' I said. 'That seems highly unli— Actually, that seems perfectly plausible. For one thing, the nuns themselves complain of inexplicable draughts making doors bang shut. And for another, the Udney girls practically told me so. They said their father wanted a covered way from the castle – Hopekist Head – to the chapel. Always having had one before, would certainly account for his not wanting to do without one suddenly.'

'And the mother – when she demanded a new house – demanded a modern one with no such things,' said Grant. 'Well, she would. If she had found out about all Mr Udney's "orphans", she would want a house with one front door and a clear view of the drive, wouldn't she?'

'And she did find out!' Alec said. 'She found out from Father Dixon. Or she found out and went to him, but one way or another she discovered that he had hidden the scandal and she left the Church over it.'

'And here's another thing,' I said. 'It makes sense of the strange noises I heard. Creaking and groaning. There were unseen doors opening. What a fool I've been!'

'Let me just check that I've got this clear,' said Hugh. 'Udney's legitimate daughters decided to kill the housekeeper-nun, the son in India and, eventually, after a lot of shilly-shallying, the daughter. But in that instance they failed.'

Grant, Alec, Donald and I all leapt to our feet and made a single choreographed lunge for the telephone. Alec got there first.

'Sister John?' he said, once it had gone through, 'It's Alec Osborne. Where's Sister Mary? Lanark, you mean? Is she attended? I don't mean by nurses. She needs a guard. We're coming back, Sister. But you need to organise shifts of two at a time and guard her. We shall be there by sundown.'

He broke the connection.

'What now?' I said. 'The Chief Constable? The Fiscal?'

'We've been here before, Dan,' said Alec. 'Trying to convince a copper of some outlandish tale.'

'McLintock?' I suggested.

'Even with the perspicacious Constable McLintock I wouldn't know where to start,' Alec said.

He lifted the earpiece again.

'Operator?' Udney, Waterside, Carstairs Stop, please.'

'Why did they let her live?' I said. 'Why haven't they tried again?'

'Let's hope they haven't,' said Alec. 'It's ringing out but no one's answering. Come on Dandy, let's go.'

27

They were at home when we got there, the four of us in Hugh's Daimler. I had put my foot down about Donald and foresaw having to make it up to him in some lavish way.

The solitary housemaid answered the door and showed us into the drawing room where the three Udney girls were gathered around a meagre fire, looking as pretty as angels in the lamplight.

'Hell-o,' said Bena. 'Who's this you've got with you?' Her tone was bright but all three of them were on their guard.

'Are you the one who went to India?' said Hugh. 'Well, I'm here to tell you that Sooty Asher was a friend of mine and I shall prove what you did if it takes my life to do so.'

Bena barely missed a beat before she answered. 'You know nothing of the jewel in the crown, I see,' she said. 'Hypothetically, if one *were* to commit a naughtiness there, one would simply buy off everyone who might be troublesome.'

'Naughtiness?' said Hugh, and I trembled to hear him.

Verbena did not so much as flicker. 'I have won,' she said. 'We have won. The hospital is closing. We are selling Hopekist Head and this place and all the rest of it and we are moving somewhere more to our liking. What is more, if you quote me I shall deny it all.'

'What about the convent?' I asked. 'Is that closing too?'

'We fervently hope so,' said Daff. 'Bloody place. There is no paperwork to show that our benighted Papa actually gave it in a gift to that trollop. And that means she couldn't give it to the Church. But fifty years of diocesan habit – if you'll pardon the pun – is rather difficult to unravel.'

'No paperwork?' I said. 'Because you finally found the last of it and destroyed it?'

'I?' said Daff, with a hand pressed to her bosom. 'I, Mrs Gilver? What an extraordinary suggestion. It was Ernie Arnold and Chick Tiddy. I thought you knew.'

'No one will believe that those two could either pull it off or would have any reason to,' I said.

'Au contraire,' said Bena. 'Dr Glass and Sergeant Gibb have sworn to it already. Oh, Daff! I so much want to revel in it. Shall we? Shall we tell them all? I don't think anyone would believe them if they blabbed, do you?'

'I can scarcely believe it myself,' Daff said.

'I don't even know what you're talking about,' said Cinty.

Her sisters both grinned at her and Daff shook her head fondly.

'I know you don't, you sweet little goose,' she said.

'Oh do let's tell them!' Bena said. She turned back to beam at Alec and me. 'Gibb and Glass will do, say or hide anything we ask them to.'

'What?' said Cinty.

'Cinty led Dr Glass on—' Daff said, but her sister interrupted her.

'You told me to be kind to him and to the inmates,' she said.

'And you certainly were, darling,' Daff said. 'He's absolutely round your little finger.' She turned back to face us. 'Cinty led Glass on, as I say, and I led Gibb on. They lapped it up without questioning. Can you believe the gall of them? As though either one of us would look twice at either one of them! I was almost sick, sneaking along to his hovel to hold hands and coo.'

'I think we were there once when you arrived,' said Alec.

'And,' I said, remembering Debrett's on Gibb's bookshelf, 'he was looking to better himself to deserve you.'

'I know,' Daff said. 'What a scream.'

'So it was *your* idea not to clear up the mess in the sacristy and chapel?' said Alec.

'The passageway was full of that dratted paint,' Daff said. 'We felt sure if masons and carpenters set to they'd find it and then questions would be asked, you know?'

'Won't they turn on you now?' I said. 'Gibb and Glass?'

'Dr Glass wouldn't turn on *me*,' Cinty said. 'I didn't *do* anything.'

'It's true,' said Daff. 'She didn't. She sat with Papa. And no, Glass and Gibb won't turn. Pride, you see. And besides, Glass would be struck off for the pistols – as it stands we've taken the blame; saying Cinty felt unsafe at the hospital and took to leaving one loaded where she could get to it easily.'

'What?' said Cinty. 'Daff, I *never*.'

'Poor weak woman,' Bena said. 'No one will judge you harshly for it, my pet. And as for Gibb, he'd lose his job and his house and be a laughing stock. No, everything's fine in that quarter.'

'But why didn't you just try to dissolve the trust?' I asked. 'Or trusts. Why not just ask nicely? Why did you have to go rampaging around in a convent, killing people?'

'On Christmas Eve, as your father lay dying,' Grant put in.

Cinty, always the most tender-hearted of the three, put her head down at those words, although the others simply smirked at us all.

'Because it was you, wasn't it?' Alec said. 'In the convent chapel, in a habit?'

'Well, I was busy in India myself,' Bena said. 'But yes, of course it was us. And as to why . . . when Mama died we found her diaries. Most interesting. She had written it all down. We found out that it was real.'

'All these years it was real!' I said. 'Good Lord, you knew before Mother Mary did, didn't you?'

'You tell me what we knew,' said Bena. 'What have *you* made of it, Mrs Gilver?'

'Your father married her,' I said. 'Amaryllis Asher.'

'Top marks,' said Bena. 'We reckon *she* thought it was merely a romantic gesture. She might have thought Father Dixon was performing some kind of blessing! And when it was over, and she was given somewhere to stay, she confessed her sin and embraced the Church. Father Dixon heard her confession.'

'But could she take orders if she was married?' said Grant.

'That's a very good question, whoever you are,' said Daff. 'As to whether Mother Mary was actually a nun, whether she was free to be a nun . . . I have no idea. But certainly she was a married woman. Our mother wrote it in her diary and we knew if any papers had survived, they'd confirm it.'

'And so,' I said, 'Ultan Asher – properly Ultan Udney – was your father's heir.'

'Oh jolly well done,' said Daff. 'Yes, that's more or less it. We found papers, letters, pictures – all from the Indian boy.'

'And so Bena set off to take care of him?' I said.

'What?' said Bena. 'Lord, no – this was years ago. Aren't you listening? It was when Mama died. That was when we decided to start our life of good works – helping the sisters, helping the doctor, setting up an orphanage in Hyderabad. We laid our plans carefully and thoroughly.'

'Your plans,' I said.

'Plans to kill your brother, destroy his birth certificate, destroy all record of his parents' marriage, cause a scandal at the hospital and terrify the nuns into leaving,' said Alec.

'What are you talking about?' said Cinty. 'All we did was destroy records.'

'Oh dear,' said Alec. 'I'm afraid not, Miss Udney.'

'And it went off . . . I shan't say without a hitch,' said Daff. 'There were some sticky patches but we took care of them.'

311

'It's not the first time, is it?' Alec said. 'You've killed before.'

Bena gave him a look of intrigued interest. I did too.

'What are you talking about, darling?' I said.

'A great many things about this case don't make sense,' said Alec. 'And the sad tale of George and little Sandy Molloy is one of them.'

'Good grief!' said Bena. 'Are you some kind of psychic? How on earth did you cotton onto that?' She was truly astonished, but she sounded tickled rather than horrified.

'It's true then,' said Alec. 'You killed Rose Molloy!'

'Hypothetically,' said Bena in the same drawling voice that made me want to smack her, 'if some jumped-up little nobody suddenly started acting as if she was *your* sister you probably would want to take care of matters, wouldn't you?'

'Hm,' I said. 'You're trying very hard to sound brisk and practical, Miss Udney. But it's not really just about money and property, is it?'

'Well, we've no wish to be a laughing stock either,' said Daff.

'It's more even than that,' I said. 'This hurt you, didn't it? Finding out that your father truly loved Amaryllis.'

'Rot,' said Daff. 'He was a lifelong philanderer. That's all.'

'He loved her,' I said. 'He called all his daughters after flowers in honour of her. You were all named in remembrance of that first love.'

'He loved us too,' said Cinty, sounding tearful.

'He loved us *only*,' said Bena.

'And yet look at how you repaid him,' said Grant. 'As he lay dying. Christmas Eve!'

'We weren't to know he'd choose that night to die,' Bena said. 'The plan was set and it was too late to change it.'

'*That's* where you went?' Cinty said. 'When you told me you were overcome with emotion and had to leave his bedside?'

'In a nutshell,' said Daff.

312

'There's one thing I'd love to know,' said Alec. I thought I could guess what he would ask but he surprised me. 'Hypothetically. I understand that you started a fire and desecrated the little box room to cover your tracks. To hide the fact that you were searching for papers.'

'Don't forget the brainwave about the big footprints!' Daff said. 'Unfortunately, that ruddy McLintock saw through them and so we had to fess up to them being fake.'

'Look, never mind that now!' said Alec. 'Did you really keep Mother Mary inside the chapel so that she died there?'

'What?' said Cinty.

'And if you did, how did you manage to stay in a burning building for longer than everyone else and survive?'

'But didn't they see you?' said Grant.

Bena shushed her with an impatient wave of the hand. 'Hypothetically,' she said. 'You do remember that this is all hypothetical, don't you? And that we'll deny it all if you try to spread such a vicious lie about us?'

I glanced at Cinty. It struck me that she was not at all likely to back her sisters up on any of this. I wondered why they were not more troubled about her.

'Daff,' Bena said, 'I'll let you tell them. It was your brainwave.'

'Gas mask,' Daff said. 'You couldn't see a thing because of the veil unless you looked at me straight on. From behind and the side I looked the same as the rest of them. From straight on I daresay I looked a little strange.'

'You looked,' Alec told her, 'like a monster. You know you did, because someone saw you.'

'Ah yes, a mute madman saw me. I'm hardly trembling. Now, Gourlay, you see, was our second string in case anything went wrong with the other two. Ernie Arnold led him out and he followed like a lamb.'

'But I don't understand why you were there at all,' I said. 'You'd done your work with the paint and matches by midnight. Why were you still there when the chapel burned down?'

'Good grief,' said Bena. 'Do you always talk everything to death like this? It's very dreary.'

'I don't mind, Bean,' said Daff. 'Although you're quite right. She quizzed everyone to shreds last week. It was utter tedium.' She turned to me. 'But the night of the fire was *thrilling*! I couldn't have dragged myself away for a pension. Of course, I knew damn well Old Mother Mary would act the hero. As soon as she saw me, she sent the others out. She didn't want a scandal to take down her precious orphanage, you see. I knew she'd try to tackle me. But she didn't stand a chance. Once she *finally* left off ringing that bloody bell, I made short work of her.'

'You stayed inside the chapel to kill her,' I said.

'And everyone thought she was overcome by the fire,' said Daff. 'Yes. Our father was right about passageways. They are extremely useful. It was the perfect murder, really.'

Hugh had been speechless for so long that I started a little as he spoke.

'Why are you telling us all this?' he said. 'Why aren't you running away? Why aren't you trembling?'

'Haven't you been listening?' Daff said. 'Who would believe you? Gibb will deny everything, Glass will deny everything. The passageway is cleaned up. Tiddy and Arnold are dead. Ultan is dead. We all have alibis for it all.'

'How can you?' said Alec.

'On Christmas Eve we were severally in India or at Papa's bedside,' Daff said. 'You'll say I stayed with you, won't you my pet?'

Cinty nodded dumbly.

'And on Thursday?' I added. 'When Sister Mary was attacked?'

'Cinty and I were at the hospital and then at the convent. You saw us. Everyone saw us.'

'And Bena?' said Alec.

'Bena had only arrived at Liverpool the day before. She drove herself from Carlisle just in time for breakfast,' Daff said. 'You witnessed her arriving. She certainly didn't leave her blameless hotel room in the dark of night, hare off up here, kill Tiddy and Arnold and then hare back again.' She gave us a travesty of an innocent smile. I was beginning to feel quite sick, just from looking at the two of them.

'You've been diabolically clever,' I said. 'Can I ask one question?'

Daff and Bena shared a glance and then Daff nodded. Cinty was beyond even that. She sat numb with horror. I could not say how much she had suspected and tried to deny but her life was crumbling around her and her face showed every crack and every slip.

'My question is this,' I said. 'Why didn't you kill Sister Mary?'

'On Christmas Eve?' said Daff. 'Why would we? I mean, of course we loathed her, but golly if we were to kill every one of our father's by-blows we'd never be done.'

'I didn't mean on Christmas Eve, actually,' I said. 'I meant on Thursday. But I'm interested to hear you call her a by-blow.'

'It's a kinder name than the other,' said Daff, misunderstanding.

'Let me see if I've got this right,' Alec said. 'What did you find in Sister Steven's room on Thursday?'

'What?' said Bena. 'What do you think? What have we been searching for and fearing and dreaming of all this time? The parish record, of course. The record of the marriage between Papa and Amaryllis. *Finally!*'

'Oh my God,' said Alec. 'Dandy, they don't know.'

I frowned, too confused to be sure; too confused to dare believe. 'One extra question,' I said. 'Why did you *attack* Sister Mary on Thursday?'

'I know it was wrong of me,' said Bena. 'But don't nag.

315

Honestly, if you'd seen her, prostrate on the floor at the foot of that hideous crucifix. Such a goody two shoes! Who could have borne it?'

'You idiots!' said Alec.

'Merciful heavens!' said Grant.

'They really don't know,' I chimed in.

'They're not alone,' said Hugh. And then after a pause he said: 'Oh!'

Bena's chest was rising and falling very rapidly. Daff was breathing normally but her eyes were darting back and forth as she desperately thought of what she might have missed.

'Don't know what?' she said.

'Nothing!' said Bena. 'They're trying to unsettle us, that's all.'

Cinty was openly weeping. Her fair head was bent almost to her knees. Bena and Daff, for all their usual cooing, watched her cry with not a scrap of warmth in their pale blue eyes.

'Shush now,' said Grant. 'We know *you* didn't do anything. 'You're not part of this. You're not like them.'

'I *am* like them!' said Cinty, sitting up. Her eyes were flashing. 'I'm exactly like them. I'm their sister.'

At her words, a great light broke over me. Cinty's dark eyes and fair hair made her so different from her sisters. It was all I could do to not laugh out loud.

'No you're not,' I said. 'And they know you're not. You're their half-sister.

'Your mother, after years of humiliation, seeing all your father's children far and wide, had a love affair.'

Bena laughed scornfully at my sentimental choice of words. 'Pure speculation,' she said.

'Not entirely,' said Alec. 'It makes sense of one otherwise puzzling fact.' He paused and all three Udney girls watched him with avidity. 'It troubled me what could have happened to cause a sudden rift between your mother and Father

Dixon. The obvious thing is that your mother found out about the marriage.'

'Ah,' I said. 'I see. It explains why on earth Father Dixon would suddenly blurt it out after all those years, when doing so would harm him!'

'Aha!' said Grant. 'Of course.'

It was hard to say who looked more annoyed by our crowing; the elder Udneys or Hugh. I took pity and laid it out for him. 'Mrs Udney confessed the affair to Father Dixon. And he comforted her by sharing a secret.'

Daff and Bena maintained a stony silence but their faces, bitter suddenly, gave them away.

'I am not a half-sister,' said Cinty. 'I'm an Udney.'

'And you really *didn't* do anything,' I said to her. 'You didn't so much as strike a match, did you?'

'I'm not a by-blow,' said Cinty again on a rising pitch. 'I'm not an orphan and I'm not a . . . I'm not a *bastard*!' She hurled the last word at her sisters.

'Hyacinth,' I said. 'Yes, you are, dear. All of you are. And orphans too.'

Bena hissed. It was not a word nor a cry. She actually hissed.

'Well, Cinty might have a father somewhere, I suppose,' Alec said.

'I *had* a father,' said Cinty. '*Our* father. He loved me. He told me so as he lay dying. I was with him all night.'

'I know you were,' I said. 'You are innocent and we can help you.'

She looked at her sisters, at their hard faces and then at Grant's kind smile and at whatever expression of coaxing tenderness I had managed to get onto my own face. She was so close to letting it all go.

Alec moved towards the telephone which lay on a side table.

'I can call Constable McLintock right now, Miss Udney,'

he said. 'He's a clever man. He'll be able to see that you are innocent. If you'll be a witness, he'll take care of you.'

'Don't listen to them,' Daff said. 'Stick with us, you little goose. We're going to get our own back on that filthy beast, for our mother's sake and for our own. We're going to get away from here and away from all those village faces that look like ours, staring at us and smirking.'

'Not *my* face,' said Cinty.

'We shall go to the south of France,' said Bena. 'Wouldn't that be lovely?'

'Rather extravagant for three penniless by-blows,' I said.

Again Daff Udney gave me a swift look.

'Papa wasn't a beast, Daff,' said Cinty. 'He had feet of clay. But we are all sinners. And he truly loved me.'

Bena snorted. 'I'm sure he did,' she drawled. And she smirked as she went on, 'if he hadn't been dying he might have shown you exactly how *much* he loved you.'

'You horror!' I said.

'Plain speaker, Mrs Gilver,' Bena said. 'Cinty is a pretty girl and was no relation to him.'

As Cinty grasped her meaning she looked, for a moment, as though she might be sick and then she slapped her sister hard across the cheek and marched over to stand just behind Hugh. A moment of ghastly silence followed. Daff broke it.

'Penniless,' she said. 'What did you mean, Mrs Gilver? We're very far from penniless, I assure you. And what did you mean by calling us by-blows? What are you hinting at?'

Alec, Grant and I all looked at one another deciding who would get to pick the plum and tell them. Then I turned to Hugh.

'You say it,' I said. 'For Sooty's memory.'

Hugh gave a curt nod. 'Now that your Papa is dead,' he said, 'and his male heir is dead too, everything belongs to his only surviving heir. His only legitimate daughter. Marigold Asher. Sister Mary.'

Hugh and Alec grabbed the two fleeing Udney sisters with no difficulty at all, at the cost to Hugh of a bite on the hand. He dined out on it all spring. I telephoned to McLintock and delivered a report of a succinctness I will never stop being proud of.

'Tiddy and Arnold, Constable? The fire and the breakout and the attack on Sister Mary? Two of the Udney sisters did it all. Bring handcuffs to Waterside now.'

Meanwhile Grant sat with her arms around Cinty Udney, stroking her hair and murmuring to her.

'What was your mother's maiden name?' she said. 'Templeton? That's lovely. Better than Udney anyway. And your middle name? Louisa? "Louisa Templeton". She sounds like a very happy and contented young lady. And her first pleasant task will be to tell the doctor he doesn't need to close his hospital and to tell those sweet nuns that their order owns everything around them as far as the eye can see. Wouldn't you like to visit Sister Mary and tell her that? And wouldn't you like to be there when George Molloy is let out and reunited with his little Sandy? He will be let out, won't he? Now that the truth about how his poor Rose died has come to light. Wouldn't that be a lovely thing to do? What would you wear to carry out such solemn duties, Miss Templeton? Say it was in the springtime and it was a pleasant day? I could dress your hair for you, you know.'

And so as the sound of Constable McLintock's whistle began and we saw him come pelting up the drive on his bicycle, I was almost laughing.

319

Postscript

It was months later that the final puzzle was solved. We got an invitation to a wedding, Hugh, Alec, Grant and me. Of course, Hugh would rather have died than attend and Alec said he could do without it, so it was Grant and I who set off in my Cowley down into the valley and up onto the moor, to the rebuilt and rather splendid chapel at St Ultan's, to witness the marriage of George Molloy and the woman we had barely learned to call Miss Morag McKechnie.

'Morag Molloy!' said Grant. 'Isn't it awful? Not that "McKechnie" was any better.'

'Neither one a patch on "Sister Anne",' I agreed.

'Do you think they'll be happy?' Grant said. 'The former inmate of an insane asylum and a fallen nun?'

'I think they've got as good a chance as anyone,' I said. Privately, I thought George Molloy had shown a stubborn streak that might be unwelcome in a husband, but Sister Anne was the best judge of it.

'It's very romantic,' Grant breathed, as she inspected her hair in a compact mirror. It was staggering: so short at the back that it twinkled like that of a boy fresh from the barber and with a row of curls along her forehead that looked painted on. My mother would have taken the vapours if one of her maids had been seen outside in such a state – or in its equivalent in the day – but if the choice was to let Grant wear the latest fashions herself or allow her to foist them on me, I found the decision very easy.

'Romantic?' I said. I had found it hair-raising when the story had come to light.

'Knowing the way through the tunnel,' Grant said. 'Coming to the convent walls to talk to his childhood sweetheart and watch his little boy? Refusing to run away unless she came with him?' Grant gave a happy sigh.

'I call that blackmail,' I said. 'Imagine how poor Sister Anne felt knowing that he was living in an asylum and wouldn't leave until she gave in.'

'So ardent!' said Grant. 'Like something off the pictures. And her clinging to her veil, while her heart broke.'

'Honour like iron,' I said. 'All very well if you like that sort of thing. But rather a comfortless virtue for a wife.'

'I'd call it loyalty,' Grant said. 'She stayed loyal to her sisters even though for two months, since she heard the message in the bells up until we solved the case, she thought Mother Mary wasn't really a nun and St Ultan's wasn't really a convent. She thought all of them were tricked and lost.'

I could hardly blame her, for I had thought the same. It still seemed shocking that a married woman could found a nunnery with her husband living, but Rome had spoken and it was so.

'Hm,' I said. 'Here we are. Oh look, the gates are open.'

As we swept in, I was astonished at the change a few months had wrought. The apple trees were in full green leaf, the grass below them was like velvet and even St Ultan's, on such a balmy June afternoon, was softened to something like beauty.

When they heard the motorcar, several of the sisters came out onto the steps and waited.

Sister Catherine was there, leaning heavily on Sister Monica, and squinting. Sister John was there, arms folded. Sister Steven stood looking thunderous. Sister Julian had the grace to look uncomfortable. All of the senior sisters, I had learned, knew Mary's secret and had vowed to keep it from her daughter and take it to their graves; but only Sister Julian knew there was a passageway that came out in the laundry. She had checked it once on Christmas morning and then put it from her mind. All the time someone was getting in and two detectives were beating their heads against the question of *how*, Sister Julian – from long habit, from the memory of Mother Mary urging her to keep the peculiarities of their home to herself – had said nothing.

As we drew close, Sister Martha opened an attic window and waved a facecloth and when we stopped and stepped down, Sister Mary came forward and embraced me. No sign of the wound in her head showed behind her wimple and only a carefulness in her walk hinted at how slow the healing of the scar in her middle might be.

'Mrs Gilver,' she said. 'Welcome back. And Miss Grant, I believe.'

'Sister Mary,' I said. 'You look splendid.'

'Splendid?' said John. 'Oh dear.'

'It's Reverend Mother,' Steven said. 'As near as dash it.'

'*Mother* Mary!' I exclaimed.

'Mother Ultan,' Mary said. I noticed John and Steven both nodding, pleased by her finally cutting the ties to her worldly life and, no doubt, by her picking such an unspeakable ugly name.

'Sister Abigail and Sister Martha insist that you go straight to the kitchen for refreshment,' said the woman I would always think of as Mary, taking my arm. 'They're baking to feed the five thousand, of course. And you're bidden to go through and see Nurse Pirrie and Nurse Matt before the ceremony too. Admire the new clothes we've got all the children. They're more like little butterflies than little lambs today.'

THE END

Facts and Fictions

There was an orphanage – Smyllum – in Lanarkshire, and there still is a state hospital there that grew out of an asylum that grew out of a hospital for soldiers. There were and are numerous large houses too. But, although this story was inspired by the history of the area, Hopekist Head, St Ultan's and Waterside are entirely imaginary. Carstairs Stop is an imaginary third village I've added to the real Carstairs and Carstairs Junction. None of the characters here are based on real individuals living or dead and any similarities are accidental.

Sister Julian's Rational Laundering

It is not my intention to dally with questions of velveteen,
rayon or weighted silk in the laundry; nor to trouble myself
with such matters as how to press smocking, bias-seams,
padded items, corselets or any other frivolous items. If,
however, you desire a sound knowledge of how to care for
cotton, woolens and linens at home, draw near.

Method is the key! Careful preparation, flexibility in the
face of inclement weather, and orderliness above all things
make the difference between a good job well-finished on
washday and exhaustion, damp and disarray.

Any young woman who finds herself serving a cold dinner every
Monday, or still has wet sheets hanging down from the airer
on a Tuesday teatime, would do well to send it out and apply
her talents elsewhere.

The mended clothes and linens should be gathered together in
the scullery the day before. Mended, mind you, for any tears
will only rip further if left be. Pockets should be checked
and all flannels and woolens thoroughly shaken. This is the
time to rub stains and steep whites. A professional laundry
has a multitude of utensils, but at home you will need to
soak all items in one bath or tub. Lay the dirtiest at the
bottom and the cleanest at the top and refrain from
disturbing them. Handkerchiefs, especially in winter, should
be steeped separately in a pan of salt. Early on washday
morning, grate sufficient soap for the day, make a pint of
starch and light the boiler under the copper. It is best to
stretch lines and set props and pegs handy now, rather than
wait until the first load of wet clothes is ready for
hanging. In a professional laundry, of course, the ropes are
always there.

It is often assumed that linens and white cottons should be
tackled first. This is folly. When the copper is warm but
before it boils, woolen garments – such as habits in our
case, cardigans and jerseys in the average household –
should be washed gently. This saves them shrinking in over-
hot water and also allows the longest drying time for these,
the hardest garments to dry.

Fine wool should be agitated only lightly and the entire
garment should be supported when moving it from copper to
rinsing bath, lest the fibres stretch and spoil the line.
Woolen stockings go in after the larger garments, with more
lively agitation in the ever-warming water.

When the woolen garments are rinsed and mangled, check that
the water is clear. An experienced laundress will have no

trouble washing black woolens in water as it warms and ending up with a clean boiling copper-full, but laundry work is a skill not all possess.

When the copper boils, fill two more baths with starch and blueing ready for the whites. It is at your discretion which garments are dipped and which are simply rinsed. The order of whites is this: tablecloths, table napkins, clean teatowels, shirts, bedsheets, personal linens, handkerchiefs, infants' napkins. That is, from the cleanest to the dirtiest in strict order. The inclusion of clean teatowels assumes that they are washed daily between weekly boilings.

This ordering will allow the entire wash to be done with one copper of water, so long as the laundress is watchful and canny. If inexperience causes a problem and you find yourself with a grey copper of flat water and half a wash left to do, do not try to mend matters with more soap. There is nothing for it but to start again. Do not, however, fill the copper with freshly-drawn cold water. This is wasteful of time and coal. Instead, pour the rinsing water (sans starch and blueing, naturally) into the drained and wiped copper. This water is already warmed through by the passage of the linens rinsed so far and will come to heat much more quickly.

As the day goes on, garments dry enough for pressing can be unpegged, rolled carefully in a lined basket and replaced on the rope with later loads. Except in high summer, it is to be expected that at least some of these later items will need to be aired inside when the warmth is gone from the day. A good laundress working quickly will have her copper cooled and scullery aired and dried before the first of the woolens is ready to press and the sun is sinking.

Sister Abigail's Tripe

This healthful and tasty dish is just the thing to warm us through on a cold, damp, winter's day. Children love it, if we take care not to let them know what exactly it is. We call it cream stew at St Ultan's and the bairns cannot get enough of it from All Souls' to Easter.

Ingredients for a family.
2lb tripe
4 large sweet onions
2 pints milk
Salt and pepper
Knob of butter
1 heaped tbsp flour

If your butcher will clean and trim the tripe before you bring it home, this is an easy recipe indeed. If not, start in the morning with the kitchen windows thrown wide for a through draft. Rinse the tripe under a cold tap until the water runs clear. If you have only a pump, talk to the butcher again, or maybe have liver.

Once the tripe is clean and the odour has abated, cut it into nice even pieces and scald it quickly in your biggest pot with the water at a rolling boil. Drain and rinse again. Even more than pig's kidneys, a dish of tripe is spoiled beyond eating if any evidence remains of its purpose in God's glorious world, while the creature was living.

With your clean and trimmed tripe to hand at last, slice the onions very thin and, in a good heavy pot, put them with the tripe, milk and salt. If the dish is meant for very small children, the pepper can be omitted and added to taste at the table.

Bring the pot to a boil and then simmer as gently as your range will let you for as long as ever you can. The tripe will be edible in two hours, delicious in four and like manna from heaven after six, always assuming the fire is low and the pot is not prone to catching.

When the cooking is done, lift the tripe and onions from the milk gravy with a skimming spoon, pour the gravy into a jug and wash the pot thoroughly. Then melt the butter and add the flour to make a paste. Slowly add the milk back in, stirring all the while. When the sauce is hot and thickening nicely, add the tripe and onions and let them warm through.

Serve with floury potatoes and if the little ones want to mash the tripe and tatties in together and make a hash of it, go on and let them.

HAVE YOU READ THE DANDY GILVER SERIES?

HODDER &
STOUGHTON